Praise for previous works by Jo-Ann Mapson

"*Along Came Mary* is a wonderful novel, filled with women so real and honest you feel you've known them all of your life. It is an absolute joy to read this book; you won't be able to put it down. You'll find yourself thinking about these characters, wishing them well, long after you've closed the last page. *Along Came Mary* is another sparkling gem from Jo-Ann Mapson, a novel about women who laugh through hard times and survive whatever comes their way. Bittersweet, poignant, and ultimately triumphant."

—Kristin Hannah, author of *Distant Shores* and *On Mystic Lake*

"The feisty characters and rueful emotional wisdom of this sequel will win over all but the hardest-hearted reader."

—*Kirkus Reviews*

"A valentine to oceans of good women who survive bad beginnings and worse men. . . . A well-crafted novel."

—*USA Today*

"What do you say about a book that makes you start checking maps to see if you can go live in Bad Girl Creek yourself? I fell head over heels in love with each of the four distinct women in this book, characters so indelible, so alive, the pages literally breathe. Written with prose as clear and sparkling as lake water, this is truly a heart-stunning novel about bonding friendship, abiding love (the friendly and the amorous kinds), loss, regret, and the faint glimmerings of hope that can spark and lead to a future."

—Caroline Leavitt, author of *Coming Back to Me*

"Jo-Ann Mapson has long been a wizard of words, and in her newest novel she makes magic—a literary potion mixed with brilliant characterizations, sweet emotional resonance, second chances, and a dash of laughter. This story of starting over is told through four women so real they'll live within you; their heartaches are heartaches we've all felt; and the redeeming strength of their sisterhood will have you calling up your own best friends late in the night, urging them to read *Bad Girl Creek*, too. Don't miss this one."

—Jodi Picoult, author of *Salem Falls*

"An absorbing story and quirky, appealing characters (a given with Mapson), deepened by honest grappling with a whole slew of messy emotions and issues."

—*Kirkus Reviews* (starred)

"Well-drawn settings and interesting characters . . . a pleasant diversion."

—*Library Journal*

"There's not a woman alive who wouldn't want to spend time with the ladies down at Bad Girl Creek. Mapson's women are complex and caring, funny and fierce, strong and fragile; in short, fully evolved characters you'd want to know in real life."

—*Booklist*

"Mapson is one of those fortunate writers able to spin an absorbing yarn without neglecting the underpinnings of character and theme. . . . [A] gifted new novelist likely to be entertaining readers for many years to come."

—*Newsday*

"This is a love story with a salsa bite and a winning heart."

—Barbara Kingsolver

"A funny, harsh, visceral novel . . . Mapson's finesse with both detail and the big picture, and her appreciation for the eloquence and explosiveness of silence between lovers, make this novel an engrossing, sensuous, resonant read."

—*Publishers Weekly* (starred)

"[T]he perfect dessert for women—and men!—who like *The Bridges of Madison County,* then found they were hungry two hours later: hungry for character development, believable plot, dialogue, and language at once controlled, mature, romantic, subtle, and memorable."

—*Los Angeles Times Book Review*

Also by Jo-Ann Mapson

Goodbye, Earl
Bad Girl Creek
The Wilder Sisters
Loving Chloe
Shadow Ranch
Blue Rodeo
Hank and Chloe
Fault Lines *(stories)*

Along Came Mary

A BAD GIRL CREEK NOVEL

Jo-Ann Mapson

SIMON & SCHUSTER
New York • London • Toronto • Sydney

to Susan Morgan

SIMON & SCHUSTER
Rockefeller Center
1230 Avenue of the Americas
New York, NY 10020

This book is a work of fiction. Names, characters, places, and incidents either are products of the author's imagination or are used fictitiously. Any resemblance to actual events or locales or persons, living or dead, is entirely coincidental.

First Simon & Schuster trade paperback edition 2004

SIMON & SCHUSTER and colophon are registered trademarks of Simon & Schuster Inc.

For information about special discounts for bulk purchases, please contact Simon & Schuster Special Sales:
1-800-456-6798 or business@simonandschuster.com.

Designed by Lauren Simonetti

Manufactured in the United States of America

10 9 8 7 6 5 4 3 2 1

The Library of Congress has cataloged the hardcover edition as follows:
Mapson, Jo-Ann.
Along came Mary : a Bad Girl Creek novel / Jo-Ann Mapson.
p. cm.
1. Female friendship—Fiction. 2. Women—California—Fiction. 3. Women with disabilities—Fiction. 4. Women landowners—Fiction. 5. Women pet owners—Fiction. 6. Women gardeners—Fiction. 7. Floriculturists—Fiction. 8. California—Fiction. I. Title.
PS3563.A62 A78 2003
813'.54—dc21 *2002075893*

ISBN 0-7432-2461-2
0-7432-2462-0 (Pbk)

The efforts which we make to escape from our destiny only serve to lead us into it.

—Emerson,
"Fate," *The Conduct of Life,* 1860

Along Came Mary

Locoweed

A perennial herb six to eight inches in height, with blue-green leaves, locoweed produces up to twenty-five purple or white flowers, and bears inflated pods that can germinate for years. Other names include milk vetch, rattlepod, jimsonweed, mad apple, and stinkweed. It is reported to taste bad, but if horses are hungry enough, they will eat it to the point of intoxication. Symptoms include depression, anorexia, weight loss, blindness, brain damage, resulting in death.

Maddy

1

Hell, and the Route Out

EXCEPT FOR TWO BOYS hyped up about tonight's rodeo, the bleachers at Five Corners stood empty. Those kids in their dirty coveralls and straw cowboy hats—maybe nine or ten years old, they were already talking in the hard way of their fathers, son-of-a-bitchin' this and goddamnin' that. I even saw one of them spit Copenhagen into a Coke can. They leaped the seats as if they were the backs of broncos, and I knew what was on their minds: winning a silver buckle, taking home the big-haired rodeo queen, though they weren't sure what exactly it was you did with a girl once you got her there. It's a way of life they were indoctrinated into straight off the baby bottle. Forget about the long-legged cranes that migrated through the sandhills; the university, where they could expand their minds; the highway leading out of town to brighter lights—this was as good as it got—Friday-night rodeo, good times, and Bud Light. Even without my mama's horoscope book I could read their futures: Knock up a pretty girl in high school, buy a double-wide trailer on time, work for NAPA Auto Parts, watch ESPN, and call that a life.

Me, I needed a map to tell which town I was in. I stood there smoking a cigarette before I started grooming the collies. I felt like ten miles of bad road, and I was looking down thirty miles of it, once again wondering how in the sweet Jesus I got to where I was. We were that far from anywhere, Dalton Afterhart and me. Tonight he would play his one famous song, and the crowd would go wild because a ten-year-old hit was really something out here in Nowhere Special, Nebraska. Everyone would buy him a beer, lay down ten bucks for his CD, and have him autograph the jewel case. I'd collect the money, and then Dalton would buckle his nasty spider monkeys into custom-made saddles on my border collies and he'd turn them loose in the arena. So where the hell *was* Dalton?

"Hey there, Mary Madigan."

I looked up to see Belmont Monty, the rodeo announcer, coming my way. He wasn't satisfied with calling me Maddy like everyone else; he had to say my whole name, every syllable coming out of his mouth like music. Monty was eighty years old, wizened as a golden raisin, and dressed in his natty Western-cut corduroy suit. I had no idea what his real name was. He'd acquired the Belmont nickname from his horseracing days, when he was a big-deal jockey and well known at the track. Then he had a wreck or drugged a horse or started taking drugs himself, or whatever else it is people do to fall so far from grace that they end up working here. "Hey to you, too, Monty. Looking so sharp there I might have to kiss you."

He grinned, a big, white, false-tooth smile.

Mentos, my female collie, whined from her tether, and Slim Jim, my male, trembled all over with happiness. My dogs adored this man, and why shouldn't they? He was a good man. It was something a person could tell just by being near him. He reached down to rub their ears, and they groaned with pleasure. "Where's Dalton?"

"Damned if I know. Said he'd be here an hour ago. Guess he's still drinking his lunch at Five Corners."

Belmont Monty squinted at me from behind his thick-lensed glasses. "Want me to go beat on him?"

There was a sight I'd pay to see—five-foot-nothing Monty whaling on six-foot-tall Dalton. I shook my head no. "He's been later than this. He'll be here when he gets here."

Monty patted Mentos one last time, then adjusted his cowboy hat and moved along to check on the others. I admired the old man, the way he got ready for each rodeo like somebody was there with a clipboard rating our performances. Once when Dalton was being a dickhead deluxe, I spent the night in Monty's trailer. He made me a pot of green Chinese tea and sat up with me while I cried about men in general. I asked him did he have any kids, and he said God, no, he hoped not. Monty claimed to love three things, in this order: horses, dogs, and redheaded women, only when the first two items on the list weren't available. After that night Dalton was a peach to me for two solid weeks.

People like Dalton, who had had a chance at the spotlight and missed, there was a dressing room for them here at the Great Western Rodeo Company of America. We started out every year near Blanco, New Mexico, with mesas on one side of the road and locoweed on the other. You couldn't pasture horses there, but some cheap-ass always tried to save a buck on hay, and there was a long-drawn-out scene of suffering before a cowboy grew *cojones* enough to shoot the horse that ate the locoweed. Why God couldn't see fit to add a few trees and some grass to that landscape was beyond me, but I guess God had his reasons. Even third-rate rodeos were an addiction. Cowboys got asked for autographs; kids like the ones in the bleachers looked up to them as heroes. Those riders brave or stupid enough to ride bulls earned cash, sometimes a fairly decent amount. Of course occasionally they drew a longhorn that flicked them off as easy as a booger, and they went to the hospital, where—whoops!—it was adios long-term memory, but for some people that could be a good thing.

The players in this rodeo were like slow-falling stars, but stars all the same. They attracted gaggles of groupies, girls who screamed and pulled up their T-shirts and showed everyone their wealth. Then there were roadies like me, who didn't fit in anywhere—we came and went so often hardly anybody noticed.

I got out my various brushes and started working on Slim Jim's glossy black-and-white coat. Border collies come in the short- and longhaired varieties. Jim's was crazy long, prone to tangles and burrs, collecting particularly in his ruff. He stood still for the brushes, but let me come close with a fingernail and he carried on like he was being ax-murdered. Mentos's coat was thinner, silky, a beautiful sign of weakness in her breed. She was easier to groom, so I did her last. I liked them to look their best, so I finished them up with a mist of Show Sheen, and I remembered to outline their strangely blue eyes with some Vaseline to keep the dust out.

The dog-and-monkey show consisted of two overly intelligent dogs running with two of the vilest primates known to the animal world trying every which way to get loose. It went like this: Ten white sheep and two black ones were released into the arena. Immediately my collies started cutting the sheep into herds, because that's what they knew. The monkeys, screaming and clapping their hands, appeared to be cheering them on. From the stands all this looked hilarious, particularly with a six-pack of beer in your gut. But the monkeys were terror struck, and my collies were and are simply obsessive about work. There could be nuclear war going on up there on their backs, they'd still cut sheep. They wanted those black sheep out and separate from the white ones so bad it looked like Birmingham in the sixties.

All the time Dalton told me how the crowd loved our act. Just listen to them laugh, he'd say, and if that didn't convince me, how about the money we got paid? He'd pull on his leather gloves and unstrap the monkeys and toss them back into their cages for bananas and some kind of herbal Valium concoction to keep them quiet until the next show. My collies were allowed to sit and watch the events, but they had to be leashed or they'd try to herd the horses, the bulls, and the clowns; if it had legs they considered it fair game. At that point things took a turn for the serious. Me. I climbed the stairs to the crepe paper–draped stage and sang, a cappella, our national anthem, and tried to think of something besides what the words mean. It was just something I did. And when people got teary and clapped too soon, I knew enough not to take it too seriously.

For instance, this one time in our travels, we stopped at a Wal-Mart that was having a plant sale, and I bought all these four-inch pots of indoor greenaroo. Dalton got a big kick out of that, me going "domestic." Soon enough all the plants mysteriously died. I think he sabotaged them with coffee. Dalton was jealous of everything I liked, even my clothes, especially my deerskin leather jacket with the red-white-and-blue-beaded fringe my grandmother Fawn made me. He hated the fact that I had Indian blood in me and he did not. Next I got these cactus plants, special food, and a book on how to care for them. I bungee-corded them to the window in the trailer, and on the first of every month I fed them an eyedropper of plant food. At present my paddle cactus was sporting a fat little bud! Every day I checked on it, and I told that plant, Spike, if you can manage to bloom in this crazy environment, maybe I can too.

FIVE CORNERS ROADHOUSE was this hokey, hogan-shaped building that badly needed a new roof. Not that it mattered much in the summertime, but come winter I imagined the place leaked like a sieve. There was a wooden hitching rail in front of the parking spaces. Even a few ratty horses tied up. Nothing worth stealing except for this seventeen-hand black-and-white paint horse with a ton of chrome. Inside the bar all the rodeo cowboys were drinking, which was what I'd've liked to be doing, but drinking made me do stupid things, like have sex with total strangers or agree to five-year-long singing gigs with men like Dalton or—duh, what do you know?—both, so I avoided the bottle, though I hadn't quite got around to doing the AA thing. On the sign outside Five Corners, faded plastic letters announced that the Lou Peltier band played every Thursday through Sunday. I wondered if he was a distant relation to Leonard, one American Indian who stood up for his beliefs enough to stay in jail and not rat out his brothers. It killed me how Bobby Dylan could sing one song and get Hurricane Carter cut loose. Unless Clinton grew a conscience—and how likely was that?—Leonard would rot in the slammer until he was an old man crippled by phlebitis. Underneath the regular sign, in those plastic letters they use on movie marquees, it read, TO-NITE ONLY DALTON AFTERHART. Whoop-de-fecking-do. Just then, the door swung open and out came Dalton himself. It says in the Bible that man is created in His own image.

I hoped that was an exaggeration, because if not, Lord God, what a specimen! Imagine Kevin Costner with an overbite, a beer gut, and a little bit blonder hair, age fifty-two, but looking older. Now cut his vocabulary in half, give him a shorter, fatter Johnson that only works half the time, and the bank account of some ordinary Joe. Take away manners, and throw in a Ph.D. in sweet talk, paint a mean streak down his back, and you have Dalton Afterhart, who professes to have authentic Cherokee Indian blood! First time I met him in Tulsa he asked me to call him Chief. I told him that sounded even dumber than anything I could ever have thought up, and I had a lengthy history of dim. I am one-quarter Creek Indian, one-quarter German, and the whole other half of me is a terrible combination of fighting Irish and Sicilian Eytie, thanks to Daddy's parents' scandalous union. I didn't tell anyone anything when they asked me why my last name (Caringella) was so unusual. I just said, *Gee, isn't that a coincidence, your name sounds pretty fecking weird to me, too.*

"You feed those monkeys, Maddy?" Dalton slurred as he tried to light his cigarette. He was way buzzed, having trouble with the lighter, and I was banking that even with a pot of coffee in him he wouldn't be sober by the time he needed to perform.

"Hell, no. They're not my monkeys. You feed the little bastards."

"Those monkeys pay for your cigarettes, let me remind you."

"Relax, Chief. I tuned your guitar."

He stopped in his tracks, the cigarette hanging from his lips, and gave me a smile. Nobody knew this but me, but Dalton was going deaf and he could not tune that beat-to-shit Gretsch to save his life. He fancied himself some Willie Nelson clone, on the road 365 days a year. I guess he thought the world would eventually give him a trophy for his time, and my tuning the guitar would go down in history as a small contribution. "That's what I love about you, Madigan," he said, using my middle name, which I preferred. "You're thoughtful."

Dalton was the only man who ever said "I love you" to me besides my daddy, and my daddy sure as hell didn't say it anymore.

"Oh, get over yourself," I said, and went to tune the guitar before he realized I was lying.

WELL, THE NIGHT DIDN'T STAND STILL for thinking, and Dalton did not get sober enough to sing. In fact, he must have had some secret bottle stashed back in the trailer because when I came to get him for the show he was dressed to perform but passed clean out. He'd apparently bumped into a few things along the way, too, because the frying pan was on the floor, and so was a bagful of onions, and the silverware box I kept all straightened was upside down, and I nearly broke my neck stepping on spoons and knives. Then I saw my jacket. Mother feckity! It was covered with vomit. My paddle cactus was out of its pot, and the bud, which was just starting to unfurl a silky yellow blossom, lay crushed in the sink. I cradled it in my palm for a moment and then tossed it in the trash. Using a dishrag, I wiped each bead clean and tried to get out the worst of the stain, but the deerskin had soaked too much up ever to look good again.

I sat down on the bed and took Dalton by the shoulders. I shook him hard, I threw water on his face, yanked his belly hair, screamed in his ear about what a worthless piece of shit he was, and all the while he smiled and rolled his eyes. His limp form in that horrid parrot-patterned Hawaiian shirt fell back on the bedding like he'd just finished a day of hard labor. Jimmy Buffett after too many margaritas. I was killing mad. If we didn't do the act, we didn't get the paycheck, and we needed gas money just to stay with the rodeo. Outside the trailer I heard the collies whimper, and I pictured them cowering. They hated fighting, and could tell when I was in a bad mood without me saying a word. The monkeys, who were probably hooked on the herbal Valium, rattled the bars on their cages and screamed that ear-piercing squeal that meant they knew it was almost show time.

I asked God, *What have I done in my twenty-nine years to deserve this?*

He answered, *Don't go there, Madigan. The answer will take too long and you can't spare the time.*

So I rinsed the vomit off my hands. I swept up the dirt,

picked up the silverware and the onions. I took out the leather gloves, the special saddles, said a Hail Mary, who had never let me down. Some Christians will tell you that praying to the Mother of God is pagan, blasphemous, and downright wrong. To them I say, Excuse me, and just who taught Jesus his pleases and thank-yous? Give the woman some credit. I harnessed up my dogs. Mentos was such a good girl that she looked at me with her wide blue people eyes and lifted a front paw when I went to adjust her cinch. Slim Jim stood tall; like a good soldier, he knew the drill. Then came the monkeys. Thing One and Thing Two was what I called them. Their little biting faces were pure evil. At first they looked real cute, like wrinkly old grannies, but if you gave them a half second they'd transform into aliens with razor-sharp teeth like in that movie about the gremlins.

They despised the saddles, the straps, the stirrups, the buckles, and the cinches that kept them tethered to the dogs. They were trembling by the time I got the second one buckled in—and they'd each had nine peanuts as bribes. I wanted nothing more than to let them out, but the thought of that paycheck kept me going. Lately we'd been eating only one meal a day to save up cash. I changed into Dalton's Hawaiian shirt, tied it above my belly button so my silver navel ring showed, grabbed his ratty old guitar, and headed out the trailer door just in time to hear his cue.

It wasn't that big a crowd tonight. Maybe sixty people. The rodeo arena looked so different in the dark, somehow more genuine. Once when I was really broke I did exotic dancing in this club in Tulsa, and the way they made me up and lit me I swear my own daddy could have walked in and not recognized me. That was a lifetime ago—how could I say that and not yet be thirty years old? I let the dogs into the arena. Mentos ran to the left, Slim Jim cut right. I let them circle twice, and then I lifted the gate for the sheep.

The crowd went berserk as the dogs began to work the arena. The monkeys squealed like they were being stomped to death. Two beefy women stood up in the crowd and started yelling about animal cruelty. They were wearing white T-shirts with big red splotches on them, I guess made to look like blood.

I prepared myself for whatever came next—a paint gun, a bullet, or the afterlife.

My identical twin, Margaret—I called her Maggot; she called me Mary Magdalene—could not hold a tune if it came in a bucket. In all other ways she was a superior human being. Maggot worked in a day care center, tending the babies. *I pray for you, Maddy,* she'd said to me more times than I could count. *I pray that your music lifts the spirit, that you find a good man, and that our Heavenly Father blesses you on a daily basis.* I'd get so mad at her I wouldn't return her phone calls or answer her letters, even though she never played such games. Singing was the only thing that ever came natural to me. I wasn't afraid of solos, or opera, or even the national anthem. People heard my voice warble on "and the l-a-nd of the free" and assumed I was choking up on patriotism, but it wasn't true. Politics had failed me every step of the way. Maggot was very patriotic. She voted in every election. July Fourth was her favorite holiday, and she was purely mental for fireworks. Because of her dying, it was hard for me to sing that anthem all the way through. Dalton always said, "Madigan, you keep that wiggle in your voice, it's fuckin' brilliant." Feckin' Dalton. Sometimes at night when I woke up next to him and he was sleeping on his back snoring like a ripsaw, I got the urge to crush a dozen bananas, rub them over his privates, and turn the nasty-smelling spider monkeys loose.

"Stop the insanity!" one of the protesters yelled, and I thought, Huh, using that spiky-haired power-workout chick's slogan isn't very original.

"Shut up, you dyke!" a cowboy told her, and a beer bottle flew through the air. Like thunder, the grumbling that rumbled through the crowd increased, and the air felt heavy and ugly. But the dogs kept running, the white sheep moving like a beautiful stream, the black sheep behaving like the hunted. I hated this act, I hated the activists, I hated Dalton Afterhart and his drunkenness for leaving me in the bull's-eye of this evening, and I missed my jacket, which I knew would forevermore smell like his beer and nachos sick-up.

"Animal cruelty!" the dykey girl's friend yelled, and the beer-bottle cowboy and his pal rose to bodily remove the two women, who from the looks of them, were ladies who would not suffer such interference without protest. They screamed and fought, but the crowd booed them down. My collies continued to herd the sheep, the audience clapped, the monkeys wailed; I got a headache that said, *Have one drink, Madigan, just one, and then I'll leave you alone.*

Then Belmont Monty went to the mike. He said, "Ladies and gentlemen, Dalton Afterhart, singing his Top 40 hit, 'When You Stopped By.'"

Only it was me climbing up there to the spotlight with the beat-up Gretsch with its duct tape–covered holes, and wearing Dalton's Hawaiian shirt, all smelly in the armpits because no matter how much deodorant he rolled on, he reeked. I tossed my black hair back over my shoulders and smiled, leaning into the mike. From this far away the scar on my mouth didn't show, but every time I pulled my lips across my teeth, I felt it just the same as if it were still in stitches. "Good evening, folks. I know you were expecting Dalton, but he came down with the flu. I hope you'll put up with me singing his song, though, and I do have his CDs for sale, autographed, and special for tonight to make up for the disappointment, one dollar off."

"When You Stopped By" was so pathetically easy a song, and I had heard it so often, that I could play it in my sleep. Dalton sang it in the key of G, because for anything else he'd need a capo, and he lost them too often to keep track. My voice was higher than his, so I barred the chords, sang it in E-flat, and tore things up with some fancy chord inversions just to keep from boring myself to death. It told an entire story start to finish, not just one good chorus where you sang the same refrain over and over. It had this mysterious ending that made you want to know what happened the next day when the couple involved woke up. I shut my eyes and sang.

Lately I had the urge to see Mama again, even though she didn't seem to share the inclination. Pretty soon I'd turn thirty, though, and I kept on thinking that since it was the end of my twenties, having lived through that decade of madness, I should touch base with the woman who gave birth to me. Mama was in Oklahoma, living on the edge of the reservation again with her sister, MayAnn. My dad, well, I'd come to learn it was best to leave some people alone in their grief. Between us there was Maggot. Gone, but not gone. I'd've given anything to trade places with my twin before she died. It's not that I didn't like myself; it was just that at this stage of the game I would have liked to walk in Maggot's shoes and, however briefly, see the world through her eyes. Like now, under this summery Nebraska sky, so wide open. To me it looked like a dirty gray sheet, and made me think of chintzy motels and bad sex. Maggot, she'd probably have seen tempera paint on crisp white paper. The first brushstroke of something beautiful enough to frame. She might have turned to me and said, *Mary Magdalene, the Lord hath made some real beautiful stuff down here,* and I would have answered right back, *Yeah, but for every pretty thing there's five cosmic mistakes He should be thoroughly ashamed of,* and she would go on to say, *Never end a sentence in a preposition,* and I would have fired back, *You just did,* and then we'd hit each other and start laughing. . . .

I had—still have—this famous temper. Maggot had endless compassion. People in need of comfort were drawn to her. Seemed like everyone but the horny gave me a wide berth.

And the song I was singing: It made me think about how when I met Dalton years ago I thought he might be the answer to my prayers. I needed somebody older to keep me from doing stupid things, and to demonstrate how to behave in public, somebody to slow me down and help me grow out of my wildness into well, maybe a lady, like Maggot was. But it didn't work. Well, it kind of worked for a while, but then it was like this Chinese cook I once dated said—*sanpaku*—everything got out of whack and I saw that mostly what Dalton was was an old drunk who liked firm young nookie because it helped him forget he was growing old. So I had this feeling inside me of my heart tapping its foot, and now my fecking cactus wasn't going to bloom, and the jacket that my grandma made by hand with tanned hide and hundred-year-old trade beads was ruined by an alcoholic's poor aim.

When you stopped by
It was fall. All the falling autumn leaves

Decided not to fall after all. They hung around
the trees
Making canopies of red. Lacy dreams of gold
and green,
Colors soft enough to make a bed.
So what's a man to do
When he meets a girl like that,
But hang around her life; maybe ask to hang up
his hat.
And somehow the years collide,
And lovers grow from friends.
Like that day when you stopped by
I never wanted it to end. . . .

When I finished singing you could've heard a pin drop in the arena. Not even Slim Jim howled. *God,* I asked, *did I sing it wrong? Were my fingers barred wrong on the frets? Was I singing the jokey lyrics I made up when I was bored to death, pissed off at Dalton and his pretentious delivery? Had I totally lost it?* He didn't answer. Oh, what did it matter? I got paid no matter what. Feck it; all's I had to do now was sell the CDs, sing the national anthem, and I could go to bed—if I could shove Dalton over enough so I could lie down.

Then the most amazing thing happened. Everyone got to their feet, like America commanded they do with the anthem, only I hadn't sung that yet. They clapped and they clapped and they would not stop. I felt tears in my eyes. I just stood there until Belmont Monty came over and patted my back and said, "Maddy, sweetheart, maybe we should have the national anthem now, and you can sell the CDs afterwards."

I looked down to make sure my fly was zipped, and it was. Then I whispered to Monty, "Does this mean I did good?" and the mike caught it. Monty said, "Yes, honey, you did right fine," and the crowd laughed.

So I went ahead and I sang the anthem. For once I made it through "land of the free" without the wiggle interrupting my voice.

LATER THAT NIGHT, when I was trying to balance the monkey cages and the collies and get back to the trailer, the girls with the phony bloody T-shirts showed up. I looked up from the cages and there they were, kind of scary, like biker chicks, hands in fists at their sides, and I felt this unreasonable urge to start laughing, but immediately saw that this would not be the best tack for somebody five four and 120 pounds to take.

However, Caringellas were not quitters, so I planted my feet and stood my ground. "Something I can do for you ladies?"

The smaller one took a step forward. Right then I got the impression the bigger one had bullied her into speaking first. "What you're doing with those monkeys is animal cruelty."

I sighed. "I couldn't agree with you more. Only they're not my monkeys. They belong to the guy who's passed out in the trailer over there. Why don't you go take it up with him if you can wake him up?"

"And the collies," her friend added, moving toward Slim Jim, who growled low in his throat. "It isn't morally right to force dogs to wear saddles and chase sheep."

I held up a hand. "Hold on, Babe. The saddles are one thing, but border collies are bred to herd sheep. I swear, if these two don't get to herd something on a daily basis, they rearrange their food dishes. It's in their blood—"

That's when the first balloon hit me. I thought it was full of water, but then I looked down at my belly and saw that the parrot shirt was covered with red. A quick sniff told me it was probably food coloring, but by then I was royally pissed off. Then the second balloon hit me in the left tit, and the third missed me but caught Mentos in the eye, and she started yelping.

"You call yourself animal lovers?!" I yelled, and just like that I shifted into fight-club mode, knocking the smaller one to the ground and kneeling on her chest in two seconds flat, and I heard the satisfying crack of a rib under my knee. She huffed hard, then bitch-slapped me across the face and once again I saw red, but this time I felt a slow trickle down my cheek, and reached up to touch real blood—mine. She must have been wearing a ring. I doubled up my fist and landed one on her chin, and then I leaned back and hauled Mentos by her collar to the girl's face. "Look what you did! You could have blinded my dog! Get out of here, you coward, and take your asshole friend with you or I'll kick her butt, too."

One more knee, this time to the belly, then I shoved her off and looked for her friend, but surprise, surprise, the bigger one was nowhere to be seen. I was breathing hard as I found a hose and wet a cloth, gently daubing Mentos's face clean. She had the eye half closed, and I knew if I told Dalton I wanted a vet to look at it he'd argue she was just a damn dog and one eye was plenty, then go drink whatever I would have spent on her vet bill.

Belmont Monty came over with my pay as I was sitting there hugging Mentos, trying to calm her. He whistled. "Lordy Jesus, you're all cut up. What in hell happened here, Maddy?"

"Had a little run-in with the animal lovers."

"Those girls in the bleachers?"

"If you can call them girls. I had my doubts, but I didn't check their panties."

"Two against one? You're such a little bit of a thing. How did you manage—"

I cut him short before he had me laid out in an ambulance, headed for intensive care. "Monty, can I have our pay?"

"Sure." He counted it out and looked at the cages with the screaming monkeys. "You—uh—sure you don't need any help with those—uh—primates?"

Poor Belmont Monty. He was too old for this. He should be living in some nice little one-bedroom apartment near the Los Alamitos racetrack, where he could watch the six A.M. workouts in peace. If I'd've said yes, he'd pop a coronary on the spot. "Relax, Monty, I'm all right. This is just a scratch."

"Be a shame to add another scar to that pretty mouth, Hon."

Yes, it would be. I folded the bills into my pocket. "It's nothing a Band-Aid won't fix."

Visible relief flooded his face. "Well, then, I'm gonna grab me a beer. Hope Dalton's feeling better. See you two in Cheyenne."

He toddled off into the night, headed for Five Corners and

beer, billiards, and boobs—the three B's, which made up the brotherhood of man.

I trudged back toward the trailer, but there was a lot of traffic, pickups coming in with the radio blasting C&W; feed trucks going out empty, headed to suppliers; travelers ogling the sights; and the locals all juiced up and ready to party. What stopped me was a yellow Ryder truck. It was probably just somebody's weekend rental, moving furniture from one residence to another, but since McVeigh blew up the Murrah Building, to me every yellow van was a potential bomb. I couldn't move.

Mentos whined, Slim Jim danced around me, and the bastard monkeys shook the cage bars Jonesing for their nightly dose of herbal Valium. I knelt down in the dirt and howled out loud for my sister, who did nothing to deserve having her life erased at age twenty-five just because some idiot was mad at the government.

So many things I wanted right then that I couldn't have—like my family around the dining room table in McAlester, with fry bread on one side of the platter and fettuccini on the other. I wanted to hear Daddy arguing the merits of saying the rosary and Mama saying horseshit to all that, and smell her burning sage at dawn and blessing the four directions. I wanted to wake up drenched in sweat because it was 105 degrees outside, and see Maggot sitting there with not one hair out of place and her shirt buttoned all the way up to her collar, a peaceful smile on her face because she loved her life like it was winning the damned lottery.

When it happened I was sleeping in a Super 8 with some dirtbag whose name I don't even remember. I woke up with a start, thinking what the hell was that dream I was having, or am I getting the flu, or maybe this is a heart attack because of how much cocaine I did last night, and then I felt it—the bottomless pitch into loss, and immediately afterward the phantom ache of my lost twin rising like bile in my throat.

The driver's-side door of the Ryder truck opened, and an old man got out. He looked at me, tipped his ball cap politely like it was every night of the week you saw a sobbing, paint-soaked girl kneeling in the dirt with two monkeys in cages and twin whining border collies. He hurried off to the bar because if he didn't need a drink before, he sure needed one now. I told the dogs to sit, picked up the monkeys, and went into the trailer. Dalton was still asleep. I emptied his wallet and found three hundred dollars. The rat bastard was holding out on me! I left him enough for a bus ticket, shoved the rest into my pocket, gathered up my cactus plants and my ruined jacket, found my toothbrush and shampoo, and my photographs of my sister. I tipped a generous amount of the herbal drug into the monkeys' bananas, and at the very last moment before I closed the trailer door, I unlatched their cages and whispered, "He's all yours, boys."

Then I closed the trailer door, unhooked the hitch, stood there for a second, and sucked my sore knuckles. I wadded up some Kleenex onto my cheek because it was still seeping, and I told Mentos and Slim Jim to load up in the truck's cab. Mentos's eye was swollen shut. "The first vet we come to, we'll get that taken care of," I promised her. I meant it. They were such good dogs; they minded so well it broke my heart. I gave them each a Milk-Bone, then popped the tab on a Diet Coke and drank half the contents down, enjoying the carbonation burn against my tight throat. The three of us headed out into the night, not toward Cheyenne and the next rodeo, but toward Oklahoma City and a different kind of showdown—one that was five long years overdue.

Rick

2
Professional Laryngitis

NANCY JANE MATTOX.

A better man would have gone after her.

He would have stopped her in the weed-filled parking lot of that overpriced mom-and-pop grocery. Held her, and this part's important, tight at the elbows, because even though Nance is small, she's strong and will fight. He'd have held on until she was finished calling him every name in the book. Then he would have said he was sorry, meant it; admitted he was wrong, meant that, too; and just before he explained that his tragic flaw was possessing the maturity level of a thirteen-year-old, he would have kissed her.

The kiss, you see, is vital. With Nance Mattox so much hinged on kisses, especially the see-you-later kind. Nance grew up with a slate of stepfathers as interchangeable as tube socks. She had no clue as to who her biological father was. Her mother was prone to divorces the way some people catch every cold that comes along. I think Nance viewed all men as apt to bail out at any second. I'm sure my behavior during our three years of living together didn't help. All I knew was the woman was mad for lips against lips, a quality I learned to appreciate in record time, if for all the wrong reasons.

She would have craned her neck this way and that, avoiding me, but eventually I would have landed one on her pout and changed her mind. I'm taller. I do push-ups every morning to maintain my upper body strength while at the same time avoiding carpal tunnel syndrome. When I set my mind to something, I generally attain it. This job, finding a vintage pressing of Paul McCartney's *Band on the Run,* an affordably priced first edition of Pynchon's *Gravity's Rainbow.* When I want something I go after it. Usually. And if there's one thing I know how to do, honestly, it's kiss.

Instead.

I stood fifty feet away as if I was up to my ass in quicksand. I watched the only woman who's ever come close to being my soul mate (as close as I let anyone shoulder up against that big brick wall inside me) sit down on the rickety, bait-splattered steps in the fancy jeans I always used to tease her about, splay her knees in a most unladylike manner—which of course gave me an immediate hard-on—and whip out the cell phone she lives and dies by.

She made a call.

I figured taxi, but Nancy said, "I love you" even before she said hello.

So who in the fuck did she love besides me?

Then she started crying.

God. When women weep, I completely shut down. Emotional scenes reminded me of my mother, who cried in order to get me to baby-sit the neighbor's retarded child, to take my ugly cousin to the junior prom, and to promise to major in pre-med in college when all I ever wanted was to be a writer. Not a journalist, a *novelist.* The real thing—Jack London, Jr. Ambrose Bierce without the mysterious ending. A hetero Gore Vidal. I wasn't totally egomaniacal; I would have settled for a small niche on the midlist. Instead I ended up in journalism, writing a weekly column on Portland's music scene. I supervised a herd of freelancers who hadn't mastered the basic rules of punctuation, and tried to get them to turn their six hundred words in on time. On Wednesdays at eight P.M. we put *After-Hours* to bed. Then I turned the calendar page, and for one nickel-plated hour I marveled at how far removed my job was from a satisfying career before I began the process all over again.

Next Nancy did call a taxi. Then she threw her beloved twenty-first-century digital technology into the bushes and started walking. She has this amazing butt. To look at it you'd think it was total muscle, but it's got the perfect amount of give to it. Even though baggy jeans are in style, Nance'll wear hers tight forever. When I looked at her rear pockets, the tips of my fingers tingled, because of what I knew. Like how to lift her up when we were getting busy, so that I could move deep inside without hurting her. Where to press to maximize contact, and send her into that squealing song that makes my eyes cross and renders me incapable of any communication beyond a smile. Imagining another man's hands in that area—well, that really pissed me off.

So of course I had to follow her. Just to make certain she was safe.

She waited by the roadside until the taxi arrived. It took fifteen minutes. During which time anything could have happened: bear attack; kidnap by woodsman gone mad for lack of companionship; hell, she'd lost so much weight she could have been picked up by a hungry owl, her Italian shoes and all. But none of that happened except that I stood paralyzed thinking up various scenarios. Stomping out there and yelling back, which never worked. Logical explanations, which should work but don't. Whether or not I could find a bar open this early in the morning, one with a television set and Alaskan amber in a bottle. Doubtful. All I intended to do was wait until she was safely settled in the backseat with her seat belt fastened. Then I'd catch some Z's, shower, and do what I set out to do when I came here, which was interview one of the fundamental musical legends of the sixties, James Vernon Taylor, aka "Moose" when he was at Milton Academy; "String Bean" during the years 1966–67; "JT" for obvious reasons, and the nickname he's best known for, "Sweet Baby James," which is a complete misnomer. Taylor wrote that song for his nephew, son of the late Alex, who died in 1993, but did most people care to get details like that right? I cared. I spent days on research, seeking out that one unique element that would become the focal point of my piece. Once, in my youth, I'd seen the late John Fahey, onstage, interrupt the show to adjust his guitar when it went out of tune. *I tune because I care,* he used to say. It mattered to him. It mattered to me. I believed small details like that made my stories come to life—at least until Don, my twenty-nine-year-old editor, got that weird frown and said, "I don't think people are really interested in this stuff anymore, Rick." Don made six thousand dollars a year more than I did just so he could hand me shit like that and ruin my plans for the evening while I stayed late to dumb down a piece I'd worked eight hours to write smart. He had a red Fender Stratocaster guitar in his office. I'd never seen him do anything with it but polish it. The job he walked into straight from copyediting was supposed to have been mine after my boss left, but somehow I ended up on the other side of the desk, shaking his hand, saying welcome to my magazine, have at it, and would you mind ruining everything I've worked for years to get right? This wonder child, who'd been working nights, was now my boss. But was he satisfied with his great good luck at skipping over years of paying dues? Of course not. Not until he had his little buddies on board, and he'd changed the tone of the magazine entirely. Undone all I'd worked for. He never said so directly; rather, he let me know in subtle ways. Like assigning me to cover *Lord of the Dance,* and giving one of his Gummi Worm–eating freelance pals the sit-down interview with Courtney Love.

Job satisfaction was one thing; the love of a good woman, another, even if she sometimes was a pain in the ass. I watched the taxi taillights disappear into the Douglas firs down that dark stretch of highway we had driven only hours earlier, when I was able to envision a different outcome—Nance naked in my arms, us making love in the shadow of St. Helens—a kind of necessary balm for all the shit that had been going on in my life lately.

Of course, Nance had no idea about the shit factor. I never told women things of that nature. Apparently my "unwillingness to share" was one of my failings. *Does your tongue get paralyzed?* Nance used to ask me. Women wanted so much, and words to go along with it, too. She made me dig in my heels the same way Don did when I tried to talk him out of cutting my articles by six inches.

I watched the cab until it disappeared. *Someday I'm going to leave you for good, Rick.*

Okay, maybe I deserved to be left.

You're mean, Heinrich. No one can hurt me the way you do.

Could I help it if she handed her power over to me like it was a tray of chocolate chip cookies?

I do not hand my power over to you. You manipulate me into begging for attention. There's a difference.

Maybe it wasn't a power thing. Maybe it came down to the simple difference between the sexes. Women offered up their hearts; men ran straight to jokes the minute they felt theirs throb in response. Or it could have been simply that I was a scoundrel. Like she said.

Scoundrel.

Ha. She hated it when I laughed at her, but come on, who in the year 2000 used words like "scoundrel"?

Only fascinating women.

Which is why after the cab didn't screech to a halt, and Nance didn't jump out and return to me, I walked over to the store and rummaged around in the bushes until I found her cell phone. Typical scoundrel behavior. I sat down on the steps in the same place she'd been only moments earlier, but it was cold wood again, boards and nails in need of paint. No trace of Nance.

Except in the last few numbers she'd dialed. So I scrolled through them. Deleted the local number, which had to be the taxicab company. But the previous number—the one with the 831 area code—that brought out the reporter in me. Who besides me could she say, *I love you* to?

Dammit all, those were *my* words.

Which is why I then pressed redial.

"Don't push me, Nancy," the voice on the other end said. "I need time. How is talking now when I'm angry enough to pitch the phone into the ocean going to do any good? Jesus, the journalist! What were you thinking? That all the heartache he pulled on you was history, or was this just about sex? Tell me, why is it you'll sleep with him but not with me?"

After he stopped yelling at Nance, I said, "Greetings. Allow me to introduce myself. I'm the journalist. Name's Rick. Also, I didn't sleep with her, though I sure wanted to."

There was a deafening silence. Then, "What the hell are you doing with the woman I love anyway?"

"Allow me to set the record straight," I said, and what followed was a most enlightening chat.

I learned enough to know that I'm not about to let her go to a jerk like that. Nance deserved better. I might not have been the better she deserved, but she was not ending up with that judgmental buffoon. Not if I had anything to say about it. I'd go see him. We'd talk. But I'd wait until everyone involved calmed down. Which might take a little while.

After-Hours was never going to win any Pulitzers. You could find stacks of the magazine in supermarkets, coffeehouses, and music stores, as well as in gutters, where it did a decent job soaking up our state's famous rain. We reported events in the tried-and-true style: the one-sentence intro intended to draw the reader's attention followed by quotes from the performer—all of which had to be approved by the publicist—then a few exchanges of interview questions, a brief tour through his or her body of work, and winding it up with a reminder of the upcoming gig. We weren't allowed to use curse words, to rake locals over the coals, and when it came to poking fun at political targets, policy was strictly hands off. For this I got paid enough to have a life that included car payments, a PPO that questioned every claim I submitted, and let's not forget Don, who spent every working hour riding me like a bad case of zits. Lately, when I couldn't stomach having to interview 'N Sync, when Howie Mandel's publicist was on the phone wanting to know could he swing a cover story, unemployment was beginning to sound like a viable alternative. I entertained fantasies of writing up my resignation, walking out, and spending the day in Powell's, walking the aisles of books in silence, hanging out with real writers, even if they lived only in the pages of their books. Imagining that was like having this compartment inside my brain I could comfortably travel to and still manage to write my articles.

A newsroom office offered about as much privacy as taking a shower on national television. Reporters typed into computer terminals that were set five feet from one another. The guy next to you caught a virus; it was yours by the end of the week. The girl two desks over broke up with her boyfriend; before lunch everybody knew the gory details, down to what piece of crockery got thrown and which body part it hit. Nobody except Don merited an office with a door. A reporter had to win three Pulitzers and cure cancer to get an office, but who really wanted a windowless cubicle? Which was why the arrival of the sunflower bouquet instantly became everybody's business instead of just Nance's and mine. Her card read: "Sorry about Washington. Hope you got the photo anyway. Be happy, Rick. I'm going to try to be."

E-mail I could ignore, pretend I never got. Flowers, well, to a guy, that was cause for pause, major snickering among the ranks, because they'd automatically assume they were from my mother, or it was my birthday, an occasion for daylong teasing and black balloons. I set the sunflowers on what passed for my desk among my other tchotchkes and continued working on the Taylor interview. I'd pared it to fifteen hundred words, incisive questions, scintillating responses, and the telling detail here and there that elevated the piece to three-dimensional. What with consulting sources, piecing together the timeline, separating fact from inference, it had taken me the better part of a week. I pushed myself to edit every sentence until there was nothing left but muscle. I was just about to send it to Don when those flowers arrived. I tucked the card back into its envelope and considered the arrangement. Three tall stalks, tied in a blue ribbon, set into a cobalt glass vase with florist's foam in the bottom to supply the water. One for each unhappy year, no doubt. In Spanish the word for sunflower is *girasol*. If you called someone a sunflower in Spanish, you weren't talking about a strong-shouldered person who rose above the earth to face the sun. It was sort of an insult, like calling someone a sycophant or a social climber, proving that nothing could be taken at face value. Linguistics, in my opinion, ruined everything.

Surf the Net and you'll discover that sunflower seeds were

the favorite food of chickadees, bluejays, titmice, evening grosbeaks, goldfinches, nuthatches, and the pine siskin, as well as mockingbirds. They made a good snack food for humans, but if you swallowed the hulls you could end up with diverticulitis, like my buddy Ben, and that could mean corrective surgery and a special diet for life. No argument, the color yellow was cheerful on a gray day, and even brightened up a nice day, too. As flowers go, the sunflower was a manly bloom. Nance knew that. They stood proudly on their woody stems, heavy heads held high, but I suspect that on some level they also poked fun at my ambition.

Back there in Washington, on our ill-fated venture, I waited in the lobby of the hotel for Mr. Taylor until two hours past our agreed-on meeting time. Finally I got tired of sitting around and insisted someone at the desk ring his room. This beefy guy in a muscle T-shirt came into the lobby and told me the interview was off. No reason, Mr. Taylor had simply changed his mind. The bodyguard—maybe thirty, at least 250 pounds—flexed a biceps. "Run along," he said, as if he were talking to some teenage groupie seeking an autograph.

"We had a confirmed appointment," I countered.

"Now you have a canceled appointment."

"Can I at least get a photo?"

He looked at me like I was gum on his shoe. "Call the publicist."

I sighed. "Look, I don't want to drag this out any more than you do. I was promised an interview and a photo shoot. My story's due in two days. Can't you work with me here?"

He looked at me unblinking and said no.

I wanted to deck him, but I flipped my notebook shut and got in the Saturn and drove home. I turned the stereo on as loud as it could go without blowing out another set of speakers to my CD of choice: Emmylou Harris's *Red Dirt Girl.* Who needed James Taylor—a man idiot enough to leave Carly Simon with that incredible mouth of hers—the whiny songwriter whose late work drew in the over-forty crowd like a free subscription to *Consumer Reports*?

I wrote the piece the way I always do; on first draft everything gets in—my own ideas mixed in with the facts, emotions coloring the piece, any residual anger of not getting my questions answered allowed to burst into flame, the description of bodyguard boy none too flattering and filled with speculation of steroid abuse. Though it was far from a time-effective journalistic technique, it worked for me. When interviewing, I left the tape recorder turned off and relied on extensive notes. No tape meant people came to trust me sooner. Sometimes they revealed drug problems or copped to chronic illnesses, and in one memorable case, a celebrity cheating on a spouse. When they asked me not to include those details in the piece, I honored their wishes. Nevertheless, putting them into my first draft led me to interesting places, and sometimes provided the one defining detail that gave my article an edge. I backed up my files, naming them *a, b, c,* and so on until I'd edited down to the proper word count, finessed the transitions, and emerged with a final draft that was worthy of going into the queue. Don edited me. He slashed-and-burned like the forest service. But this piece was so tight I figured it didn't need anything except a headline.

When I'd pitched the story to Don, explained how great it was going to be, he'd responded, "It had better be, Heinrich, or you can pay your own travel expenses." We stood on opposite sides of the journalistic riverbank, Don and I. Whatever subject I considered worthy of a story he called outdated or, worse, "easy listening." If it wasn't about GWAR or Kirk Hammett, it didn't merit ink. At first I tried explaining our demographics to him, then I figured the positive feedback I'd get from the James Taylor interview would show him. Sure, Taylor was a musical grandfather by today's standards, but his concerts sold out, and he did not give interviews. Not only would this profile put me in Don's good graces, *he'd* look good. That in turn would ease the pressure on me. Not that I was in trouble, just fielding the usual crap—call this publicist you pissed off, your freelancers are late, glaring typos, et cetera, et cetera—it wasn't so much a matter of the next promotion that came along being mine. I planned to outlast Don and his red guitar by example. So I combed the Internet, pulling a little from this web site and a little from that one, patching Taylor's words together like one of my mother's hokey

Oklahoma quilts until I had a sort of secondhand interview consisting of Mr. Taylor's words. And it was good stuff, the piece among the best I've ever written. I documented my sources, cited each web site I'd taken his words from, sent it into the queue, notified the photo department we needed a picture, and then I went downtown and drank Amber Ale with Ben. We listened to a new folkie group consisting of three guys and one girl with shaggy armpits and a whirly-twirly skirt. She sang about loving the earth in such a committed way I expected her to dump the contents of their tip jar back to the soil.

"Behold, a dirtette among dirts," Ben said, referring to the girl in the group. He told a mean tofu joke, and once again laid out the plot for his great American novel. "It'll be a bestseller, man," he insisted. "Blow their minds. Sell to the movies. I'll have so much bank I'll be golden."

Reporters all had novels. Ben's simply floated closer to the surface. Mine was deeper down in my gut, lodged there like undigested sunflower seeds. The story had been there so long I could no longer tell if it was guilt or inspiration. I drank my beer, listened to the music, but those flowers Nance sent kept accusing me.

Honesty had been Nance's thing. Mine too, I thought. But in the year that she'd been gone, all my boundaries had blurred. I'd lied to women just to get them to go to bed with me, and then never called them again. I'd written seductive e-mail to one girl, and when it failed to get a response, I copied it and sent it on to the next one. I'd promised my mother I'd come home for my birthday and then flaked out at the last minute. When my dad ended up in the hospital, I should have flown home, but weaseled out of it, rationalizing that since it turned out to be angina, a phone call sufficed. From time to time, I told myself to call Nance, at least end things in a friendly way, but somehow I couldn't dial the last digit of her number.

Had I ever sent her flowers? Once. A Hallmark thing I ordered off the Net. Standard bouquet of dyed carnations and daisies; flowers she hated. Got free air miles for it. Never used them. Now she worked on a flower farm. Probably picked her own bouquets.

I'd sent the story to Don an hour before deadline.

"Got the Taylor thing," he said in the hallway as I was putting on my jacket.

"Good," I said. It wasn't a compliment any more than a dog raising his leg at a fire hydrant was a friendly hello. "See you Monday," I said.

He stood there looking at me for way too long.

Monday morning the sunflowers were still upright in the florist's vase, but the water had turned murky. Before I could sit down, Don called me into his office.

"Here's the thing," he said.

"What thing?"

"Your Taylor story. It's an okay draft, but it lacks bite."

"What do you mean, 'bite'?"

He rubbed his chin, which featured a thin beard and, seen in the right light, looked rather Amish. "He's an old coot. Nobody cares how many platinum records he sold. What I mean is, where's the dirt? You worked on that thing for a week. Surely in that time you managed to uncover something interesting. Like, wasn't he a heroin addict? Do something with that. Punch it up."

I took a breath. "There's no source to back up that rumor. I didn't get to where I am by writing stories based on innuendo."

He patted me on the back. "Look, dude, I'm not saying it sucks, just that it's bland. Put something in about the heroin, and the response will be humongous. We want it to pop. To get calls. That's what I'm after."

I hadn't been called a dude since junior high. "I don't think I can do that."

"I figured as much," he said. "Which is why I handed it over to Ethan. You two will share the byline."

Well, I'd walked into that one. He answered his ringing phone and I started off to my desk, my upcoming weekend thoroughly trashed. Ethan was one of Don's pals, with multiple facial piercings and a set of Bose headphones. He was an adjective-crazed skateboarder, and there was no way I'd share anything with him, especially not a byline.

I turned back and knocked at the open door of Don's office. He was sitting in his chair polishing the Stratocaster with a chamois cloth. "Can you even play that thing?" I blurted out before thinking.

His laugh reminded me of one of those toys Nance used to buy for her dog, a high-pitched squeaking that really got on my nerves. He demonstrated for me just how well he knew the guitar, and even without an amp I could tell he was good. "One more thing," he said as he set the guitar back into its display stand. "I forgot to tell you that while you were away, we had a meeting and made a few shifts in the paradigm. I'm changing you from days to evenings. Really, it's a compliment. You've been at this game so long we need you to start training the future."

"Excuse me?"

His phone rang, and he answered it. Gave me enough time to think up a dozen reasons I should remain working days, all of which I knew he'd shut down. When he hung up, I asked, "I suppose this means weekends, too."

"Sure, occasionally."

"Why am I not surprised?"

"Dude," he said. "You and I are finally on the same page. Awesome! Take the rest of the day off, but be back by four, okay?"

"I don't think I can be back by then," I said. "In fact, I don't think I'll be back at all."

I had to hand it to him. He never even blinked. "Well, nice working with you. Don't let the door slam you in the ass on your way out."

If he'd picked up the guitar again, I would have had to kill him.

Back at my desk, I packed up my stuff and ignored the ringing phone. Who'd be calling a dinosaur like me? The Spice Girls? Hanson? I was about to let it go to voice mail when I decided to take it one last time, thinking against all odds it might be good news. "Heinrich, *After-Hours* magazine."

"Oh, honey," my mother said. "Thank God. I tried to get you all weekend. Your father's in the cardiac unit. He had bypass surgery. Everything went fine, but the doctors said we're not out of the woods yet. I know I'm imposing, but can you please take some vacation time and come home? For a few weeks, maybe?"

So. Richard senior had finally had the Big Kahuna. The phone call I'd spent much of my life fearing had come. "Sure, Mom." I cradled that phone in the crook of my neck for the last time as I logged onto the Net and made my reservations.

IT WAS RAINING OUTSIDE, beading up on my leather jacket. The first flight I could book was a redeye. I wandered through the plaza, downtown, circled the City of Roses sculptures, checked out the homeless guys who were happily drinking the dregs of other people's Starbucks coffee. One beggar rode an ancient bike with a basket, in which he always had a kitten, never a grown cat. I didn't want to think about what happened to the kittens when they grew too old to work his scheme for him. I sat down on a bench and clutched Nance's cell phone, which I always carried with me. Had she still been in my life, all it would have taken was one call. She would have set aside whatever she was doing to cheer me up. Made me a wonderful dinner, taken me to bed, worn me out, washed my back in the shower, explained that there were *so* positive aspects to quitting a job at age fifty, that some would say this was "the opportunity of a lifetime" instead of a poorly aimed shot, and it was important to go home and be with my dad, that family was blood, and times like these you had to be there, and I'd do fine, really I would. But Nance wasn't here. It was ridiculous to imagine I could have beaten Don at his game. The little ferret was untouchable. Apologies would only make me look like a chump, and I wasn't sorry. As for working nights and weekends, the truth was, I was too old to keep crazy hours with no nights off. At the same time I knew any paper or periodical I approached would put me on the same schedule. Journalism was an industry where nobody except little twerps like Don got breaks. Behind his back we all told jokes, but from now on, it would be his name on the masthead of *After-Hours,* not mine.

And my father? We'd never gotten along all that well, but I didn't want to think of him dying. I wondered how much it hurt to have a heart attack, that whole left-arm thing, and how long it would take his ribs to knit back together after the surgeons had cracked him like a walnut in order to work their magic. Suppose he developed complications? Or didn't make it? How could my mom get on by herself? My brother lived twenty miles away. He'd take care of her. But my parents had been married fifty-two years. When a longtime partner died, the other half of the couple caught a case of the dwindles, and usually died soon after.

I spent the remainder of the day arranging to have my things put into storage—books, CDs, clothes. After Nance left I'd kept the space pretty spare. I informed the leasing agent I was out of there, to use my security deposit to make up the difference in rent and have the place cleaned. Ben had been looking for a car, so I gave him the keys to the Saturn, and he gave me a postdated check. How frightfully easy it was to dismantle a life.

I called my mom from the airport pay phones, staring at women who traveled wearing platform shoes and hip-hugging jeans. They looked so young, out there strutting their stuff. Meanwhile, my dad was getting blood transfusions, and he'd be in the CCU until the threat of pneumonia passed. Yes, my brother was there with her, and my sister was driving down from Maine. Everybody was just thrilled I was coming home. It was a sad reason to have a family reunion, but a reunion regardless.

I listened to her babble on, thinking of the way Don's fingers had traveled up and down the guitar strings, how he had that complex chain of notes committed to memory, while I had to keep checking my ticket to remember which gate my plane was leaving from.

"Fly safely, honey," my mother said.

"Get some rest," I said back.

At midnight I heard the rattle of the newspaper dispenser clanging open and watched the guy empty it and load up the new issues. I spent a quarter to buy one, and flipped pages until I found my article. Don had kept his word. Ethan had skateboarded all over my writing. There were six inches allotted to the heroin question—no proof—just enough tawdry speculation to give James Taylor ample reason to refuse all interviews for the rest of his life. And there on the byline, right next to Ethan, was my name.

That was it. All bridges burned. Career conflagration.

Beryl

3

Postcard from Palmer

May

Dear Bad Girls of the South,

To answer your smart-alecky questions, yes, we do have summer here in Alaska. Do we ever. Imagine a four-month-long holiday, where instead of the sun setting it gently touches down for an hour or so, then lifts again, like a hot-air balloon. Everywhere you turn there's a music festival, an outdoor craft market, a wildflower nature walk, some kind of celebration of all that light. And yes, it's vegetarian heaven, the produce freakishly mammoth, and the cabbages worthy of documentaries. Along with all that come tourists, whole flocks of them with lapdogs and cameras and campers with decals in the windows—just like Bayborough-by-the-Sea, only we have more parking. And please don't worry. I'm fine. Sometimes I get so busy that I forget to write, that's all. You guys are in my thoughts all the time. I miss each of you beyond reason. How is Leroy? And that old carrot pillager, Duchess? I'll bet you guys are selling so many cut flowers right now you hardly have time to plan for fall. Which fertilizer will you use this year? How many poinsettia orders do you figure you'll get? Did you plant that pink variety again?

Earl's in Anchorage tonight, playing guitar at Bear Tooth with Scott Kiefer. I'm here alone in our Palmer cabin, just me and Verde and this moose cow that's decided that our front yard is Moose Motel 6. I wish I could fall asleep. I bought myself a silk eye mask (just like Zsa Zsa Gabor!), but it doesn't fool my internal clock one tick. As I write this, I'm drinking coffee and staring at the mountains from the picture window, these huge granite crags. Every once in a while the moose twitches her ears. It must be annoying to have mosquitoes dogging you every minute. It's hard to imagine winter is only five months away, which by the way is Verde's latest word. Anyway, see you soon, probably before this card arrives since our mail travels by dogsled, I think. By the way, Pheebs, your aunt was wrong when she called the Iditarod a dogsled race. It's a *sled-dog* race—they do all the work. If you get stuff like that wrong, Alaskans nail you. When I get to the farm, let's stay up all night and talk. We have to celebrate Phoebe's last few days as a single girl, but sensibly, no more of that hospital business, you hear?

Love, Beryl

P.S. XXXXX (X-rated kisses from Verde!)

Phoebe

4

The Language of Horses

AT FOUR A.M. I woke to the sound of Leroy Rogers carrying on. Ness's horse had his own vocabulary. He'd nicker when he was about to get fed a warm mash—this low, chuckling gurgle that seemed to come directly from his neck. Whenever David Snow and Ness rode David's horses onto the farm, Leroy brayed his outrage like a jealous donkey. If anybody drove the tractor too close to Leroy's land, Leroy screamed in fear, and try as I might, I couldn't come up with any words to describe that sound besides "awful."

"Mares can call a foal from across a pasture with one well-placed whinny," Ness had told me. "Every baby can pick out his mother's voice, no matter how many horses there are."

Well, having shoed horses for twenty years, Ness ought to know, but at four A.M. I figured Leroy whinnied because he was spoiled rotten and knew his stall was a hundred feet from a house full of easy marks.

Pretty soon I heard Ness groan from her bedroom.

A year ago she'd stolen Leroy from her ex, the same man who'd infected her with HIV. Not exactly a fair trade in my humble opinion, but Ness had made a kind of peace with her life. She went to church. She hung out with David Snow, the gay screenwriter who lived deep in the Valley. They both carried the virus, but David was sicker than Ness. When he had bad spells, she nursed him. Spent the night and everything. By now David probably knew more about Ness's personal life than I did, which sometimes ticked me off. Ness and I used to tell each other everything. We'd vowed never to allow men to come between us, but then I'd gone and agreed to marry Juan, heaving a boulder into my own glass house. Ness insisted she and David weren't lovers, but did a woman have to have sex with a man in order to love him? The two of them were always trotting off to the movies, antique hunting in Sierra Grove, or headed to gallery openings, stuff Ness had never seemed interested in until she met him. Sure, she still drove the tractor around the farm, depending on how well she felt, and she'd eased out of regular shoeing work in favor of the flowers we grew. Loving horses was as much a part of Ness as her cornrow braids. She was one of us, a Bad Girl. But I was starting to wonder if David might not be running a close second on her list of favorite things. She'd surprised us all by making a gift of Leroy to Florencio, our farm foreman. Florencio was so old about all he could manage was taking Leroy on stately walks, but that horse had never been so immaculately groomed. Leroy had a damaged history the same as the rest of us. Ness said that Jake used to beat on him for no good reason. In the old days, every chance I got I had slipped Leroy sugar cubes. Still, he never accepted the fact that his next meal would arrive without reminding everyone, which was no doubt why he thought that four in the morning was a perfectly reasonable time for breakfast.

I heard the screen door slam, and Leroy started in nickering hello to Ness. Then things were so quiet I heard the ticking of my late aunt's Ansonia clock. It wasn't all that valuable an antique, but the reclining brass figure gracing its side looked enough like my aunt for her to fool me into believing the clockmaker had designed it in her likeness. Sadie had a million stories. She was always telling me tales, citing her sources whenever I doubted her. Russian, Prussian, Persian, or Czech, each story seemed designed to assist me through some difficult aspect of childhood. Her stories were like fairy tales on steroids, a wild mix of her travels and a lifelong penchant for reading. Uncle Remus meets Agatha Christie, the two of them go out dancing, end up in a blues club in New York City, drinking too much, exchanging phone numbers they'll lose on the subway. It was as if the refrain to each one was the same: *Welcome to the real world, Phoebe, where if happy endings are just out of reach, at least the journey is interesting.*

I had tucked my brown hair behind my ears that morning, the day of my wedding. It had grown so much this summer that it now touched my shoulders. "I'm going to style it myself," I had told Ness. "Juan likes it plain."

Ness had given me a look, and soon we were off in the LandCruiser to Cecile's Comb-out, where once a month she had her braids attended. "You're going to adore Gabriella," she said.

Right.

Forget my crooked spine, how gimpy I walk, or all my years at Shriners' Hospital. To make me feel truly crippled it took a beauty salon. For one thing, all those different products lined up on glass shelves out of my reach. Then there were the endless shades of nail polish. So many reds it boggled the mind, and now all these strange colors, too, like blue, glitter, or that scary black. Sixteen different kinds of brushes to choose from, when all my life I'd bought the same brand when the old one got too ratty. I was definitely out of my element. For the first time in a long while, I wanted my wheelchair, some familiar surroundings instead of this vinyl swivel chair with the hydraulic lift.

"Feels like I'm going in for an oil change," I explained to Gabrielle, who was the first six-foot-tall black woman I'd ever met with waist-length red hair.

"Close your eyes and relax," she said as she gave me a wash and towel-dry. Her hands felt wonderful on my scalp. My hands felt wonderful, too, because Tiffani-with-an-*i* was massaging my cuticles with some kind of lemon balm before she did my manicure.

"Lord Almighty, girl," she scolded. "What do you do all day? Dig in the dirt?"

"As a matter of fact," I said, "that's exactly what I do," I said, and I told her about the flower farm and the clay sculptures.

"Don't be telling me no lie," she said, looking at my wheelchair.

"Honest. You should come to our Fourth of July sale." I groped in my pockets for a flyer to give her after the appointment.

Gabriella held her shears up and said, "Hold on, everyone. I'm getting an idea."

Tiffani sniffed. "Better run while you can, Phoebe. Nothin' good ever come of Gabby's brain trying that hard."

"You hush," Gabby said. "Stop interfering with my muse."

Cecile's Comb-out had a sound system that played R&B, jazz, and some really good stuff from the sixties. When Aretha's "Freeway of Love" came on, all the stylists stopped whatever they were doing and danced. These women! They moved their hips so fluidly that I wondered if their bodies had higher water content than mine. Gabriella knew all the words, and the backup, too, every "ooh-whee" and "yes-yes." Tiffani had the better voice. She sang over Gabriella until Gabriella got mad and threw a towel at her, and Rahkelle, the girl who managed the place, told them to knock it off or she was going to put on Michael Bolton. After everyone screamed and made remarks about his impossible hair, they shut up and got back to work.

"What your hair needs is encouragement," Gabrielle told me as she massaged some shiny-looking gel into it. With her fingers she crimped it into marcelled waves, turned my chair, and made me look in the mirror. "Now. What do you think of that?"

What did I think? I looked like a flapper. Like the daughter of some 1890s Mexican don. Like a woman who was surer of herself than I was. I touched a curl and pulled it out to a slightly softer length. "Preciousness?" I said, using her full—and despised—first name.

Ness smiled at me from the next chair over, where her braids were being gently patted dry. "Pheebs, you look like a gangster's moll. Juan is going to rip your dress off and throw you down on the buffet table."

Tiffani held up my hand and showed me the blood red polish she'd painted on. "Such dainty fingers," she said. "You get another coat of color, then a topcoat of clear. Your nails aren't done until they have that topcoat, honey. It's like the right jewelry."

She pronounced the word *jew-la-ree,* and I smiled.

Rahkelle stepped in to apply my makeup, and like a good girl, I shut my eyes, pursed my lips when she said to, just generally surrendered to the paint and potions other girls lived by. In the background Aretha sang the anthem of strong women everywhere: *Be strong. Have faith. There's another land a-waiting by and by.*

IN MY ROOM I lay in the dark as still as I could manage, trying not to be hungry though I was, or sick to my stomach, though that possibility lurked right behind the hunger. Most of all I tried not to think about Juan, and how thanks to Central Coast fog and a four-car pileup as he drove back from dropping my mother and her new husband at the airport to catch a plane, he was gone in the time it took for three cars to rear-end the one that braked for a perfectly good reason: a lost dog, a pedestrian who misjudged the traffic, an anonymous deer in search of superior browsing, all that polished metal and chrome crumpled, and the man I loved, who was always reminding me to put on my seat belt while forgetting to put on his own, delivered his wedding-day kiss to a windshield instead of to me.

SOME DAYS I DID ALL RIGHT. I lay on my left side, like Lester had told me to, imagining my chest cradling my compromised heart instead of it bruising against my ribs. Other days I tossed and turned, and each minute passed so slowly I felt as if I was dream-running to escape all manner of beasts. The real danger wasn't my heart, though I'd put it through a lot over the last year. However seasoned it had become, it beat steadily. The problem was my imagination and the dark alleys it liked to explore. In that split second before Juan hit the windshield, what were his thoughts? Did he die on impact, as the paramedics insisted, or had there been time for him to feel the awful pain? Did he really and truly love me, wheelchair and all, or had there been some pity involved? Was he sorry we hadn't gotten to say our "I do's"? Would our marriage have lasted?

Not that it mattered now.

Think of a nice Aunt Sadie story, I told myself. One with no great lessons except how to be still and patient and wait for the flowers to bloom. Okay, then, how about you pretend you're having a hot-rock massage at the Post Ranch Inn. You smell the heat of the sun hitting the bark of the oak trees. Listen to the roar of waves in the distance. Whales are swimming by, their rubbery skin impervious to the salt water and the new calves are learning to—

The screen door banged shut, and a cuss word rang out as Ness stubbed her toe on something. I heard her slowly ease my bedroom door open. I spent so much time in the dark that, like a cat's, my eyes had adjusted. She looked so beautiful standing there in her nightie, the hem damp with dew. She squinted as she checked up on me. In her kente cloth headwrap, she looked regal and African and stronger than any tree I could name, including redwood.

"Phoebe," she whispered. "Are you sleeping?"

"Huh?" I mumbled, as if she'd awakened me.

"Never mind. Go back to sleep." Ness yawned, then trundled back to bed.

Outside, Leroy was quiet for a change, his muzzle stuffed full of hay. Imagine a meal being enough to make someone that happy. It would never work on Nance, another of us Bad Girls, who'd lately turned up her nose at any food besides Diet Coke. The house I'd inherited from my aunt went still like it did in the long hour just before dawn, when stray thoughts traveled as deep as dreams. I'd been awake for so long that I figured I might as well watch the sun come up—the sunrise might qualify as my one thrill for the day, actually. Then I'd go back to sleep, really I would, since that was the extent of my agenda, and more important, my capabilities.

"Alone," I whispered to myself. It was a word I tried out now and then. Same went for "dead," which I preferred to "passed away."

IN SADIE'S JOURNAL she wrote about her weddings as if they were senior proms, as if marriage were nothing more than a wonderful excuse to buy a fancy dress, drink champagne to excess, be the center of attention, and get lots of really great presents. Yet every once in a while, tucked between those descriptions of designer gowns and costly bottles of bubbly, I found something like this:

> K's family all decked out in formal wear, tuxedos they owned, not rented, my poor father standing back from the crowd in his Sears off-the-rack. The string quartet playing every note perfectly, their bows moving in unison, like syncopated tree limbs. K, so drunk that when the minister asked, "Do you take this woman . . ." I saw him shrug a little before his brother elbowed him and he remembered to say, "I do."
>
> Kenny kissing that woman—his one last fling, a young man's folly . . .
>
> The scent of the old roses in the garden nearest the house—they're my roses now, too.

Even now that passage haunted me. I had worried and wondered, was it fair to marry Juan when my heart had already chalked up one infarction? Would I burden him with my medical problems? Though it was pointless to consider, I continued to work those questions over in my mind.

At six P.M. on that summer evening, in the same garden of white roses where Sadie had married the faithless Kenny, under a bower Nance had made festive with gold ribbon and hundreds of fairy lights, Juan and I were supposed to tie the knot, jump over the broom, and recite our vows. Instead my mother married her new love, Bert. "Want to know how we could make this day truly special?" she asked as she sat on my bed and watched me dress.

I cringed, picturing some horrible conga line or sing-along. "How?"

"A double wedding! Bert and I, and you and Juan. What do you think, Sweetheart?"

"Mother, surely you're joking," I said.

"Oh, honey," she said. "It's such a great idea. Let's do it. Bert and I have a plane to catch, so there's no time to waste. . . ."

There was a moment of hesitation during which she realized I wasn't kidding and I realized she wasn't either. Into that moment stepped my Juan, smoothing over the moment and sealing his fate. "We must respect our elders, Phoebe," he insisted. "Let them marry first."

I threw Sadie's silver-backed hairbrush across the room. Why did I have to share with her? Why now, on this day of all days, was I supposed to act like the adult and let her be the child? "No," I'd said, but Juan drowned me out. "I can take the newlyweds to the airport," he said. "Then we'll have the day to ourselves."

If he hadn't been there, I would have stood my ground, but it seemed wrong to start out my marriage by messing with Latino traditions. "Fine," I said. "But you hurry back."

"Absolutamente," he insisted. "I'll send them off to their honeymoon, then take our vows and dance until the sun sets."

I understood what he meant, even though I couldn't dance unless somebody held me up so my feet didn't touch the floor. That day turned in my mind like a kaleidoscope: a flash of Mother's pearl earring glinting inside steel gray helmet hair. Her cheek painted with a youthful blush. Her face unable to contain her smile. "Mother," I'd said, "you make a beautiful bride," and she did, in her cream-colored silk suit, her lipsticked mouth thanking everyone who wished her well in this hurry-up, late-in-life romance. The tension in my stomach loosened as I imagined us from this moment forward healing the mother-daughter rift we'd always tiptoed around, cut short by Juan's quick and easy good-bye. It was twelve miles to the airport. Maybe he even said that he'd be back before I noticed. That would have been like him.

I was dancing with David Snow when we heard the sirens.

LYING ACROSS THE ARMREST of my wheelchair was my wedding dress; a simple Mexican peasant cotton design that Nance insisted wasn't fancy enough.

"Oh, look!" she'd said longingly as we flipped through the different frocks on the rack in the bridal boutique in Bayborough-by-the-Sea. "Seed pearls and satin."

The sample dresses, size ten, were like stepping inside a circus tent. The salesclerk apologized like mad when she brought in some flower-girl dresses. After Nance and I managed to stop laughing, I started trying them on.

"Do I look as absolutely titless as I feel?" I asked Nance, knowing she would tell me the truth.

"Yes."

"You do not," the salesclerk soothed. "You look radiant."

"Don't settle for something you don't love one hundred percent," Nance preached as I pulled them over my head one by one, trying to worship them and falling short of the altar.

"Are you talking about dresses or men?" I prodded her, because I knew she still carried a torch for her ex, Rotten Rick, the journalist she refused to talk about, though she'd been dating my brother, James, for a year now.

"Dresses," she fired back, gathering the rejects in hand so I could try the next and the next.

Then the clerk handed me this tea-colored *quincenara* dress, and said, "Just give this one a chance."

Last chances—somehow they always worked out for me—my heart attack not causing too much damage, coming out of the coma remembering my ABCs, making up with James, and us pooling our resources to run the farm together. The minute Nance buttoned up the back, I knew it was the one. "This definitely doesn't look like a flower-girl dress."

"I don't know," Nance said. "There aren't any seed pearls. It looks kind of ordinary. I mean, it's not like your wedding dress has to be wash-and-wear, Phoebe."

"We can stitch on a few pearls," the clerk suggested.

But I loved it just the way it was. Plain. Honest. I bought it. Tried it on numerous times for all the Bad Girls, and at night I'd dreamed of having perfect legs, stepping gracefully like a heron down the garden path to my beloved.

Maybe thinking wasn't as dangerous as grieving, but it held its own level of peril. By giving selfishly into my pain, I could ignore all the problems here on the farm. Such as Nance, who ran on frenetic energy and migraine pills. Diet Coke couldn't be blamed for all that. Her size-four jeans hung baggy, and I wanted to bring up eating disorders but she never lit in one place long enough for me to get around to it. She'd bring us tea and two of the Staffordshire cups, take one sip, and make a face. "Gag. Tastes like bathwater. I need a Diet Coke," she'd say, and then run off to the kitchen leaving me feeling as if I were a child left behind to have a solo tea party while Mom ran off to a cocktail party and the baby-sitter had phone sex with her boyfriend. The day Nance brought me cranberry juice in a Waterford goblet full of crushed ice, I knew something huge was up. "How are you feeling today, Phoebe?"

"The same as yesterday. I hate my life, I don't want to ever see my mother again, and I'd appreciate it if you didn't try to cheer me up."

"Oh, that wasn't my intention at all," she said.

I could see it in her face, some major good news she was bursting to tell me, but she wasn't sure how I'd take it. That's how all the Bad Girls acted around me. Like I was something made of glass so fragile one misplaced word would shatter me. "Nice crystal," I said, holding the Waterford up to the light. "If you like a drinking goblet that can double as a free weight. What's the occasion?"

Nance set hers down on the bedside table and stared at the carpet. "Phoebe, please don't hate me," she said quietly.

"Why would I hate you?" I said. "I love cranberry juice."

She blinked her big eyes at me and I could see the happiness lurking in them. "It's, well, it's your brother."

I felt my heart seize. "Is there something the matter with James?"

"No."

"For God's sake, Nance, don't scare me like that. If it weren't for James; I don't know . . ." It wasn't a sentence I dared finish. James was essentially running the farm while I lay here in bed. "Then what is it?"

"He asked me to marry him, and I said yes."

I swallowed hard, the juice astringent against my tongue. It would have been easier to watch movie footage of Juan's wreck than to hear her words, because they meant the impossible: Life was moving on. Life didn't care about my grief. It hadn't even stopped for one minute to feel sorry for me, and now I couldn't deny that. I put on my best happy face and handed my friend my empty glass. "I think that's wonderful, Nance."

In her hands the glass caught the sunlight. "I'm thinking about this for my crystal pattern," she'd said. "What do you think? Is it too clunky? James put his foot down when I showed him the Fostoria. I'm trying to compromise, but I miss that delicate engraving. Oh, Waterford's all wrong. I know it is. Dammit all, I have nine goblets of different patterns, and I can't commit. Phoebe, I need you to tell me something. I love James. He's everything I ever dreamed of. But sometimes I think about Rick, and I don't think I'm over him. Do you think maybe I really don't want to get married?"

I had to answer, because I knew what vacillating cost. "You tell me." I listened and drifted into memories. Nance popped migraine pills and washed them down with the Diet Coke. Seed pearls. China patterns, crystal. Sometimes it was hard to hear while I was mourning my own wedding-day dream, but when Juan had died, the world hadn't stopped turning. I wanted the Bad Girls happy, and that was that.

Nance had her heart set on the dream wedding—satin, platinum, designer labels, the subtle undercurrent of sex sanctioned by the church's blessing, her motley assembled family all starched and spit-shined like we were actual relatives instead of friendly impostors. I would rise to the occasion. She and James had been on-again, off-again for so long that behind their backs Ness and I referred to them as Zelda and F. Scott sometimes. Zelda talked crazy, like how great it would be to have a cigarette, if only they didn't stink and give you cancer, and if a woman age forty had a baby every year for three years, the odds were good that she could live long enough to see them safely into their mid-thirties. And oh, my God, had she remembered to tell the bakery she wanted real butter cream frosting, not that Crisco fluff?

I'd never gotten to taste my cake. Six tiers covered with candied violets, and spun-sugar angels on top. Inside, a decadent chocolate cake with a tart raspberry filling. "Chocolate in a wedding cake is supposed to be bad luck," Nance had told me, but did I listen?

"Horse poop. Chocolate's chocolate, and I bet some greedy person who wanted all the chocolate for herself made that up."

"Don't say I didn't warn you," she'd kidded, and at the time we'd laughed because I was a regular slut for chocolate, I loved Juan, and I felt certain my lucky heart was so full I could enjoy both, and in retrospect everything looked like a neon warning sign.

Juan and I had fitted together. We'd become the "us" I never imagined, like those Russian nesting dolls Beryl Anne had sent down from Alaska for a wedding present. Alaska mail was so weird that even though she'd sent them Priority Mail, they hadn't arrived until yesterday. When I opened the box I indulged in some illegal crying, not because I didn't like them. When Beryl had moved out of our farmhouse to live with her beau, Earl, we knew we were going to miss her, but I had no idea that it would hurt this much to have her up there in the Great Land. Women friends—I hadn't had my circle very long, but our bonds were strong. Of the four of us Beryl had been the quiet one, mysterious, but full of insight. Leave it to her to find this wedding gift. There were only three dolls to the set, so intricately painted I had a feeling they cost a small fortune. Lacquered to a high gloss, they nested one inside the other. The husband doll in his tuxedo and cravat was the largest, and he went on the outside, with the bride doll fitted inside him. She looked dreamy eyed, and her hands lay against her white lace bodice as if she was hiding a surprise. Inside the bride doll was this tiny baby doll, absolutely naked except for a cranky expression painted on her face, like she was saying, "Time for my bottle!"

I wasn't going to get a happy ending, but that didn't keep me from rewriting my life while I lay still trying to heal:

Just for the time it took to have our wedding, God gave me legs, and Juan and I danced. "I love you, Juan," I said. "So, so much. I have the most wonderful secret to tell you. Tonight, as soon as we're alone."

"Yeah?" he said to me, a smile playing across his face. "What is it?"

"It's the kind of present you don't have to unwrap. But you will have to wait for it."

"Tell me now, Cara. *You know I hate waiting."*

"I think I'm pregnant."

His face, stricken and thrilled all at the same time. "Don't tease a man that way, DeThomas. It's not funny."

"Juan, I'm not teasing. I think I'm really, truly pregnant. And did I mention that I love you, and that my name's Nava, not DeThomas?"

"I love you, too, Señora Nava. And if you're pregnant, I'll drive you crazy making you take vitamins. Now, tell your husband, what makes you think you're pregnant?"

"I have all the usual symptoms."

"Did you take a test?" His eyes looking directly at me, as if no other world existed outside ours. In them I could see a future that included several dark-haired babies, all with straight, strong spines and perfect legs. Maybe enough children for a soccer team.

"I bought one for us to take together, tomorrow morning."

His smile again. "This day is full of surprises. Your mother and Bert. The fog lifting just when we said 'I do,'" and then he pressed a hand to my belly. "Now this."

I pressed my hand on top of his. My ring glinted. "Let's slip out right now, Juan. Let's go to my bed."

"Our *bed. And tomorrow we'll take the test."*

And it could have happened that way if my mother hadn't showed up. If Juan hadn't insisted we let them go first. I was a woman drowning in a sea of "if onlys." I touched the nesting dolls, still cradled in their packing peanuts in a box on my bedside table. Was Beryl's choosing this set some cosmic coincidence, or all those miles north of California, could she sense what I only suspected? Of course, it might have been just nerves. I hadn't thrown up or anything. But with three missed periods, either I was racing into the earliest menopause on record, or I was pregnant with Juan Nava's baby.

Lester, my doctor, was going to pitch a fit.

Maddy

5

Nightwalker

A COUPLE OF YEARS BACK, this tornado ripped through Oklahoma, killing forty-four people and injuring eight hundred. A thousand homes were flattened to rubble. The newspaper photographers had a field day—dead horses bloated up like sausage, babies wedged into trees, close-ups of the one china teacup that made it through intact. During that whole season of calamity people camped out in the school gym waiting for Clinton to send federal funds. Right around then Mama left Daddy and moved in with her sister, MayAnn. Lots of Indians in this part of the country had big bucks, but Mama and MayAnn were only quarter-blood, and MayAnn looked totally German, plus they both had married "white" men. Basically what they had to show for their heritage was good complexions, and long, dark hair that men still whistled at.

MayAnn had left Herbert, and now instead of a brick-front ranch house she lived in a double-wide trailer on five acres of nothing. Out front there was a plastic child's swimming pool for her bloodhound, Big River. Sometimes River got called in to work, and Auntie fired up her gold Chevy Impala, and took him to search for lost children or dead bodies or whatever needed finding. Mostly though, he lay on the porch looking mournful and drooling, the exact opposite of Mentos and Jim. The tornado leveled MayAnn's barn, but it spared her trailer. It emptied River's pool and flung it into a tree, and turned up her vegetable garden better than any backhoe. Auntie sent me a photo of herself standing by her place with her arms up in the air like she was saying, "Doesn't this beat all?" Behind her two ratty Appaloosas stood in the corral. Where the barn had been, the ground was pummeled, just whaled on, like Bigfoot had passed through. That tornado was the first break anyone in my family caught in so long, somebody should have baked a damn cake.

I expected there'd been some new building going on since I was here last. But the Oklahoma weather had aged everything, making it hard to tell what was new and what had been there forever. In Nightwalker, a typical small town, everybody knew everybody's business. I figured by the time I hit MayAnn's, several old ladies would have written down my license plate and called one another, just to be sure I wasn't some collie-toting serial killer.

The place smelled the same, loblolly trees and scrubby fir, every now and then a mountain of horse manure that needed to be hauled away, and scribbled all over that, the heavy scent of imminent rain. MayAnn's Impala was parked nose-out in the carport, a faded American flag duct-taped to the antenna. Big River sat on the porch regarding my truck with little enthusiasm. Slim Jim and Mentos were itching to get out of the truck and give River the once-over, but I took hold of their collars and told them how it was going to be.

"You behave yourselves while we're here, and Auntie will give you dinner. Screw up, and you'll have to sit in the truck. She serves that canned dog food. Think it over and get back to me."

My dogs looked up at me as if they were receiving orders about going into war. Last night we'd slept at the Pump & Pantry motel just outside Broken Bow, Mentos and me in one bed, Slim Jim in the other. We could've driven all the way here, but I was so wiped out after seeing that Ryder truck I didn't even turn on the motel television. We slept until the people staying next door got into an argument. I lay in bed awhile, hoping they'd settle down, but they were both so intent on winning I could tell it would keep on until checkout. The dogs and I shared a package of beef jerky from the vending machine. I gassed up the truck and drove slowly.

"Go easy on Mama," I said as I cut the engine. "And maybe she'll go easy on us."

I said a quick Hail Mary, got out of my truck, and stretched my arms in the humid air. MayAnn's plug-ugly horses whinnied from the corral. The aluminum roof on the new barn was already pitted, likely from hail. Somebody'd mucked the place out not long ago, but to the side of the barn the manure pile stood four feet high. I climbed the fence and petted the Appys. The smaller one shied and took off bucking around the corral. That could mean it was going to rain, or maybe the idiot horse had caught a wild hair. One thing I knew for sure, unless Mama had gotten a job, she was home, because it was time for *All My Children*. Both MayAnn and Mama had a king-size investment in Tad and Dixie's marriage, the one union on earth they considered unbreakable. It was the source of most of their bickering. Instead of knocking on the trailer door, I opened it, went inside, and sat down on the couch to watch the show with them.

Aunt MayAnn was drinking a Diet Coke. A bag of pork rinds sat on her lap. Mama was just sitting there, her thumb keeping place in her horoscope book. Onscreen Tad was trying to convince Dixie that he hadn't meant to sleep with the schizoid lawyer chick, that his infidelity was the result of the evil Dr. Hayward spiking the punch with some crazy Viagra-type drug called Libidizone.

"See?" MayAnn said, beseeching her sister to listen. "Mr. Mind of His Own was encouraged by bad medicine in the punch!"

"MayAnn," my mother said, eyeing me without a blink. "Tad's own hands pulled down that lawyer's silky panties."

Oh, that look of hers! When we were kids, Maggot used to warn me, "Mama's got the steely-eye thing going again. Make sure you picked up your clothes." Mama and MayAnn were never huggy women, but I expected a smile from one of them, at least. As if Tad and Dixie were right there in the room and she'd been hired to mediate their reconciliation, Auntie MayAnn got up to fetch me a Diet Coke, all the while talking to the television. "Give him another chance, Dixie. He's a good man, plus he's rich."

Mama snorted with laughter. "Any halfway decent lawyer could get her half his money. Maybe she should hire the one he slept with."

My aunt looked at her sister. Mama stared back. With both of them so thin, Mama's long dark hair braided into a thick rope, MayAnn's black hair its twin, and the stubborn set of their mouths, they might have been two halves of the same mirror image instead of born two years apart. "Nita," MayAnn said, "you have a hard heart. What's Dixie going to do with a bunch of money and no man?"

My mother tucked a tissue into her sleeve and sipped on her Diet Coke. "Well, she could build a nice house for herself, or maybe start her own business. She could tat a lacy tablecloth and serve lunch to friends who won't lie to her. Maybe even get herself a couple of border collies and hit the rodeo circuit."

"Ha-ha, Mama," I said. "Very funny."

Mama sighed. "Mary Madigan, you look like you slept in those clothes. Where have you been, and what brings you out here to Hooterville? I hope it isn't money, because as you know, your father took all mine."

Auntie folded her arms across her skinny bosom. "What she means is 'nice to see you.' Maddy, Sweetheart, you all right with that Diet Coke? I might have some root beer around here."

"I'm fine, Auntie. Thanks for asking."

"I have to agree with your mother, Maddy. You look about done in. You in trouble with the law again? You been stealing cosmetics?"

"My God," I said. "Are you ever going to let me live that down? The last time I stole anything was in junior high."

"Last time you got caught," MayAnn said, giggling.

"I am not in trouble! I have just ended my affiliation with the rodeo, if you must know. I thought I would come look up my family to say hello. Or maybe that's a crime, I don't know."

Mama looked at me again. Her poor face. It used to be so smooth, always laughing. Grief had tormented her into old age. Her mouth had pursed into those lines like a cranky schoolteacher gets. I wanted so badly to reach out and pull her to me. I wanted to feel that warm brown skin against my own, smell her sweet smell, tortillas and perfume and the strong-woman smell, feel her hands drawing me close, combing through my hair. But since we lost Maggot, she hadn't liked being touched. She didn't talk a lot, and when she did, she said harsh things that hurt. If I was real lucky, by the time this visit concluded, Mama might tell me she liked my cowboy boots, and then ask me where I was headed.

"I don't like that dark color of lipstick," she said to me. "I never did."

I wiped my mouth clean with the back of my hand, revealing the scar from where I had my stitches.

"Mother of God, what happened to your upper lip?" Mama asked me. "Where'd you get that scar?"

In a large pot on the stove, something wonderful bubbled and simmered. I got up to investigate and saw that it was hominy and chilies, with some kind of meat I couldn't identify and hoped wasn't goat. I stirred it, replaced the lid, and lowered the fire to simmer. Of course it was a damn scar. Because I couldn't afford plastic surgery, a crooked white line erased the bow on the left side of my upper lip. Why else would I put on purple-black lipstick every damn day? I knew if I answered her question, my mother would have all the bait she needed to categorically dismiss each moment of my life since I'd left McAlester. I tried hard to come up with a good lie—dogbite, horse threw me into barbed wire, a car wreck where I went through the windshield. No way was I telling her it had come from Dalton Afterhart's fist and too much alcohol—on both sides of the argument. "It's nothing. I fell off a horse. Doctor who stitched it up said it would fade in time."

"So you've left this rodeo adventure?" MayAnn said. "You stayed with it so long I thought maybe it was working out. What happened?"

"She broke up with a man," Mama said. "Am I right?"

I clutched my Diet Coke, the can nearly empty and the contents heated to room temperature. "It was nice while it lasted," I said.

"Maybe you should take Dixie to lunch," MayAnn said. "Trade boyfriends."

She and Mama tittered, and I wanted to smack them both. They were fine ones to talk, MayAnn divorced for the second time. "At least I had the brains not to say, 'I do.'"

I threw the Coke can into the trash and walked outside to check on my dogs. Big River hauled himself up enough to slobber all over my hand. I took him over to the truck to meet my guys.

When you introduce collies to other dogs, there's always the chance they'll see them as something to be mercilessly herded. Of course, the same held true when they encountered cattle, goats, chickens, children, butterflies, running water, lawn mowers, brooms, and tree limbs, depending on how hard the wind was blowing. I worked with Slim Jim about this constantly, but still he had to run through the list. And if Jim said, "Chase," Mentos'd run until she dropped.

Maybe they could sense the family rejection in me, but they only yipped a little and then lay down waiting for me to give them something to do. I was tired of fetch, so I got out one of the jars of bubbles I always carried and sat on the porch steps blowing them and letting the guys give chase. River looked up at me as if I was insane. "You're a working dog," I told him. "Can't you tell this is called any port in a damn storm?"

He huffed his muzzle, and all the wrinkly skin rearranged itself. I blew bubbles until my cheeks felt as stretched out as Dizzy Gillespie's, but the collies outlasted the whole jar. They needed two walks a day, forty-five minutes each, plus a training session I wasn't up to just now. Part of me was wondering what Dalton was thinking about suddenly finding himself in a trailer with no truck to pull it, and whether a man who'd barf on my jacket was capable of missing me. Maybe all along he'd been one of those rat bastards who said *I love you* with as much intent as *Sure, I'll be glad to fix that dripping faucet; I'll get right to it as soon as I feel like it.* Another part of me was four years old again, hoping against hope that my mother would chuck me under the chin and say how nice it was to see me, how pretty I looked when all's I looked like was the staircase to hell.

I told the dogs to get in the child's pool so they'd cool off. It was two o'clock, and the June sun above was beating down hard. No trace of wind for a break. Sweat beads rolled down my neck. They dutifully stepped in, and stood there trembling. They hated water unless it was to drink. I wanted to get in the water myself. By the time Auntie MayAnn came out of the trailer, it was starting to rain, but the air was already so humid the rain didn't make much difference.

"So," I said. "How'd things with Tad and Dixie end up?"

She shrugged. "Have to wait until the next installment. Those damn soapers won't give you an ounce of satisfaction. They draw out the story until I forget why I gave a hoot in the first place. Still, I can't stop watching. I like your hair long," she added, as if I'd been here a month ago and changed the style. "It softens you."

"Thanks."

"Your dogs, or the man's?"

"Mine, ma'am. Purebred border collies."

"Huh. Appear not to trust water."

"Yeah, they're beautiful, but they have some brainless ideas, and water being dangerous is one of them." I motioned them out of the pool, and they took off like the devil was at their heels.

MayAnn held out a hand to the rain. "Only going to get hotter."

I knew that. I knew which kind of clouds meant what kind of weather; I knew the precise way to get a border collie to move; I knew when my period was due; I knew a lot of useless damn facts, but I didn't know how to get my mother to speak to me like I was alive and worth her breath.

MayAnn took in her laundry off the clothesline and hollered at the horses to stop cribbing, which they did, momentarily. "Supper won't be for hours yet, Mary. Drive me into town so I can get some fabric."

I looked over at the Chevy, which appeared to be in running order. The rain had reduced the American flag to a limp hankie. "Mama coming?"

MayAnn petted River and told him he was a beautiful red boy. "She's deep in that horoscope book." She got into my truck and waited.

Mentos and Slim Jim looked at me expectantly. I hated to tie them up almost as much as I hated to ask my mother to look out for them. I snapped on their leashes and staked them near the scary child's pool. "I won't be long," I hollered into the trailer, and petted the dogs, knowing full well they had no sense of time—you're either there or you're gone, capital *G*.

Windows open, we drove down wet roads, some gleaming tarmac, others dirt. The rain brought out all kinds of scents from scrub bushes to the oniony perfume of warm Oklahoma air. I read someplace that's because the rain encourages this special kind of bacteria to bloom. All's I knew was it reminded me of Dalton's armpits after we'd have sex, a not entirely unpleasant scent, but strange, and male. On either side of the road the summer grasses grew so thick I could almost hear the insects munching. Plenty of new trees had been planted, pine mostly, but they hadn't had the time to grow tall. All kinds of horses grazed from behind fences, ignoring the rain. One little farm featured goats; another had a llama the color of peach brandy. Every now and then a clutch of silver rural mailboxes broke up the earth tones, so bright it made me squint. Like most small towns, the business district had a hotel with awnings, and if you blinked, you'd miss it altogether. We drove by Bazley's Baked Goods, the place Maggot and I used to run into for free cookies when we were kids. "Oatmeal raisin," she always said, a pint-size health-food nut case. For me it had to be chocolate chip or I'd go without.

"Turn there," Auntie said. "Park in the lot by the fabric store. Come in with me."

I didn't bother to cover my head from the rain. Neither did Auntie. She walked straight to the good cotton, fingered every bolt, and then moved to a table of flannels marked half price. "What are you making?" I finally got the nerve to ask.

"A quilt."

Auntie made them every so often, to mark special occasions. "What for this time?"

She hiked three bolts under each arm and made her way to the clerk. After she gave her orders, she ran her fingers over the ribbons in the display. "For your sister," she said. "What with that dedication ceremony coming up in February, it'll be cold, so I'm thinking flannel."

I took deep breaths and tried to imagine that my sister was a few miles away from here, working hard at her job, or sitting at some desk making important phone calls instead of buried in the rubble of the Murrah Building. I could see her alive, breathing, smiling as she spoke into a telephone to reassure a child's mother. Hers was one of the bodies they hadn't recovered. I held that picture in my mind as long as I could, and when the other, horrible picture replaced it, I did not cry. Auntie MayAnn eyed me suspiciously.

"What?" I said.

"You tell me, Mary. Last time I saw you, you were half drunk and yelling something about 'I'm never coming back to this effing hellhole, and you all can sit there on the porch and cry until you mildew and it won't bring Maggot back.' Did I get it right?"

"Pretty much." In my mind's eye I saw Maggot asleep on her side of our bed, hogging the childhood quilt we'd shared. It was a Lone Star pattern, flour sacks for the white parts, blue and brown calicos, with a diamond of orange where you'd least expect it, like the embers of a fire. That was how MayAnn made her quilts, with surprises, so you could look for them when you were sick or feeling sad. That flannel she had the salesclerk cutting was soft enough to sleep next to without a sheet.

"That'll be seventeen ninety-five," the clerk said.

Auntie took an old twenty-dollar bill from her pocket and smoothed it flat on the counter. "I get some change," she reminded the clerk.

We left the fabric store in silence. MayAnn looked in all the shopwindows, told me who was new in town, who had descended from what family, who had blood, who was on the brink of bankruptcy, and who was doing the extramarital fandango. At the antique store she stopped and pointed to a potbelly stove. "Ha! See that worthless piece of crap?" she said. "I sold that stove to the man who runs this store for fifty dollars, and it's rusted clean through on the bottom. Now he's got it marked three times that. Pure fool."

"Didn't you used to keep a plant in that?"

"All the time," she told me. "When the last one died, I thought, okay, that's enough dead plants. Sell it and buy some silk flowers."

We laughed, and for a moment, everything was good.

Of all places, MayAnn steered me into a teahouse. There were frilly curtains on the windows and small rickety tables. Last time I'd been there it was a mom-and-pop diner, I think. For sure it was the same waitress. Susie.

"Order something," my auntie said. "You don't look right. Are you on drugs again? I hope not, or else that votive I light for you every Sunday is a waste of a good quarter."

"I am not on drugs. I'm tired and I'm hungry, that's all. I realize how bad I've messed up. I don't need a fecking inventory of my past offenses. I remember each and every one of them just fine." Susie the waitress did not bat an eye. I took my time looking at the menu and tried to think what I wanted besides vodka and lemonade. "Do you have real coffee?"

"Sure."

"Coffee for both of us and the sandwich plate, too. White bread. Thanks."

"No problem, honey," she said, walking off to fix my meal.

What with all this feminine decor, antique paintings of mothers with babies, and fancy old silverware, it felt as if the room were closing in on me, demanding to know my reasons for being here. "It's been almost five years, MayAnn," I blurted out, my heart beating in my chest like one of her Appys kicking the fence rail. "Pretty soon I'm turning thirty. I quit that dead-end rodeo job, and I'm thinking maybe I'll look for a real job someplace near you and Mama."

She laughed. "Mary Madigan, what kind of job you think you're going to find out here in Nightwalker? Museum tour guide? Maybe if you go to Tulsa you can find something worthwhile."

"Then you're saying Mama hasn't forgiven me."

"Honey, why do you take this so personal? It's herself she can't forgive."

"But I'm her daughter, Auntie."

"She knows that."

"I didn't kill Maggot, the bomb did."

There. I'd said it. The ugly truth we didn't utter out loud for fear of grief grabbing us all by the throat and running wild again. My twin, unlucky enough to go to work that day, died on April 19, 1995, at 9:02 in the morning. Well, we *hoped* she'd died at 9:02, because if it took longer than a minute, none of us cared to know.

Aunt MayAnn took hold of my hands and squeezed. She looked me in the eyes. Hers were opaque, unreadable, like a shark's. I had my father's eyes, more of a hazel color, quick to well up, determined not to spill over. "Maddy, some people don't get over grief, they make a bed in it."

Susie set my order down.

"You enjoy that sandwich, hon."

I stared at it.

Auntie said, "I kept thinking River'd be the dog who'd find her. He knew her so well. We found all the babies, but not Margaret. His paws were all tore up, but he wanted to keep looking. It was like he knew she was in there." She shook her head and tapped her spoon on the table. "Maddy, explain to me why that boy thought a bomb could do something good."

I stared at the crustless bread and imagined it would be easier to swallow a mouthful of mud than a sip of coffee. "I don't know. He was angry at the way his life turned out. He blamed the government." My voice trailed off. Inside my chest it felt like my heart had beat itself to ribbons on my rib cage.

Auntie sighed. She opened the fabric-store bag and laid out her material from light to dark, and then reversed it. "Sunshine and Shadow," she said. "That's a good, simple pattern. Margaret would have liked that. I think that's the way I'm going to piece this one."

Neither of us had the courage to cry. She let me pay the bill.

THAT NIGHT AT supper I served up the hominy and handed everyone a napkin because that's what a good daughter did, respect her elders. The door to the trailer was propped open, and the flies had finally gone somewhere else. The rain had stopped, but a bigger storm was coming, one of those all-nighters Oklahoma was famous for. We watched the clouds roll in and the sky darken. I could smell that coppery scent in the air that meant a lightning show. The dogs lolled on the porch, their bellies full. I blew on the surface of my stew and waited for it to cool enough to eat it, but it stayed so hot for so long it was like the stuff was witched.

I'd met this man once, an older guy, kind, with little professor glasses, way too smart for the likes of me. It was the first time I'd sung in a karaoke bar, and I was half crocked when I did it, this B.B. King song anyone can sing when they're drunk. He was from the West Coast, and I think he might have been somehow attached to the music industry, because when I was done singing, he invited me to his table for a drink, and started talking about how well studio work paid, and so on. It was a bad time in my life, and I remembered asking him was all this attention because he wanted to go to bed with me, because if so, he could shut up and take me to his room right then. I did that a lot back then—pick up strangers. Sex was like a shot of morphine, guaranteeing a good night's sleep. But he didn't take me to bed. I asked him was he gay or something, and I remember he smoothed my hair off my face and said how if I cleaned up my act, someday he'd hear my voice coming out of the radio. I laughed so hard I got tears. Then he told me about the Pacific Ocean, how it was warm all year round, and how good it felt to swim in the wintertime. By then my tears were flowing in earnest. He wiped at them with a napkin and quoted some Indian guru who said that depression was like a tidal wave: It could crush you if you tried to stand up to it, but that if you rode it, sort of bodysurfed it, it might actually turn out to be a place to find all kinds of new ways of looking at things. He left money for our drinks, kissed me on the forehead, and hauled ass to the airport. I used his tip to buy myself another drink, and ended up eighty-sixed from the karaoke bar. I never saw that man again, or the ocean, and my voice coming out of a radio was like a dream I'd had when I was spiking a fever.

Auntie ate her stew, her spoon making irritating little clicks against the bowl. Mama pushed at hers with a piece of cornbread until it was soggy and disgusting. There was nothing to do in Nightwalker except watch TV. Mama and MayAnn hadn't turned the set off all day. It was reruns of *The Newlywed Game, Extra,* and then *Wheel of Fortune.* The box yammered continually, as if there was this whole other world ready to be entered into at a moment's notice.

"You didn't eat much," Mama said to me. "Five years away. I suppose your tastes have gotten all fancy."

"Nita," MayAnn warned.

"Maybe she's pregnant," Mama said.

I glared at her. She'd gotten pregnant with us when she was twenty-three and had been married to Daddy for a year. Sometimes it seemed that her biggest fear had been one of us getting knocked up out of wedlock. No, not one of us, really just me. "I'm not pregnant," I said. "I'll run into town and buy a pee test if you don't believe me."

Up she got from the table and scraped the contents of my bowl back into the pot. She stood at the sink and washed my bowl clean. When she set it in the rack it felt like I hadn't been there at all, like she'd erased me. "I don't know about how you run your life," she said, "but around here we can't afford to waste food. Around here, we go to Mass every Sunday, and we dress in clean clothes. . . ."

I felt myself beginning to lose it. Inside old chunks of history fell against one another, and when they collided sparks shot out. I shut the television off. "Dammit to feck and back, Mama," I said. "I'm sorry I didn't die. I'm sorry it was Maggot instead of me. Instead of both of us."

She walked over to me and slapped my face. "Don't you *ever* say that." Then she stomped outside, and it was just MayAnn and me sitting at the table.

"Oh, very nice," MayAnn said. "Well, you got her to talk to you."

I wanted to cry.

MayAnn pulled me into her arms and hugged me close. Her bones were sharp and her embrace too hard. I willed the tears to come to me, now that I was in a safe place; but my sorrow had dried up, leaving flint and shale among chunks of broken heart. I thought of abandoned dogs on the edges of highways, that scared look in their eyes as to which way to go. Women who slapped their toddlers in public when they misbehaved instead of comforting them with a soft word or a dollar toy. It was a slide show my mind played to me when I felt worthless. It was what made me drink. When MayAnn let go, I found my purse and applied my purple-black lipstick until my scarred mouth felt like my own again. I whistled to my dogs and told them to load up into the truck cab. I said good-bye to Big River, the only one who looked truly concerned to see me go. Then I walked over to the fence where my mother stood with her back to me, and I put my hand on the fence rail right at her shoulder. The damned Appys nipped at each other trying to get to me, sure I had treats.

"Mama," I said, speaking to her back. "You win this round. But I will never stop trying to get you to love me. I won't come around. You're free to stay alone inside your miserable shell forfecking-ever, but I love you anyway. Good-bye."

I backed out and was five miles down the road before I noticed that MayAnn had taped the American flag to my antenna.

THE PUMP & PANTRY MOTEL was full up, so I had to stay at a Super 8. The clerk behind the registration desk was maybe eighteen, East Indian, and glued to the television watching a baseball game. "Give me the room at the very end, will you?" I asked as I laid down my thirty-six dollars.

"If you bring someone into your room you have to pay for them," he recited as he shot me the key.

"So noted," I said.

Some motels, no matter how worn they were, I felt happy to be there. The shower might be old, but it was scrubbed clean, and the wrapped bar of soap was mine alone. This room was the other kind. The bed sagged in the middle. The pillowcases didn't match the sheets. A cardboard sign taped above the basin said: DO NOT UNDER ANY CIRCUMSTANCES DRINK THE WATER. I bought some bottled from the vending machine and poured it into a bowl for the dogs. I braved a shower, scrubbed my hair, brushed my teeth without rinsing, got into bed, and said a few Hail Marys. God, well, I was mad at God, but I loved Mary, all peaceful in her blue robes, unafraid to stomp snakes. I bet she hadn't fallen off the wagon when her mother was mean to her. The Blessed Virgin Mother was Daddy's favorite part about being a Catholic. He lit daily candles in her honor while my mother shook her head at what she called that ritual madness. Then, when Maggot died, my mother had turned Catholic with a vengeance.

What with car headlights coming and going in the parking lot and the rain pounding down, neither the dogs nor I could sleep. The bar/restaurant across the street was using the Super 8 for overflow parking. Poor Slim Jim felt required to growl at every car door shutting. I said "Shh" so many times I was sick of it and got up and looked out the window.

At the bar end of the restaurant a sign advertised a karaoke contest. I didn't particularly feel like singing, but walking over there and ordering a drink was sounding pretty great. In fact, if any day called for a drink, this one qualified. Even though I'd quit cold turkey four years back, and hadn't slipped once, alcohol was my constant companion. In my dreams I drank and felt the rush of heat down my throat, loosening my belly, flashing fire at the inside of my knees. Some days I woke with the chemical aftertaste on my tongue and a walloping headache. That made me nostalgic for those old days where I sang for anyone; I danced dirty; I slept with whichever man asked me to be his that night. Not one of them failed to tell me how good I was in bed, not once. I laughed at them, not remembering the first thing about it, but grateful all the same for the compliment because their words proved my existence, gave me some kind of worth.

"You guys stay here," I told the dogs.

The night air was cool. My clean hair tickled my bare shoulders like fingers. The door to the bar opened, and out poured a kinder world: Music I understood. I'd worked in bars, serving drinks, mopping up, making friends with the guys in the bands that came and went. Other girls went for drummers, but I always sought out the rhythm guitar player. We'd drink, kiss a little, and I'd end up singing my heart out in the companionable smoke, the friendly smell of spilled beer, and so much laughter that I loved going there, had to be a part of it all. This bar before me was your typical Oklahoma watering hole, duded-up cowboys in tight jeans, and gum-chewing women with big hair, pastel eye shadow, and Western-cut blouses that, so far as I can tell, flatter nobody. On the karaoke stage, some tubby guy in snake boots was murdering the bejesus out of a Kenny Loggins song. I listened until he finished, waiting for the crowd to start throwing rocks. Instead, they clapped and hooted, and he took a bow. Were they deaf?

I asked the bartender for a greyhound, and he made it in two seconds. It sat on the bar in front of me, sweating in the glass, waiting for me to throw away my years of sobriety. I had my hand around the glass when some guy with greased-back hair and wearing a shiny gold shirt grabbed the microphone and yelled out were there any last minute entrants, because if not, the judges were ready to close the karaoke contest. A hundred dollars prize money, he said, and somehow I found my hand up in the air, waving, *Me, me!*

He gestured me up onto the stage. The crowd was hammered, clapping for anything, and so they welcomed me warmly. When the technician asked me which song I wanted, I was tempted to do Tubby's, just to show him how to hit the right notes. But there were so many great choices: Aretha, old swing stuff, Billie Holiday, Janis Joplin, and buckets of blues, from sharecroppers to current stuff. I looked for an old favorite, "No One Ever Tells You." Amazingly, they had the Diane Schuur and B.B. King CD. I pointed, the techie loaded it into the prompter, and I clutched the microphone like it was Dalton's neck. After a hoarse beginning, I threw my troubles into the words, heedless of how it sounded. Sing how you feel, more than one guitarist had told me. Get what's inside and hurting you out and into the words. Well, tonight I was tired and angry, and singing an anthem for the hot, hard night and my unforgiving mother, but most of all, for that cold drink waiting for me on the bar.

"No One Ever Tells You" is a Carroll Coates and Hub Atwood tune. My daddy had it on CD. I can't remember when it was first recorded, or who sang it, but I challenged anyone to find better heartbreak lyrics. Calling it a song wasn't right; it was more of a blues poem. I read in a magazine that Duke Ellington used to say that by using the energy it takes to pout, he wrote his songs, sometimes in as little as fifteen minutes. I gave this song five years. Inside that time was Dalton and our countless fights; me missing Maggot; and not drinking when I wanted to so badly that I felt actual pains. When the synthesizer got to the part where B.B. performs his guitar solo, instead of standing there waiting for it to finish, I threw in a new verse, all my own:

No one ever tells you
That love is just like dope
That the first time that he screws you
Your soul fills up with hope
And no one ever tells you
There's no drink to wet that dry
When he cleans out your bank account
And leaves you alone to cry. . .

On the chorus I cranked the song up two entire octaves. I made the words shiver, the same sick way you feel when you're coming down off coke. I gave every single sharp a tap on the way back down, like I was crushing vertebrae. I finished by speaking the last word, "before," into the microphone like it was the only truth that could be counted on, and before the music ended, I handed the mike to the techie, who sat there open-mouthed staring at me. People were screaming for me to do it again, but all I could see was my drink waiting, and I wanted it more than I had ever wanted anything in my life. On the way to the bar, some old guy picked me up and swung me around, told me I was Patsy Cline reincarnate. Then a cowboy came up to me with tears in his eyes and asked if he gave me twenty bucks, would I please sing "Ruby, Don't Take Your Love to Town." His girlfriend hauled him away before I could answer. The announcer took my arm and steered me to the judges, who sat at a table littered with beer pitchers. One of them handed me the hundred-dollar bill. I stared at the green face of the dead president and thought how with this bill, I could buy drinks all night, or I could get myself a bottle and take it back to the Super 8 and drink myself to sleep. I could call my father in Tulsa and tell him to leave the door unlocked, or I could turn west and just keep driving. So many choices before me that I felt overwhelmed. I ran into the ladies' room and looked at myself in the mirror, my eyes wide as a startled animal's, my heart beating crazy like in my coke days. But it was Maggot looking back at me from the mirror, her sweet smile as twisted as the wreckage she died in. *Mary Madigan, what are you doing here?* she asked me. *You think this bar is the place you're supposed to be?*

I stuck the money in my bra. The hardest thing wasn't turning away from that beautiful drink, it was the moment Maggot's face faded into a smeary mirror and girls behind me jostled to reapply mascara.

TULSA IN JUNE, when it's not even miserable hot yet, is pretty hard to take. When Daddy sold the McAlester house, he moved into an apartment above the Italian restaurant he owns. It didn't have air-conditioning, but people really liked his food, so they came to eat late in the evening and sat at tables outdoors. Once, when Dalton and I were passing this way, I knocked on the door, bracing myself for the hot garlic aura when he opened it.

"Margaret?" he said, as if he'd just been thinking about my sister, and the look on his face did me in. In the background I could see how he'd pared his life down since the divorce. All his good furniture was gone. The apartment was decorated in thrift-store generic, featuring a plaid couch with furry arms and a butt depression where he must have spent his time off. It depressed me to death. A single lamp with a cracked shade, resting on an endtable of chipped Formica patterned in phony wood grain, cast a ring of dusty light. Atop that table there was also a statue of a Mary with her nose broken, courtesy of one of his and Mama's better fights. Of course, Daddy had his television set on, some religious station asking for "love offerings," because to say, *Send us your money* was too fecking honest.

"Dad, it's Mary," I remember saying, while Dalton waited for me in the truck.

But Daddy wasn't sober, and he couldn't make that work in

his mind. "Margaret, you look skinny. Let me run downstairs and get you something to eat, make you some dirty spaghetti."

Dirty spaghetti had been Maggot's favorite dish—garlic sautéed in butter, and then whipping cream added to make white sauce. I gave up and played along. "Maybe later, Daddy. How are you doing? You okay?"

He smiled. "I have my health, the job, and the church. . . ."

Once Daddy mentioned religion he'd talk for at least twenty minutes, making his way through every station of the cross. I studied him. He was in his late fifties, but the booze had made him look older. His once-black hair was graying. Blue-eyed Italians have strange eyes to begin with, somewhat icy, and with the dark ring around the pupil. If such a thing was possible, Daddy's eyes had faded to an even paler shade. They reminded me of really old dogs' eyes, cloudy with cataracts.

"Let's you and me go to Saint Teresa's and light some candles," I told him, and I took his arm and walked him to the church, a block away, where I watched him light votives and chant his hopeless prayers.

NOW, YEARS LATER, I sat in the rear pew of the same church, watching my father do that very same task, only he had no idea I was present. His movements were so practiced and repetitive that it was as if he had worn a rut from the restaurant to the altar. The candle flame cast his shadow on the wall, making him look like the giant he'd been to me during my growing-up years, when our family was intact. When Maggot or I had fallen out of trees, or we'd skinned our knees crashing bikes, Daddy had been there to soothe us, to check our bones for breaks, to make sure his girls were okay, and to make us spaghetti. Then came the day one of us wasn't there, and what was left of him was this old man kneeling to pray. Inside, I felt my rusted-out heart move one step closer to compost. I watched for as long as I could, then I left him there, still kneeling.

Rick

6

Hero School

SIX YEARS BACK, when I was forty-four, I saw a used leather bomber jacket in the window of a vintage clothing store in downtown Portland, and I had to have it. An outward and visible sign of the inward and hidden me, I thought. Shabby but durable, something that would never go out of style. But now, as I walked down the jetway into the terminal, my fellow passengers stared at me like I was a bum. Life on the West Coast had imbued me with a perpetually casual attitude. Apparently such was not the norm in the travel hub of Tulsa, Oklahoma. I took the jacket off and held it over my arm, and at the same moment spied my sister at the gate, waving.

Karen was the baby of the family. Other people made do with e-mail, but Karen wrote actual letters, several pages long, sometimes with illustrations in the margins. On my birthday she sent me a box of homemade cookies, wrapped in wax paper, clear across the nation from Maine to Oregon. We didn't see each other often, so when I pictured her I generally saw bony knees, buckteeth, and a twelve-year-old meticulously plotting a community fish tank. She was forty-four now, dressed in one of those gauzy import store shifts, a purple scarf across her shoulders. She looked old enough to be somebody's mother, and I tried not to let on how much it shocked me. "Little Ricky!" she said, crushing me in a hug. "You look like you've been run over."

"Thanks," I said. "Try getting any sleep in coach. Is there a place to get some decent coffee in this airport?"

"Dad's fine," she said. "Thanks so much for asking." She steered me to the nearest coffee cart—it wasn't Seattle's finest, but it beat the brown water they served in flight. After my first sip hit bottom, I said, "I could tell from your face he wasn't dead. And I fully intended to ask about him as soon as I had some coffee."

Karen picked at a scone she'd ordered. "It's a toss-up who's crankier today, you or him."

"Who wouldn't be cranky after having a saw taken to his rib cage?" I said as we made our way to the baggage claim.

"So what's your excuse?" she said. "Or are you turning into Dad just like I'm turning into Mom?"

No one knew better than me how critical my father could be. His examination of the world was never ending. Whoever said engineers retired didn't know Richard Heinrich, Sr. "How are you turning into Mom? Did you go back to church? Experience an insatiable need to favor your middle child over the others? Oh, wait. You forgot to have children, didn't you? What a bad girl. Shame."

Karen made a face at me. "I knew there was something I was forgetting. All I meant is we're middle-aged, Ricky. You, Ronnie, and me. Our parents got old, and lo and behold, we got old, too."

I grabbed my duffel off the carousel. "Age is only important if you dwell on it. Most days I feel seventeen. I'm ready. Let's go."

Karen touched my arm. "That's all your luggage?"

The subtext of our filial bantering surfaced, wet and shiny as a shark fin. Karen sensed I was in the middle of a major life change. Losing a job, breaking up with a girlfriend, flunking a class I needed to graduate—she could tell things like that long before I confided in her. "Look," I said. "Either I can fall apart on the airport floor and tell you the whole story, or we can go see Dad in the hospital like good children and I'll tell you everything later. Your call, sister."

She looked at me unblinking, and I saw crow's feet at her

temples. "The doctor says this surgery could give Dad ten more years."

I suppressed a groan. Sons weren't supposed to feel like this, but I was having trouble mustering enthusiasm at that much more time for him to disapprove of me. "Great," I said, and we looked at each other and started laughing. "Don't say anything at the hospital," I warned.

"Are you kidding?" she answered. "I'm barely keeping things together as it is."

THE PROMISE OF sharing a joint later with my sister fueled me to enter the cardiac unit. The hallways were clean, the floor buffed. Patients with IV poles and deep looks of concentration made slow laps. Here everyone had a private room, and had they been able to get out of bed, they would have enjoyed a nice view of some trees, Oklahoma architecture at its most efficient, and the brightly colored flow of traffic. My dad looked gray behind his oxygen tubes, his body propped into a sitting position courtesy of the electric twin bed. He wrinkled his forehead when he saw me, and I bent down and kissed his cheek. "Hey, Dad," I said.

My brother, Ron, stood up to let me have his chair. He said hello to me as softly as he could, in a funeral director's voice that meant, *I'm the good son because I was here when the shit hit the fan,* and P.S., *You still owe me money for that blown head gasket I sent you money to fix when you were stranded in the middle of Egypt, pal.*

"Where's Mom?" I asked.

"Where is she?" my father echoed.

"Daddy," Karen said. "She's taking a nap, remember? We made her go home to get some sleep. Ronnie, you look wiped out. Why don't you go get some lunch?"

"Rick," my father said, reaching for my hand. "Thank God you're here, son. Now I can relax."

Well, that was enough for Ron to stomp out of the room.

"Don't get yourself all excited," Karen said, smoothing Dad's covers. "Rick's not going anywhere. Come on, Dad. You're supposed to rest."

He dutifully shut his eyes. I watched my father fight falling into sleep, like I used to when I was a kid and afraid of missing something. It struck me how a twin bed was roughly the same dimensions as a casket, and if your father lay in one, you couldn't help think about death. As a child I'd expended major effort trying to disengage from the people who created me, only to discover that when it appeared they were about to leave the planet, harder than anything I wished them back.

Karen switched on the television, keeping the sound muted. We flipped the channels from tennis matches to CNN to some Japanese cartoons. After twenty minutes Dad was snoring, so we headed for the parking garage and that shared joint I'd been holding out to myself like the proverbial horse's carrot.

"Homegrown?" I asked.

She nodded.

"What do you do in winter?"

"Grow it indoors. You know," she warned as she lit the joint, "Ron will figure out we're stoned. He'll start in preaching about our lost souls."

I inhaled deeply and held my breath before answering. "Ron gets his high from the Lord; I get mine on weed. What's the difference?"

Karen took the joint back. "Last time I checked, possession of Jesus wasn't a misdemeanor. You know, Ron's lucky," she said. "I kind of envy him God's compass. The idea of a permanent true north."

I gave her a look. "Now you *are* sounding like Mom. What's wrong? You and Lincoln on the outs? Or did you get tired of peeing in an outhouse?"

She shook her head no and breathed out a wisp of smoke. "I adore Lincoln. We're great. I love my life. It's incredible."

"After twenty years," I said, "the only incredible thing is that you two can still find things to talk about."

My sister tapped out the joint in the ashtray and waved the smoke out the window of her car. "Oh, advice from Mr. Relationship. What happened to Nancy?" she asked. "I loved that girl."

"Give me a break. How could you love her when you never met her?"

"It's the weed talking," she said. "Let me rephrase. I liked you better when you were with her, so I suppose I loved her by default."

"Well, she's long gone," I said. The weed was doing tricks on my head, too, and I was having trouble following my sister's logic. "It's just me. This is now. That's the way it is."

"Now?" Karen echoed. "I'm sitting in a car getting high with my favorite brother who's turned into a pinchy hard-ass. That is an unacceptable now."

"I beg your pardon? I'm supposed to take criticism from an eternal hippie?"

"Yes."

"Why?"

"Because I'm happy."

"Oh, a happy hippie. That makes all the difference."

"Let me tell you something, Little Ricky. Hauling my own water makes me appreciate every drop. Twenty years with the same man, I've learned a few things about love."

"Like what?"

"Like how love changes from nonstop passionate sex and fantasies to enjoying your work and sharing the days with your partner. Love is the person who'll wipe up your barf and drive fifty miles to the market to buy you Seven-Up when you have the flu."

"Karen, you sound like a greeting card."

"Do I? Huh. Maybe that's where all the sentimental copy comes from, writers who spend twenty years in a happy relationship. All I know is I wouldn't change my life one iota."

Her words babbled into and out of my ears like a brook. "How do you know I'm not better off without Nancy?"

"Look at you, Rick. You've turned into this game player. You don't talk, you tease. Teasing's cute when a guy is twenty-five, but at fifty, and I mean this with the deepest love, Sweetie, it's kind of pathetic."

I was quiet a few minutes. We had to get back into the hospital pretty soon or Ron would come looking for us. He'd be the type to call the cops on us, too. I didn't know if I was supposed to thank my sister for the joint or the buzz kill. "I need a nap," I said. "Are you okay to drive me home?"

WHEN I WALKED UP THE DRIVEWAY to 639 Miller Street, I noticed that the shutters on the house were still painted colonial red, and that some of the louvers were missing. The junipers near the front door had grown tall and scraggly. My dad had kept them trimmed to a perfect rectangle during high school. I used to hide my smokes in one of them, reach in and grab them on the way out during my senior year, when I made A's and B's only after my father threatened not to pay for college. Being grounded for three years, you develop this huge interior life.

"Richard," my mom said at the front door, wiping her hands on a dish towel. "Honey, it's so good to see you. Come in, come in."

I kissed her wrinkled forehead, and Karen slid past us into the kitchen. My mother's skin felt like parchment. I guessed Oklahoma City was about as far from plastic surgery and fancy gyms as a person could get. "I'm fine, Mom. Just need a good night's sleep, that's all. How about you? Are you doing okay?"

My mother snapped the dish towel into thirds and set it next to the pile of laundry on the kitchen table. After a lifetime of white shirts and blue or brown slacks, my father's clothes were now brightly colored, some of them even plaid. Karen was already at work folding things into neat piles.

"I'm fine." My mother took me by the arm and led me to the kitchen table. "Sit," she said, "and let me feed you something."

She took a macaroni casserole out of the oven and set it down on a hot pad. Apologies to Proust, this was what childhood smelled like to me—carbohydrates, cheese, and slices of hot dog. She poured me a glass of whole milk and sat down next to me. To her a clean plate was the strongest proof of my love. I blew on the first spoonful to cool it, and caught her staring at me *that* way—figuring I'd had my heart broken again, she was gathering sage advice to soothe me. It wouldn't be long before she started buying me stuff I didn't need, things she couldn't afford, well-intentioned junk I had no place to keep since I'd let my rented condo go and put the detritus of my life into storage.

"Hey, that looks yummy," Karen said, but Mom was busy at

the sink, or maybe her hearing was going, because she didn't answer.

"Get it yourself," I teased. "Since you weren't the firstborn son and haven't produced any grandchildren."

"Very funny," Karen said. "Do you know how much cholesterol is in that thing?"

"You let your brother eat in peace," my mother said.

Karen stuck her tongue out at me, and I returned the favor.

I was still a little high. All I could think was Richard the man was lying in a hospital bed stapled together while Richard the boy, the *fifty*-year-old boy, sat filling his belly with starches at the same table where he grew up. I counted myself in terrific company—Thomas Wolfe, Ralph Waldo Emerson, and Richard Heinrich, Jr.: a novelist, a philosopher, and a has-been journalist. The drag was, those guys were celebrated, even though they were dead. I, on the other hand, only wished I were.

It was definitely nap time.

That night after hospital visiting hours ended, Ron and I watched the local news and then a baseball game. My sister sat in my father's recliner, crocheting something out of blue yarn. When I asked her what she was making, she answered that she wasn't sure yet, leading me to believe she'd found time to finish that joint without me.

Ron talked back to the television and chewed out the players who "weren't trying hard enough."

"It's a game," I said. "And no matter how loud you yell, they can't hear you."

He stared at me, clearly indignant.

"What?" I said. "This comes as a surprise?"

Ron went off. "You fly in at the drop of a hat wearing a leather jacket that probably cost an arm and a leg, and I'm supposed to listen to you?"

"Well, I'm right about the TV."

"Shut up, Rick."

"Excuse me?"

"You weren't here when the doctor was telling us Dad's chances. You didn't sweat out five hours in the waiting room lering if there was enough healthy tissue left for the bypass to work."

"You're right," I said, hoping that would end it. But he only took a breath before continuing.

"You don't have a wife and kids to support. You still owe me for your blown head gasket when you were stuck in Podunk, Wyoming, and I wired you enough cash to fix your car, money I could use," he said while Karen pulled the crocheting up to her face to hide herself lest she be drawn into this confounding discourse.

"Fine," I said. "Whatever it takes to shut you up." I whipped out my checkbook and handed Ron a blank check. "Fill it in for whatever makes us even," I said. And I got up and went to my old room and shut the door.

Ron's and my old room still sported the saggy twin beds we'd abused ourselves in as adolescents. It was a big-enough house that I should have been rattling around it like a jellybean in a jar. Instead I wanted to get in a taxi and go back to the airport. The house was so small that the closed door only muffled my brother's and sister's voices.

"Look at that pitcher," Ron said to the television. "Arm like a girl. Could he throw any more directly to the batter?"

Maybe it was leftover from the pot, but I thought I could hear Karen's crochet hook loop itself angrily through the yarn. "Hasn't Jesus taught you anything?" she told him. "Girls have perfectly good arms."

As soon as I'd left for college, my younger brother got rid of all my music posters. He sold my black light, which still pissed me off, because by now the thing would be a classic. Ron was everything I was not—a Republican, religious, a family man, and a career salesman. He went into insurance straight out of high school, won salesman of the year five times, and now sat on this empire constructed basically of people's fear of disaster. He lived twenty miles away, in a house with a pool and his wife, Shawna, and the grandkids my parents doted upon as much as Ron allowed. Alison and Robert had narrow boundaries. They attended parochial school and weren't allowed to play video games, because consorting with public education and electronics was equivalent to shaking hands with the devil. Every Christmas, Ron sent photos. The kids looked like they'd been taken back forty years to shop at a dusty department store. I never knew if the presents I sent even made it into their hands.

And Karen, at the other end of the spectrum, well, maybe she was happy in Maine, where she and Lincoln fished for a living. They made everything, including their soap. They grew vegetables, canned jelly, tanned moose hide; it was the complete back-to-nature scene, or as Ron would call it, pagan. I wondered if I should go home with her, pitch a tent, get a job in a cannery, eat a lot of fiber, give my muscles a workout, and rest my brain.

Mom had taken down our corduroy curtains and replaced them with miniblinds. The walls had been painted builder's white. I looked through the bookshelf at Ron's things because I'd taken everything of mine with me. *The Art of War,* which was really a book on how to be cutthroat in business, a monster-huge tome called *Jane's Ships,* and every issue of *Hot Rod* published during the seventies. I took *Jane's Ships* to bed with me. About ten pages into it I realized that the same way that some people are afraid to fly, I didn't trust the ocean, and that got me thinking of Nance.

She loved beachcombing more than shopping, I think. Weekends I was on deadline and she didn't have any shoots, she'd sometimes drive to the Oregon coast. She picked up shells, those Japanese fishing floats, and collected pieces of driftwood. Filled her car up with that crap. She'd come home smelling of salt and wood smoke, drifty and remote. Scared me. I felt the distance between us and knew it was of my own creation. For all the good times we had together, for most of it, I'd had my foot on her back, kicking her away. I mean, she'd ask me to take time off to be with her, and I'd bark, "Hello, where's your autonomy in this relationship? Can't you entertain yourself?" *Autonomy*—that word nearly always ended the discussion.

I tore the covers off the bed but still felt trapped. I pulled up the blinds, opened the window, and let a full Oklahoma moon shine in. I set *Jane's Ships* down on the floor and shut my eyes. Either it was the pot or the ghosts of the past that wouldn't let me sleep. I was home, but it wasn't my home, it was a house, owned and clear, in which two aging people lived, one in cardiac care and the other at his bedside, worrying herself to death. Their fifty-year-old boy lay motionless in bed like the terminally ill, but he was only terminally confused. Somehow that felt worse than a fatal diagnosis.

Two weeks passed, and our routine became a comfort. Ron took the early visit shift; Karen and Mom drove over in the afternoon. I volunteered for evenings because Dad and I could turn on the TV and not have to say much to each other besides "Can you fluff my pillow?" and "What time is it?" and "When will your mother be back?" His nurses were attentive. One of them was so cute I wanted to ask her out, but when I spotted a diamond ring on her left hand, it seemed like too much trouble, so I didn't even bother to flirt.

Dad's progress was textbook. They pulled out various tubes, and like when I used to come off being grounded in high school, he received little privileges. From broth to pudding to an actual meal, and with each increment he grew crabbier. One day I took Ron's morning shift, and it was as if he'd fallen down off the ladder. I called in the cute nurse. "Is it just me, or does he look gray to you, too?" I said.

It took her a half a second to get worried. "You might want to call your family over," she said.

Dad's cardiologist suggested blood transfusions, and said that if we each gave blood, a direct donation—family blood—was safer than a stranger's.

"I'm ready," Karen said. "Call the lab and tell them we're coming down."

"Rick," Ron asked me. "Is it safe for you to donate?"

"What? Do you think I have a disease? Thanks, Ron. I bet I can give two pints to your one."

"Listen to you two," Karen said. "Shall we get your Mickey Mouse Club ears out of storage?"

"He's testing my testicles," I said.

"I am not trying to do any such thing, and there's no reason for vulgarity."

"How is saying 'testicles' vulgar? Half the people in the world have testicles. And the other half?"

"Boys," my mother said.

When I looked at her face I knew I had to let the comment go. "Never mind. The lab's waiting. Let's go."

Karen lay back against the chair pumping her rubber bulb while healthy, organic blood drained from her strong arm into the plastic collecting sack. The nurse had trouble finding a vein on Ron and had to stick him several times. The nurse was a bubble-blond hottie, and when she slid the needle into my arm I entertained an unseemly thought or two. "What do you think of my veins?" I said, in order to hassle Ron.

"Nice and plump," she answered, winking. "Just the way I like them."

Oh, she was corn-fed, I could tell. She had dark eyes, and that hair color was natural and healthy, and I wanted to run my fingers through it. A gold chain disappeared into her cleavage, and I was imagining what kind of charm dangled from her necklace when Ron hit the floor in a dead faint.

"Oh, Lordy!" the nurse said, abandoning me to tend my brother. She hollered for help, and in a minute's time the place was pandemonium, and suddenly Karen wasn't looking so hot, and the next thing I knew she'd barfed all over the hottie nurse.

So I didn't ask the blond out; Dad only got two units of family blood, and the rest was some stranger's. The lab told us never to come back, that there were plenty of other donors who didn't cause such scenes. We rode the elevator to the cafeteria in silence. In line for coffee, I noticed Ron was near tears. "It's not that big a deal," I told him. "Let it the fuck go already."

He looked at me, ashamed, tears in his eyes.

I shrugged. "So tell him it was me who fainted," I said. "He's already pissed off at me. What's one more failure on my part?"

And by God, or in spite of him, that's exactly what Ron did.

WHEN DAD WAS RELEASED from the hospital, Ron returned to his insurance empire. Karen headed back to Maine, eager to see Lincoln and resume fishing. She stood in the driveway leaking a few sentimental tears and trying to hug me. "Ricky, will you be okay here without me?"

"I'll spend a few more days, do some yard work."

"Then what?"

"Head back to Portland. I can get a job like that," I said, and snapped my fingers.

She pressed a bag into my hand, snuggled close and kissed my cheek. "Don't smoke it all at once," she said, and then got into her car for the long drive north.

I watched her car until it was out of sight. In reality I had no plan beyond trying to take it easy so the pot would last long enough to allow random thoughts to drift into my empty head. I figured that with luck, one of them might have a career attached to it.

AS SHE SAT ON THE COUCH, my mother leafed through *Catholicism Today* and said "Uh-huh" as if the article was making a point so illuminating that she wanted to share it, but didn't dare speak up while the men were watching sports. On the coffee table a crystal candy dish held butterscotch toffees—my favorite. When I went looking for a beer in the kitchen, I noticed she'd stocked up on my favorite cereals—three boxes worth of apple-cinnamon Cheerios, like I was moving in to stay. Instant claustrophobia descended. What was it about home that turned a mature adult into an eight-year-old?

My mother was nearing the end of her magazine.

My father had set up a TV tray next to his recliner. On top his medications were lined up in amber plastic bottles. Any minute his watch alarm would sound, and my mother would fetch him a glass of water. Then he'd sigh dramatically and make this noise as he swallowed each pill, as if he were trying to force life down his unwilling throat. Then Ron would call, and they would each get on extensions so they could talk to the good son who would end the conversation by telling Dad he was praying extra hard for him, and Mom would sniffle and tell me what a wonderful man that Ron had turned out to be.

"Think I'll go to bed," I said, and hightailed it up the stairs before my mother could offer to bring me clean towels.

I HAD BREAKFAST AT TEN—apple-cinnamon Cheerios—blamed sleeping late on the time change, drove my dad's Caddy around town, and ate lunch someplace different every day. I was home by two, which allowed me to park in front of the TV and watch the Cartoon Network on cable. Droopy Dog, Foghorn Leghorn, Rocky and Bullwinkle; the adventures of my childhood made sense. If you saved the maiden, busted the criminal, exposed the evil Russian influence, you could stop the Cold War. They may have been cartoons, but they were heroes. My father had brought me up to be a hero. I'd failed him in more ways than I could count. I didn't fight in Vietnam. I wasn't curing cancer. The words I'd written were already decomposing.

Late afternoon, when the classic cartoons gave way to contemporary crap that didn't interest me, my dad returned home from cardiac rehab. He'd visit with his cronies from the old days at the factory, where he'd put in forty years of tool-and-die manufacturing genius. They were old men, too, tottering unsteadily, dressed in the same bright clothing. They mall-walked to stay in shape. They played bridge or poker or rummy or slapjack. They sat around the living room telling old war stories and pretended to be surprised every time. When they left, my dad sank into his chair and looked sad.

"You want to take a walk around the neighborhood with me?" I'd ask.

"Nah," he answered every time, sounding distracted and angry.

Sometimes I took a nap, or read until dinner—*Jane's Ships*—I could now recognize a Dreadnought at fifty paces. Other times I ducked out and took a walk without him, and at the end of the street, where the trees were thick and one empty lot awaited its new house, I'd light up a joint for a few hits to get me through the rest of the day. We ate supper—almost always a casserole—watched more TV, and my mother patted my knee until I felt it jerk up in reflex when her cupped hand got within two inches.

"Whoever she was, Richard," she whispered to me, "she didn't know what she was throwing away."

What could I tell her? *Oh, yeah, she did?*

Pretty soon I was smoking a joint every night before bed, which made my dreams these watery cartoon landscapes, with Nance calling to me as a recliner swallowed me up. As her voice floated away, I realized the error of my ways and called out to her, but she could no longer hear me. Mornings I woke stunned to find myself in the narrow bed, and the first thought to cross my mind was, Whoa, am I late for school?

Sometimes I took her cell phone out of my jacket and ran my fingers over the numbers, touching places where her fingers had traveled, wondering what they were doing now.

This particular morning, however, the noise of a motor woke me. I peered out the window and saw my dad struggling to push the power lawn mower across the backyard. I hurried downstairs and found my mother. "He's not allowed to do that yet, is he?"

She dried our morning dishes and put them away in the cupboard. "No. But he woke up insisting. Maybe you can talk some sense into him. God knows he won't listen to me."

He wasn't making a great deal of headway. Haphazard lines of higher grass he'd never tolerated from me way back when yard work was my job zigged across the yard.

I pulled on a T-shirt and walked into his view, making a gesture for him to cut the motor, but he only put it into neutral. "Dad," I shouted over the roaring of the lawn mower motor. "Pushing that old dinosaur is going to bust all your stitches loose. Turn it off."

The expression on his face said he'd rather mow over me, but he relented. "Look at this grass," he said with disgust in his voice. "Somebody has to see to it."

"Dad, you're eighty-four years old. You have the money. Hire a gardening service."

He mopped his brow and stared at me. I expected a lecture. He said, "You know what, Rick? They tell you the pain of a heart attack feels like indigestion. That's a damn lie. What it feels like is being crushed to death. I couldn't get my breath. The pain was so big I felt like something was eating me. Unforgettable while it was happening, but now, well, I only remember the idea of it. Like your mother used to say when she was in labor."

"I'm sorry you had to go through it," I said. "Her, too."

He waved his hand. "Why apologize? That's what it means to be a parent. Sometimes it hurts, and other times you're proud."

One little jellyfish tentacle of a word, but it still stung, and I imagined that showed on my face. "Ron's done great," I said. "His kids, job, marriage. He made it all work, didn't he? And Karen, so she's a little unorthodox, but you just have to look at her to see how happy she is. That should make you proud."

He laughed. My own father, standing on the unmowed lawn leaning against a piece of equipment bearing blades that separated us. I expected it, but I wasn't ready for what he said next. "I was afraid I'd wake up incapacitated. Unable to take care of your mother. Then I saw all of you kids, rallying around her, and I knew I could die then and she'd be taken care of."

"You're not dying, Dad. The surgery was a success."

"You're not listening to me. I'm saying I'm ready for it when it comes. It takes all the pressure off."

I squeezed his upper arm. "Let's go inside and get a cool drink."

He pushed me away. "You never took the easy way out of anything, did you, Rick? Always had to hike the hard road. I bet you think of yourself as a failure. You think I see you that way, don't you?"

A car drove down the street, and my father turned to wave. Here in his world, everything was a known quantity. "Well, don't you?" He pushed away from the mower handle. The smell of cut grass made my nose itch. "I love Ron and those grandkids to pieces, but if I hear the Lord's Prayer offered up just one more time on my behalf, he'll tip me over the edge, you know what I'm saying?"

I was too shocked to reply.

"I always wanted to try my hand at writing. Bet you didn't know that about your old man, did you? But you'll do it for me, won't you? Tell all those stories. Take the hard road."

I wanted to reach out and grab hold of him, to tell him it

wasn't too late, but in my heart I knew it was beyond late—for my father, possibly even for myself. He went into the house and I mowed the shit out of that lawn, did the best job ever.

"THOUGHT I'D RUN OVER to that memorial for the bombing today," I said as my mother poured me a cup of coffee. "Idea for a story. Take home a freelance thing. Might as well write this trip off on my taxes."

Mom looked up at me. "I think that's a lovely idea."

Immediately I felt stricken. Karen had been gone only a week. We'd been to the mall to buy me new bath towels and the kind of transistor radio you can take into the shower and not get electrocuted. Then there was the device for heating up shaving cream so it came out at a soothing temperature every time. All these presents could mean only one thing: Mom was wise to the employment situation and me. I poured the Cheerios into a bowl, the same as I'd done yesterday, but today they seemed different.

She said, "Will you be here for dinner?"

"I don't think so. I think I'll catch a redeye back to Portland. Unless you want me to stay longer."

She took my cup from me and rinsed it, set it in the dishwasher rack. "No, I think we'll be okay. But I sure appreciate you using up your vacation time like this. I don't know how I would have gotten through this without you kids. But will you do one thing for me, Richard?"

"Name it," I said.

"Call your father more often. I know the surgery was successful, but nobody knows the future." She smiled, and her eyes glinted with tears.

"I can do that," I said, and gave her a hug.

I went on-line on my dad's computer and booked a 10:00 P.M. flight. I packed up my duffel—clothes clean, ironed, and folded—and said my good-byes. I took a cab to the memorial, thinking I'd waste the day there and call a cab when it was time to be at the airport. Any other visit, I'd have felt this giant sense of relief, as if I were Steve McQueen taking the motorcycle ride over the barbed wire in *The Great Escape.* Today, however, my exit felt disappointingly normal.

THE FIRST THING THAT CAUGHT MY EYE was how the bronze gates had tarnished along the edges. Evidently people felt the need to touch them. Nance would have known how to photograph that so a ghost imprint of a hand showed on the metal. The June sun beat down, and I rolled up my sleeves as I walked around the place. On the reverse side of the walls the architects' mission statement read, "May this memorial offer comfort, strength, peace, hope, and serenity." Nice words, but no way. The 168 empty chairs were arranged precisely, awful enough to raise the hair on my neck. I didn't know anyone who'd died in the explosion, which struck me as odd, since my parents had lived here their entire life, and me, eighteen years. I glanced around at the people visiting and tried to guess which ones were tourists and who among them might have lost a loved one. Mostly they were people looking, cameras in hand, which struck me as a little crass. I wasted time with a minor fantasy about finding some heartbroken youth mourning his first love, trying to figure how that might provide entrance into a worthwhile story. Publishing freelance paid next to nothing. But it was as if the nasty editor part of me knew how to argue down story pitches so well that I didn't get far. Thought about my dad, whom I'd sent *After-Hours* every week without fail, even though he never said, "Good work," or "One helluva story." Strangely, I didn't mind that anymore.

Then I spotted this woman standing at one of the chairs. She had long black hair pulling free of its braid, and little strands of it were whipping into her eyes from the wind. She also had two black-and-white dogs beside her, one leash in each hand. They were so alike and standing so still they looked like a matched set of statues. She ran her hands along the chair and laid her cheek against its back. I noticed how the security guard took a step closer, but didn't tell her to stop. I wondered if that meant she'd lost someone here. If that was what people did, found the chairs that stood for the person who died and touched them for comfort. She stood up, and I could clearly see her mouth moving, her wide lips lipsticked this funky purple women assume guys like and don't. I watched her set her shoulder bag down on the grass so she could embrace the chair again. Weird. I glanced over at the walls. The carved 9:01 represents the moment before the bombing happened, when the Ryder truck was parked on the street and people inside the Federal Building were working, when McVeigh allegedly made his escape. The reflecting pool and the empty chairs separate the 9:01 wall from the other, which reads 9:03, the moment after the bomb went off. That ominous missing minute is what got to me. I thought how if I'd lost somebody in the bombing, I'd probably throw myself in the pool trying to find that one minute, sure that could change everything.

Well, with all her touching of the chair, one of the dogs' leashes slipped from her grasp. The dog took off running after a squirrel. Nance's dog was always running off, and she'd yell in this fishwife tone, which did absolutely no good and made me cringe, thinking that this was how she'd talk when she was old and how could I live with that? So I wasn't much for dogs, really, and I didn't plan to run after this one unless it headed into traffic. The black-haired woman turned and then called out, "Jim, come *now,*" and stood waiting. Her legs in the tight jeans—well, it made for a nice tableau, so I kept my eyes on her. She put a finger in her mouth, whistled like she was calling a taxi, and damned if the dog didn't make this wide loop and come back to her like he'd choreographed the entire deal. Squirrel forgotten, he sat at her feet, looking up adoringly. She took hold of the leash, patted his head, then dropped the leash and walked fifteen or so feet away. The dog waited. She turned, released him with a hand signal, and he came to her side and sat quietly until she once more picked up the leash. Then they walked back to the chairs. Whole thing couldn't have taken more than three minutes, but it was long enough for her purse to get stolen.

The security guard began checking trash bins. Anyone who walked by, she asked if they'd seen it. When she walked over to me and said, "Excuse me, a beaded tan leather purse? Have you seen it?" I don't know, something happened.

Up close her eyes were this greenish color and so sad I

wanted to give her some good news. She never once let go of the dogs. I shook my head, and she started to walk away, then I called her back.

"Let me check the men's room for you. Sometimes thieves take the cash and throw the purse away. Don't ask me how I know this."

She tried to smile. "Thanks."

And I got lucky. I found her purse stuffed in the used paper towel bin. Suede, beads, it looked handmade, like something you'd buy at a Trading Post. I wiped a glob of hand soap off it and took it out to her.

"You found it?" She squealed with delight and dumped the contents on the ground. Whoever the thief was, he only wanted her money, because everything else was there, tampons, cigarettes, hairbrush, and sunglasses, even her driver's license. I figured now was when the tears would come, but it was something else entirely.

"Mother feckity!" she yelled skyward, at a decibel level that nearly punctured my eardrums. "That was all the cash I had in the world."

"You could get an advance at an ATM," I suggested.

She stared at me. "Hello? An ATM? Don't you have to have a damn bank account to do that?"

"Well, yes," I started.

"Freaking yuppie," she said and scowled at me.

"Listen, I didn't take your money, Babe, I found your purse for you. In some women's books, that makes me a hero."

She lit a cigarette and blew smoke at me. I thought of how hard I rode Nance until she gave up smoking. For some reason this pissed-off chick exhaling in the shadow of the survivor elm tree stirred me in a different way. I reached for my wallet. "Here. I've got fifty on me. In the name of heroism, it's yours."

Of course that left me with an empty wallet, but I didn't think she'd accept money from a stranger, which showed how little I knew. "Thanks," she said, and grinned around the cigarette, and started to walk away.

After a moment I picked up my duffel bag and trailed after her. "What are you going to do now?"

"What do you mean, what am I going to do now?"

"You have all my money. Don't you want to buy me a drink for being a hero?"

"Not particularly."

"Where are you headed?"

She thought a moment. "I'm going to buy a full tank of gas for my truck, then drive to New Mexico. I have friends there. They'll let me work until I earn enough traveling cash. And I've pretty much had it with Okla-fecking-homa."

"I've never really explored New Mexico," I said, trying to stall her.

"Your loss."

I took her arm, and she stopped dead in her tracks. Runaway Jim, with his weakness for squirrels, growled at me. I let go. "I just want to talk to you."

"For God's sake, what about?"

"I'm a reporter."

She threw the cigarette down on the grass. "Oh, and are you a *crime* reporter by any chance? Are you going to get my five hundred bucks back for me by writing a fecking story about how lowlife Oklahomans rob visitors to the fecking bomb memorial?"

God, her mouth. "Actually I'm not a reporter anymore. I got fired." Why in the fuck had I told her that?

She sat down on the grass and looked at her watch. "Make it snappy, former reporter. I have to get the hell out of Dodge before dusk, or I am going to lose my damn mind."

"Do you eat with that mouth?"

She laughed. "Among other things. Clock's ticking."

"I was wondering, by any chance, did you lose somebody in the bombing?"

The momentary willingness to listen to me was replaced by her digging into the depths of the leather bag. She found the fifty dollars and threw them in my general direction. The laws of physics prevent paper from being an effective weapon. They scattered around me. I picked them up and ran behind her, all the way to her truck. I figured I had to follow, because this was going to be a much better story than the memorial.

"THIS SONG'S FOR MY STALKER," she said into the karaoke microphone, and proceeded to win her second contest of the night. I'd spent the night following her from bar to bar, whistling the loudest of anyone when she sang. She wasn't just good. Lucinda Williams came to mind, with a little bit of Rosanne Cash and k.d. lang thrown into the mix. She liked going on last. Knew that was the power position. She was so good that when she sang it erased everyone else's efforts. And she didn't care, and that was the biggest part of it. I sat there listening to her, wondering where on earth she'd come from, what kind of childhood she'd endured to give her that attitude, and how it was she could get those two dogs to mind her like she was God. The judges always asked her to do an encore when they handed her the prize money, but she'd only laugh and head on to the next bar with a paying gig.

At bar number four, I realized my ten P.M. flight had left without me.

Onstage Mary Madigan Caringella—"Call me Maddy, she'd said"—was winning her third contest (the bar before this one was rigged, in my opinion), and by my count, she was up three hundred as the judge handed her the cash. She pointed a finger at me. Her stalker. I walked up to meet her. "You rocked," I said, and meant it. "Where are we headed next?"

"Time to call it a night, Hero Boy," she said. "You look like the type with a credit card. What do you have? MasterCard? Visa?"

"One of each, actually."

She patted my arm. "Good. I'll let you pay for the room."

Phoebe

7

The Magic Lantern Show

In the distance I heard the faint sound of a siren on the highway and wondered if the fog had caused one of those infamous Central Coast chain-reaction accidents where, like dominoes, cars rear-ended one another and snarled traffic for hours. Nance hadn't been kidding when she told me I'd get bridal nerves, but mine were more than pure selfishness—when it came to my mother I was cynical and as barn-sour as Leroy Rogers. Please don't let it hold Juan up, I prayed, with no thought for anyone but myself. I looked at the string quartet my brother had hired and wished the guy with the cello would push his hair out of his eyes, and that the waiter had worn pants that didn't show his ankles. Worst of all I sat there in my wedding dress waiting for my groom to return from driving my mother and new stepfather to the airport and thought, Damn, don't I look pretty!

And next thing the wind kicked up a little, and the roses in the vases at each guest table fluttered, and for a moment I smelled them so strongly the air felt like incense, and then just as quickly the breeze stilled, and the air was plain old oxygen, and Lester had taken off his jacket and placed it over my shoulders, and I'd said I wasn't cold, but thanks anyway. Then I'd felt the hair on the back of my neck stand up and how the gooey gel the hair-

dresser had used made my curls feel fake like something you'd line an Easter basket with, and my doctor asked, "Are you all right, Phoebe?" and somehow I knew I wasn't even though nobody had told me yet.

"You cannot allow yourself to get upset, Phoebe. Your heart can't take it. Lie down now, rest. I'm going to give you a shot to help you calm down."

"No, not a shot, no, it can't be good for—"

"Hush, hija, *the doctor knows best." Florencio, standing by my bed, where James carried me after Beryl arrived, having driven right past the wreckage. Rosa massaging my hands, speaking Spanish words Juan's mother might receive as a comfort, had she not been in the car with him. I'd tried to marry the man I loved. Thanks to my mother interrupting things, needing a ride to the airport so she could make a connection for a flight to some fabulous island, I'd taken out what was left of the Nava family, totally obliterated them.*

Could I stay healthy enough to take a baby to term? What if the farm went belly-up? Say the baby survived. Would I ruin him bringing him up without a father?

Lester cleared his throat as he walked into the bedroom. "Hello, Phoebe. Preciousness called and said you upchucked your breakfast again."

"For crying out loud, Lester," I said as I tucked the sheets in close even though it had to be eighty degrees outside. "So I get sick to my stomach every once in a while. It's not like it happens all the time."

"It shouldn't be happening at all, Phoebe."

Nance sobbing. James trying to soothe her while paying attention to me.

Ness running her hands through my marcelled waves, combing out the stiff curl with her long horsewoman's fingers.

"I'm here, Phoebe. David is, too. We're not going anywhere. We'll be here all night."

Oh, my God. How was I supposed to get through the darkness?

Beryl, still dressed in her traveling clothes, lying down next to me, saying nothing, just holding me in her arms. Toward morning, people trailing back into a bedroom full of wedding guests who stayed too long. Wedding presents that I would never open. All that catered food outside that had spoiled while waiting for me to lift my fork. The way that one syllable boiled out of me: "Out!"

Out. All of you, now. Take your well-intended pity and go home. *Locking eyes with James. He loved me enough not to make me beg.*

LESTER SAT DOWN ON THE BED and put his head in his hands. The sigh that came out of him was monumental. I knew I wearied him. I wasn't the kind of patient he saw once a year for a routine checkup and worked in when she got bronchitis.

"Lord help us," he said.

I steeled myself, because I knew he was about to use some Latin word for abortion.

"Three months is pretty far into a pregnancy to have the full gamut of options. At best this would be a high-risk undertaking. The odds of carrying to term are not in your favor. Given your heart, there's no question, you'd have to remain in bed for the duration. The delivery would have to be a C-section, but no general anesthetic. This complicates your current medications, too, Phoebe. The risks are—"

"All I want to know is would I have a chance?"

"There are always chances, Phoebe. But you need to think about this in terms of your own health."

I HAD LEANED ON MY CRUTCHES and watched James walk our mother down the garden path toward her groom. Bertram Martin Dunlap, born in Hilton Head, South Carolina, now residing

in East Lansing, Michigan, had made his fortune selling drugstore sunglasses. This was my new stepfather, old Bert, in his navy blazer with the bright yellow silk handkerchief blossoming from the breast pocket. Khaki pants, flashy white shoes, and Charles Nelson Reilly spectacles completed the outfit. I thought how freeing it must be that when a man grows older, he can dress any old way he feels and not give one poop what people think, and wondered how Juan would dress. One thing for certain, when Bert smiled at my mother, it was apparent that he loved her. The look she returned was hopeful, but there was a question lurking beneath—am I worthy of happiness? For a moment there, I had to bury my face in her flowers and try not to cry.

Juan looking at me, smiling. I crooked my index finger and sent him the tiniest wave. He mouthed the words "I love you, Phoebe," and—whoops!—all my held-in tears threatened to spill.

"SYMPHONY FORTY-ONE," David Snow said as the portable CD player he'd brought over to keep me company began to play. "How perfectly, wonderfully sad."

"How can sad be wonderful?" I said. "That I do not get."

"It's Mozart, Phoebe. He specialized in the dark mood. Who could blame him? He lived to be thirty-five, died penniless, and worked at the whim of monarchs who didn't know from taste. And yet, such genius. Incredible, don't you think, how he captures just how you're feeling?"

David sat across from my bed on Sadie's chaise. He belonged in all this opulence, in this sorrowful, brilliant music. I didn't know squat about Mozart, but I liked the way the harp sounded, as painful and honest as if someone were plucking each vein in my heart. David hummed along and didn't miss a note. Listening with him was like how I imagined dancing would feel. Two people moving across the flagstones, their bodies warming the air.

The weather didn't take its toll on David they way it did on the rest of us. He moved slowly, calmly, as if the very air was rich and thick as molasses, and every step confection. I wished I could bottle his calm and use it like hand lotion.

My mother setting her champagne glass down and embracing me. Still dressed in her wedding suit, she'd changed from her Italian pumps to walking shoes. I'll call you the minute we get back. Enjoy your wedding, dear. I wish we could stay for the ceremony, but this was the only available flight.

That's why God invented videotape.

"Don't stay up too late, and remember to take your medicine."

Bert, clearly anxious to get to the airport, shook my hand. "Have fun," I said, waving, and I meant it.

"Vamanos," *Juan said, and they headed toward the car.*

"Hurry back," I called out, and for just a split second I had this niggling feeling that I should go with them, that it was important, but then Lester called my name, and I forgot all about it and embraced the man who only months ago, when I was so sick with pneumonia I'd fallen into a coma, had saved my life.

Out the French doors of my room—Sadie's room—I saw the UPS truck speed away. The Bad Girls must have told the new driver to go around back and avoid me. The truck—it could have been his. The steering wheel he touched. The radio set to Monterey Jack's drive-time show out of Sierra Grove. I could live to be a hundred, and just a glimpse of that brown truck with the gold letters would make my heart race. Nance had sewed sheer curtains for my window since I was confined to bed, but I could still see out. The curtains were supposed to be soothing, keeping the summer sun from flooding the corners of my room, glinting painfully off the mirror. How could I tell her it didn't matter to me if it was day or night?

One sultry dusk when I was crying as softly as I could, I saw Nance and my brother outside, dancing to a music that played inside their heads. No doubt they were practicing for their upcoming nuptials. It hurt to watch, but I couldn't look away. Had

Juan had the radio on when he was hit? Was Monterey Jack interviewing Bill Frisell? Was it Pledge Drive week, and people calling in just to make Jack hush up and start spinning discs again? What would be an apropos jazz tune for the final moments of your life? "A Nightingale Sang in Berkeley Square"? Maybe Beryl would know what a nightingale looked like. The eucalyptus branches swayed above my brother, Nance safely tucked into his arms. In the heat of that summer night, the air was filled with the scent of jasmine, so strong it made me want to vomit, not for the first time that day.

TRIPWIRES TO BE AVOIDED:

1. The brocade-covered chaise where we'd once made love.
2. The lacquered dresser with half its drawers cleared for Juan's things.
3. A towel flung across the backrest of my wheelchair that could have been the last one he used.

I imagined I heard the squeak of the shower turning off. Juan stepping onto the bath rug, just around the corner, whistling "I Cover the Waterfront." His strong hands rubbing his thick brown hair dry. Him standing there naked, his perfect body glistening with droplets of water the towel had missed. Sometimes I had caught them on my tongue, just not often enough.

NESS CALLING TO ME, time to eat dinner. Every night we sat together, our plates on trays set up in my room. We opened the French doors, and the outdoors came in, for as long as it took for us to finish our food, anyway. Duchess lay on the porch and sniffed at the breeze. Leroy danced in his corral in anticipation of his next walk, or a handout. The carpenters took advantage of the relative cool to get in a few hours' work on James's house. To the west the ocean sparkled in the sunset, and tourists wandered Bayborough-by-the-Sea dazzled by the wealth and beauty of the village as they felt the cobblestones beneath their tennis shoes.

They stared into real estate office windows at properties that were the things of high-priced dreams, and out of reach or not they were living their lives. Bayborough: Every season brought its own treasure. And what did any of that mean, any of it, when Juan wasn't a part of it?

THAT FOG. *Drifting onto the patio, that strange smoke-like mist settling ankle-high, infiltrating the fields, it had no place at a summer wedding. Florencio and Segundo lighting the lanterns, switching on the rented heat lamps.*

"Lester, can you believe this? I'm overdosed on happiness. I feel almost hyper." Juan, hurry back.

"There's no one who deserves to be happier," he said.

Hormone surges, I thought. I am a pregnant bride. Scandalous.

What the hippie minister had said: "A life without love, without the presence of the beloved, is nothing but a mere magic-lantern show. We draw out slide after slide, swiftly tiring of each, pushing it back to make haste for the next."

Goethe. Sadie's journal.

Inside me that ember of selfishness. I hoped that the minister wasn't using up all the good stuff he'd arranged for Juan and me on my mother and Bert.

Nance and Ness, so lovely in their lacy blouses and the golden silk pants we'd decided were much more flattering than traditional bridesmaid dresses. The empty seat where Beryl Anne was supposed to be sitting concerned me, but she'd called from Seattle, saying the plane was delayed.

THE PLANT BERYL BROUGHT ME was an Easter cactus, Latin name, *Rhipsalidopsis gaertneri*. It was supposed to bloom in spring and, if conditions were good, fall. A native of Brazil, its paddles were green, so we didn't know whether it would bloom red or pink. We had to wait. I unburdened my heart to that plant: *I'm lost,* I said. *Mired. I loved him more than breath. Where are the maps that explain how to survive this hurt?*

Hey, it answered. *Try having had the rain forest yanked out from under you. I haven't seen a single goddamn parrot around here. Do you have any idea how hard it is to sit in this dry, lifeless place day after day, working on flowers?*

EVERYONE APPLAUDED *when Bert slid the band on my mother's finger and she transformed from Rita DeThomas, widow, into Mrs. Bertram Martin Dunlap, bride. Even I felt the shimmer of that magic-lantern moment. When they kissed I must have had another hormone surge, because tears came forth entirely uninvited and didn't stop until Juan touched my arm.*

"Cara? *What's with the crying? This isn't like you."*

I wiped my eyes. "This is your last chance to bail out, Nava. Maybe you should take it."

He kissed my forehead. "No way. As they say in my neighborhood, you're stuck with me por vida, *but listen. Mami's feeling sick again. I'm going to drive her to her sister's house."*

His mother had just gotten over the flu, and at her age a relapse was a serious thing.

"I'll be back in a few minutes."

"Okay," I said, but I felt like crying again.

Juan went on talking while my mother and Bert shook hands with well-wishers.

"So I was thinking since my cousin's house is only about a block from the airport, why don't I drop your mom and Bert off on the way? It'll give me a chance to talk to them a little, you know, get to know them."

Juan looked so handsome, his dark skin against that starched white cowboy shirt, the embroidered roses at the cuffs, mmm-mmm, that I could hardly take my eyes off him.

Chinese lanterns strung in the trees, just waiting for enough darkness to fall so they could be lit.

I kissed Juan's mother on the cheek. She rattled off some Spanish I didn't understand, and then she folded a lace hankie into my hand. It was so thin it felt like gauze. "This is too beautiful," I said, and tried to give it back, figuring it for an heirloom I didn't deserve. Mrs. Nava was dark-eyed, tiny, bird-thin, except for her smile, which was enormous. "Hoy pa'unos y mañana pa'otros," *she said, and gently tucked it back into my hand.*

"What's she saying?" I asked my soon-to-be-husband.

"That she loves you already; you're family. And," he grinned, "that she expects babies very soon."

*I laughed, and leaned over to whisper into her ear, "*Bambino *on board."*

I think she understood me.

A BAD WEEK, we called it. Throwing up all hours, not sleeping. Lester assured me that one sleeping pill wasn't going to hurt the baby, so I took it, landing in a dream I never thought I'd have again. Sadie, in her mermaid outfit, tears gleaming on her cheeks, reached out to embrace me.

"Darling?"

"Don't you 'darling' me. Sadie, you knew and you didn't tell me. How could you let this happen?"

"Hush," she said. "Juan's here, he's safe now; a little confused, but with time that will pass. Things take a while up here. You remember how scared you felt when you started college? It's kind of like that."

"Sadie, what am I supposed to do? Lester said the pregnancy is going to be high risk in capital letters. I can't get through this without Juan. I don't even know if I should be trying."

"I have no answers for you, darling. Not even a promise. Only what is, and how you choose to go forward from this moment."

"Sadie?"

"Yes?"

"Take a fucking hike."

BERYL AND EARL were coming up the driveway! Oh, Beryl Anne Reilly, my curly-haired, wry-smiled, plain old even-tempered, bird-obsessed Beryl. I wanted to run to her, pick her up in my

arms, and swing her around. "Hey, Alaska!" I called out. "That must have been one annoying flight, from the look on you guys' faces. Welcome to my last few moments as a single girl."

But instead of coming to me directly, Beryl pulled James aside and said something that erased the smile of welcome from his face. He bent to say something to Nance, and whatever it was, it caused her to clap her hands over her mouth in a terrible way.

Smooth as ice, David taking my arm.

They all knew something that I didn't, and clearly it was a bad thing. I shivered. Right then a kind of stillness came over me, and I swear I felt the baby move inside me. It was just a small flutter, like the wave of a fishtail working against the tide. I wondered what a three-months fetus looked like. In the books it would probably show one of those big-headed blobs with a dark spot for an eye, but I knew better. My baby, even if it was only the size of a berry, was perfect. Its eyes were coffee brown, like Juan's, and it had his thick jet lashes. Its hands were perfect, with waxed-paper skin and palm creases in which a fortune teller would find only good news. It had fingernails the size of a pinhead, and infinitesimal moon-shaped cuticles. It flexed its tiny joints as it swam and waited to be born, and then handed to its father like the gift that it was.

I knew then. Without knowing, I simply knew.

I APOLOGIZED TO GOD for believing him to be without gender. Surely that important a job meant he or she; how could a Supreme Being create such a diverse world without some sense of sexuality? And probably he was indeed a he, because a she would never do something this appalling. I bargained: *Lord, let him be paralyzed; who more than I knows how to deal with a body that works only halfway? Let him be in a coma; I can wait, even if it takes years. You'll see, I'll sit by his bedside and play Mozart, Juan will hear the music, and he'll come back to me the same way I came back to him. I will pray. I'll light Chinese lanterns every night at six-thirty, and the shadows that play across his handsome face will be enough, Lord. I'll learn to drive a UPS van and take over his route until he gets strong enough to*

do it himself. Please, God, everyone says you are merciful and just; now prove it.

ANOTHER BAD WEEK. Per Lester's instructions, I lay in my bed on my left side, which was supposed to be easier on my heart. Ness brought me breakfast trays with fruit, a custard dish of vitamins, and, in a crystal vase, one small cut bloom fresh every day. "Cut flowers are for funerals," I said. "Take them away."

"I grew them," she fired back. "They're staying."

She sat on my bed and read to me, even though that was hard for her, out of children's books that Earl had sold her back when Beryl still lived with us. "I hate children's stories," I told her.

"Tough titty. I like them."

When she finished reading and got up to leave, I said, "Hey, don't forget the flowers on your way out. And you can take the cactus, too. I can tell it isn't happy here."

Nance flitted in and out, but it was hard for her to light. From her I heard farm progress reports, and came to believe that organization could solve almost any problem. She also gave me synopses of whatever concert she and James had attended the night before: Manhattan Transfer, BeauSoleil, and Ladysmith Black Mambazo. "Phoebe, we need to plan the fall boutique," she said, clipboard in hand.

"You handle it."

"I need your input."

"Ask James."

"Would you like to see my new photos?"

"Not really."

"Oh."

Every time James entered the room, Nance found an excuse to duck out. My brother brought me new packages of clay, and a beautiful maple breadboard on which to work it. "Look at these new metallic colors they came out with. Nice, huh? Maybe you should play around with them. They'd make nice Christmas ornaments."

"So give them to Martha Stewart."

"Phoebe, you have to—"

"Lie here and breathe," I said. "That is the extent of it."

"Mother is desperate to speak to you."

I looked over his shoulder into the fog that never left my room. "Do not put her calls through, James. I swear to you that if you do, I will get out of this bed, call a cab, and disappear out of your life forever."

He dropped the subject, and sat there twiddling his thumbs.

"Go run the farm, James. Can't you see I'm very busy here, growing a fatherless baby I probably won't be strong enough to lift?"

"Self-pity isn't very terribly attractive, Pheebs."

"You think I don't know that?"

"We love you, Phoebe, all of us."

"Oh, yes, the all-important *love.* Is there anything in this world a person can count on less?"

"Well, I brought you a book. I'll just leave it here on the bed."

James wouldn't let anyone else tell me. He sat me in his lap, while all around us the wonderful music played and that astonishing cake glittered on the table waiting to be cut with the silver knife and melt on the tongue like communion. My girlfriends cried. One by one the guests heard the dreadful truth repeated like a child's game of telephone. The cookbooks, blenders, the odd silver salad fork; new sheets to pull snug over a mattress we'd already shared, ceased to be presents. "It's not just Juan," James said, probably figuring that the first blow might as well contain all of it, that hearing the pain all at once would be easier to bear. "His mother, too, Phoebe. Beryl and Earl stopped to help. She says they died instantly, that she's sure they didn't suffer."

"Give her a tranquilizer," Nance insisted, the bottle already in her hand.

Lester reached in and pushed her drugs away. "Absolutely not. James, carry Phoebe into the bedroom, and Phyllis," he said, calling to his wife, "fetch my bag from the car. Hurry."

I flailed my arms, beating my brother with my fists. James took it all. He never once let go.

ONE MORNING I WOKE UP, my cheeks wet with tears, and turned my head to see the Easter cactus looking pretty bad. Poor old *Rhipsalidopsis gaertneri*. Beryl had planted it in a chipped container, no dopey ribbon on it, no "Deepest Sympathies" swizzle stick stabbed into the soil. I decided that if the baby was a girl, I would name her Sadie, after my aunt, and call her Sally. Up close I could see that each paddle of the cactus was outlined with a deep purple, similar to Nance's lipliner. There were fine hairs there, too, but no thorns. It needed water. I tipped my tumbler into the pot and watched the soil take a greedy drink.

Wait.

Why hadn't this occurred to me before? Nance wanted a baby. James wanted Nance. I could persuade them to adopt Sally, or Sam, as the case may be. No matter what happened, there was a way out of this.

I LEAFED THROUGH *A CHILD IS BORN* and tracked the baby's evolution. Sometimes, when it occurred to me that what I was studying was akin to tabloid fodder, I was ashamed. The photographs captured a time of life that was supposed to be private, not even glimpsed. I stood at the precipice of all I'd lost, staring, and felt the urge to take a swan dive. I hadn't yet revealed my plan to my brother, but I knew he'd accept. Only a matter of months, I told myself. Then, who knew? Maybe I'd go to Europe. Take a world cruise.

Or simply check out.

Beryl

8
Farm Journal

June something

I can't think about the accident because it makes my blood pressure go up, and I can't talk about the accident because that makes everyone cry, so I try to write things down about the accident here in my journal, but reopening wounds that are just beginning to scab over seems like a bad idea. I'm not a lofty thinker like Phoebe's aunt Sadie was, and I can't make sense of why it happened, or tell a great story that delivers a message. I'm Beryl Anne Reilly, ex-convict, husband killer, bird lover, former Bad Girl, and paramour to Earl. These pages won't end up anywhere except in recycling, which is just where they should end up. All the Bad Girls think that five years in jail taught me wisdom. Ha. It taught me survival—that the more you can do for yourself the better off you'll be. I can rewire a greenhouse, but I can't make this awful sad time any less awful or pass any faster. We are pathetic. I'm obsessed by a truth I want to unburden but dare not do so. Nance doesn't even pretend to eat anymore. Preciousness has a permanent groove in her forehead from frowning. And Phoebe, well, she might just be doing the best of all of us, but God, how I wish she could cry and carry on and break all the windows. Now this business with her being pregnant, and who knows what that will do to her heart? There are times I go nuts. I mean, *nuts,* like riding my old bicycle deep into the valley as fast as I can pedal because it feels like the fingers of old ghosts are right at my shoulders, and I can't get away no matter how far I go. What I wouldn't give to release this pain all tidy and practical, like an owl expels his pellet of mouse bones. I try to be kind to everyone, and usually I am, but sometimes I snap at people who don't deserve it, like Florencio. I try not to lie, but I'm lying every single minute. Are necessary lies any less terrible?

I don't believe in God. I kind of vaguely believed after my mother died. But when my father went, and I was left with my stepmother, well, God and I permanently parted ways. So how do I explain this urge to confess—and say I *did* confess—to *whom?*

Phoebe will hate me when she finds out what I didn't tell her about Juan's accident.

July 4th—Independence Day Sale

Earl and I were supposed to be back in Palmer now. We'd be headed downtown for the Fourth of July parade if we were. I'd planned to enter Verde in the pet competition. Found him a trapper's felt hat at a fabric store. Got him a toy shotgun. There's a fireworks display in Anchorage, not to mention the start of fishing season, but since Juan's death, everything's changed, including the tilt of the earth.

Here is what I do: I work all day with Florencio, and all night we girls take turns sitting with Phoebe until she falls asleep. Last night, when I finally came to bed, I whispered to Earl, "Save me. Tell me something good, something that will help me find the strength to make it through this. I am fresh out of hope, we are missing summer in Alaska, and I haven't been honest with anyone."

He took me in his arms. "Beryl," he said. "You're honest with me. What happened happened. By the time we got there, nothing could be done."

"But—"

He pressed his fingers to my lips. "He's at peace now. With each passing day Phoebe will hurt a little bit less. The salmon will be around for a while longer. Next year I can fish my ass off.

I think we need to stay here, or more specifically you do. And you need to keep your blood pressure down and your beautiful mouth shut."

Then he ran his hands down my body and he touched me in all the places that remind me how lovers can temporarily heal each other of just about any pain. His fingers were so gentle that if I closed my eyes, it could almost have been a dream. When he moved into me, it felt like a hug that had just been promoted from friendly to glorious. He laughed that when we make love I keep my eyes open, but the truth is, since Juan died I'm afraid to shut them even to sleep. I felt guilty having wonderful sex in this house with the mantle of sadness still so fresh and the silence we keep out of respect. But did that stop us? No, we continued, greedy for release, quiet in our efforts, and after we finished, I cried for the first time since the accident, facedown and noiselessly into my pillow. Earl rubbed my back and stayed awake until I felt calm again. I slept all night in the crook of his shoulder, and when I woke up next morning, he hadn't moved.

If there had been men like this in the world before, were they in hiding?

A bird mates, lays an egg, keeps it warm, feeds the baby, teaches it to fly, and the cycle continues. If I'm so lucky and this is what I get, what does that mean Phoebe is?

This is why I believe in birds more than I do God.

Tuesday

Florencio and I spent all day in the greenhouse. I replaced the corroded wires with new stuff that will last twenty years. Juan's death has aged him. A couple of times I saw his hands shaking as we connected wires. The moment everything was ready, I told him to push the button on the control panel, and his face lit up brighter than the lights. The electrical inspector who came out to sign off on our work automatically told Florencio, "Good job," and I sensed it was better to let him think that a man had done it than to correct him. He had that look—anything a woman put her hands to had better be a recipe.

Sometimes I think he's right.

Wednesday

Why do so many people want flower arrangements for Fourth of July? Ness and I stayed up all night making 250 baskets filled with red and white carnations, blue bachelor's buttons, and asparagus fern. Since Juan's death flowers make me sick. We Bad Girls went to the memorial service held in the Catholic church in Salinas. Phoebe didn't ask to, not that Lester would have allowed it. The scent of flowers and incense and sorrow in that little church made me sick to my stomach. Earl played a duet with Bighead, some adagio that had me in tears. The service was said in Spanish, and I was glad I could tune it out. The scent of those flowers got in my hair, clung to my clothes like cigarette smoke. The latest rage in floral design is "posies," which are flowers bundled into a fat bouquet of flowers that is round on the top, and the many stems are cut short and tied with satin ribbon, and stuffed into this little glass cone called a "tussie-mussie," which I think sounds like baby talk for a tampon. I don't know how many were in the church that day, but for the Fourth of July, Ness and I did ninety-three posies. Nance came up with the idea of poking a handful of sparklers into the flowers, and—voilà!—you have high Valley style, not Martha Stewart but darn close. Ordinarily Nance would take advantage of a sale to offer crafts, soaps, nut breads, and the like, but this year we all agreed we should just quietly sell the arrangements and get it over with.

All that day Phoebe wouldn't talk to anyone. Lester came out and sat with her for a long while. Afterward he walked out to see us, and Nance asked, "Well? Is she doing better? How's the baby? Is her heart all right? You'd better not hold anything back, Lester, or I will personally make you sorry you did."

I handed Lester a tall glass of lemonade I'd made that morning with fresh lemons and mint and cracked ice, and thought about what it meant to hold things back, and how I wouldn't blame him one iota if he thought it was best for Phoebe not to know. I handed one to Nance, too, and watched her set the glass down without drinking. "I'd like to send a therapist out here for her to talk to," he told us, "but she said no so vehemently I let the subject drop. I have to tell you, ladies. I thought I knew how hardheaded Phoebe was, but I'm afraid I've gravely misjudged her."

Nance started in on how therapy was a good thing, and Lester quickly picked out two floral baskets, one for his office, one for his wife, and hauled ass. I love that man, even though he still pesters me about getting that eye exam, which is a total waste of time and money, since here I am way over forty and I don't even need reading glasses. But Nance is the one who needs to be in therapy.

When he left, Ness went, "Huh. Think maybe he wanted to send that therapist out to talk to all of us?"

Like Earl told me to, I bit my tongue.

Same day, later on

Has DeThomas Farms earned a reputation since last Christmas or what? Between preorders, walk-in traffic, and farm tours, we ran out of flyers for the autumn sale. People asked if they could sign up for holiday poinsettias now, and Nance started a list right there on the laptop computer James bought us. I asked, "Is it a good idea to commit to Christmas poinsettias when things are so iffy?"

Nance, the only one of us who can figure out how to work the computer, said, "Hell, yes, we are committing to poinsettias. They are the one big crop we can count on. They make it possible for us to be sitting here on our butts working while the rest of the world punches a time clock."

And Ness said, "Poinsettias, ick. I secretly never wanted to see one again."

We all agreed. During the afternoon lull Ness said, "Beryl, sometimes I hear Phoebe carrying on in there. Talking to that plant. I'm concerned."

"At least she's talking to something," I said.

"We should bring her more plants," Nance said, in that hopeful tone she uses for everyone except herself. All she'd eaten all day was iced coffee and a half a banana. She wouldn't even drink the lemonade because I'd used real sugar instead of calorie free. "One at a time and really picky varieties—orchids and ferns and all the kinds that need babying?" Nance said, peering at Ness over her glasses. "Precious?"

"Babying?" Ness said, cranky from the heat and probably

too much sugary lemonade. "Could you have chosen a more unfortunate choice of words?"

Nance got all huffy and said, "You want to climb down off your high horse, Miss Never Makes a Mistake?"

She sighed, and I snapped at her, "Enough with the friggin' sighing already! For God's sake, I am sick of the almighty sighing around here!"

Ness said, "Oh, that's rich. Complaints from the queen of sighing. Sister, you don't know the half of how annoying it is."

"I do not sigh," I told her.

"Yes, you do. Nance does it even more than you do."

Nance said, "Bullcrap. Give me a for instance."

Ness held out her fingers and ticked off, "For instance, try breakfast, lunch, and dinner. I figured it was your alternative to eating. Why don't you sit your skinny ass down and spill all about what's bothering you. You don't eat enough food to keep a butterfly alive. What's got your undies in a knot, girlfriend? Is it James, or is it Rotten Rick?"

"I'll thank you to not mention that rat bastard's name in my presence," Nance said, and then clammed up tighter than ever. She snubbed us for the rest of the sale, and was the first to go indoors when we ran out of arrangements. "Shall I go after her?" I asked, and Ness said, "No, leave her be. She's either praying for Phoebe or in there doing the poor girl's nails. Either way it's a good thing."

Then *she* sighed. I laughed, but she didn't notice. She straightened all the plant sale money and asked me, "Do you think Nance is anorexic?"

"I think every woman I've ever met is at one time or another," I said. "When I was married to J.W., I wore a size four."

"Oh, Beryl, do you think Phoebe's going to make it?"

"I hope so," I said, "but if I was in her place I might not even want to try."

So it's a good thing it's Phoebe and not me.

And just thinking those words made me so sad right then that I felt sick to my stomach, and I sighed. Ness is right. I'm a hateful, lying person. I don't deserve to be a Bad Girl.

Thursday

Earl took our rental car to Sierra Grove to check on his properties today. Get this: In addition to the bookstore and the coffee place, he owns a bed-and-breakfast in a Victorian house, and three smaller houses up the street! Once I peeked in his checkbook, and the balance was $168,000. I wanted to ask him more about the properties, but he had plans to gig with some musician friends up north in Benicia, and said he'd be back in a few days. "Hang out with the Bad Girls," he told me, and handed me some money. "Take gentle care of Phoebe."

He says that every day. I have three thousand dollars in cash in my wallet.

And he kissed me long and deep, like he does some mornings in Alaska, when the sun is up so high in the sky it could be this intrepid little housecat that's run far, far up a spruce tree, and not even a sexy fireman can coax it down.

It is odd to be loved. Not just the great sex, which floors me, but *loved,* respected, treated with care, my needs anticipated, and to have become part of someone's life so deeply you want to know everything he did that day, even his smallest thoughts. Especially while Phoebe lies there not daring to move, keeping her emotions reeled in so she won't jeopardize the baby. What are *her* smallest thoughts? Where are the arms to hold her at this time when she needs it most? In the afternoons I go into her room and lie down next to her. I snuggle up close and stroke her hair, rub her shoulders, hum songs.

Mostly she tells me to go away, but occasionally she'll let me stay.

Beyond that I have no clue what to do to make things better.

Friday night, late

Why didn't Florencio and Rosa have other kids after their daughter drowned? Why don't Nance and James just elope? Why does Phoebe insist on going through with a pregnancy that could kill her? Why can't I get quit of the feelings of guilt that I know more than anyone else does about Juan's death?

Where is Earl?

Saturday night

Nance and James went to the movies. Here is what I think: Nance is trying to run this romance by the books. She makes James call her for dates. They have dinner out. They attend movies, plays, performances, gallery openings, and then they sit in the living room and discuss them like college students with a chaperone. I've seen them kiss, but he never spends the night in her room, and she comes back from his place by dark. If I didn't know better, I'd swear she was trying to regrow her virginity. I am keeping count of how many calories she takes in while in my presence. Today I saw her eat one slice of toast, no butter, no jam. We use diet bread around here, so that is forty calories. Forty. She powers down the Diet Coke—zero calories, zero sugar—and lemon and pees every ten minutes, so it's likely she pees out the forty calories and then her metabolism just goes berserk and starts eating up the muscle. She just looks like death warmed-over, and if I say word one about it she hightails it out of here in her Rodeo. On the other end of the spectrum, Duchess is putting on weight. Here's what I think. I think every time Nance feels the urge to eat, she throws Duchess a biscuit.

Ness is spending the night tonight with David Snow. Now here is a mystery that truly could use Nancy Drew. What do a gay white man with HIV and a hetero black woman with HIV have in common that requires spending the night? Possibilities include: medication, a love of old movies, popcorn, and someone to sit next to in the dark. David's got six horses, but between the two of them it would take three shifts to exercise them all, and there are days David's too frail to walk to the john, let alone ride a horse. Horses only need new shoes every six weeks, and Ness is over there five out of seven days a week. Ness is a born-again Baptist. David claims to be Sufi, which according to Phoebe's aunt's dictionary means a Muslim mystic, and from what I learned in prison, Muslims were kind of down on the female race. I could be wrong. I'm wrong about a lot of things. Like stabbing a husband instead of walking away. Like thinking I can save every winged thing on the planet just by loving them. So maybe it's like Ness says, they love each other as friends, and stay up all hours to talk, or maybe she goes there to avoid

Phoebe's bad moods, or maybe, just maybe, they have decided to have sex with each other because who else would understand the other person's needs better than each other? Maybe this is menopause. Or maybe I am just so freaking paranoid my mind is going a million miles an hour.

Lester came by earlier and took Phoebe's blood samples. He gave her a thorough going-over, and she fell asleep right after dinner. Earl still hasn't called, but I'm not worried. Sometimes in Alaska he goes off for a few days by himself, and he always comes back with some kind of memento for me—a piece of jadeite, a feather, pressed wildflowers. I miss sleeping with him, though Duchess is good company. The old girl's muzzle is dusted with white hair. I miss Verde. When I called the vet he said all was well, and that my bird was rapidly becoming spoiled, like he wasn't spoiled before?

Looking at Sadie's portrait is disturbing. What the hell was she thinking when she posed for it? That is a very smart-alecky smile. Almost accusing.

I should stop drinking so much coffee—I might be starting to get a little paranoid.

Later that night

Oh, I had the most terrible dream! Earl had gone hiking alone, even though I'd begged him not to. It was rainy out. He hit a patch of loose rock and slid hundreds of feet. When he stopped, his back was broken, and he called out but no one heard him. Even asleep I kept trying to fix a different ending to the dream. The Lassie ending: If he'd had a dog, maybe he could have taken hold of his collar and gotten dragged down the mountain to safety. The Eagle Scout ending: If he'd hiked with a partner, one guy could have gone for help, leaving markers along the way, like Hansel and Gretel. The Alaska ending: Earl died of thirst, or got eaten by a bear, or fell into a crevice in a glacier and froze and no one found him for a hundred years. The only constant was that I wasn't there, and I knew I would never be able to forgive myself, which is just how Phoebe must be feeling.

What really happened

I have lived my life with too many secrets zipped inside me. Some, like what my stepbrother did to me when I was sixteen, I felt I had to keep, or I stood to lose my family. I kept the awful truth to maintain a hold on the world, and thinking one went hand in hand with the other. And what I wouldn't give to sit him down now and ask what did he think he was doing. Other secrets, well, here I am all grown up, and I see how keeping secrets made my path a narrow, rocky place instead of soft and beautiful and stretching endless before me. There are no good secrets. Not a one. We should know if our kids are molested or our lovers are unfaithful and who killed Marilyn Monroe and how much the government knows about global warming and who's really responsible for drug trafficking. It's my fault for letting those things inside me keep me from so much of my life. Then I could excuse it because I didn't know better. Now the only thing I know for sure is that I can't hold this inside any longer:

The day after Juan died, people had slept on couches if they slept at all. They were making phone calls, pots of coffee, crying, trying to think what to do to make this terribleness easier to bear. I went outside to clean up. Last thing Phoebe needed to see was the wreckage of her wedding. The patio looked like the scene of a crime—plates of half-eaten food, chairs pulled halfway out from the tables, full wine glasses, and forgotten wraps. The minute the first shot was fired, everyone had run. I began scraping dishes when I heard a sound I know well, birds fighting. When I turned to look, the blackbirds were all over the cake, gorging themselves.

I hate to think what might have happened if I had a shotgun.

Oh, I hate lying to Phoebe. I'd told her that Juan and his mother died instantly. It wasn't a complete lie. Mrs. Nava probably did die quickly. People who don't wear seatbelts usually pancake into the tarmac. Juan, on the other hand—Earl said the minute he heard that moan coming from deep inside him he knew he wasn't going to make it. I didn't know. His face was a ruin. Like someone had taken a mallet to it. Because his car was old, and didn't have airbags, on his way through the windshield the steering wheel crushed his chest. There was so much blood he couldn't have had more than a teaspoon left inside him. Later that night, I heard the same noise coming out of Phoebe, which convinces me that there's more than one kind of hemorrhaging.

Tuesday

Earl says he needs to go to New Mexico, and do I want to stay here or come along. Am I terrible for wanting to go?

Sage

Varieties include perennial, annual, bush, and groundcover. Flowers vary from white to yellow, pink to red, lilac to purple, to a deep, true blue. Some are aromatic, others flavorful enough to use in cooking. Sage makes a fine tea said to loosen a chest cold. Commonly used by native peoples to "smudge," or cleanse a new living space. Gather sage in the wild, as some believe that paying for the herb ruins the spiritual aspects of the ceremony. Bind into a bundle, light the end, and allow to smolder. Thoroughly permeate each room, removing any negative energy by wafting the smoke into each corner until you've created a "sacred space." Sage is easy to grow, but can, without care, overtake a garden.

Rick

9

Wild About Harry

THIS IS NOT SEX, IT'S ART.

Madigan Caringella makes love the same way she sings. Things begin with a slow, grumbling start. Then, finger by finger, she slides her hands down my ribs, looking for the missing one she insists God took to make her kind. When she lets me inside, she sheds her skin. Gets on a first-name basis with every nerve. Together we move in a hopeless quest to touch every part of each other simultaneously. Then she takes hold of my heart and squeezes. When she lets go, believe me, I swear my heart has never felt so alone in its life.

"You stay in the shower one minute longer and I swear I'm letting the dogs in. Dammit all, Rick, you're hogging the hot water, and we have to get on the road."

"Be out in a minute. I'm thinking."

"In a minute, my ass! Is it my fault you stay up half the night writing poems while normal people are sleeping?"

"I don't write poems. I've never written poems. I'm writing a novel."

"Whatever! All's I know is you and that fecking notebook are inseparable, and Ana and Lee are expecting us today and we have to leave now, or we won't get there until midnight. I'm sending Mentos in to lick your legs. Here she comes. Hot slobbery dog tongue . . ."

I groaned, and it struck me that was the noise *I* made during sex, and for a moment I wondered if that particular sound indicated pleasure or bewilderment.

Fact: Just looking at Madigan Caringella made me hard.

Fact: The first night she let me into her bed we'd screwed ourselves silly all the way to first light.

Opposing point of view: Something felt off.

Supporting evidence: I didn't need an emotional attachment to enjoy myself in bed.

Overall impression: What's better, mediocre sex with someone you love, or gold-medal sex with a relative stranger?

Fact: Maddy wrung me out after knowing me less than twelve hours.

Consideration: Did that make her immoral? Or me?

Possible conclusion: This girl lived one step closer to the animal kingdom. Like those wiseacre collies of hers that sat on the floor witnessing our unlikely alliance with something close to alarm—as if they knew the future neither of us could see.

After the fact: I held on to her and slept, and that part was good. But when I dreamed, it was of a woman who became a bear. The she-bear furiously swiped a claw at me, and instinctively I threw up my hands to cover my face. When I lowered them it was no bear at all; it was Nance, saying, "Stop looking at me like I'm freaking Cinderella." She used to say that in the mornings after we'd made love. I couldn't help it. My smile was a purely autonomous reaction to her glow—the way her skin took on the light, her messed-up hair, and the smart things that came out of her mouth—I'd found the whole package pretty compelling.

Addendum: Maddy didn't make me smile. She made me take long showers and run the water as hot as I could stand it on my lower back. She made me look in the mirror and wonder who the fuck the tired unemployed guy was looking back.

Definite conclusion: I was in trouble here.

Startling new information revealed: Old stingy Rick, who'd

buy a cut-rate Valentine's Day card if it meant saving a quarter, was laying down the cash to get us both to New Mexico.

WE DROVE THROUGH what appeared to be the worst part of Texas, and it was hot inside the truck, smelling entirely too much like dog. I was tired of all Maddy's tapes, and my back felt wrenched, particularly on the right side. Maddy laid out our route over breakfast, we decided on a time for breaks, and I did my best not to lecture her on her driving at eighty-five miles per hour. Around one in the afternoon we'd lunch at whatever diner struck her fancy. Had to be a diner. If Jell-O wasn't on the menu, she'd complain. "That stuff's made of ground-up horse hooves, you know," I told her.

"Shut up, Heinrich," she said, wiping her mouth with a napkin. "I've had enough disappointment in my lifetime. Don't you go ruining Jell-O for me, too."

"Tell me more about that disappointment," I said. Frequently.

And every time, she'd answer, "In your dreams, paperboy."

I suggested I drive, and that way she could nap.

She bit into her cheeseburger and answered me with a full mouth. "The dogs are used to me driving."

"They could ride in the truck bed."

She set the burger down and glared at me before swallowing hard. "Do I look like one of those fools who puts her dogs in the truck bed and hopes for the best? Do I?"

UNLIKE NANCE, who had to pee every hour on the hour, Maddy drove a long time without stopping for a break. When we crossed the New Mexico state line, things greened up a little, but mostly it was wheat-colored prairie rolling on and on, anonymous and barren. Every now and again a windmill dotted the landscape, or there was a picturesque falling-down barn, or some tidy ranch house surrounded by a few dusty cattle. Whatever was left of the Old West wasn't doing so well financially. I indulged a fantasy about holing up in a converted barn and writing the novel I'd felt surfacing the summer after I'd graduated journalism school.

My first decent assignment had been an article on country-and-western music, which offered me a glimpse into the underbelly of the business. I polished up my six hundred words, had someone over me edit them to dust, and learned that being a journalist and a writer were two entirely different endeavors. Eventually it was me in the editor's seat, and I moved on to cover music I actually liked, but the intrigue of Nashville's darker side had never left me.

I had a million first lines—"They call me Rocket, and they throw me roses." "When you can't speak the truth, try singing about it." "The night I took the stage at the Bluebird Café, a chorus of ghosts with better voices than mine sang backup." The hero's quest transported into modern-day circumstances, the folkie/country scene in deep, dark detail. Rocket—Tim Rochert—would be as charming as hell. I'd employ Hemingway's spare sentence structure. Engineer one of Steinbeck's unflinching wars between men and other men. There'd be the woman who was bad for Tim—whom he, of course, wanted—and the good woman who'd stand by patiently waiting to save him from himself. The story would coalesce in a style both understatedly elegant and subtly elegiac. The book cover would feature the honey-colored body of a Gibson guitar set on its side, its curves recalling a woman's reclining body. . . .

Maddy waved a hand in front of my face. "About two more hours, Mr. Sandman. You need to stop?"

I shook my head no and watched a fine sheen of sweat form above her upper lip as she grinned. Her dark hair was pinched back in one of those alligator clips women favor these days. The wind had tousled it so much it looked like bed hair. Her stretchy tank top was rolled up under her breasts. So far as I could tell, she wasn't wearing a bra. I thought about sex with her; how she was the first woman to flatten me in bed, just take the starch clean out of me. It was scary, compelling, and I fantasized grabbing hold of the steering wheel and pulling us over so we could do it again, right then, on the side of the road. *Later,* I told myself. In the dark all I cared about was losing myself, and holding on to Maddy was a good place to do that.

GALISTEO, NEW MEXICO, as viewed from the passenger seat: One Catholic church, adobe exterior, rotting wooden steps, painted white crucifix on the roof, said paint peeling in a manner so photogenic it would make a best-selling postcard. A general store, also adobe, advertising homemade tamales, hand-cranked ice cream, plumbing fixtures, and genuine turquoise jewelry. A horse farm, ripe with the smell of manure and an impressive fly population. New fence surrounding a sprawling ranch probably owned by a movie star, some guy who flew in once a year in his private plane and pretended he was Buffalo Bill with GPS.

On Calle Gordo, Maddy parked her truck behind a low red adobe wall. Wildflowers bloomed against it in a riot of colors—purple, yellow, and a healthy wallop of red. We got out of the truck and looked around while the dogs stretched their legs. A few scattered domiciles offered housing to people foolish enough to try to make a living here. Maddy led me up a stone path to a duplex with wooden gates. We'd missed her friends Ana and Lee after all. They'd left us the key and a note: "Back tomorrow. Make yourself at home. Don't drink the tap water unless you boil it first—it will give you the runs." I took a swig of my Dr Pepper. It was bone-dry out here, and I wished I'd bought a six-pack.

"How'd you and Ana meet?" I asked as Maddy folded the note into her pocket.

"Powwow in Billings."

"Powwow, huh. Is she Indian?"

"Yes, she's Indian."

"Really? What tribe? Are you an Indian?"

Maddy frowned at me. "Criminy, Rick. Stop acting like a damn reporter. Ana's my friend. I'm her friend. So we have a little blood. Does that make us something special?"

Several things about Mary Madigan Caringella intrigued me. Besides the way she behaved at the Oklahoma memorial, and how intensely she went about the act of making love, she appeared to always be in forward motion. Driving, eating, arguing, singing—God, that voice of hers reached all the way down to my soul, and then it tugged—I got the impression she had lived her whole life with one foot outside the frame, like she was reaching for a present she might feel more comfortable in because this one sucked so bad it gave her the willies.

"Be that as it may, I usually like to know a few things about the women I live with."

She jiggled the key in the lock. "And you do know a few things, don't you? You know I like Jell-O, and you know better than to touch my belly button. You know I can go three times in one night, while you, my out-of-shape companion, need encouragement to get to the final go-round."

"Hey, I crossed the finish line, didn't I?"

She leaned over and kissed me. "You're going to love this place. It's a writer's dream come true."

"How's that?"

"Look at it," she said, shoving the warped door open. Red tile floors, thick white-painted walls. A *banco* with cushions. A woodstove, a fireplace, and the rattiest-looking upholstered chair I'd ever seen. Made me long for the BarcaLounger. "Old, isolated, picturesque. Plus Ana's ex-husband Harry is buried right outside the kitchen window. You can't get much more inspiration than a body in the garden. I think I'll get our stuff out of the car."

While Maddy dragged in her clothes, I stood looking at the garden. Someone had planted vegetables on top of old Harry. Pole beans, staked tomatoes, and squash blossoms lay heavy on stems in the direction she'd pointed. Soon they'd wither and produce fruit. I wondered who'd eat them, because I had no plans to ingest something that harvested its nutrients from a corpse. Of the few things I disliked in this life, dead bodies were at the top of the list. Women who withheld the truth from me ran a close second, and overly smart dogs came in third.

Maddy threw her clothes inside the door and stepped back outside. "Let's go exploring," she said. "No, let's check out the general store. Or maybe we should shuck our clothes and sit in the river."

Why did she have such trouble standing still? I knew it had something to do with that chair at the bombing memorial, but that was only part of it. "How about we just sit for a few minutes?" I suggested.

"I guess." Maddy poured bottled water into a bowl for the collies. "But before it gets dark, I want to show you every inch of this town."

From what I'd seen, that would take about fifteen minutes. I sat down on the porch and took off my T-shirt. "How did Harry die?"

"Cancer, I think."

"That's too bad. Was he very old?"

"Forty-nine."

"That's young." *Younger than me,* I almost said.

"To some people, I guess."

"You told me Ana was living with Lee."

She refilled the dogs' water bowl. "She was and is."

"Well, how'd all this tending a dying ex-husband sit with another man?"

She laughed, the dogs drank, and then ran off investigating the rooms, dripping water on everything, including me. "You big goof. Lee helped *nurse* Harry."

I shook my head and thought of James, my phone pal, and wondered if he was screwing my ex-girlfriend at this very moment. Not that I lived in Portland anymore, but would Nance come back to nurse me if I was dying? I shuddered in the summer heat. "Sounds kinda flaky to me."

"To help somebody you once loved die? I think they call it humanity."

"Hey, two whole sentences without a cuss word. Where's the nitro?"

For a second she looked at me with blind panic. Then the glare returned. "Feck you, Rick."

"Feck?" I couldn't help but smirk at her unique slant on cussing. The endless stream of it, as continuous as AM radio.

Madigan cocked her head. "You are one uptight white boy. Harry left Ana the duplex in his will. Why the hell shouldn't she bury him outside a place he built with his own hands? It's a beautiful place to spend goddamn eternity, isn't it? I mean, lots of people don't get a choice. You know, Rick, I thought New Mexico might cure you, but now I'm not so sure."

"Cure me of what?"

She snorted and walked past the garden. "If you have to ask, you're worse off than I thought. Come on, doggies. Let's go exploring."

"I'm not invited?"

She flipped me off and kept walking.

Whoa. I picked a few wildflowers and stuck them in the empty water bottle. Then I lined up her cactus plants on the kitchen windowsill.

Maddy was gone three hours. In that time I had a mild panic attack about selling my car to Ben without checking the Blue Book price. I placed our toothbrushes in a glass in the bathroom. I did a load of laundry, making sure to separate the whites from the colors. I walked down to the general store and bought a dozen tamales, two pints of cinnamon ice cream, bananas, milk and cereal for breakfast, and for lunch, a locally produced white cheese and fresh tortillas. I sat on the wall and stared at the sky until the sun went down. It took a while, but it was a cosmic sunset, all shades of purple and a nicely contrasting orange.

When Maddy came back, she fed the dogs and took a shower. I stayed outside on the wall, pondering my circumstances. As of today I was living in northern New Mexico, home to an inordinate number of meth labs, a fact I knew from UPI and my years as a reporter. The state was also popular with movie stars hiding from LA smog. Hell's Angels loved New Mexico, as did heroin dealers, wealthy Texans, and the Mexican Mafia, reported to control the town of Española.

I had no clue what a white guy from Portland via Oklahoma was doing here. None whatsoever. I had a pocket full of cash, I was sleeping with a girl I knew nothing about, save for her incredible body. She might kick me out tomorrow, just like that, and at some point I'd probably have to go back to my parents' house, where my father's feebleness and my mother's generosity would deliver me yet another stomach-wrenching ride in the guilt arena. I was over fifty—I played the movie in my head of what life was supposed to be like at this stage—nice house overlooking the water, new car every two years, beautiful wife and two-point-five children graduating college, social security—well, the only problem was, that was somebody else's movie. Certainly not mine.

By now my mother had folded up my clothing and set it into a box between layers of tissue paper. My father was probably still bitching over hiring a gardener, taxing his health in order to jaggedly cut his own lawn. If I thought Oklahoma was strange, Galisteo was fecking Mars. But for the first time since I'd left my job, I felt I could take a breath and my lungs inflated all the way to the bottom. Indoors I could hear Maddy singing, her gorgeous voice tempting me, but I planned to wait until she called me before I went inside.

"I'M TELLING YOU, MAN, this computer's a good deal. Brand new. Windows ME, a DVD player so you can watch the director's-cut movies. Active matrix screen, ten gigabytes, and 128 megs of RAM. All that's missing is the box, and how bad do you need the box? A grand, man, you can't find one for that in the store."

"Where exactly *is* the box?" I asked the short Mexican guy in the white T-shirt who spat in the dirt and looked away. We were standing on a street corner in Albuquerque, having just exited the overpriced Gateway store, and were almost to the truck when he called us over.

"Hey, you want this computer or not? I can't spend all day standing around in the sun, man. I got me a skin condition."

"Who are you? An ex–Gateway employee?"

"Rick, just buy the damn thing, and let's go eat lunch," Maddy said. "Think of all the money you'll save on your little paper notepads."

"Ha-ha, Maddy. I'm laughing myself to death." I peeled off twenties and offered the guy four hundred. "I know it's hot," I said. "This is all I have."

He called me a variety of Spanish names, but he pocketed his money. I wrapped the laptop in my jacket, and took it to the truck where the dogs waited. It was the first time I'd ever knowingly bought something stolen. My father was right keeping me grounded all through high school; way back then I'd left my moral compass in the woods, and apparently I'd never gone back to look for it.

"What are you going to write about?" Maddy asked me as we sat in the truck thirty minutes later, eating tacos so greasy my fingers were slippery.

"You," I said, reaching over to wipe hot sauce from the corner of her mouth.

"Very funny," she said, batting me away. "What are you really going to write about?"

"I don't know. Me?"

She laughed and divided the last of her taco into equal halves and fed it to the dogs. Then she wadded up her napkin and smiled. The sun was setting behind her left shoulder. When she smiled like that I could forgive her almost anything. "When we were kids? My sister read more books than anyone I know. Me, I can't sit still for anything like that. Can't imagine writing. I don't even make shopping lists. I say what I need in alphabetical order, and that's how I remember. Apples, cornflakes, Kleenex, tampons. It's a good system."

"Where's your sister live?" I asked. "What's her name?"

She sighed and scooted over closer to me. Her hand on my thigh was warm and strong, promising good things to come. If we were truly lovers, it might have meant something profound. "Holy Mother of God," she said. "Will you look at that sky? Have you ever seen anything that color outside of a paint box? People say once you spend time in New Mexico, the light holds you prisoner."

We were almost home before it occurred to me that I had heard the history of mesas, planned a trip to Acoma Pueblo, and was half drunk on the smell of sage on the wind but that Maddy hadn't answered my question. She was far better at skirting the truth than I was, and I had spent my life working my craft. Like a turtle she could slip inside this prehistoric shell, and nothing I said or did could penetrate it. Maybe that was what kept me here. I made up my mind that whatever it took, sooner or later, I was getting in. It would be better than any sex. Any guy worth his salt could convince a woman to take off her clothes. But open her heart? That took skill.

That night while I was working on the laptop, she slid over and wrapped her arms around me. Started nipping my ears. Followed up the nips with that hot tongue. "Come on, Rick, it's late. Take me to bed."

I shrugged her off. "Take yourself. I'm trying to write."

More kisses, more hot tongue on the back of my neck. "The laptop's not going to walk away in the night. You can write tomorrow."

I sighed and set the computer on the bench. "Didn't we do this yesterday?"

"So," she said, "maybe I want to do it again."

I palmed her face. It was beautiful, even the scar on her lip. But it wasn't open the way Nance used to lay herself out to me. It wasn't vulnerable, and maybe it would never be. "What's the matter?"

She sat up and turned toward the window. "I'm bored."

"Not a very compelling reason for sex."

Her dark eyes shone. Something was surfacing, and sex was the only way she could keep it at bay. She looked down at her hands and said huskily, "Just take me to bed, and don't ask any more questions."

"Okay," I said, "but all I'm going to do is hold you."

While the computer hummed on the *banco,* I did my best to distract Maddy from whatever was bothering her. I rubbed her back while she cried. Whenever I thought she was empty, she howled again and the tears started all over. I tried my best to go with it, but the reporter in me was busy adding up two and two. Mention of the book-reading sister. The chair at the Murrah site. The way Maddy never ordered a beer. Eventually she fell into sleep like she'd been sledgehammered, but it was a long time before I did.

ANA I LIKED RIGHT AWAY. She was dark, short, and hyper—always gardening or beading, knocking at the door with vegetarian dishes she wanted us to sample. Lee was tall and chunky, with white hair pulled back in a ponytail, and Lee was a woman, which made the whole thing with poor Harry even more intriguing, but if I asked questions I'd be called all those woman-hater names so I pretended I wasn't surprised and no matter how much Maddy jabbed me in the ribs and teased me, I refused to react. "I have no problem with lesbians," I told her. Really, I didn't, so long as it was me they were dipping in honey. What bothered me the most was how from the back Lee could have been mistaken for a man. Was it some unwritten rule that one half of a lesbian couple had to turn asexual?

Lee didn't really talk unless circumstances forced her. Couldn't draw her out with anything—she didn't ride horses, she ate what was put in front of her, and worked on her jewelry. Some mornings she'd climb a tree and smoke a joint, but she never invited me to join her. Mostly she kept to herself, working on silver pieces to sell at the weekend markets. She treated Maddy and Ana the same strange way.

"We have a lot in common," I said to her one afternoon when the girls were out riding horses they'd borrowed from the farm down the way and Lee was sitting in the courtyard polishing a load of belt buckles. "Working the way we do," I added. "Both of us are pretty focused."

Lee squinted at me and continued polishing.

"I like your stuff," I said. "Really. Needlepoint turquoise is becoming a lost art. The painstaking setting of the stones, the silver work—"

"You can't afford not to like it," she said, interrupting me, and took it inside.

After that we nodded hello when we saw each other, and on the few occasions when we had dinner together, we listened to Ana and Maddy as if they were our better halves, like we were two retired guys whose brains had turned to mush.

MOST MORNINGS I SLEPT in until the dogs woke me, and then I let Maddy sleep and walked them down by a creek whose currents were deceptively swift. The female border collie stayed by my side, but Jim felt compelled to bring me all manner of soggy treasures, and to shake himself dry all over my jeans. They weren't bad dogs, exactly, just dogs with definite needs. When they didn't get those needs met, they let you know the level of their unhappiness by destroying things, like the secondhand dictionary I bought on one of our treks into Albuquerque.

This Maddy found hysterically funny. "That's a riot," she said. "They're telling you to stop using big words."

"I don't use big words."

"Yes, you do," she said, and proceeded to quote directly from my hopeless first chapter. "'Saturday morning, Tim deviated from his normal route, perambulating down Main Street in search of the titian-haired woman he'd seen in the bar the night before. . . .' Come off it, Rick. Why not just say he took a *walk?* And what the feck is titian-haired anyway? Some kind of Greek god? How can a person have hair like a Greek god? I mean, weren't there a bunch of different hairstyles back then?"

I seethed. "Titian means her hair is brownish red."

"So say brownish red." Madigan stepped through the torn dictionary pages and began making a peanut butter sandwich. That was about the extent of her culinary skills. "You want half of this?"

"No."

She smiled. "Okay. Remember, I offered."

"Seems to me you're always offering things I don't want."

The smile left her face as quickly as it had arrived. "Excuse me? What is that supposed to mean?"

"Just out of curiosity, which one of us has a journalism degree? Did you even finish high school?"

Maddy threw the sandwich down on the counter. On her way out the door, she said, "Well, pardon the feck out of me for taking up valuable airspace around the famous fecking writer who lost his damn job."

The screen door banged shut. While I picked up the torn pages and smoothed them flat, the dogs stared at me, those big blue eyes accusing. "She was spying," I told them. "Am I just supposed to let that go?"

They whined to be let out.

Maddy didn't return. I abandoned the dictionary and took

the dogs outside to find her. We walked over the footbridge down to the creek. The water was ice cold, but the dogs didn't mind. It wasn't deep enough to drown somebody, but if a person lost her footing, who knew what could happen. Over and over I called her name. No answer. I wanted to hear her sing again. If I needed anything, it was the sound of her voice. That in itself was a story. If she came back, no, *when* she came back, I'd apologize and take her out to dinner, let her order anything she wanted, even lobster. I'd say, "Let's drive to Santa Fe. Have dinner someplace nice. Listen to some music. Run down to the general store and buy a paper. Take those damn dogs with you and tire them out." That was better than "I'm sorry."

BACK AT THE DUPLEX I fed the dogs her sandwich. I went to the store for the paper and circled possible dinner choices. I leaned out the front window of the duplex, hoping to see her making her way along the red dirt road. Got a pinch in my neck and had to quit that.

Finally, at dusk, I heard the screen door creak open. The collies were so happy to have her back, they were fairly skipping, showing off for her attention. I watched them and thought of Nance and that Labrador she kept, Duchess or whatever its name was, and how just before Nance left me she'd confide in the dog, tell her about her day, and how that damn dog seemed to listen. It was old and smelly, a real albatross. Maybe it was dead by now. Ana and Lee were in Arizona all week, selling their wares at some Gem Show they said was worth the long drive. Thanks to Harry acting as compost, the vegetable garden was flourishing. We had ripe tomatoes, monstrous zucchini, and sunflowers gaining about six inches in height per day. I thought about how I had absolutely no clue what to do with myself until Maddy got back.

"Forgive me," I said when she walked through the door.

"I'll try," she said, and ducked into the bathroom.

While she showered and changed clothes for dinner, I turned on the computer, highlighted the entire chapter it had taken me a week to write, all fourteen pages, then I took a breath and hit the Delete key.

"JESUS WEPT," Maddy said, as we made our way through the crowded streets of old-town Santa Fe. "I've never seen so many people in my life. What happened to this town?"

This was a question I sure couldn't answer, having never been here myself. "Seems all right to me."

She snorted. "It's turning into Los Angeles."

I'd been to LA. "No, it's not."

"Yes, it is. Stop arguing with me."

"I will, but that doesn't mean you're right."

We passed a number of places I wouldn't have minded exploring: a weaving store with blankets in the window, several dozen galleries, a bookstore with a poster of Georgia O'Keeffe on the back of a motorcycle, and the Cowgirl Hall of Fame, which was really a restaurant and I could tell would have perfecto cheeseburgers. Maddy stopped in front of the Catholic church and watched the remains of a wedding party being photographed for posterity. Latino family—lots of bridesmaids, tough-looking groomsmen, and four flower girls.

"What do you think, Caringella?" I asked. "That part of your future?"

She fired back, "Part of yours?"

I laughed.

A low-rider in a purple Impala drove by, his car rocking on hydraulics. Everyone in the wedding party turned to look. We passed a rare bookstore and ducked into a dusty-looking bar, dimly lit and smelling of beer. "Find us a table," Maddy said. "I have to pee."

The only remaining table was so far off to the side one of us wouldn't be able to see the stage. I took the better chair, figuring I'd offer to switch with Maddy halfway through the set. A waitress came by, and I ordered a Coke for Maddy and a beer for me. "Who's playing?" I asked.

"Whoever shows up. You want some chips and salsa?"

"Sure, thanks."

It was a rough-looking crowd, except for the curly-haired woman sitting alone at the table nearest the stage. My reporter's instinct kicked in, and I knew she would be the one person I'd seek out after this concert, that somehow I could tell her remarks would be the ones I'd quote in my story, if I had one to write.

"Chips?" Maddy said when she returned. "What the hell is this? I thought you were buying me dinner to make up for being such a dickhead."

I sighed. "I am not a dickhead, and this is called an appetizer."

"Pardon me for not being a cosmopolitan. Where I come from food like this is called the main event."

"Really? Okay, Maddy, I'm calling you on it. Where did you come from?"

She looked me dead in the eye. "Same place you did. Loserville."

Just then the guitarist came on stage. He wasn't anybody I knew, but he had a nice guitar, looked like a custom-made acoustic. Within his first three notes chills ran up my neck. We'd lucked out; this was going to be a good show. I tried to think who he reminded me of—Leo Kottke before he got old. Pat Metheny when he performed a solo, but there was some other stuff in there, wildly innovative stuff, and it was driving me nuts because I could almost recognize it.

Maddy offered me the basket of chips. "Want some *appetizer?*"

I leaned over the table. "Be quiet," I said, placing my fingers over her scar. "Do not speak. Just sit there and listen. Order whatever you want for dinner."

The whole time the guy played, he never said a word. Twice, when he took a break to drink a glass of water, he sat down at the table of the curly-haired lady. Obviously they were a couple. He touched her shoulder, and she looked up at him like a woman in love. It was something to watch.

"Look at her hair," Maddy whispered. "What color would you call that?"

"Brownish red," I said. Definitely not titian.

Maddy

10

Step One All Over Again

As I sat down at the table and crossed my legs, there was no denying the vibration in my hand. The curve of glass felt dangerous. When I set it down, my palms went clammy, but they were nothing compared to my skin. It was as if the pores had opened too far and sucked in everything in the room—other people's arguments, stale cigarette smoke, the ghosts of past nights when bouncers had to eighty-six drunks right and left, and women sat in alleys crying big boozy tears they'd otherwise hold inside. I never knew when the longing would hit me, only that when it did I was in trouble.

Get up, take a walk, the reasonable voice inside me insisted. *Tell Rick your problem. He'll understand. He'll take you somewhere else.* But he'd been so mean to me earlier. Saying did I ever graduate high school. So I wasn't book smart. Things between us were fragile. Plus I didn't want him to know I was a drunk. *Pride talking,* the sensible voice said. *Pride only gets you in more trouble. Shut up,* I told it. *Mind your own fecking business.*

Like some psychic forced to examine a future she'd rather not see, I sat there and let the panic roll over me in waves. Plain and simple, bombardment was the enemy's secret weapon. If it overloaded me with sensation, crowded my personal space with need, it pushed me toward the colored bottles behind the bar until I was so close I could only focus on the world by looking through them with a kind of Mr. Magoo clarity. The memory of the taste in my mouth was so strong I could almost smell it. All I knew was that deep down I was sad, and the recollection of my drinking days set my mouth to watering, and the desire for the taste on my tongue was huge. One drink would take care of all that, just one swallow. I thought of my greyhound in Nebraska the night I won the karaoke thing, and how I'd left it on the bar untouched. I would have given anything to drink that drink now. In a minute, maybe less, my jittering would be replaced with a soft-edged calm. In that calm state I could be anyone, my father's favorite daughter, my sister's perfect twin; I could even be the woman Rick wanted. "Ready to order dinner?" I asked him. "I don't want to eat alone."

Rick pushed the complimentary chips and salsa toward me. "It's early. Let's wait and order after this set," he said, and turned his focus toward the stage where the guitarist played—doodled, really. The guy was so good I could tell he was just fooling around—playing some old Fahey thing, jazzed up with a strange barre chord I couldn't figure out. He wasn't planning on going into overdrive for this small a crowd.

I picked at my hangnails and thought about how I was throwing mere chips toward that empty cave inside of me. How the demons that lived there laughed at the gesture, and threw the chips back. They weren't above finishing other people's drinks. Turning tricks if it meant the kind of treat they liked. I could be sober eighty fecking years and still they'd be my constant companions. I could feel them lying there, performing silent aerobics, and staying in shape waiting for the magic word to cross my lips: *alcohol*.

In my lap I squeezed my hands into fists. My knuckles were white from clenching the demons' throats closed. Rick sipped his beer like he didn't really care if he drank it or not. I emptied my Coke before any of the bubbles had a chance to go flat. All around me were people who could drink rum, bourbon, scotch, and vodka, their demons having been to charm school. Maggot drank. Oh, yeah. She took the sacramental wine at Mass. She toasted friends at their weddings with champagne and prayers. When we were fourteen years old, I'd gotten so drunk I passed out. My friends left me at the high school in front of the tennis courts, where the lights were burned out. Anything could have happened—rape, murder, death from exposure—but all that did was my sister found me and sat with me while I heaved and cried, and then she cleaned me up and took me home and didn't even give me a lecture.

The Chinese cook I dated for a while used to tell me his AA sponsor periodically reminded him to HALT. What it meant was don't do anything when you're Hungry, Angry, Lonely, or Tired. I was all of those. Hungry enough to steal chips from other tables. Angry at myself for having an alcohol problem in the first place. Lonely enough that the way Rick's hair fell into his eyes made him look so good to me, I might even have been kind of falling for him a little. Tired simply went without saying. I pretty much hadn't slept through the night for at least five years.

That was why when the guitar player began his rendition of Steely Dan's "Deacon Blues," I got this wild hair and marched my butt up there, sat down next to him, and opened my mouth to sing. I loved that song, even if it was about dying in a car crash. The trouble was, everyone sang it like some jazzy, cool tune, when what it required was sharp, jagged edges. If some aging rocker like Joan Jett had recorded it, it would have gone platinum all over again. Maggot, I knew, would have sung it like a hymn.

Sometimes my sister'd drag me to church, and I'd listen to her singing all that crap about crossing over the river, Jesus waiting onshore like her new best friend. It just stunned me how she could keep her faith. Maggot attended all the parishioners' funerals, from the way-old people she didn't even know to guys who made a career of wreaking havoc on their livers, and whose families acted all shocked when it came time for the drunkard to pay up. The Chinese cook used to tell me, "Buddha says all life is suffering." "Even when we're in bed?" I'd tease him. "Knowing that in mere minutes it's going to end?" he'd answer. "Yes." No fecking duh. Maggot told me the afterlife was the human reward for earthly struggle. I wondered whether she had time to recognize her own exit, or if as everyone keeps telling me, there wasn't time to know what was happening. Horse manure. How long did terror take to register—a nanosecond? I knew she had her arms full of as many babies as she could manage, half of them already dead, and it was likely she was reaching for another. She knew she was on her way out because I knew, and I was and always would be her twin.

When we finished singing, people clapped, no more enthusiastically than before, but from what I could tell of Santa Feans, enthusiasm was a felony. Back at the table, Rick's frown looked permanent.

"May Jesus forgive me," I said. "You want to tell me what did I do now?"

"That song, Madigan. It's 'Deacon Blues.' A legend. You just *walked* up there."

I sipped my now-watery Coke. "This isn't Carnegie Hall, pen pal, it's a bar."

"The artist didn't invite you."

"The *artist* is slumming. Look at him—don't you wonder why he's playing for *tips* when he could be in concert?"

"Excuse me?"

"Heinrich, don't you know who that guy is?"

"I suppose you're going to tell me."

"Nobody knows his real identity. Some claim he's Pat Metheny. Others say he's Bill Laswell, you know, that guy who plays bass on every decent underground CD. Surely you've heard of him."

"Of course I have. Laswell produces Buckethead, the guy who wears the KFC bucket and the mask. He won't let anybody interview him."

"You're getting exceedingly warm, my friend. Did you know that Buckethead was offered a job with the Red Hot Chili Peppers, and turned it down? Imagine, us choosing this bar on this night in this town, and you with a story handed to you, and no stinking newspaper to publish it in. Guess you'll just have to enjoy the experience, like us regular people do, while paying for my dinner."

Buckethead, ha-ha. I didn't know who he was any more

than Rick did. But he was practically slobbering at the possibility. Buckethead was only a name to me. I'd listened to his CDs only because the Chinese cook was obsessed with them. Rick was sitting up and staring hard at the guitar player, who was now beginning to show some of his more intricate chops. The Santa Feans didn't even notice.

"A question," I said. "Is it against journalism ethics to perform a spontaneous duet? Are you planning to call the music police and have me arrested?"

Heinrich leaned back in his chair and folded his arms across his chest. If there had been a television in the place old Rick would've started watching even if all that was on was an infomercial hosted by Judith Light hawking zit medicine. Anything to keep from talking to me. Fifteen minutes went by. I was getting the silent treatment but good.

"I'm beyond kind of hungry now," I said, but Rick refused to make eye contact.

"Hmm. Think I'll go ask in the kitchen if I can wash dishes for my dinner." Another ten minutes.

"Okay, Heinrich, I give up. Will you be nice to me if I never sing in public with strangers again?"

No response.

Now, Dalton may have been a full-blown drunk, not to mention an asshole, but whenever we listened to live music he got all animated, generally ended up onstage singing along with the band, leaving dollar bills in his wake. And he always fed me. I felt in my jeans pocket: a tube of wine-truffle MAC lipstick, two quarters, and a dog whistle. I reached under the table and gave Mr. Heinrich's thigh a stroke. "I'm prepared to make dinner worth your while."

He took hold of my wrist and deftly moved my hand away.

"Sorry for living, but the graveyard's full!"

I thought of Maggot flinging that childhood chop my way, her words as harmless as pillow feathers. What happened to the bodies they couldn't recover? Did they incinerate in the second blast, the one that took the rest of the building down? Ashes. What comes after ashes? Is it dust? When you sweep it up, where does dust go? What happened to the silver bangle bracelet she never took off? The goofy colored shoes she bought just to make the day-care kids laugh? That freckle we both have on our left tits?

Clear across the bar I could smell the bourbon this wannabe cowboy was drinking.

AFTER THE SET ENDED Rick hightailed it up to the stage to talk to *the legendary player of the legendary song*. I wondered if he flashed his defunct press pass. Everybody was clearing out of the bar except for that redheaded woman who was clearly waiting for the musician. I liked how she was dressed, Levi's, sandals, and a smooth leather jacket you couldn't tell was expensive but probably cost more than my truck. Ever the bad-mannered intruder, I went over to her and stood near the edge of her table. "Pardon me, but I'm curious. Have you ever in your life heard your hair described as 'titian'?"

She looked at me, paused for a moment, and laughed. Just then the waitress arrived with a tray full of food. Apparently playing the bar gigs included free eats, because there were two cheeseburgers, two huge salads, two orders of fries, and so forth. Rick and the legend were deep in conversation. The redhead looked at them, sighed, and said, "Once Earl gets to talking, he can take a while. It's a shame to let this food get cold. By any chance, are you hungry?"

"Are you kidding me? I'm trying not to drool. Mr. Cranky over there promised me dinner, but so far all I've gotten is attitude and a verbal citation for singing."

She smiled. "Earl and I loved your voice. So far as I'm concerned, that song will never be the same unless you're singing it. Do you work solo, or are you in a band?"

"Neither. I was just dinking around, but thanks for liking it. Do you sing?"

She laughed. "Not one note." Earl and Rick were sitting on the edge of the stage deep in chat. "What's your name, Sweetie?"

"Maddy."

"Well, Maddy. Why don't you sit down and keep me company, and this cheeseburger before it gets cold?"

"Seriously?"

"Sure. If Earl's hungry, we'll order from the hotel room service. My name's Beryl. Beryl Anne Reilly."

I didn't need to be asked twice. "Thanks, Beryl Anne. This is the first nice thing to happen to me all night."

We inhaled those burgers. We ate all the salad, even that purple stuff I never quite knew whether to call lettuce or cabbage. We giggled, drank Coke, and she told me about the farm she used to live on, "in California, right along the coast. We grew flowers," she said as the waitress refilled her Coke. "Some afternoons when the sun was hot, the whole place smelled wonderful, like roses and lilacs and honey all mixed up into one delicious perfume."

Her face grew kind of sad as she explained it to me, and I figured maybe she was homesick. "Well, New Mexico mostly smells like poor people," I told her. "But it's got halfway decent soil for growing things. I have a little garden—nothing that would win any awards, but it's colorful."

"I'd like to see it."

"Really? I could draw you a map on this napkin. You'd have to keep your eyes open, though. I mean it's a real blink-and-you-could-miss-it kind of place. Don't expect the Hilton."

"Earl and I have been traveling too long," Beryl said. "All these fancy hotels are starting to look alike. I miss the creature comforts. My kitchen, my parrot, not to mention my old roommates on the farm."

"Tell me about that," I said. "I can't wrap my mind around living with a bunch of women. Didn't it get crazy sometimes, like when everybody was PMS-ing?"

"Sometimes," Beryl told me. "But most of the time it just felt safe. We'd make dinner together, have long talks, and dream up new ways to market stuff. I loved it."

She ate her dinner, quiet for a while. Rick was now holding Earl's guitar, and Earl was showing him that barre chord I didn't know. I wanted to jump up for a better look, but I wanted Beryl to keep talking, too. "So what were they like, your friends? All the same age? Did you work outside the flowers—you know, like regular jobs? I've never seen the Pacific Ocean. Jeez, listen to me! I sound like I just snorted a line. I'll shut up now so you can eat your dinner. You don't have to tell me anything else."

Beryl set down her knife and folded her napkin. "That's okay. I want to. First there's Phoebe. She's just incredible. Such spirit. And Ness, tall and black and filled with sass. She had this beautiful horse and went and gave it to the foreman on the ranch, because she said he needed that more than she did. Then there's Nance. Imagine a Southern belle in total revolt. Dress her in name-brand everything, Italian shoes. She has a dog, a Lab, the sweetest, kindest pooch on the planet."

I abandoned my burger to flip open my wallet and show her photos of Mentos and Slim Jim as puppies. "Here are my babies."

She fawned over the pictures and told me about her cursing parrot. "Verde doesn't mean it," she insisted. "He's what you call 'a product of his early environment.'"

"I know exactly what you mean! Once Mentos peed on Rick's Birkenstocks—which you may not know are the holy grail of reporter footwear—and he took her chin in his hands and logically explained why she must never do such a thing again, which of course she did the very next day!"

"Rick is a reporter?"

"He was until he quit. Well, secretly I think he might've gotten fired. He's very mysterious, you know." I arched my eyebrows to drive the point home.

Beryl was quiet for a while. Then she said, "Earl's big on mystery, too. What is it with men? Where does that stuff come from? Cereal box decoder rings?"

"Comic books," I said. "They all want to be X-Men."

We laughed, sputtering Coke, and momentarily, our mystery men looked up at us. Then it was back to the serious talk, no girls allowed. I no longer cared. My belly was full, and I'd nearly forgotten about the liquor bottles behind the bar. That Beryl didn't have a drink on the table helped. The later the hour, the more the cleaning crew gave us dirty looks, and the funnier everything seemed until my cheeks hurt from laughing. Beryl and I both reached for the last fry at the same time.

"Break it in half," she said, and I did.

"You must miss your farm girlfriends," I said. "How long are you in town for?"

Beryl's face went sad again. "That's kind of up in the air."

UNDERNEATH THE SOIL Harry's corpse fed the squash plants first. His bones sent strength up to the yellow blossoms forming along the thick green vines. Old Harry had plans for those crooknecks, the *prolific*—a word Rick had used in his new chapter—zucchinis. Harry whispered to me, too. He told me to stuff the blossoms with cheese and breadcrumbs, to fry them in real butter, and to make certain to eat them while they were still hot. Harry may not have been on earth, but he sure wasn't done with it. Maybe this was his way of making reparations for how shitty he'd been to Ana, hurt her enough to make her leave him and turn to women for kindness. Maybe he was saying thanks to her for coming back. Otherwise, how had she found it in her heart to nurse such a bitter man? Was there anyone on earth I would postpone living my life for to see them through to the end?

FROM INSIDE THE DUPLEX I could hear the murmur of Rick's voice. He was a dickhead some of the time, but I was starting to like the parts of him that peeked through his gruff outside, especially when I made him laugh. Then he looked like a kid to me, one whose life had been filled with meat loaf and green beans, and science projects that turned out so good he won second place. He made me happy in bed, but he could be really annoying with the fecking endless questions. How many did a person need to ask? At what point did the story come together? This writing thing of his—when was the story whole enough that you could sit back satisfied, like after a Thanksgiving dinner? Last night he hadn't come to bed at all, just stayed up all night at the computer writing God knows what. I kept quiet, hugged Mentos, and tried to sleep. I could practically hear the big words he was typing. Well, I'd had nights like that, when singing was more important than breathing. Maybe it was his way of coping.

Who cared? Right now it was a brand-new day, ninety degrees and drier than rocks. I tilted my face to the sun and drank in the summer, because I knew it wouldn't last any longer than what we did in our bed.

AT THE END OF THE NEXT WEEK, I'd forgotten about Beryl and Earl, but Rick hadn't. He left me weeding my small garden of rich red soil, and went in search of Maybe Buckethead, as he called Earl.

"Rick, give it up," I said. "Think about it. If the guy wears a bucket and a mask, it probably means he doesn't want to be recognized. What makes you think he's going to change all that for you? Don't blow his cover."

He stood by my truck trying to shoo the dogs out. The minute he'd opened the door, they leaped inside, sure they were going to be left behind. "You don't understand, Maddy. That night at the bar, we connected."

Connected. What did that mean, exactly? "What is so important that you can't wait? Maybe they'll come by on their way out of town. I told you I gave Beryl a map." What I was thinking was how Beryl and I had connected, that I was starting to think maybe women did that, as they got older. Which meant I was doing that, getting older.

"I'm just going to cruise by, invite them here for dinner," Rick said.

"Which you're going to cook," I yelled as he drove my truck north up the highway, spraying a giant rooster tail of dust.

BERYL SET DOWN THE TROWEL I'd given her and petted the dogs, who were most unhappy that we were gardening instead of taking them for a walk. She looked toward the open window of the duplex. Rick and Earl were indoors, poor Earl no doubt being asked five jillion questions. Every once in a while someone would play a guitar lick, then it would get quiet again. "It's too bad they're missing this sun," she said. "Me, I just can't get enough of it. Too many winters spent inside, I guess."

"I'd apologize for Rick if I thought it would do any good," I said. "I never met a man who likes to talk that much, except this one career meth addict. He was a total blast when he was high; I mean he'd try anything I suggested. Bungee-jumping, white-water rafting, rock climbing, sex in a phone booth. But the rest of the time I spent ducking out of the way of his fist. That is the one thing I will never understand about men, that hitting thing. Ever had a guy try to hit you?" I asked.

Beryl frowned, which she did a lot. "Maddy, is New Mexico the right place for you to be? Are you happy here? Are you safe?"

I jammed my trowel into the soil. "Well, there isn't a whole lot to do here, and the amount of hand lotion you have to rub into your skin is beyond belief. But it makes a nice pit stop. To tell you the truth, after five years with Dalton, I was ready for a break."

She touched my arm. Her skin was so pale it freckled instead of tanned. "And when you've had your break? Where will you go?"

I shrugged. "I'll figure that out when I have to." I took a deep breath, all the summer scents filling my nose. "Like Candide said, 'We must cultivate our garden.'"

Beryl shooed Mentos out of the row we were weeding. "Have you and this Rick been together long?"

"A couple of months. Why?"

"Nance, my roommate on the farm. She once had this reporter boyfriend named Rick. He was from Portland, and I only saw his picture once, but he could have been this guy's twin brother."

A pang of jealousy stabbed me in my throat. God knows why, but I wanted to pound this Nance. I yanked at the roots of one very stubborn weed. "Really?"

Beryl sighed. "I hate telling you, Maddy, but I feel I have to. Nance got her heart broken by that man. Big-time broken."

I laughed. "By Hemingway reincarnate? I know his type backwards and forwards. He's the big, brooding, the-world-has-wounded-me type. He's not going to hurt me. Besides, I can walk away from this in a minute." I flung the patch of devil grass in the air, and Mentos took off after it. She'd catch it, too, eat it, and throw it up later, probably in the bed, hopefully on Rick's side.

"You said that he lost his job. Do you know the details?"

"Only what I read in the laptop files, ha-ha. I think it was something about libel, which is a fancy word for attacking or demeaning someone, in a written or spoken statement, that damages that person's career or character, but you probably know that. I looked it up in what was left of the dictionary after Mentos and Jim ripped it apart. Hey, Beryl. Did you ever copy off other kids' papers in grade school? I did it all the time. Did you know that's called plagiarism? I never thought it was a big deal, but apparently it is to newspapers. I fecking hated school from day one. My sister was a straight-A student. I wonder if a person can go to hell for copying. Or lying, or dating meth addicts, or having way too many sex partners." I laughed nervously. "Why am I telling you all this? Did you take psychology classes? Are you secretly a shrink?"

Beryl set her handful of weeds down on a paper sack. She was old enough to be my mother, but when she looked me in the eye, there was nothing but kindness there. "I read a lot while I was in jail for accidentally killing my husband."

I stared at her, my mouth open in shock. Then I leaped over the row of plants and gave her a hug and a hurrah. "Good for you. I have no doubt the rat bastard deserved it."

"I haven't told you the details," she said.

"You don't have to. I can tell just by looking at you he was a freak."

"It was still wrong."

"Ha. The only thing wrong was you doing time for it."

She sat back on her heels, and we both looked up as a small plane passed by. "Somebody else probably would have stabbed him eventually. J.W. was always pissing people off. It's funny how in retrospect I see dozens of ways I could have left. But while I was with him . . . I don't know. It was like I was wearing blinders. He'd pay attention to me, and I felt like the most important thing in the world to him. Then he'd drink too much, or go into one of his moods, and wham! I panicked. The castle was burning, but where was the fire? Wherever it turned out to be, whoever had set it, it was my fault. I'd just hate to see you in that sort of situation. You're a kind person, Maddy, and you can sing your socks off. Earl was talking about you to some of his buddies in Taos. How you should record a demo."

I popped another plant out of the pony pack. It was cool in my hand, that perfect, sterile dirt that had helped it grow from seed to seedling. Now I was going to tuck it into some earth with history, and it would have to try hard to fit in.

"Well, Rick told me this big story about how his new boss had it in for him, and how he was always trying to make him look bad, some other guy wanted his job, blah-blah-blah, and how they trashed this one thing he spent a lot of time writing, and it made him look bad, so the endless hassles didn't seem worth it, and so he quit without trying to clear his name, even though it was that word, you know, *libel*."

Beryl tamped the earth around my seedling, her fingers gentle against the ball of roots.

I thought of McVeigh using his fingers to tuck the pieces of the bomb together. The Oklahoma papers covered every aspect of the bombing: McVeigh's family under endless investigation, how it was all bad news no matter what the reporters turned up. Maybe McVeigh would rot in prison exhausting appeals, although lately the papers insisted he was leaning toward execution. If he was after martyrdom, he wasn't going to get it from the Caringellas. Maybe the other inmates would take him out like they did Jeffrey Dahmer: internal justice. I'd heard my mother say once that she wanted nothing more than to watch the baby killer put to death, and early on I'd echoed her feelings, yet whenever I thought of the person who had to push the sodium pentothal into the IV tubing, my stomach turned, and all I could think was that Maggot would have visited him in prison. She would have stood outside on the night he was scheduled to die, her candle burning, singing "Amazing Grace," her voice steady to the last note.

Beryl said, "Do you think he was sabotaged?"

I suspected he had more help than just that one guy. If he died the story would never be told. Within the circle of gun nuts what he did would elevate to legend, fuel the sick fire already burning across America.

"Maddy?"

Oh, yeah. She meant Rick. "Well, say he was. Maybe it's not such a bad thing, having your life turned upside down. How much more of an educational experience can you get, really, learning how a few words from an article can cost you your good name?" The way Beryl Anne was looking at me made me nervous. "What?" I said. "Is this about me copying elementary school papers? My sex partners? Do you think I'm going to hell or something?"

Beryl scratched her nose, leaving behind a streak of dirt. Mentos nosed her shoulder, and she took time to pet her neck. "A person has to believe in hell for something like that to happen," she told me.

"And you don't?"

"Sweetie, I don't even believe in heck."

I loved that she called me sweetie. Had anyone outside of a bar—drunk, penis in hand—ever been that nice to me besides my father? "Why not?"

She arranged the pulled weeds from smallest to largest. "Think about the hardest things you've endured. How you survived them. This whole business of God's damnation—forget the flames and brimstone. Hell is nothing but a void. Being alone."

"What about heaven?"

Beryl brushed off the knees of her jeans, which were dusted with earth so red it looked like she'd knelt in paint. She got to her feet, walked down the property to the shade of our cottonwood tree, and started looking for a stick to throw for Jim. She took her time picking. Her pitching arm was strong. We could have been on the same team, kicked us some girl butt. The stick spun end over end, and my good dog sprang from the patchy grass to catch it in his teeth. The sun hit Beryl from behind, illuminating her in leaf-fractured light that did something strange to her curly hair, bleaching the ends of it white. I missed my sister so badly it felt like somebody'd cut my guts out with a knife. Beryl turned to me, smiled, and there were tears in her eyes as she said, "A person never knows when the one they love will be yanked from the earth. The one minute you begin to take it all for granted, it will disappear. You have to cherish every single moment. How about you, Maddy? What's your idea of heaven?"

I shrugged, and for a moment I thought, It's wherever my sister is now.

LATER THAT AFTERNOON WE TOOK A HIKE. "I love this part of New Mexico," Beryl said.

"I don't know what there is to see."

"Oh, lots. Just open your eyes, Maddy."

To my dogs these long expanses of red dirt staining their feet was the ultimate nirvana. All they had to do was drop their noses and breathe in the history.

"Look," Beryl said, pointing out every plant and wildflower, telling me its history. "Did you know that prairie grasses sustained the buffalo? Now they're practically extinct. There's this heirloom seed place in California. They catalog every seed in hopes they can keep them from becoming extinct. Every single thing that grows has a dozen uses." She plucked enough sage leaves from various bushes to tie into a bundle using my ponytail scrunchie. "Smell this."

The scent made me miss my mother so bad that I had to turn away before Beryl thought I was some kind of nut case, which, when I thought about my mother, I guess I was. "You're not supposed to pick that without a purpose," I said. "Cooking, or you know, a ceremony."

"I didn't know that. Well, let's burn it sometime." We walked a mile or so, taking sips off the water bottle I carried. "You know the farm I told you about?"

"Yeah."

"Phoebe, who owns the place, is pregnant. Her boyfriend died a few months ago in a car wreck." She peeled leaves from a branch of sage down to the stem. "She had health problems to begin with, and now we're all really scared about her making it through the pregnancy. Ness, she makes sure Phoebe eats and gets enough rest, but rest is only part of it. She misses Juan so much, but to grieve openly could hurt the baby."

"Wow," I said. "She can't even cry?"

Beryl shook her head. "And then there's Nance." She turned and looked at me. "Rick's old girlfriend."

The hair on the back of my neck quivered. "Yeah, yeah. I'm listening. Go on."

"She's got this eating disorder. I think it might be anorexia. So I'm just going to say this outright, Madigan. Not to hurt you, but maybe to warn you. I know it's none of my business what's going on with you two, Maddy, but Nance spent three years with him. She loved him. He took all that for granted. One day she asks about their future and he dumps all this trash on her, like it's her fault for wanting a commitment. In my book, that's abuse. Are you ready for something like that to happen to you?"

"If I had enough heart left to break after Dalton, I might be worried." I touched my chest. "Only enough room left in the organ for my wonderful doggies. Rick Heinrich will never penetrate the chest wall!" I took off running, and the dogs happily gave chase. We made a wide circle, startling some rabbits, then came back to Beryl, winded.

She handed me the water bottle. "I think there's still some heart left in you to break. If you need to get away from Rick, promise me you'll try the farm. They're great women. And they'd love your dogs. Pets are practically a requirement to living on the farm."

She handed me a pamphlet—*DeThomas Farms: Flowers, Fine Gifts & Heirloom Poinsettias*. I stuffed it in my pocket.

"Don't throw it away."

"I won't." But inside I was thinking, Yeah, right, me living with a bunch of women, how fun could that be? Still, how weird that Rick was this Nance's ex. Six degrees and all that. I wondered what broke them up. Mr. Cranky was incredible in bed. That part would be hard to leave. He didn't get all pissy about eating dinner at the same time every night. Still, he could be a prickola sometimes. I wondered what he'd said to this Nance to make her leave him. Could a man give a woman anorexia? How much did anyone know about another person, really?

The day was fading but still warm enough to raise the sweat and soak my tank top. A slight breeze coming through the canyon felt chilly, although I knew it couldn't be less than eighty degrees. Pretty soon the sky would go purple, and the famous

New Mexican clouds would part like a curtain and show us the stars. My sister was up there with them, far from the reaches of fired reporters and right-wing idiots. "I'd like to stick my feet in the Pacific Ocean."

"Right across the highway from the farm. Go now, while you're young and mobile."

"Mobile? Ha." I squinted into the sun. "I'm broke, Beryl. Rick's the one with *dinero* to burn. I came here to work the Saturday Market for Ana and Lee so I could save up a little cash. Earl's rich, isn't he? It's funny how the people with the most money hide it so well."

I could see her shoulders stiffen. "His money was a complete surprise to me. He lived—still lives—a simple lifestyle."

"I'm sorry. I didn't mean for it to come out that way. Sometimes I shouldn't be allowed in public."

"Hush. It's all right. I'm glad I liked him before I found out," she continued. "Otherwise how could you ever know your feelings are real?"

"Don't ask me. I don't know how anybody can trust feelings. So how did Earl get rich," I asked. "Did he earn his money from his music?"

"He's got his finger in a lot of pots."

"I have to ask, but don't answer if you don't want to, Beryl. Is Earl Buckethead?"

She looked at me unblinking. "I don't really know. I have my suspicions. Then I see an advertisement that Buckethead's in concert, a thousand miles from where we are. 'Tis a mystery. My turn, Maddy. Are you in love with Rick?"

"Good God, no!" I plucked another strand of sage from a gray bush and added it to our fat bundle. "Half the time I hardly even like him. We're friends, I guess."

Beryl nodded. "We're going to lose the light if we go too much farther."

"Yeah. I guess we should turn back. I kind of hate to, you know?"

She smiled. "I do."

The dogs had to be whistled for six times before I resorted

to yelling, "Biscuits!" even though I hated lying to them. Then they came flying toward us, tongues lolling, and we turned toward home.

Halfway there Beryl stopped me. She placed her hand on my arm. "Maddy, you ever decide you need out of the Rick situation, or any situation, go to the farm."

"I'm telling you, Beryl, I'm fine."

She kicked the dust from her shoes. "If ever a time comes when you're not."

WE STEPPED OVER THE THRESHOLD into the house. Earl and Rick sat on the *banco* and floor respectively, Earl with his guitar and Rick with his hot laptop. The room smelled more of guy than it did New Mexico, and I got the urge to burn the sage bundle right then. I never could figure out how men reeked up a place just by sitting in it. Maybe it was a hormone thing, or maybe their bodies were impervious to soap.

"I feel like cooking," Beryl said.

Rick looked up from his pages. "Gee, and Maddy kind of had her heart set on canned soup again."

"No dinner for you," I said. "No matter how good it is."

He smirked. "For your kind of cuisine, I can wait."

I never could tell if he was making fun of me or if he was just the kind of fool who couldn't let his smile loose for fear it would unhinge him. "Yeah, no kidding you can wait. Till the cows come home if you keep talking like that to me."

"Apologize," Earl said. "That's no way to speak to a woman."

Rick looked up, startled. "Sorry."

He could have been apologizing to either one of us.

Beryl laughed and gave Earl a kiss on his cheek, so then I did, too. His expression never changed. His hands were never still on the guitar strings. He plucked out the strangest melodies, and whoever he was, he kicked guitar ass.

We girls walked down to the market and perused all two of the aisles. Beryl wouldn't let me pay for anything, even though I had brought money along.

"Save it," she said. "When you need it, it will be there."

"Oh, God," I said, dropping the cilantro on the counter. "You're leaving tomorrow, aren't you?"

THE NIGHT THEY LEFT I COULDN'T SLEEP. Rick and I got into a big fight.

"Who forgot to fill up the pitcher that filters the water?" he asked.

"Beats me," I said, as I sat on the floor beading a necklace with tiny fetish animals.

"Now I have to brush my teeth without rinsing," he said.

"And this is a mortal sin? Use Coke," I said. "There's a six-pack of that in the fridge."

"Coke rots your teeth. Why on earth would I brush my teeth and then expose them to a sugar-filled drink with no nutritive value?"

I opened my mouth. "Look in this mouth," I said. "Do you see one single filling? No. My mother fed me Coke in the bottle, Buddy Boy, and I have perfect teeth."

"Yeah, I know," he said. "You're always using them to bite me during sex," he said. "What's that all about, anyway?"

I could feel the heat rise in me. Ten degrees, maybe. "Are you complaining about how I make love? Are you really standing there registering a complaint? Have I ever once turned you down? Can you say the same to me?"

At that point he walked out the screen door and let it slam behind him. I could have dug him a place next to Harry, I was that mad. But I went back to my necklace and beaded three more before my eyes started to cross from tiredness. I filled up the damn pitcher, too.

Now Rick lay next to me, flat on his back, his eyes fluttering with some dream I knew wasn't about me. I leaned on my elbow and watched him for an hour or so, and then I remembered the sage bundle Beryl Anne had made, found it in the kitchen sitting inside a teacup. I lit the end of it, and blew on the embers until the smoke wisped outward. It smelled like dope, and I got a pang for another sloppy high I wasn't allowed. I swirled the smoke around Rick's body until the trails looked as if he were part of his dream, a little bit of that world leaking out, visible. When he woke up he looked at me and said, "What the hell is burning?"

"Sage bundle."

"And the reason for this is?"

"I'm smudging the meanness from you," I said. "One last-ditch attempt to save whatever this relationship is."

He hoisted himself on his elbow and stared at me, waving away the smoke. Without his glasses I figured I was no more than a blur. "Give me that," he said, and took the bundle from me, stubbed it out hard in a cup on the bedside table. "Come here," he said, and I did. He kissed his way down my body, real kisses, with kindness in them, and it was like falling down a cliff, mentally scrabbling for some kind of hold on rock that crumbled as I tried to grab it, and eventually not giving a care where I landed. He was good at making love, better than all the other times. So how could that Nance woman leave that behind?

August

Pretty much every morning I peeked into Rick's computer files. After sex Hemingway slept like the fecking dead, and when he woke up he didn't want to talk to anyone for at least two hours. I set the laptop on the table and continued beading necklaces and earrings to sell while I read his stories, plus I was curious to find out if there was anything about this Nance person. Clearly the introduction of Earl-Maybe-Buckethead into our lives and the departure had given Mr. Heinrich much to write about. They had been gone for a month now, but Rick kept on tooling the story sentence by sentence. Occasionally there'd be this asterisk by a paragraph, a note to remind him to "flesh out" a section. Weird phrase, but it piqued my interest:

"How does he do it? Coax the same noise out of that guitar that Madigan makes when she's slick with sweat, using bodily sensation, trying so hard to get past whatever it is that haunts her . . ."

What exactly did that mean?

Some days I wanted to slap some sense into him, say, "Rick, go get a job helping kids learn to read. Volunteer at a homeless shelter. Come work the Saturday Market with me in the sun on the steaming asphalt and learn to count change. Whatever soul you have is so dried up and buried under your anger it's in danger of blowing away. Harry's got more soul than you do." And then he would write something like "Maddy lives her life so fully in the moment that I'm jealous," and I'd see him in a whole new light, and something inside me would quiet down, and continue waiting for the rare night he'd wake me by reaching for my body.

His novel appeared to be on hold.

A weird thing he did: He'd pee outside in the garden every night when he thought I wouldn't notice. Peeing on Harry, as a matter of fact. What was that all about? Could a live man really be jealous of a dead one?

I WROTE MAMA AND AUNTIE A POSTCARD that I got free at the inn where Beryl and Earl had stayed. Auntie would think I was doing so well that I could afford a nice hotel in the middle of nowhere. Mama would look up from the horoscope book and tell Auntie I was still the same old Mary Madigan, selfish, giving my body to strangers, and not going to amount to anything. Auntie would go out on the front step to feed the bloodhound vitamin supplements, and yell to my mother, "Nita, why can't you give that poor girl a break?" And whatever the rest of the conversation was, I was glad I wasn't there to hear it. Meanwhile Tad and Dixie's marriage had no doubt hit another bump, and some poor soul in Pine Valley caught amnesia, and my mother would have a lot to say about how if somebody was lucky enough to catch that disease, why on earth would they try to get rid of it?

New Mexico wasn't the land of enchantment; it was more like the land of coming to terms.

I SWORE RICK COULD GO A WEEK without eating and not feel one pang of hunger. When he ate, it was strictly for fuel, and he could make a meal out of the weirdest things, like Brussels sprouts, which no one is supposed to like, or a bacon-and-raisin sandwich. As for me, after Beryl left, nothing filled up the groaning emptiness. I craved bread, spaghetti, potatoes, and all the carbohydrates in sight. I might've had five pounds extra on my thighs, but my soul barely clung to my bones. Nights were hard. The indigo sky, for one thing, and lightning off in the distance. The utter quiet of living in a place with no neighbors besides coyotes and the occasional lynx. We only got one radio station, and it was in Spanish. While Rick slept I'd go out and sit in the garden and talk to Harry—the one man who didn't talk back to me or tease me.

What do you do with yourself when you feel like you're going to crawl out of your skin, Harry? Unfortunate choice of words. Sorry. What I meant was, how does it feel to be dead? Do we pester you with all our noise? Can you hear us having sex? Do you watch and think how utterly stupid it is to make such a big deal out of bumping our bodies together? Would you even want to do that anymore? What's on the other side, Harry? Where is my sister?

Probably Harry had buckets of wisdom to offer, but every time he told me the same things: *I could use a little water. Help, the rabbits are digging under the fence.* And most annoying of all: *This is the life, Madigan, lying here growing things to feed the people you love.*

Feck.

One of his old riding buddies stopped by one afternoon to ask the whereabouts of Harry's grave. I stayed indoors beading while Rick chatted with the guy. He wanted an ear for his war stories, and Rick ate that kind of thing up with a spoon. "You should have come out, Maddy," he told me later, when I was taking the dogs out for one last pee before bedtime. "Guy goes way back, knows a lot of New Mexican history."

I'd lived enough history, I figured, to not have to subject myself to some old drunk's recollections. A glint in the garden caught my eye. It was a pint bottle of rum—Harry always was a fool for rum. New Mexicans did stuff like that: leave full bottles and packs of cigarettes and even racing forms on their friends' graves. Odd as their customs were, they were kind of endearing. I went indoors.

Rick typed on his computer. I made some toast and ate it buttered to within an inch of its life. While I took a shower, Rick turned in. He slept, the dogs slept, even the earth went quiet as she renewed herself in the lack of sunlight. I tried to. I lay on my back and stared at the plaster until 1:30 A.M., when it seemed imperative that I go outdoors and check on that rum bottle.

There were no good reasons for me to fall off the wagon that night. Rick had been fairly nice to me that day. Thanks to Saturday Market my money bundle was fattening up nicely, and in a few weeks I could haul ass to someplace else out of this one-horse town wrapped in adobe like leftovers. Yep, that's what I'd do, as soon as I figured out where that better someplace might be. But I cracked the label anyway. I inhaled the resiny scent of rum and tilted the bottle to my scarred lip and drank it down. "Fire in the hole!" Dalton used to yell when he started drinking hard stuff, warning his liver to soldier up. Friendly fire. My old flame. The house of blue lights.

I told myself that I was nicer with one drink in me—maybe Rick would forget writing his whodunit of the legendary guitar player for half a second and look at me like I was something special instead of his now-and-then sex partner. He might lean over the tabletop and say, *You know what, Mary Madigan? If I'm not careful, I might be falling in love with you.*

Yeah.

I told myself it was because I missed Maggot, that I couldn't face the world without my other, better half. Asked God for the jillionth time what he was thinking leaving me here and taking her. But that was the stupid crap every drunk hauled out when she got tired of climbing that same old sober-to-no-place staircase, reciting that same old tired jargon, and swollen with pride, believed that just this once she could do it—tame the untamable. God didn't bother answering questions like that.

Rick

11

Reaping Harry's Bounty

"WHERE ARE THE CLEAN CLOTHES?" I hollered from the bedroom out to the front room, and when Maddy didn't answer, I raised my voice. "Maddy? Did you hear me?" Now that summer was over, short-sleeved T-shirts no longer cut it for me. "You plan on doing laundry anytime in the foreseeable future?" I peered down the hallway, catching a glimpse of one jean-clad thigh. Maddy sat cross-legged on the *banco,* beading necklaces. She sat there a lot lately, even though Saturday Market was over, and very soon Ana and Lee would arrive to reclaim the duplex.

She looked up from the beads and eyed my nakedness, clearly unimpressed. "Did you say something?"

"Look at me. What's missing?"

She set her beads aside. "Do you really want me to answer that?"

"I'm out of clean shirts. Also, clean pants, socks, and whatever the hell else I happen to own."

"So wear something dirty. It's not like you have to punch a time clock."

I was starting to shiver and determined to make it stop. "How about I'm used to my clothes smelling nice? How about that you agreed to do the housework if I paid for the groceries?"

She sighed dramatically and threw the necklace down on the floor. I heard the beads scatter and watched the dogs slink under the kitchen table. Maddy drifted past me to the hallway where the washer and dryer were gathering cobwebs behind closed doors. I knew how to work a washing machine. I folded my T-shirts better than she did, in thirds so they looked as if they just came out of the package, while Maddy folded them in half so there was a crease down the front that took half a day to shake out. It was the principle of the thing that got to me—her housework in exchange for my buying the food—and why should I hold up my end of the bargain if she wasn't holding hers? I heard the lid of the washer snap up and the water start to run into the washtub. Hurray, I thought, clean clothes in an hour or so, but deeper inside me I wondered, At what price? Maybe I'd go outside for a while, check on Harry. Fall had come quickly in our little town, and the first frost had arrived a few nights ago, announcing that winter was on its way in. I zipped up my cleanest dirty jeans, threw my jacket over my bare skin, opened the front door, and was met by a swirl of white.

"Maddy, come look. It's snowing." And it was. A light swirl of flakes eddied in our courtyard, melting as soon as they hit the ground. I leaned against the adobe wall. Snow sifted down onto the garden, burying the last of the summer vegetables I'd refused to eat, covering poor Harry. Harry and I had become friends, of a sort. I told him the truth, and he, very kindly, did not pass judgment.

She came out onto the porch, followed by the dogs. They pushed by me, racing around the yard leaping up now and then to snap at the falling snow. She watched them for a long while but didn't scold them. "Yeah, yeah, snow. I've seen it. Next comes ice. Then car crashes, and then Christmas."

I took hold of her glossy black ponytail and gave it a gentle tug. "You're in a fine mood, Oklahoma."

She stepped quickly to the left so that her hair fairly whipped out of my hand. "I'm the same as I always am, Portland."

I could have asked her if this was the other end of her mood swing, but I kept my mouth shut as she went back inside and I assumed returned to her beading.

So, Harry, I said. You're finished being vegetable fertilizer. What's next? Do you lie there all winter, pondering what you did wrong in your lifetime, or is it too cold to think? I can't believe those women dumped you straight in the dirt, no coffin or anything. That's lesbians for you, practical, no frills. Still, you're under a lot of dirt, so you must have a pretty high R insulation rating. Close to R-30, I'd say. Listen to me, I've never even built a plywood sailboat cruiseworthy of the gutter. My dad would be able to tell you, though. Old Richard, nothing slips past him. What was your dad like? Did you guys have a close relationship? Did he teach you adobe? Is there one guy in the world who gets along with his father?

Periodically I did call home. I was an ace at leaving messages. Always made sure to call when I knew they'd be out—at Mass, mall-walking, dinner with my perfect brother. Couldn't really handle a lecture on aimlessness while I was in the middle of writing this story of the mysterious guitarist. Was Earl this Buckethead fellow or wasn't he? Why, with talent to burn, did he drop in to bars in the middle of nowhere and play for tips? How come Maddy knew so much about the business, who recorded with whom, and most of the names I'd never heard of?

She was moody as hell lately, didn't even want sex. The good part was it allowed me to work quietly. She took long walks, spent a few nights sleeping on the floor in the living room. Got all cranky when I asked her about it. Not interested in kissing. I wondered what was up with that girl. The collies were like barometers, skulking around out here, waiting for her to cheer up. I whistled to them and led the way down to the stream. What the hell, a little break might even be good for me. *"Andale,"* I said. "Let's leave your mama to her mysterious funk and go pee on rocks."

Buckethead Story

Earl's a man you wouldn't look twice at on the street. You'd expect to come across him in a hardware store, trying to find hinges, or at Kmart, buying his kid a fishing rod. Camping at a

KOA, Earl's the guy who'd help you pitch your tent but wouldn't take the five bucks you offered in thanks. The last place you'd expect to come across him is onstage, coaxing shred from an Ibanez Iceman. He hammers on and pulls off as easily as cracking his knuckles. Plain dude, flashy music.

He doesn't give interviews.

I don't have his permission to write this.

Sometimes rules must be bent for the greater good. He's sitting across from me, in my front room, in Galisteo, New Mexico, the so-called land of enchantment. People here swear the earth hums. The famous blue sky is filled with those trademark white clouds artists spend a lifetime trying to capture. It's Georgia O'Keeffe and D. H. Lawrence and the Catholic Church. It's the state with the highest traffic-accident death statistics across the nation. Earl agrees to talk—to my girlfriend.

I note the muscles in his otherwise skinny forearms. How his fingers, always in motion, travel independently of his conversation—a built-in counterpoint. He smiles when his lady passes by, a redhead who smiles back. But when he plays, his face changes, and it's clear this music comes from some place we mortals only dream of visiting.

MMC: So what do you think of these wonder boys who pop up on the scene now and then, a sixty-thousand-dollar guitar in their hands, pay the right stations to play them, getting all this hype?

B/E: Hell if I know. Talk to me about music, Sweetheart. I've heard you sing. It's always been about the music, and it will continue to be about the music until the planet explodes, don't you agree?

MMC: Yeah, I do. When did you pick up the guitar?

B/E: When I was a kid. I watched a lot of black-and-white movies. Listened to their soundtracks, wanted to copy them.

MMC: I love black-and-white movies. Any favorites?

B/E: *Godzilla.*

Laughter. The sound of two bottles opening. Beer for me: E prefers cream soda. Wish we had a TV. Surely there would be a Godzilla movie on some channel and then I could capture his reaction . . . maybe even get him to pick up the guitar while I tape him.

> B/E: There was something about the way he walked. How he had to fling his body from side to side to get anywhere. Clumsy as he was, he should have lost all his battles, but if things got tough, he just blew fire and cleared the path. Pissed off but honest.

> MMC: Is that why you only play small places? You don't want anybody "messing with your monster"?

A few notes plucked from the high E string followed by the high B—endless double-stops—Chuck Berry kind of thing. Elementary scales, then his fingers move rapidly and the notes spill almost faster than the ear can catch. A string breaks with a loud ping under the pressure. He laughs.

> B/E: Being anonymous allows you to concentrate on the music. Less interference.

And then like an idiot I tromp in and ask him what's wrong with making money, doesn't everybody crave fame? He looks at me, and I know I've blown it.

> B/E: You want to know why I don't give interviews, man? Because sooner or later, what we're talking about stops being about the music, and I get asked that very same question. Turn that thing off. I'm done talking.

Sound of feet scraping, a door opening, Earl calling, "Beryl Anne!"

HARD FEELINGS? I'd promised Earl not to use his name, or otherwise provide any clues to his identity were I to sell the piece. Yet I knew that would be the first change any sane editor would insist on. Just like Don, back in Portland, he'd ask, *Where's the hook? Readers aren't going to care that you sat knee-to-knee with a legend, that you know what he looks like, what his real name is, if you don't spill it in the article.*

And if I said, *Buckethead,* what would that get me? Word of mouth travels fast in the music world. I could take this piece to any of the slicks, one of them would be happy to print it, and it would sell copies, maybe even go on to be one of those collectible issues that fans will pay fifty bucks to own. They might offer me freelance work. With a slip of the pen I could out Earl and rationalize it. Hey, no big deal, it would have happened sooner or later. But nothing I wrote subsequently would ever come close to this story unless I turned into one of those slimebags who got the subject drunk enough to reveal secrets, and of course, me, being their buddy, would promise not to write about that—until I got back to my keyboard.

It occurred to me that I was only going to be fifty years old for a short time, and next I'd turn fifty-one. The hair at my temples was streaked with gray. The other day I'd found my first gray pubic hair, truly a defining moment worth writing about. How long could I write about new music before I turned into the old hack that refused to grow up? Became a joke instead of Robert Hilburn? What did I want to do with my writing anyway? A newspaper feature with a certain word count no longer applied. I was free to write any way I liked. I'd told Maddy I wanted to write a novel, but even without her pointing out how leaden my words were, I knew what I'd managed so far sucked.

Interview questions. Notes in the margins. I was obsessed with the truth of the answers when what spoke to me was what was in the margins. I closed my eyes and rubbed them. Saw those petroglyphs that Maddy and I ran across out in the desert on our drive here. The recurring hand shape, like some ancient god warning whoever passed this way to stop. The spiral, like the mortal coil of a man's life—he travels so far, then adios. But what truly annoyed me was that infuriating flute player, Kokopelli. When I had too much to drink, his I-told-you-so song rang in my ears for hours. That other night, when Maddy'd been trying to use my body as Kleenex, I heard the flute player long into the night. His music made about as much sense as a mockingbird, a New Mexican Pied Piper. I hit Save on the computer, put the machine into hibernation mode, and without telling Madigan where I was going, I drove into town for whatever distraction I could glean from my meager surroundings.

"WE'LL BE BACK DAY AFTER TOMORROW," Lee told me over the phone when I woke up with a king-size hangover I'd earned all on my own. "We've rented your half of the duplex to a professor from the community college. Rick, are you listening to me?"

"What's he teach?" I asked, my eyes still closed against the brilliance of the winter day.

"Anthropology."

"Great. He can dig up Harry and write a thesis on why relationships don't last."

"You're an ass, Rick."

My head throbbed, and I fumbled on the bedside table for the glass of water Maddy took to bed with her every night. I knocked condom wrappers to the floor, pinched myself on one of her hair clips, and then found the glass, which was empty. "Lee, Sweetie," I rasped. "I won't disagree with you."

"Good, because I'm not in the mood to argue. You guys can stay a few more days, but we really need the place soon so we can repaint it. Is that a problem?"

"Not at all. Thanks for the heads up." I hung up the phone and put my face under the kitchen faucet. I knew that if I drank the water without filtering it first, a close relationship with the toilet would follow. I also knew how little I cared. Slowly, as my body rehydrated, I realized that Maddy wasn't here, that the house was empty, even of dogs.

I used to think that being surrounded by women would be a kind of utopia. That being the only man in the midst of three of them—including the lesbians—would feel kind of like Saturn, surrounded by devoted rings. Even long-distance, Ana and Lee pulled at me from an entirely different direction than Maddy. Imagine three separate tides, each one equally intent on getting her way. They bickered among themselves and replaced their own faucet washers. The time when I wanted to have sex with all of them had long passed. Now I just wanted some peace and quiet and some notion of my purpose on earth. It was past time to move on from here, even without the anthro prof's imminent arrival. The only man who truly belonged here was Harry, and I wasn't interested in bunking with him. Maybe California would be a nice place to spend the winter, but I didn't know what Maddy wanted, and I surprised myself that I considered her wishes. Lately she got up in the night and stayed away from bed until the wee hours. During the day she'd disappear. I hadn't dismissed the possibility of astral travel. Instead of the two of us making some kind of future plans, I spent half my day trying to find her. And then there was the small matter of the empty rum bottle I'd found in the trash. I'd half convinced myself that she'd found the gift that character left on Harry's grave, and dumped it out. Poor Harry. I hoped she'd at least poured it into the dirt, so he could get a whiff of what he was missing.

I wandered all three streets of town looking for her. I checked inside the church, where only two votives were burning, and a veiled woman knelt praying to the statue of Mary. I walked to the store, where I bought myself a Dr Pepper and Maddy some Cherry Coke, her favorite liquid refreshment, too sweet for my tastes. I smiled at the old lady behind the register. She smiled back. All summer that had been the extent of our conversations, because my Spanish didn't go beyond *holá,* and I hadn't tried to improve. In the lobby of the inn where Beryl and Earl had stayed, nobody had seen Maddy recently, but maybe a couple of days back, in the bar? The bar? Her truck was still in the drive, so I knew she had to be within walking distance, but how far did that walking distance stretch? Clear to Madrid, the hippie town that has lots of atmosphere but never-ending plumbing troubles? To Texan-invaded Santa Fe? I sat down on the front porch, next to her beading supplies. I fingered the fetish beads she bought by the handful so she could crank out three or four of those necklaces a day to sell at Saturday Market for twenty-five dollars each. Onyx turtles, tigereye horses, coral bears, turquoise birds. Saturday Market had been a successful venture. In addition to earning several thousand dollars for Ana and Lee, of which she'd receive a fair share, Maddy had also managed to sock cash away. She kept her bills rolled up like a drug dealer's in a purple felt Seagram's bag. I had no idea how much she had, but it probably wasn't over two grand. If I left without her, how would she get along? Who would she go to? Some guy who'd treat her like dirt, smack her around for her smart mouth?

I plucked a glossy black hair from her stained deerskin jacket and held it up in the sunlight where it shone blue. *Glossy*—what kind of word was that? A combination of floss and gleam? It was the precise word for her hair. At night I liked to gather it in my fist and pull her to me, showing her where I wanted her mouth. Sometimes I breathed into the nape of her neck, inhaling the long black threads, feeling them tickle my throat. When she slept her hair fell down her back like river water.

When Maddy rounded the corner on horseback, riding that fat Appy the lady from the inn encouraged her to exercise, she was wearing a T-shirt and jeans, and the temperature couldn't have been much above forty. The dogs flanked her, their breath visible in the chill air. "Hey," I said. "We have to talk."

Maddy looked down at me. "Fine," she said. "It's about time we did something together besides fuck."

Her words came out sloppy, and I wondered if she'd been drinking. When I was a kid and my father drank, he'd round a corner and loom large before me in the same unbalanced way. We kids tiptoed around him, fearful that one wrong step would result in chaos. He'd been white-knuckle sober for years, but I realized I still behaved the same way toward him, and further that Nance, having been raised by an alcoholic parent herself, understood that. Maybe our codependence had dovetailed so nicely we hadn't tried to outgrow it and relate in healthier ways. Maddy was an unknown quantity. I'd assumed the reason she didn't drink was because it made her sick. For her to use the real *f*-word instead of her usual "feck" meant we were entering mood-swing territory.

"Lee called. We have to move out in five days. Want to go to dinner and talk about our next stop?"

She sighed and lay down on the horse, letting the reins drop from her hands to the dirt. I hated how much she trusted animals not to injure her. I fought the urge to gather the leather up and lead the horse home. "Not hungry," she murmured. Then she laughed, a little crazily, like tears weren't far behind, and she slid off the Appy to the ground, losing her balance only once and recovering nicely. "Think I'll take a nap."

"What am I supposed to do about this horse?"

"He'll be fine. Just need ten minutes. That's all."

I watched her stumble inside, the dogs following. Definitely alcohol. I could smell it when she walked by me. But why now, and what was I supposed to do about it? I pulled myself up onto the horse's back and rode him back to the stables. Felt good to see the world from his back, that few extra feet up.

While Maddy slept, I did the laundry. I separated the darks from the whites. Made sure the water was cold. I added the detergent first. In the pockets of Maddy's jeans, I found a folded-up pamphlet for the flower farm that Beryl had mentioned. I recognized Nance's touch—her style of photography, her flowery approach to writing copy—right away. How weird was that? Of all the possible pocket contents, something from my old girlfriend? I leaned against the washing machine and studied the layout. She was still the queen of adjectives. She wouldn't have lasted a week in the newsroom. But somehow I could tell that what she'd written would sell flowers. Sunflowers. For a moment I recalled every moment of our ill-fated trip to St. Helens. That promising beginning when I held her at the airport. The vibrating tension between us in the car. I'd never wanted to make love to her so much as at that moment. Knew that when we did, the past year's separation would drip off our bodies like sweat. What would have happened if I'd put her plane ticket on my credit card? Told her she was beautiful, that she mattered, that more than anyone else in my life, including the Beatles, I loved her best?

I checked on Maddy, who lay on her back, mouth open,

snoring softly. I pushed the hair out of her face, tucked the pillow under her head, pulled off her boots, and sat there watching her. God, she looked so young—no more than twenty-five—she *was* young. I liked her, a lot. But take on some messy substance-abuse problem? Why would I want to? I wondered for the bazillionth time what had caused her to drink, and worried momentarily that it was me. I pictured her at the Oklahoma memorial, trying to find her purse. We'd begun there, two people who bumped into each other and found themselves Velcroed together. But there was more than that. Her voice, for one thing. When she let herself go, she sounded as soulful as Etta James. When she sang "Deacon Blues" that night in Santa Fe, it was as if someone had injected my veins with jet fuel. The hell of it was she didn't even know how good she was, and worst of all, she wasn't really trying to apply her talent. She was fooling around, wasting time. I wondered what she could accomplish if she believed in herself. Recorded? Her voice was distinctive. She'd never once pestered me with questions about Nance, not even when she carried that flyer in her pocket. She believed me when I told her the circumstances of me losing my job. *Go write the novel,* she said, that whole God-never-shuts-a-door-without-opening-a-window deal. She let me know when I was showing off with the fifty-dollar words. All I'd given her was me, me, me—my life, my wants—and I thought of her working those Saturday Markets alone, hawking stuff to tourists while I slept late and played dilettante writer if the mood struck. Whatever was currently going on with Maddy, maybe she needed a drink to stand her life. My so-called life was made up of a whole lot of experiences, some of them interesting, some of them boring and trite, one or two even defining, but Maddy, since Maddy, my life *was* a novel—a book I'd fork over twenty-five bucks to read in hardback without a complaint.

I remembered a journalism professor in college, his dictum that a good reporter never lets a story get away, that he should commit to following it to its inevitable conclusion. Outside snow was falling again. The washing machine reached the end of its cycle and beeped. Next to me a beautiful girl stirred in her sleep. Harry was as silent as ever, but suddenly I had a craving for vegetables that I knew was entirely his doing.

Beryl

12

Road Journal

BY THE TIME WE LEFT NEW MEXICO, Earl had his feathers in a ruff, like Verde in one of his Garbo moods. To calm him down we visited every used bookstore between Albuquerque and Flagstaff. He bought some first edition John Nicholses, and three signed copies of Paul Gallico's *The Snow Goose*. "Beryl," he told me, so excited. "In ten years these will be priceless."

Ten years. I wondered where I would be then. That look on Earl's face—he could have been a ten-year-old finding a Mickey Mantle baseball card in a pack of gum. This "relationship" of ours—neither a marriage nor two people working toward anything definite, something else entirely—had taught me several facts: Without dust jackets most first editions are not worth the asking price. Breakfast is indeed the most important meal of the day—without it, a man's blood sugar plummets and mood swings follow. Only solitary walks can ease that, and being left behind in a strange place didn't agree with me anymore. I lived for the way Earl looked at me on his return—like I was a sight for sore eyes, and the quiet huff of breath just before he kissed me, like he was letting out his air to share mine. Most important, when it came to playing the guitar in public, never ask Earl why he plays under different names, especially when it's clear he doesn't need the money. These subjects are not only taboo, they can be cause for days of silence. Yes, it's wonderful when the silence breaks, and great sex follows, but after the dust settles, you're left feeling like you carved a year off your life span with all the worrying.

SUPPOSE I WAS AT BAD GIRL CREEK versus riding next to Earl on this freeway surrounded by cars going ninety through godforsaken country where not even cacti thrive? I'd be working my butt off on the hateful poinsettias that would go on sale at the end of the month. Tending to the temperature gauges, fretting over light. Such needy flowers I didn't miss, but my friends were a different story. Here was how I pictured them today when I looked out past the red rocks and allowed my eyes to relax and go comfortably blurry: Nance is talking on the telephone while typing into the computer and, with the sole of one foot, petting Duchess. "Absolutely not," she tells whoever is on the other end of the line. "That delivery date won't do at all." After a pause, she says, "Well, I suppose, if that's the best you can manage, but we expect a sizable discount for our trouble."

While the bread she's making completes its second rise, Ness lies on the couch, a magazine she's not reading open on her lap. Maybe it's *O,* the magazine with the affirmation bookmarks you can read to feel better about yourself, and Ness is thinking about how once illness becomes the center of a person's life, the simplest words are like a great book distilled, condensed to a catchphrase as pure as rain. *Live large. Be of use. Leave this planet cleaner than when you arrived.* Or she might be dreaming of riding horses, forgetting everything but the thrill of a good hard gallop.

Phoebe? With each passing day, her belly grows heavier, and her dark eyes appear a little more vacant. She keeps her mind empty because if she thinks beyond eat, sleep, grow a baby, she'll crumble, and she's made it six months so far, only three to go. She knows that dwelling on miracles is dangerous. All around her the plants I potted grow and blossom and emit oxygen in a steady stream of new air. The unasked questions cycle through her blood, attaching themselves to the nuclei of cells: *Will the baby have Juan's smile? Do I have it in me to be a good mother? How will I be able to love a constant reminder of everything I've lost?*

Next to me Earl is whistling *Rodeo-o-dee, rodeo cowboy, bordering on insane.* He's been on this country-and-western kick since we left Flagstaff. When I reach over and rub his neck, I feel the wrinkles in his skin that come from living fifty-one years and quietly shouldering life's disappointments, and I love him beyond reason. I know the strength it takes to open a frightened heart. To decide to take a chance on loving somebody and not getting it right is painful as a stab wound. He groans his thanks for the massage, briefly interrupting his humming. On the dashboard a plastic Godzilla stands on its hind legs, mouth open, jagged teeth exposed. He loves Godzilla, a little crazily, I think, but in whatever hotel we sleep tonight, I will nestle into his shoulder and place his hand on my breast. We might make love, or that touch might be bond enough. Every day we have together, even when we argue, I see as a wonder. Enough food to eat, and a choice of menu. That's the security of money. This good man beside me, who smiles like I am a newly discovered planet that changed his orbit, and now he's seeing new constellations instead of the same old stars.

ACCORDING TO HILDEGARD'S *PHYSICA* (an herb book written God knows when but rediscovered in 1859) ferns are more than attractive foliage: They actually repulse evil. This makes them an excellent choice to give new mothers with infants because the devil, always on the lookout for souls to claim, will be forced to safari through frond after hideous frond so as to find a baby. I don't believe in the devil, but when Phoebe gives birth, I'll make sure to bring endless bouquets. Maidenhair, leatherleaf, and fiddlehead. In a way this baby is all of ours—Ness unable to have one without passing on her HIV infection; Nance wanting one, but so nervous and thin I can't imagine her withstanding the rigors of pregnancy, not to mention the in-limbo thing of getting stuck between Rotten Rick and James. And me, at age forty-six, with the right guy at last, and my eggs too old to coddle. I have to make do with smiling at other people's babies in supermarkets.

I think of Phoebe nonstop, and when Earl is finished pouting about Rotten Rick's interview technique, I'm going to suggest we head back to Bayborough. If he says no, maybe I'll ask him to drop me at the nearest airport, because that's how badly I need to see her. After that horrible nonwedding, I couldn't wait to get away. Now there's no place else I'd rather be.

WHILE I ATE MY PATTY MELT I thought of Madigan. She reminded me of myself at her age—that wild-horse craziness that insisted she ride the rogue beasts, stupid risks taken just for the adrenaline rush, hooking up with selfish men to see if she can turn them into nice guys—she didn't yet know that it was easier to walk on water or grow a third eye. I hoped she'd taken my advice, ditched Rick, and was heading west to see the ocean. I wrote mental postcards to her, things I'd never truly commit to paper, never dreamed of mailing.

> *Dear Maddy,*
>
> *The salt of a man's body is toxic unless you love him and he loves you back. Then it becomes an essential mineral.*

> *Dear Maddy,*
>
> *It's possible to have the most wonderful sex just by kissing. Kissing might even be the most intimate part of it. When you're a kid, and you go to church, and the minister who's trying to scare you into not having sex says, "Your body is a temple," he's right. Why couldn't we listen? Be careful whom you invite inside because your body is a Taj Mahal, built out of love for love, and only the best man deserves it.*

> *Dear Maddy,*
>
> *Help, it's four* A.M. *and I don't know where Earl is. He said he was going out to get some air, and that was six hours ago. Should I call someone? Who?*

Dear Maddy,

If I had a daughter, I know she would be just like you—the stubborn, willful kind you can't tell anything to. She would break my heart, but also be the balm that heals it.

Dear Maddy,

Did you know that if you take the flower of clover, mix it with some olive oil, and use it as eye cream, it not only staves off wrinkles but also clears your vision?

But instead I chose the least-faded postcard of the Grand Canyon and penned this quickly to Sadie's farm.

Dear Bad Girls,

If a girl named Maddy shows up, blame me. I met her in New Mexico. Didn't think much of her choice of men, but the guy thing seemed temporary. A little young, but she's our kind of people. If it counts, she gets my vote as a wonderful addition to the house. I'm fine. You all had better be fine, too. Northern Arizona's beautiful.

Love, Beryl Anne

I WANTED TO WRITE MORE IN MY JOURNAL, but the view from the hotel room window in downtown Los Angeles was ugly, noisy, and made me miss the clean, fertile scent of the farm's compost heap. Earl laughed when I got so hysterical about him being gone.

"Were you really worried?" he asked me. "Sweetie, sometimes I take long walks to feed the music."

He stroked my face and made love to me for hours. His hands—those toughened fingers, their octave reach—made me temporarily forget how afraid I was. Sometimes, though, things inside me were wound so tightly I worried. I missed Verde. Probably by now he was whispering love poems to the kennel attendant's earrings. I looked out the window and squinted to see Earl walking down those mean streets and all that happened was I got a halo around my vision, as if the sun was perpetually in my eyes. I do not like LA. Too bright, too dirty, and everyone seems to drive a fifty-thousand-dollar car.

"Beryl, when will you believe that I'm never going to leave you?"

I wanted to hold him to his words. I wanted to say, I believe you right back, but just look at the world, and how quickly things change. I was so afraid that what happened to Phoebe would happen to me, that even now, with him right there in front of me, I couldn't stop pouting.

"What can I do to make this up to you? You want to go shopping on Rodeo Drive? You want to visit the Huntington Gardens? How about we turn in the rental car and take the next flight home to Alaska?"

"Take me to Bad Girl Creek," I said, knowing the risks were enormous—Phoebe in her pain, my wonderful boyfriend out there loose in a world full of women just aching for his kind of love. "I might stay a couple of weeks, Earl. Is that okay?"

The look on his face before he caught himself and forced a smile. "We've already missed the birch trees turning golden. Losing their leaves entirely. But not the first snow. I'm telling you, Beryl, it comes down like chilly confetti chastening the red berries, turning the bears all soft and sleepy. Are you sure this is what you want?"

I couldn't listen. I loved Earl with all my heart, I missed having a house to call my home, but I couldn't shake the feeling that Phoebe needed me.

Or maybe I needed her.

Three weeks. Twenty-one days. One week shy of a month. Earl and I had never been apart longer than eighteen hours—the time it took for him to get back from one of his really long walks.

"I'm sure," I said. "Let's go."

DUCHESS AND I STOOD ON THE PORCH and watched him drive away. The garden was mad with color—gold and yellow and russet mums in bloom. The potted plants sold better than the cut flowers, but either way, when set among dried flowers, they screamed autumn. I thought how California needed that, its seasons being hard to separate. You'd think colored ribbon would work for those arrangements, but it was actually plain old wheat-colored raffia that did them justice. Nance's touch, I knew. I thought of the construction-paper turkeys I used to make with the kindergarteners, back before J.W. and prison and my life went downhill. A pencil tracing of each tiny hand, then cut out colored-paper feathers for the turkey's tail. It seemed like somebody else's life.

It was too early in the morning for anyone to be up. Nance might be working at the computer, but everyone else was nestled into sheets, finishing up dreams. I stood there trying to ground myself, to believe I was really here. Then I opened the screen door, fully aware that I was inviting chaos into my entire being.

"Who's there?" I heard Phoebe call out.

"What's she doing awake this early?" I asked Duchess, and Duchess, in her infinite dog wisdom, knew better than to answer that question.

Phoebe

13

Tisanes, Tinctures, and Tea

ONE PERFECT MORNING, as dreary as all the others, while I lay in my bed growing a baby that broke my heart, Gabriella showed up uninvited. Ness was spending the night at David Snow's, so I couldn't blame this little surprise on another one of her attempts to cheer me out of grieving for the man who had almost been my husband. Nance, as usual, was holed up in her room, flipping through bridal magazines and making a career out of not eating anything remotely caloric. Beryl had been gone for months, and I missed her. I hadn't spoken a word for more than a week. It was a regular house of mental challenges, and any psychologist worth her salt would have made a killing sorting us out. The last time I'd seen the redheaded hairdresser was the morning of my fateful wedding day, and I didn't appreciate the reminder, but when she stood in my bedroom doorway with that grin on her face, holding a hot-pink caddy full of hair products, what was I supposed to do, call the cops?

She took one look at my belly and whistled. "Honeybun, all you need is a palm tree to sprout out of your navel and you could call that thing an island!"

"Excuse me?" I sputtered.

"I bet Ness fifty bucks I could get you talking again. A body can't help but smile about winning a fifty. Besides, you're not the only girl to so unfairly lose the man she loved. You might try looking at your situation this way: Your man left you part of himself in that baby. Well, enough. The past is history, the future's a mystery. All we've got is the ordinary now, so let's get started. Girl, your hair is looking so bad I don't know if I can fix it in one visit. Also, even if you don't feel like talking to me, I have a lot of gossip just burning my tongue to tell you."

I raised myself up on one elbow. Even that small effort caused me to huff. "Fine, you won your damn bet. Now leave."

Gabriella put her hands on her hips and looked at me hotly. "I beg your pardon?"

"I said you could leave now. No pity hairstyle today."

She shook her head and her intricate copper beaded earrings jingled. "Nope. I heard your hair was all bed-raggled so I come to do your do."

"Bed-raggled? Don't you mean bedraggled?"

"I most certainly do not." She dumped the contents of the caddy onto my bed. Curlers, brushes, pins, and little bottles of potions spilled in every direction. "That's a terrible word! Sounds like something that belong in the trash. Well, Sweetcakes, all I know is when my clients can't come to me, I go to them. And your hair needs me, so hush now."

She pulled a chair and a basin over and proceeded to wash my awful hair. I had been spraying it with this supposed dry-cleaning stuff, but the smell made me barf, so two weeks ago I'd kind of stopped. You name the problem, my hair suffered from it. Excessive oil, rat's nests, split ends—my "do" was a cornucopia of follicular dilemmas. Sometimes it lay so hatefully against my scalp I considered shaving my bed-raggled head. Gabriella turned my neck this way and that. "I've seen worse."

There was a frightening thought. "Then go work on them."

She *tsk*ed, lathered me up twice, and while she was at it, she massaged my neck. No one had touched me like that since my wedding day, and my emotions clambered up from deep down in that well where I stored everything I didn't have the strength to deal with. It felt like a lover's touch, not perverted, but her fingers knew exactly where my muscles were knotted, and gently coaxed them to relax. She prodded patiently, and as my sore places waved the white flag of surrender, tears slid out of my eyes. For months I'd been holding them in, but now they seeped out of me, like a tub quietly overflowing. How could I hate somebody who knew what my body needed better than I did? Without a single sob I made one quiet waterfall of a mother-to-be.

If the baby lived. If I even wanted that.

"Oh," she said. "What's wrong? Did I get the water too hot?"

"No. Could you please get me a towel."

She ignored me. "You know, most people make the mistake of washing hair in too hot of water. That just plain annoys the scalp! I myself prefer this lukewarm temperature, though a cold rinse can stimulate the roots. What scent do you prefer, Phoebe, almond or herbal? I brought both."

I sighed, remembering the bath products Nance had given me. How I'd washed my body with them on my wedding day. With each swipe of suds my skin tingled because I knew that later on Juan's fingers would travel there. I was already pregnant, and a touch sick to my stomach, but back then, sexual desire beat soda crackers for calming nausea. I was still able to move on my own two feet then, even though before the day's end that mobility had ceased. I'd been in this bed ever since. Up until this week I'd been allowed to get up and into my wheelchair to use the toilet, but last week Judi Jenkins, M.D., my Barbie doll of an obstetrician, had taken away the privilege. From now on I was supposed to call for a bedpan. As Nance would have said, "F that, up the stairs and backwards." I crept to my chair and from there to the john, and no one yet seemed the wiser. Sometimes I worried I'd end up dead on the toilet like a female version of Elvis, but asking my friends to empty my pee for me? I didn't think so.

"Almond," I whispered. "I used to like almond."

"Well, then. We will almond you up and down and eight ways to Sunday."

She popped a bottle top, and I smelled the sweet scent of orchards, a hint of Jergen's lotion, and, oh! my wedding day. Under my heart the pain throbbed like a broken rib. Gabriella ran a wide-toothed comb through the conditioner in my hair so easily it felt like silk. I wanted all this softness away from me; it hurt too much to feel this good. But I kind of enjoyed the pain of remembering: It was like looking in a photo album and seeing happier times frozen on the faces of friendly ghosts you'd never stop missing—like how I felt about Sadie. "Listen, Gabriella," I said. "Really. You must have clients waiting. Better things to do."

She bent close and pressed her dark cheek to my pale one. "Imagine if one woman would do this for another woman just one day a week, how much happier we all would be. Plus, there's my fifty bucks to consider. Ha-ha."

"Ha-ha. You aren't by any chance looking for a room to rent, are you?"

"No, ma'am. I got me a nice little ranch house and a nice little husband who does just what I tell him like a house elf. If I say, 'Honey, I been craving me a birdhouse to pretty up the garden,' off he goes to the garage and starts in hammering. He likes to cook Italian, too. I like this farm, but your room's a little too Chinese for my taste, however. That feng shui crap can be overpowering."

"They're my aunt's things."

"Your aunt?"

"Sadie. She's dead. She was that simple kind of elegant, good cheekbones, dressed in tailored clothes. She could do the Chinese thing or any other thing and get away with it. What I wouldn't give to have her style."

"Let me guess. She had a pageboy hairstyle, parted on the side."

How did Gabriella know? "Did Ness tell you about her?"

"No. Those kinds of ladies come in for their trims every six weeks, and they don't ever once ask what it costs for a deep condition. Not too shabby in the tip department, either. When did she pass?"

"Two years ago." I didn't tell her that I felt ready to join her.

Gabriella patted my arm. "If you were to decorate this room by yourself, what style would you go for? You don't strike me as a traditional type, all that dark scary furniture and brocade draperies. Or shabby chic, which is when it costs a thousand dollars for a table that looks like it set outside for a decade."

Shabby chic? Paying an exorbitant amount for peeling paint? That was how my heart felt most of the time, but when it came to surroundings that reflected the real me, I had no idea. "I had an apartment before I lived here. Frilly bedspread, courtesy of my mother; white furniture, pretty much the same. Mostly I didn't care what was around me, I was so glad to be on my own. I thought that Juan and I would figure that stuff out together. You know, scatter some of his Mexican stuff around, mix in my aunt's things, and . . ." I patted my beach ball of a belly. "Ask the baby. But before we could do much more than this, he died."

"It's a start," Gabriella said.

"Jeez! What are you, one of those desperately cheerful people? Because if you are, I can tell you right now no matter what you do for my hair you're wasting your time on me. The time when I saw the glass half full was a light-year ago."

Every barb I sent out she ignored. "You got a cradle for the baby yet? Ness's granny make the wee one a quilt?"

I felt myself stiffen under her hands. I knew one thing about the child: It was bad luck. Nights when I couldn't sleep, I'd think, What if God offered me the chance to exchange it for Juan's life? What if I could never ever get pregnant? It didn't take me half a second to say, *Yes, let's do it that way. Take it back.* "Don't you know it's considered bad luck to buy baby things ahead of time?"

"Um," Gabriella said. "I can see how you might feel that way, but not everybody does." She reached her hand over to lay it on my belly. It made me crazy when people did that, as if Juan's baby was some good-luck stone they could touch without paying a fee. In return they received great fortune, and what did that leave me with? But Gabby lifted hers so it hovered above, as if her fingers were listening to my skin, and I swore I felt a tingle. "This baby be telling me she wants to see that cradle. And she wants bright colors in her quilt—oranges, reds, deep purples, taxicab yellow, none of that pastel bunny shit."

"Pastel bunny shit"? What the hell did I do to deserve a morning like this? Wasn't my life crappy enough already? "Oh, right, you can tell all this after putting a hand to my stomach."

"That and more, child."

"Well, what else?"

She rinsed the conditioner from my hair. "Don't rush me. We'll get to it next visit. Right now I need to cut some of these split ends. Practically need a lawn mower is what I'm thinking."

Another visit? I'd have to go through this *again?* Maybe I could pretend to be unconscious. "You know I'm not going to tip."

"Don't expect you to. Just be still and let me work my magic."

"I might throw up."

She laughed. "Well, if you do, turn your head and aim for the wastebasket."

AFTER THAT SHE CAME EVERY WEEK, armed with new products, whatever fruit was in season, and a steady stream of luscious, endless beauty salon gossip. Tiffani with an *i* had gone to Maui on a vacation for one week, a Hawaiian Holidays special. Instead of coming back after enjoying her off-season bargain, though, she'd fallen in lust with a native surfer in his late fifties, and now she was living with him in one of the only Victorian houses on the island and working part-time at a resort doing manicures for tourists. No more stench of hair straightener, dye, or bleach; her nights were filled with plumeria and ripe mangoes and passion. Rahkelle, who owned the salon, was furious, because without Tiffani, she had to haul her fat butt out from behind the counter and start painting nails again. But who was Rahkelle to complain when she was doing the horizontal mambo with a pilot she met in a bar, can you imagine? Well, not doing it *in* the bar, exactly, but what did she think at her age, dating flyboys who'd only break her heart? Maybe it was all those years of inhaling acetone. Did I know that gas prices had risen a whole entire dollar for no good reason? True, the only place they were higher was Alaska. And by the way, this so-called California energy crisis was some crackpot Republican scheme to ease the president's conscience about ripping up the Arctic Refuge, and where was it the poor reindeer were supposed to graze when oil wells and cell-phone towers junked up their landscape?

"Caribou," I said, but Gabriella was on a tear and didn't hear me. Hearing her mention Alaska made me miss Beryl. She sent postcards, but a few scribbled lines weren't enough. And what she wrote—well, it wasn't anything of substance.

Gabriella talked so much I was mesmerized. If she and her little hubby had a fight, she explained the entire argument to me, step by step, then why he was wrong but would never apologize; the men in the Elkridge family did not apologize. They did, however, buy flowers, and this week she had gotten some mums the exact color of ours in the nearest field, and last week it was asters, she just loved asters, even more than roses.

"Tell him to buy them here," I said. "Hell, I'll give them to him free."

Sometimes, while she dried my hair, she talked to the baby, not me. She told the baby stories about long-ago Africa, before her ancestors were sold to the slave trade, when people were strong and game was healthy. A time before the AIDS plague had cast its pall so widely that all of Africa was in danger of becoming a graveyard. That old Africa, rich and lush and filled with singing. She aimed her voice at my stomach and explained, "Little one, once a plain woman was married to a man who had other wives. She was way, way down the list in terms of important. But, oh, did she love that man! He was a kind husband, a good provider, and he kept his wives fat and happy. One day they went looking for water, and come across a snake. Nasty snake, poisonous fellow. He bit the husband and the number one wife. Right there on the spot, they fell dead. The wife who was not so important was spared. She shooed the snake away. Grieving, she ran to an old woman who lived thereabouts, in a thatched hut, and everyone said was bad magic. 'I need to keep the flies from my loved ones,' the wife said. 'Can you help me?' Well, the old woman gave her a cow-tail switch to use for this purpose. Do you know what happened? The minute that cow-tail switch touched the bodies, they sprang back to life. Can you guess who was the most important wife then?"

"And the cow?" I asked.

"Nothing in the story about what become of the cow."

"That is extremely grim," I said. "Not to mention polygamy

is illegal. Tell me how any child of any age could possibly glean a life lesson from that little tale."

"Hush up, Phoebe. Did your hormones mess up your hearing? I guess they're running so catty-wampus you can't hear the secret in that story. Well, I got a lot more where that come from. There's a different song for every variety of snake in my homeland. In the seasons of drought the people pray and dance, and in the season of pouring rain, they dance and pray. The sky unleashes its water, and every living creature come out to drink, from the tiniest insect to the bull elephant with his mighty tusks."

She told the baby the story of the constant parrot, the one about the greedy dog, and how the spider bargained with God, and hemmed it all up with the idea that it took the entire village to raise one child, a concept nobody in America except Hillary Clinton seemed to comprehend. All this while she washed, conditioned, and styled the dead cuticle growing out of my scalp. If I complained, or tried to send her and her hot rollers packing, she told me another story.

Whenever she laughed I felt the flutter of legs inside me, as if the baby had banked off one shore, eager to swim to another. One day Gabriella picked up the only framed photo I had of Juan and regarded it closely. "Don't you just think that heaven must be the luckiest place?" she said, and, boom! she was onto a new subject.

Her offhand acceptance of Juan's death made me crazy. I knew what she was up to. With every word she was trying to lay down another layer of skin over my wounds. Well, it wasn't working. I still missed him in every fiber of my being as painfully as the day I'd lost him. In the process of growing our baby, a foot one day, toenails the next, Juan had come to rest inside me for good, had become a folktale I hadn't yet learned the words to because I was too preoccupied living it, and that hurt. Maybe I felt less alone, but no less sad.

So when I heard the screen door open so early, I expected it was Gabby showing up to "do my do," as she referred to it, and I called out, "Who's there?" expecting her to answer back, "A six-foot-tall West African woman, armed with shampoo," like she always did. Instead, Duchess nosed open my door and there stood

Beryl Anne, sunburned across both cheeks, her red curly hair hanging long and loose to her shoulders. I dropped Juan's picture on the mattress and held my arms above my bloated abdomen. Tears fell of their own free will, and I didn't try to stop them. "Oh, my God. When did you get here?"

"Just now." Beryl climbed into bed with me and wiped my tears from my face with her own wet fingers. Duchess sat on the floor and whimpered until all parties got themselves under control. "We were in LA. I told Earl I needed to be here, so we drove all night, and he dropped me off." She looked up at the Easter cactus she'd given me a week after Juan died. It was deep green, full of buds, and still ages until spring. "Look at that crazy plant, about to bloom, totally out of season."

"I can relate," I said. "There are days I have to pee so often I'm ready to do my own cesarean section, if I could get someone to bring me a garden trowel."

"Phoebe, stop that. You've never been more beautiful."

"Let me guess. In the same way those giant Alaska cabbages are freakishly beautiful?"

She kissed my cheek. "Exactly."

"You know what, Beryl? I would eat raw liver if it meant I could get out of this godforsaken bed and go outdoors. I want to feel the air on my body! I want to tend the damn poinsettias. I want to feed Leroy some oats, and I want to watch Florencio drive the tractor. What I don't want to do is sit here and have this baby."

"You'll feel different when it's here."

"I will not. Actually, I had this idea—"

"Just remain open to the option, okay? What's Lester say about this craving for sunshine?"

So I didn't tell her then about how I planned to give the baby to James and Nance. I stuck to the facts at hand. "Lester, my former friend, has sicced this fifteen-year-old obstetrician on me, and she's worse than he is! According to Dr. Judi, I can't move unless it's by ambulance, or possibly one of those harnesses they used to free Willy. Did you hear that Willy didn't want to go to sea? He decided he preferred the company of his keepers. Here the resemblance between Willy and me ends."

"Stop it, Phoebe. You look pregnant. That's all. Pretty soon the baby will be born and you'll be your old self again."

"So they tell me. Yet we both know that *they* have been known to lie."

"Oh, Phoebe. They also love you. Tell me what else is new around here. Have Zelda and F. Scott done the deed?"

"Big news on the love front," I said. "They're officially engaged. The ring is a yellow diamond, two-point-five carats, set in platinum, and it's a size four, which is now larger than Nance's dress size. Even though I fail to see much kissing and petting going on, there is more than enough planning to make up for it. Dancing lessons in the garden. Meetings with interior designers, and instead of sex, they put their Palm Pilots on the table and let them 'communicate.' The ceremony is planned for New Year's Eve. You know my brother, if he can get a tax write-off, he'll take it."

"That's really soon. The baby will be here by then. So tell me about Nance. Is she eating again?"

I looked away. I didn't want to think about that. I wanted my perfect plan to go off without a hitch. Nance and James to adopt the baby. "Some," I said. "Yeah, I think she's better." I wasn't sure, but I wanted to believe that. I wasn't ready to tell Beryl about giving up the baby. The argument that I knew would follow was more than I could handle. How did I introduce such a notion? Guess what I'm getting Nance and James for a wedding present? "Maybe the baby will be here," I said. If it lived. If I did.

"Does your doctor think it's a boy or a girl? Could you see anything on the ultrasound?"

I shrugged. "The pictures look like linoleum patterns to me. Who cares?"

Beryl went quiet.

"What can I say? I asked for Marcus Welby, I got this Nazi gynecologist."

"But it's your baby, Phoebe. Aren't you curious?"

My eyes welled up. "No, I'm terrified, and I don't want to talk any more about it."

Beryl sat up and petted Duchess, letting that news sink in. "Well, it's nearly seven-thirty. Can we wake the girls up now?"

"Check this out," I said and, feeling like a spoiled child-empress, rang my bedside bell madly until, convinced I was in labor, everyone came running.

Beryl gave me the look. "Phoebe."

"What?" I said innocently. "When you only have one perk to your name, you use the heck out of it."

"A HALLOWEEN PARTY?" I said. "Wild children trampling the plants, pestering Leroy, not to mention a lot of sticky spilled Kool-Aid. Tell me again how agreeing to have a kids' birthday party at De-Thomas Farms is going to bring us business."

With her bony left hand, Nance gestured to her computer rendering. "We decorate the barn with fake cobwebs, a paper skeleton, pumpkins. Leroy can spare a few bales of hay for a day. There's a washtub to bob for apples. We serve them grilled cheese sandwiches cut into moons and stars; finish up with cup-cakes, orange-frosted cupcakes, sprinkles. We can charge five hundred dollars."

"Jimmies," Ness said. "The correct word for sprinkles is *jimmies,* and I'd pay five hundred bucks to watch you eat a cup-cake."

Nance shot her a look. "The kids may go nuts, but within a limited area."

"Five hundred seems a little steep," I said.

"Not really," Nance said. "If you factor in the mental cost of putting on such a party yourself, cleaning up, making sure little Suzie gets to the potty on time, it's actually fairly reasonable."

"And if there are any leftover cupcakes—" Ness started.

Beryl spoke right over her. "Tell us more, Nance."

Nance flipped her rendering over to reveal a second drawing. "If some people can stick to the subject, I'd be happy to." She cleared her throat. "In the background our Thanksgiving centerpiece samples are on display, along with photographs of last year's poinsettias, and in a loose-leaf notebook, more photos, and plenty of order forms. You know how yuppie mothers are! They'll start trying to one-up each other over the poinsettias while little Buffy has a safe and sane Halloween/birthday, which the other mothers will have to outdo when their darling's turn comes around. I considered renting ponies, but there's the liability question. We could offer the parents a tour of the greenhouses, explain how we have merchandise for every major holiday. I'm telling you, Pheebs, it's like killing two birds with one stone."

"There's a turn of phrase the world could do without," Beryl said.

"I'll take Leroy to David's for the day," Ness said. "We don't need any bitten fingers. Too bad we don't have a big dumb cow or something."

"Nix that cow idea right this instant," Nance said. "At least the smell of horse poop is tolerable. So, what do you think, Pheebs?"

What did I think? I thought I would run rampant over any of those little yuppie children if it meant I got to go to a party. Even if Nance didn't, I wanted to stuff my mouth with frosted jimmied cupcakes. I also knew that the mere sight of the children would be my undoing. "What's James think?"

Nance stifled her frown, but just barely. "James said it sounded like a challenge, but he knew I was up to it."

"Ha. That's brother-speak for 'her mind's made up, I might as well give in.' Go ahead," I said. "Don't mind me. I'll just lie here like a beached whale."

"I know," Ness said. "Instead of the cow, we charge a quarter a pop to see the whale!"

Everyone laughed except me. "Thanks," I said. "I think I'm worth at least fifty cents. Seventy-five by next week."

The girls grinned at one another. Nance was the first one out of the room, clipboard already in hand, but Ness and Beryl lingered by my bed. "Glad you decided to start communicating with us again," Ness said. "It was lonely when you got all quiet."

"You shut up, you Benedict Arnold. You bet Gabriella fifty dollars to annoy me back to life."

"Actually that was David's idea."

"Well, tell Mr. Snow he's on my list."

Beryl laughed. "Fifty dollars? Have you all turned into gamblers? I'll be glad to pay half of it, Precious."

"Enough with the Precious crap," Ness said. "Doesn't anyone else around here have a secret?"

"I'll never tell," Beryl said.

"You guys?" I interrupted. "Nance looks like a wraith. Does she eat at all?"

Ness and Beryl looked at each other.

"She does fork aerobics," Ness said. "Maybe you should take that subject up with your brother. They're out together most every night. I assume he eats, since he looks the same as ever."

"I'll do that," I said. "Right after my nap. Right after something."

I was done being decent for the day. All this talk of parties and flowers had gotten to me. My afternoon would be filled with dark thoughts, and I wasn't fit to be in public.

"Sweet dreams," Beryl said, and she and Ness left me.

Carefully I rolled to my left side and felt the baby shift, finding a new position. That baby—it was neither male nor female to me—it was an albatross, an anchor, something that kept me flat on my back and thinking of doom. Dr. Judi, the eternally cheerful, said that by now everything was formed, all that was left was the final touches. The book James left me months ago concurred, though I hadn't really read the whole thing. The baby had a face, inherited features, supposedly even a personality. The lungs still needed to mature, but the skin was perfect, unblemished, covered with that waxy protective coating. Maybe somewhere there was a birthmark, or an oddly shaped mole, a unique, identifying mark. When things got too crowded, he or she would ask to come out—at least that's how it would happen for other mothers. My OB was preparing me for a cesarean. She insisted that my spine couldn't take a normal delivery. She was planning on moving me to Community Hospital of the Peninsula for the last six weeks of pregnancy, which meant any minute, though the thought of that felt unreal. The labor pains part I wouldn't miss, but six weeks of CHOP? I'd sooner give birth to quints the hard way.

And when it was born, then what? James would make a great father. He loved kids. He did the Santa thing every year for the hospital and the youth shelter. The only concern was Nance.

If Nance was so skinny she might at any given moment faint, would she be strong enough to care for a baby? If something happened, could I bear it?

Next to my bed I heard Duchess sigh and settle in for her nap. The old dog sensed when I needed her. When a bad mood came on, she flew to my side as if she could feel it coming, like a seizure. Was it all the extra heat my body gave off? I felt ten degrees hotter than the rest of the world. I swear, half the time I didn't need a sheet. I closed my eyes and the same way the baby swam inside me, I let myself drift into sleep. Since I'd cursed her months ago, Sadie no longer visited me. Juan, well, he'd never come to me, no matter how much I prayed. Every time I shut my eyes, I conjured up the sound of the shower, his whistle, and tried to glimpse his profile.

NAZI BARBIE, M.D., parted my knees and poked her gloved finger around down there. "Hello?" I said. "That hurts."

"It does not," she chided me. "I'm moving my hand very gently."

"Excuse me. I think I know what's hurt and what's gentle and what isn't when it comes to my coochie. Even if it has been temporarily taken over by an alien, this is still my body."

She snapped my knees shut, peeled off her gloves, and began to make notes in her folder. Her blond curtain of hair royally pissed me off. It was thick and shiny, cut to fall to her neck just right, never so much as a strand out of place. She was in perfect shape, and she could walk wherever she wanted to. Worst of all was her iron will, against which my threats and refusals fell like wet tissue paper. "Phoebe, it's understandable that you're feeling depressed. Once we get you in the hospital, you'll be more comfortable."

"I'm not depressed, and I'm not going to the hospital."

She looked at me with all her hours of training and said, "Oh, you're going, all right. Today, in fact. I've already called for an ambulance transport."

I sat up and felt the pull of muscles strain my belly. "Dammit all to Los Angeles and back, why are you like this?"

Her bright blue eyes blinked. "Why am I like what?"

"A female Hitler or something! What the hell is the harm of me lying in my own bed a few more weeks? An ambulance can take me to CHOP in what, ten minutes?"

"In ten minutes," she said, capping her pen and checking her watch, "you could both be dead. You with that heart, the baby arriving too soon. It could be any one of a million things. Surely Lester explained this to you when you chose to undertake a high-risk pregnancy."

"Chose"? Ooh, she made my blood boil! She'd have five babies, squirt them out easy as toothpaste, and if I was lucky—lucky, having lost Juan—I'd have this one and live through the experience to see her or him to preadolescence. *You little bitch,* I wanted to say. *You try losing the love of your life and not moving for months. You try peeing into a basin. Then we'll see how cheerful you are, you little twit.*

Instead I cried.

"So? Ready to go?" she said cheerily.

"Anything to get out of the house," I answered gloomily. "Can I at least leave my roommates a note?"

I wrote three lines and propped it against the Chinese lamp where I knew they would find it: "I am being held against my will at the damn hospital. I am *not* in labor. Do not under any circumstances call my mother."

I'd have two hours, tops, I figured, before the Bad Girls descended.

I said good-bye to the Chinese decor, to the French doors that allowed me a view of whoever might be driving up to see us. When it was the UPS truck, the new driver who had replaced Juan either had a kind enough heart to drive up James's new driveway to deliver packages, or had gotten an earful from Nance. Like a pioneer, I felt I was heading off on a recently blazed trail that would show me a new way of living. Nance and James would take the baby, and she or he'd grow up healthy and sound with my friends acting as aunts. I'd say good-bye to the flowers and find a handicapped tour of Europe. Or, worst-case scenario, my ashes would sink to the ocean floor to commingle with my aunt's, and I wouldn't be lonely.

As the ambulance drivers loaded me up, I tried to memorize my farm. I gave each stone a mental kiss of thanks. The brief view of the fields was intoxicatingly colorful. The greenhouses were slick with rain, and the brief kiss of air as I was transferred from house to ambulance spilled cool and fragrant on my face. "Easy with the cargo, boys," I told the ambulance attendants.

They were nice guys. The punky one sat in the back with me. He told me stories about his wild youth misspent in Sacramento, a place where a kid can get into a lot of trouble. He flashed his tribal tattoos at me, and said nowadays if you had a tattoo you needed to be tested for hep C. I assured him I was tattooless. When he showed me a photo of his son, a chubby baby boy with a triple chin, his eyes grew soft, and he was just like any father in the world. "You won't believe what you're in for," he said.

Beryl

14

Farm Journal

I SLICED BLOOD ORANGES, broke grapefruit into sections, quartered limes and peeled the brown furry skin off kiwis, and arranged everything on a plate. I mixed a pitcher of limeade and seltzer water, and pulled mint leaves off the stalks growing in the herb garden—something Nance herself had started from a cutting, that now, wherever there was earth to support it, had spread like wildfire. Then I went for the gold standard—chicken salad with candied pecans and celery slices. When I used to live here, Nance could never resist my chicken salad. She said her mother talked about her old family cook's chicken salad until the dish turned into a legend, and that even though she'd never tasted it herself, she knew it had to be something like this, something perfectly balanced between sweet and smoky and crunchy and spicy. I mounded it up on butter lettuce leaves because I knew the carbo load in bread would turn Nance away from the table, insisting she had a phone call to return, or a late supper planned with James, or the old reliable excuse of having eaten a late lunch.

"Dinner," I called, and Duchess, at least, came running.

Ness took one look at the table and sighed. "Oh, that looks nice. But what can I eat?"

I set her plate down in front of her. "For you, tofurky salad made with soy mayo."

"Is that it?"

"What do you mean is that *it?* You want candy and surprises, too, Precious? Well, you're getting a fruit plate. I'm going to start packing a few things for Phoebe."

She scraped her chair back from the table. "I was joking, Beryl. Relax. You've been in here for hours, chopping and mixing, and this is the first time we've eaten on the Staffordshire china since you moved out. What happened to your sense of humor? Did it freeze up and blow away in Alaska?"

"I'm sorry," I said. "I'm tense about Phoebe. I have the feeling she—"

Nance sauntered into the kitchen typing into her Palm Pilot, so I held my tongue. I thought I'd wait a bit before laying my theory of Phoebe not wanting to keep the baby on her. "Beryl Anne," Nance said. "Is that your famous chicken salad?"

I nodded.

"Oh, I am just starving," she said, and sat down at the table where we'd once shared so many meals together, happily finishing one another's plates, taking turns licking the serving spoon. She made a big show out of unfolding her napkin. "Beryl, nobody makes chicken salad like you do. Not even my snotty relatives who I've never met and by the way, who are not invited to my wedding."

"Thanks, I think," I said.

She lifted her fork, smiled wide, and pushed it around her plate this way and that. I tried to avert my eyes, to make it easier on her to take that first bite. When I glanced at Ness, she mouthed the words "fork aerobics."

"Sure is quiet around here without Verde," Ness said.

Nance nodded. "Yes, by now that trash-mouth parrot of yours would have gone through his list, I'll bet."

"I miss him, too," I said. "Did I tell you Earl's guitar playing gets him singing?"

"Really?" Ness said, and even I could tell she was just trying to make conversation. We both fell silent as we listened to the busy sound of Nance not eating.

"Think we should let Phoebe have a night off?" Ness asked, "or should we go see her again tonight?"

"I don't know," I said. "What do you think?"

But she didn't answer. We were both transfixed by Nance's elaborate ritual. She did eat the lettuce, after she'd cut it into tiny, regimented little bites. Ditto the celery. I couldn't be sure, but it looked like one or two small pieces of chicken went past her lips, but the candied pecans, which I had shelled by hand, glazed in sugar, turned into a berm at the edge of Sadie's blue calico china. She fed a little of the chicken to Duchess—nothing strange about that—but most of it she left on her plate, mashed so thin with the tines of her fork that it had turned into an unpalatable slurry. Something had to be done.

"Is there something wrong with the salad?" I asked. "You didn't eat very much."

Her smile nearly covered up her shock at my words. "I was eating crackers up in my room," she said. "I think I ate too many because—"

"Nance, how much weight have you lost?"

She flushed. "Only five pounds or so. But that's just because planning the wedding takes so much effort. There's so much to do, and then James's new place needs all this decorating so I get too busy to eat, and I drink so much coffee it speeds up my metabolism. I'll gain it back in no time. You'll see."

"Five pounds my black ass," Ness said, throwing her napkin down on the table. "Let's go step on the scale, with Beryl as witness."

"Excuse me," Nance said quietly. "I fail to see how my weight's any of your concern." She got up from the table, and her napkin fell to the floor.

Ness stood in the doorway, blocking her exit. "You're not going anywhere until we settle this. Beryl Anne, hand me that copper skillet."

"Ness, don't hit her," I said.

"In the name of the Lord, I'm not going to hit her, I just want her to look in it and see her reflection. Hand it over."

"Okay."

She held the pan, which I'd polished to a gleam, in front of

Nance's face. "Take a gander," she said. "You are skin and bones, and I am about to hog-tie you and take you to the hospital. Either you have to eat or you have to get some help, Nancy."

I put my hand on Nance's shoulder. Her bones were right there, no padding to them at all. I was afraid to imagine what she looked like naked. "Ness is right, Nance. Whatever is going on with you, it's not worth starving yourself over. If you won't talk to us, will you at least talk to James?"

Nance pulled away, and I wasn't sure if she had actually looked at herself in the shine of the copper or was looking so far beyond that image we had no idea what she was seeing. "I appreciate your concern. I had a problem for a while, but I'm better now. I have to run to meet James. Beryl, feed Duchess for me, will you? Thanks."

We stood there listening to the front door open and shut, and the sound of her Rodeo starting up.

"Sure," Ness said. "We be happy to, Missy Mattox. Nothing we slaves like better than seeing *someone* eat, even if it is a dog."

"You shouldn't have said that about the scale. She's probably terrified of the scale."

"Well, what am I supposed to say? Let's tippy-toe around the fact that your hipbones could thresh wheat?"

"What happens on her night to cook?"

"She opens a can of potato soup for Phoebe and tells me to make a peanut butter sandwich. Then she runs off, supposedly to have supper with James." Ness set the skillet down. "It's no use, Bear. She denies it, or else she takes a few bites and then skips the next five meals. If Phoebe was here at the table, I think she could get through to her, but you know, since you left and Juan died, it's just Nance and me." She wadded up her napkin and tossed it on the table, where Duchess eyed it with interest. "Hell if I know what to do."

"We could kidnap her and put her in treatment."

Ness took her chair again, and started lining up her medications. "I meant, aside from getting ourselves killed."

"Everything I've ever read says anorexia is all about controlling the uncontrollable," I said. "So what's so uncontrollable about Nance's life? From where I stand, looks like she's got it pretty good."

Ness snorted and had to stop her dinner pill regimen until she got her laughter under control. I counted fourteen pills laid out by her plate. In the mornings I could hear her gagging as she tried to get down the ones she was supposed to take on an empty stomach. "She loves Rotten Rick, but she isn't with Rotten Rick. She wants to sleep with James, because she figures if they have sex, she'll love him and forget about Rotten Rick, but James, who is no idiot, won't sleep with her until they're married—you know, he thinks it will take the commitment thing to erase Rotten Rick. This damn wedding has consumed her to the point where if one twinkle light fails to glow it will be a disaster. While I'm sure a big wedding is what Nance has always dreamed of, she can't help but feel torn thinking of doing it with Phoebe around to see what she missed when Juan died. I told her, Go to Vegas, for Pete's sake, just have a couple of drinks, say I do, do the deed, and come home married. Do us all a favor. You can imagine how well that went over."

"We could do an intervention."

"A what?"

"That's when you ambush the person with all of her loved ones, and get them to speak to her about her problem. They do it in AA."

"How is that any different than what we just did?"

"I don't know. Except that it forces the person to confront how her behavior is affecting everyone."

Ness seemed to think it over. She hung the copper skillet back up and drummed her fingers on the counter. Her mannerisms reminded me of Rick, when Earl had played guitar for him in New Mexico. I thought about his less-than-stellar treatment of Maddy, and how that night I made everyone dinner, Earl had called him on his behavior, and how quickly Rick had backed down, as if no one else had ever stood up to him in exactly that way. What bearing did all this have on Nance's not eating? Well, they'd spent three years together. And before she got involved with James, she'd seemed to eat fairly well. For a moment I fantasized what might happen if Rick showed up and saw her looking so thin. I could engineer that. I thought about explaining all this to Ness, but mostly what I had to say amounted to a long, boring bunch of facts that came to no real point. I cleaned up our plates and put the chicken salad in a Tupperware container, hoping Nance would sneak down at midnight and gorge in secret.

Ness sighed. "All this talk is making me tired. I say we let Phoebe alone tonight, and let's you and me go see David. You have to see how well he's doing these days. He loves company, especially when I bring Duchess along."

That sounded good to me. "Let me try to call Earl before we go, okay?"

She clucked. "Listen to who sounds like a newlywed."

WHEN A PERSON CALLS ALASKA, with its own private time zone, and gets no answer, she learns that endless ringing is truly what long distance is all about. Earl hated answering machines, wouldn't hear of us having one. *Let whoever it is call back,* he said. *Nothing's so important it can't wait.* I tried his cell number, but got the voice mail. "It's me," I said into the crackly void that followed the beep. "Missing you and wondering where you are. Call if you get a chance. I love you?"

Then I called Furry Paws in Eagle River and talked to Dana, who went to the kennel extension and put Verde on the phone. "Hello, Verde," I said. "Have you been a good bird?"

He answered with a string of curse words and I could hear Dana's hearty laugh.

"I miss you, buddy," I told my macaw. "Stay warm. I'll see you soon. Now let me talk to Dana, okay?"

"He's doing great, Beryl. We love having him around."

"Does he need a sweater or anything? I mean, this is his first winter. Have you guys gotten snow yet?"

"Oh, some flurries. Nothing's really stuck. Try not to worry about your bird. Just soak up all that California sunshine."

I looked out the window at the flowers in bloom. The poinsettia greenhouse was full of stock. It didn't look like fall here, much less winter. All that would change soon enough when the rains came. I remembered last year's, and Phoebe's pneumonia. This year our weather was full of grief and the coming baby. I said good-bye to Dana and set the phone on the cradle. From the kitchen I could hear Ness singing "Gotta Serve Somebody," that Bob Dylan song off the Christian album he made. Did he still believe in all that? What did it take to make the leap of faith?

Probably Earl was jamming with his buddies at that bar in Sutton they sometimes frequented. And they liked to go to this one guy's house on Big Lake. It required a boat ride to move their instruments, but in the winters Earl said the lake froze enough to bear the weight of cars, and the city maintained it as a highway. I could see him there with Paul and Annie, a fire in the woodstove, making music that serenaded the view from their window—that beautiful lake, surrounded by full-grown spruce, and whatever migrating birds were hurrying south.

DAVID SNOW LOOKED REMARKABLY HALE. He said his new medicine was a godsend, and he clasped Ness's hand the whole time we sat on the couch talking. Duchess poked around his house, sniffing antique Indian baskets, pawing at his Persian rug, wandering in and out of the bedroom. Verde would have done the same thing, but causing infinitely more damage. Still, I liked it that he didn't mind her exploring.

He had sold a screenplay to Lifetime television, and was telling us how the money they paid was going to help him afford to renovate the barn. "It's criminal what they'll pay for a hundred-some-odd pages. But I suppose once the network gets done with rewriting it, the resemblance to my words will be reduced to an outline. On the advice of my pal here," he said, and he linked his skinny arm through Ness's, "I'll take the money and run, thank you very—"

"Sorry," I said. "I'm thrilled for you about the movie. But I can't get my mind off Nance's not-eating thing. David, you came up with that great idea to get Phoebe talking. Can't you think of any way to get through to Nance? She's skin and bones. I tried making her favorite stuff, but it didn't work. Now I'm thinking intervention, but what if that just permanently estranges her?"

He smiled. "As someone who was skin and bones himself not long ago, it's hard to imagine being healthy and not wanting to eat. These new medicines give me appetite, but the long-term effects? Who knows? Maybe all she needs is vitamin B shots. What have you got to lose by trying the intervention? Get James in on it. Tell her no wedding until she gains five pounds."

"She could use more like fifteen," Ness said.

"Start with five. And tell her she has to see a shrink."

"Well," I said, sighing. "That ought to go over like a lead balloon."

He reached down to pet Duchess, who happily wagged her tail, thumping the wood floor. "Tell her," he said, "if she doesn't agree to the following terms, she'll never see this dog again."

Ness laughed and snuggled up close to him. "Didn't I tell you this man was brilliant?"

"Let's see how he does at Scrabble," I said, and dumped the tiles out on his coffee table, a mosaic of many colors, broken tiles laid every which way. "This is a nice table," I said. "Did you get it in LA?"

"Ness made it for me," he said. "She's kind of brilliant herself."

"You're blushing," I told my former roommate. "I didn't know black people could blush."

"Hush up, you cracker," she told me.

David *tsk*ed her, but he didn't tell her to stop. They were sitting so close their thighs touched. I knew how that felt when I was with Earl, as if my senses all zoomed down to my legs, hoping they'd get lucky. Ness and David behaved like two people in love, and I wondered if it was possible to be in a relationship with all the romance and none of the sex.

I won the right to laying down the first word by drawing the X. "N-e-x-u-s. Nexus," I said.

"I challenge," Ness said. "Brand names aren't allowed."

"You might as well forfeit the game right now, Precious," David said. "Nexus means 'interconnection' or 'link,' and you just gave Beryl fifty extra points."

"Damn!"

Duchess barked. David set his hand on Ness's knee, and kept it there all night. We played six games. I won them all.

LATE-NIGHT THOUGHTS:

Tonight at the hospital Phoebe was cranky. She wouldn't eat her butterscotch pudding, and told the nurse who brought the tray to go pound sand. Yes, the pudding did look like baby poop, but I bet it tasted fine. Not the best way to act around Nance, is what I was thinking. When James came by I grabbed his arm and said, "Let's take a walk, go get Phoebe some magazines."

"Phoebe doesn't read magazines," he told me as we made our way to the elevator.

"This isn't really about magazines, James. It's about Nance, and anorexia."

He stiffened like I'd told him she wore black spandex panties and favored whips.

"We all love her," I said. "But if she loses any more weight she's going to end up in the hospital next to Phoebe with a bad heart herself. We need you in on this, James. Please don't pretend it's not happening."

We were in the gift shop by the time I finished laying out my idea for the intervention. James threw money on the counter for ladies' magazines that Phoebe would make fun of and give to the nurses. The gift shop lady jumped back a foot. "Sorry," he said.

"I know how it can be," she said, trying to soothe him.

But she didn't know this. I kept quiet. Let him think about it until we got into the elevator. A bald-headed woman in a wheelchair got on, and smiled at us. When she got off at the next floor, James was crying. "How come I finally meet the girl of my dreams, and my life is this messed up? How come my sister is an emotional wreck and asked me would I adopt her baby? I'm the one who should have anorexia," he said to me. "How come all the women I love are so . . . so . . . sweet Jesus, I can't even find the words! Are you happy, Beryl? Does anything ever work out without all these life-and-death, insane complications?"

I patted his arm. "Sure. Look at Earl and me."

He sighed. "I needed to hear that."

"Anytime." I rubbed his back and we stood looking out the window at CHOP's million-dollar view of the water. *Oh, all that blue, like God's own tears,* Ness would say. No matter how far you stood from it, it was gorgeous. Nobody owned it, not the rich people in their mansions, or the people who wanted to drill offshore for oil. Well, maybe the otters owned it. Or the whales. I wouldn't mind relinquishing oceanfront property to mammals that huge and peaceful.

"I don't know what to do first," James said.

"Let's start with Nance," I said. "We'll just sit down and talk to her, like we're talking right now. We'll make a plan."

"What about Phoebe? Do you think she really means it about the baby? She told me if I didn't want it, she was going to find an adoption lawyer and make sure it went to a movie star so it could have everything it ever wanted."

"That's hormones talking," I said. "Once that baby is born and laid into her arms, she'll fall in love. You'll see."

But deep down I wasn't sure of anything. I had no idea how to cheer Phoebe up, how to make her want the baby she carried. Any second Nance might blow away in a strong wind. Despite taking care and her handfuls of pills, Ness still carried the HIV virus. And then there was me, the consummate liar: I didn't know where Earl was. To keep the delicate balance of our world from toppling down the cliff into the ocean, I pretended so hard I could have been acting in one of David's screenplays. For sure, one of us would earn an Academy Award.

Baby's breath

Delicate, graceful, and terribly romantic, *Gypsophila muralis* is a natural for wedding bouquets. Color varieties include rose, blush white, and pure white. With flowers perched on wiry stems, the plants can attain two to three feet in height. They prefer an open, dry place, and limestone dirt; can survive in partial shade, but possess no tolerance whatsoever for acid soil. Some label them herbs, others say weeds, and while it's true that *Gypsophila* can disturb native grasses, in Europe they're an excellent source of saponin, and livestock graze successfully upon them. The mode of pollination remains a mystery, but floral structure suggests wind-driven cross-pollination. A single plant averages thirteen thousand seeds. Known colloquially as chalk plant, gauze flower, and fairy plant.

Phoebe

15

Blues and Pinks

MORE AND MORE OF LATE, interaction with my belly became unavoidable. That bitchy morning nurse who was supposed to give me my sponge bath actually handed me the washcloth and told me to scrub my own funky self. And the annoying ultrasound technician loved to wheel the monitor close to my face while he swooshed the wand over my bulge, so that what once looked like linoleum patterns now definitely resembled a blind person's drawing of a human being. "Oh, look," he'd pointed out, "it's sucking its thumb. Right there you can see the baby's bottom, isn't that cute?" Thumb sucking and flashing its butt? Already with the bad habits, I thought to myself, while I pointedly ignored the screen. This baby has nothing of Juan in it; it's all my rotten genes, not to mention a few of my mother's.

"PHOEBE?" SHE SAID THAT MORNING when she called me. At the farm I had caller ID; in the hospital they'd put through a call from Charlie Manson. "I'm so glad you took my call. I've been worried sick about you ever since . . ." I heard the wiggle in her voice. "Will you at least tell me how you are feeling?"

"Bloated," I said. "Cranky. Tired of this place. But I'm all done hating you, Mother. I've moved on to hating this baby. There, aren't you happy you asked?"

"Sweetheart, you just go on and pour your heart out. That's what mothers are for. Bert and I are seriously considering flying out to see you, if you'll have us."

I sighed. I really didn't blame her anymore. I had traveled far beyond blame. Existentialism? Bah. For me it was nihilism or nothing, ha-ha. The way I saw things, the world was one big mousetrap, and every dangerous moment just reeked of cheese. What could I say to my mother, who wanted to hear my forgiveness by way of me unloading? *Don't bother? Wait until my funeral because there's no way I'm going to live through this?* I went for safety, always a big subject with Mother. "You don't want to fly in winter weather. Think of the long waits in the airport, the deicing of wings and so on. I'll call you on Christmas like I always do. Stay home and enjoy your new husband."

"I see him every day," my mother said. "This year I need to see you."

I pondered the practicality of getting a videophone installed. "How about I come see you instead?" I offered, with no intention of going through with such a paper-thin promise.

"Oh, Phoebe, do you mean it? That would be lovely," she said. "It will only take a minute to get the guest room ready. One of us will fly out as soon as you're—"

"Ready to come home?" I said, sparing us both the discomfort of mentioning the baby. I knew then that James had told her about my plan to give him the baby. Apparently brothers never outgrew the booger factor.

NANCE BROUGHT ME A BOUQUET of star lilies and baby's breath. I told her I loved lilies, and listened to her careful chatter about the upcoming holidays and kept her sitting there any way I could for as long as I could in order to participate in "the plan." Her jean jacket hung off her arms, reminding me of a scarecrow in need of restuffing.

"We've made a space for the—"

"Baby?" I said. "Nance, you don't have to tiptoe. James is

having the papers drawn up. This is really, truly what I want to do. But there is one aspect we need to discuss."

"What?"

"The adoption's conditional on you eating more than two hundred calories a day."

She flashed me an irritated look. "I'll see Lester for a special diet if that makes you happy."

I tried to reach her hand to squeeze it, but anything over the bump of my belly might as well have been on another planet. "Good," I said. "That's a start."

And then, as planned, the Bad Girls walked in with James. Ness shut the door behind her and stood next to it with her arms folded across her chest. James looked squinchily out the window. Nance sent everyone her well-raised, Southern-belle smile and tried to pretend this wasn't about her. "I didn't expect to see you all—"

Beryl interrupted her. "Nancy, it's time to stop pretending. You know why we're here. We love you, and watching you starve yourself is no longer an acceptable way to live. You're not just hurting yourself, you're hurting all of us."

Nance let go with all the usual defenses. "That's ridiculous! Didn't I eat breakfast this very morning?"

"Grapefruit doesn't count," Beryl continued.

"Look at the nutrition bars here in my handbag. Just look. I even have peanut butter flavor! Would someone with an eating disorder so much as smell peanut butter?"

Ness nudged James, and I watched my brother start to cry. "Please," was all he could manage to get out as he held up the vial of diet pills.

"Those are private," she started to say. "You have no right to," she added. "I never," she said, but apparently decided better and shook her head slowly from side to side.

"My turn, I guess," I said. "No eating-disorder program, no baby."

Then Ness delivered her line. "You have an appointment with a dietitian right here in CHOP in approximately fifteen minutes. Shall we go?"

James took her arm and walked her out the door. "Hey," I

said to Beryl just before she followed. "Will you do me a favor?"

"Anything," she said.

"I need Sadie's journal."

She kissed me. "It'll be here before you know it. Nance loves you, Phoebe. She just doesn't know how to say thanks."

Her big brown eyes filled with tears. "If you cry I will throw my bedpan at you," I said. "Go forth and make that girl ingest calories."

As soon as they all left, I begged the nurse to set the flowers on the windowsill, as far from me as humanly possible. Nance's well-intentioned gesture overwhelmed me, the scent of the lilies threatening to give me morning sickness all over again. At once the lilies began flinging their petals off like slutty teenagers, fading fast, as both lilies and the teen years do, but no less pungent for the process. I'd never really liked them much, or baby's breath. Sturdier, unscented flowers got my vote—daisies, sunflowers, and chrysanthemums with their pompon explosion. Still, the scent of the dying lilies tried its hardest to beat the hospital antiseptic smell that permeated everything from the plastic tumbler and straw I sipped my water from to the perfect hem in my bedsheets. Surely somewhere in my aunt Sadie's journal there was at least a passing reference to the lily. Of course I couldn't remember it. Reading that book was like stepping into an ever-changing story. As much as it was possible for someone as bloated as me, I turned in the bed, and slept.

"'WHEAT AND LILIES; LILIES AND WHEAT. Carry one to marry, the other to eat.' Phoebe, did you know that certain churches ordered the removal of the stamen and pistil in the lily flower, in order for it to remain virgin? And Pliny dunked them in red wine because the color white annoyed him. Let me tell you a story about Ernest Wilson and the lily. For the love of the flower, he nearly lost his life. Lugging home a vast amount of lily bulbs by mule train, he was interrupted by a rockslide. He lay in the road so the mules could pass over him, could deliver those flowers to the world. What passion, what bravery. What utter madness! Now ask yourself, what are you willing to give up for flowers?"

DINNER ARRIVED, via an overworked nurse's aide. I didn't need to lift the metal dome covering my tray to know its contents. They served me one of two things: tepid vegetable broth or overcooked vegetables. CHOP's kitchen would come in dead last in a vegetarian Pillsbury bake-off. I rolled to my side like a Marine World whale showing its belly to the crowd, and fondly remembered dinners at the farm back when it was just us girls. Homemade pizza. Beryl's chocolate decadence cake. Back when eating was a breeze, Nance's endless lectures on high protein intake. I fell asleep to the remembered pitch of her faint Southern accent, which never failed to gain in intensity when she was losing an argument. The way that girl could jaw on about things was aerobic. No wonder she stayed so slim.

My brother pulled up a chair next to my hospital bed, and I was startled back to earth.

"How'd it go with the dietitian?"

"Okay, I guess. They're setting up a program for her. You know, Pheebs," he continued. "After your heart attack, I was here every night, sitting in one of these incredibly uncomfortable chairs. Of course you may not remember this, but I believe it earns me points all the same."

I rubbed my eyelids, the only part of me that hadn't gained weight. "James. Be serious. I was in a coma. Comas don't count."

"They say people in comas remember all kinds of weird shit."

"Well, I'm starting to wish I was in a coma now. I can't get comfortable no matter which way I lay. Would you please tuck another pillow under my knees?"

He did. "I got so I even liked the cafeteria food. They make a pretty mean tuna-noodle thing downstairs."

"I'm sure the tuna would have something to say about that."

My brother the carnivore laughed, that forced and annoying *yuk-yuk-yuk* everyone had used on me since the day Juan died in the wreck. "Have at my dinner, champ. I'm certainly not going to eat it. I don't do gruel."

James lifted the plate cover to reveal a few soggy pieces of cauliflower floating in an unnaturally yellow liquid. Alongside the bowl were four packages of unsalted saltines. "It doesn't look so bad." He replaced the lid. "Tell me what you want. If you'll eat this, I'll go fetch whatever your heart desires."

"Can you really do that, James? Can you go out this door and bring back the one person in the world who made my life worth living?"

"D-dammit, Phoebe," he stammered in reply.

"Fine, I want a spicy bean burrito," I said. "And a sesame-tofu salad from Tillie Gort's in Sierra Grove, heavy on the ginger. I want blueberry-buckwheat pancakes from Fifi's, some of Ness's vegetarian lasagna, that three-bean salad Sadie used to make with the balsamic vinegar and chopped garlic. For dessert I want a pound of Godiva chocolates, no nuts, no caramel, just the darkest chocolate chocolate ones, and a banana smoothie with a shot of wheat grass to chase it all down."

He leaned back in his chair and loosened his tie. "What in hell is wheat grass?"

"You know, the stuff you say looks like cow throw-up. They serve it in Dixie cups at Whole Foods."

He groaned. "How much longer before they remove the alien that's taken over my sister?"

"Well, according to the latest ultrasound, in two weeks they'll split me open like the rotten melon that I am. And then you know what happens."

"What?"

"I presume they'll remove the baby, sew me up, and total my bill, which insurance won't entirely cover, and I will hand this child over to you and your fiancée."

He rubbed his face all over, and then concentrated his fingers on his left temple. "All that aside, Phoebe. You know what I mean. Are you going to fall completely apart when the baby comes? Am I going to have to sign papers to have you committed?"

"The only papers you need to sign are for the adoption. And you and Nance are going to make great parents. Just think—you get to start parenthood without having your sleep cycle ruined, or seeing your wife's body stitched up like Frankenstein's monster."

"The first time you said that it was funny. It's starting to sound like a political speech."

"Well, then, I must be losing my touch."

He tore the seal on one of the unsalted saltine packets and shoved a cracker in his mouth. "If I were you, I think I could see how you might be worried. I mean if it looks anything like—"

I pointed a finger, my only weapon. "Shut up, James. You are marrying a girl who weighs eighty-nine pounds. Do not even go remotely near my worries."

He chewed and swallowed, crumpled the cracker cellophane, and tossed it on my tray. When he stood up I saw the burden of all this in his shoulders. He walked to the window and pulled aside the vinyl-lined curtains. My handsome brother, who looked a little bit like JFK Jr., bless his soul, stared out toward the Pacific Ocean, something I had not been able to do since I checked into this dreadful prison. Earlier in the day Ness and Beryl had ganged up on me, too. *Juan would have loved this, Phoebe. If the baby looks like him, won't that be a comfort?* Only Nance left the subject of Juan alone. That was our deal maker; I would lay off how she was dealing with the big *A,* and she wouldn't say the *J* word. Why did everybody suddenly insist I talk about him? Was this what they meant by closure? Okay, he'd been dead nearly seven months, but did the passage of time mean anything other than I'd managed not to lose my sanity while hanging on to his baby? In my book that was called acting for the greater good. Nobody said you had to like what you were doing, you just had to muddle through.

James came back and stood by my bed. "I know we're not supposed to get you riled. Lester and Dr. Jenkins have made this abundantly clear. But I for one am pretty damn sick of all this sarcasm, Phoebe. I'm going to call Mother and tell her to fly on out tonight."

"Too late," I said. "She beat you to it."

"And you talked to her? Did you two . . . you know?"

"Patch things up?" I wanted to cry. There was no patching

up my mother interrupting my wedding day, setting into motion a chain of events that led me to this bed about to give up a baby I might otherwise have adored. "We talked," I said.

"But that's good. Isn't it?"

I didn't know, and couldn't think of a smart answer. "About the baby," I said. "Before I sign the papers I want to be sure. You and Nance have to be in it for the long haul. No divorce ten months into the deal, right? This baby needs a stable home. Loving parents. It needs to feel love from all angles. Real love, James, not just yuppie baby paraphernalia and an English nanny."

He sat down again in the chair next to my bed. I watched him reach for another saltine, then change his mind and leave it sitting in its cellophane jacket. "We'll make it," he said. "I wouldn't go through with this wedding if I had a single doubt. What about you, Pheebs? What's your next move?"

"I plan to start doing wheelchair aerobics, and as soon as I'm strong enough I'll be taking a wheelchair tour of Europe. I want to see all the great museums."

"Europe? What about the farm?"

"Screw the farm. Turn it into an office building. What do I care?"

James looked at me, aghast. "You care."

"Not really."

"Why, you chubby little liar."

I pressed my call button, and a disembodied nurse's voice came out of the wall speaker. "Yes?"

"Can you send someone in to help me tie my sneakers? I'd like to go for a run, nothing huge, just a mile or so."

James blew out a breath. "Fine, I'll run the farm. We'll take the baby. Nance and I will cuddle and rock and feed and nurse it through chicken pox and colic and whatever else comes down the pike. If it's a boy I'll take him to the batting cages and teach him to throw a fastball, even though it means someone will have to teach me first. If it's a girl, I'll pay for her ballet lessons and buy her a thoroughbred horse and warn her about the true nature of men, which is nothing short of evil. Nance will win Mother-of-the-Year, and we'll send the baby to an Ivy League school and he or she will become a doctor or a concert pianist or the next Margaret fucking Mead. You know, you going on about how you're the only one who hurts, Phoebe, flat out exhausts me. We all lost Juan. He wasn't just yours. He was somebody's friend, he was a coworker at UPS, he was Bighead's cousin, he was my potential brother-in-law, and out of all of us, you're the lucky one because you had something of his forever, that baby. But Nance and I will raise it instead. We really will. You're right. This isn't a decision to be taken lightly by anyone. Colburn thinks we're nuts, but I've had him draw up the adoption papers."

Papers? I hadn't thought of it, our names inked on heavy paper, stamped by some court. "Good. That's what I wanted to hear."

James blinked.

For once I couldn't tell if he was trying to call my bluff. "Anything else?" I asked. "Or are you finished bitching me out?"

He lifted my spoon from the dinner tray. "One more thing. Please eat the damn soup the poor thing needs to grow its final inch. Then give it to Nance and me. You're right; we'll love the baby to the best of our collective abilities. But don't expect me to feel sorry for you anymore. You may be handicapped, but bad legs don't give you the right to act like a spoiled brat."

He tugged on his leather jacket, rolled his scarf around his neck, walked out of my room, and left me just the tiniest bit speechless.

LATER, WHEN THE EVENING NURSE CAME IN and took my vital signs, she asked, "Would you like me to remove your dinner tray?"

"Not just yet," I said quietly.

She pressed her palm to my cheek. I'd bitten her head off so many times that by now she didn't bother to make small talk. Satisfied I wasn't spiking a fever, she shut my light off and left my door propped open so the hallway light cast a brilliant yellow wedge at the edge of the darkness. It was impossible to ignore. I lay there, blood throbbing through my body, every now and then my pulse running a little ragged from my brother's words. To add further insult, my stomach began growling. Oh, it was too much, this pregnancy business. Even without the complications of grief, it would have been difficult, but now? I didn't even feel like a person. My body had become a swollen host for a greedy parasite. While my life force dwindled, that creature I'd traded for the man I loved who actually loved me back grew complex organs, tied them all together, spun off cells that each had a job to do and were eager to get on with it. "You had better be worth this," I whispered in the dark. "You had better be pretty damn special and not look anything like him, or I am never coming back from that wheelchair tour of Europe. There's got to be a tour going somewhere. Mother will help me find one. And forgive me, it's nothing personal, but if it's all the same, I'd rather not be your aunt."

He or she did not move. Asleep? Like they said about people in comas, could those *in utero* really hear what was being said?

I lifted the lid off the horrid soup and, cold as it was, I drank it down. For my efforts, I received a hard kick, and I pressed my hand to the place where I could feel what felt like a rounded knee. "What more do you want?" I asked. "I've already given you my soul."

JAMES WAS BACK EVERY MORNING, waiting outside my door when my morning nurse walked out with my sponge-bath basin. "Sorry I've been such a shit lately," he said. "I'd blame it on PMS if I thought I could get away with it."

I pretended to sulk, but really I was surprised he'd backed down. What a wimp. I could hold a grudge forever, but in the spite department, James was cowering like a scared little bunny. Nance's influence, I thought. "How's Nance? What did she eat for breakfast this morning?"

"Half a waffle," he said. "And half a banana. I watched. The dietitian gave her menu plans. One of us checks up on her, and we try to hide it, but she's wise to our game. Still, she's eating. Now we've moved on to other obsessions."

"Such as?"

"The wedding. The plans sounded so great, and everything seemed doable, but lately it's gotten way out of control."

"How so?"

"Now she wants orchids instead of roses, and champagne instead of punch. We must have a formal harpist for the wedding march, and Bighead play for the reception, at which we're now serving prime rib roast. I may have inherited Sadie's deep pockets, Phoebe, but for the amount of money she wants to spend on this shindig we could put a hefty down payment on a condo in Maui."

"Nance wants a big production because she grew up poor. Think of it this way—one day of fabulous will make up for her rotten childhood."

What I didn't say was what if she doesn't get it right, if marrying James doesn't make her happy, or if she stops eating again? Didn't rehab programs for eating disorders have one of the biggest failure rates ever? Sometimes anorexics died. If the baby lost Nance, she wouldn't have any mother.

He looked at me sheepishly. "I know she's had a hard time. And she takes every little thing out on herself. Especially—"

"James. We've all been watching her starve herself for months. The question is, Why did it take you so long to see it?"

He sighed and looked away. "I meant about the journalist."

"Rotten Rick? I keep forgetting about him. I think she's as over that as she's going to get, brother. Once you slide that ring on her finger, she'll be yours body and soul."

James took a while to respond. He looked out the window and straightened my sheet, and then he said, "I hope you're right. I know it's wrong to have doubts that she loves me, but I do." He turned the chair he'd been standing in front of around and straddled it so he sat facing the chair's back. "And I have to say, you all think I was ignoring the not eating, but that's not true. All the time I'd ask her why order an entrée if she expected me to finish it. She'd tell me she was too nervous to eat, or that she'd stuffed herself at lunch. We'd go to these parties with five-star catering; she'd take one of everything and then leave it on her plate, like setting up a still life for a painter. The only things I'd see her put in her mouth were sugarless gum and—"

"Spare me the gory details," I said. "I thought you two hadn't done that yet."

"I was going to say Diet Coke. We haven't done that *or* the other thing. Clinton might not call it sex, but I do."

I pressed my fingers to my forehead, where things were feeling most unpleasant. "Those food Nazis forgot my breakfast," I said. "And now I have a headache. Any minute now Dr. Jenkins is going to show up and tell me to think happier thoughts when what I could really use is a pound of trail mix and a horse-size Tylenol."

"I'm driving you crazy," James said. "I'll leave, I promise."

"James, you're not driving me anywhere I haven't been for months now. But do I look like a shrink? You have to walk a hard line with Nance. The diet's not going to be enough. Make her see a therapist about the weight thing. And the Rick thing. Keep on her. These things tend to come back."

He frowned. "I don't want to lose her by pressuring her."

I shook my painful head. "That's not losing somebody, that's loving them. Which is worse? She breaks off the engagement and gets help, or she faints on the honeymoon before you guys can consummate the longest foreplay in the history of sex? Besides, she'll need her strength for the baby. I'm only her friend. You're going to be her husband. Keeping after her is your job. Now be a nice brother, and go give that desk nurse a hundred-dollar bill in exchange for two extra-strength Tylenol."

The nurse he brought to check on me shooed my brother away from the bed, pulled my drapes shut, and took my blood pressure. "Tell me the numbers," I insisted when she unwrapped the cuff from my arm, but she wouldn't. She made James leave, and he hadn't even been there ten minutes. "At least get me some toast," I begged her, but she told me to rest, take a little nap. Night, day, what did it matter? "Bitch," I said, but softly, because she was the one who sometimes gave me a foot rub, and how can you totally hate someone who's willing to massage lotion into a stranger's feet—feet the stranger herself hasn't seen in several months?

DOCTORS CAME AND WENT ALL DAY, a steady stream of them, taking notes, measuring my belly, touching the bumps along my spine, poring over my EKG tape as if it were the latest Tom Clancy novel. They used a lot of big words, advising each other as to what the C-section would entail, how it might "impact" my cardiac *muscle*—a much better word than heart, it seemed to me—and meanwhile I speculated whether or not my mother could have prevented my own "disability" if she'd had such a team at her disposal. Orthopedic guys, neonatologists, obstetricians in pairs as if heading off to some twat convention held on a high-tech ark. At the end of the parade there was Lester, who in better days I might have called my old pal. "Thanks for abandoning me to the Germans," I said. "This is what a person gets for paying her bills in full?"

"Dr. Jenkins got you to this point, didn't she?"

"Hello? I believe I got myself here by lying abed and peeing in a bedpan. And before you ask, no, I'm not yet convinced it was worth it."

He perched on the end of my bed and paged through my chart.

"Anything interesting I should know about, not that you'd tell me?"

He didn't look up. "I'm going to be there, Phoebe. I've told Judith I'm scrubbing in. We've scheduled you for tomorrow morning, early."

"Tomorrow? How early?"

"Someone will be in to prep you at six, and hopefully by seven we'll be done."

"Ah. So you won't miss your tee time."

He granted me a slight smile. "Something along those lines."

Big, noisy tears I hadn't known were in me chose that moment to issue forth. Lester handed me a Kleenex.

"It's normal to feel scared," he said.

"I'm not scared, I'm pissed off."

He handed me another Kleenex. "It's reasonable to feel emotional."

"You call this emotional? Try not crying for six months if you want a hint of what emotional feels like."

"Jesus, Phoebe. I think I liked you better when you were unconscious."

"Come on, Lester, give me a shot, a pill, something to quiet the panic. I think I might be having another heart thing. Get out your stethoscope and take a listen."

He calmly studied the blips on my EKG readout. "You're fine. This time tomorrow, it will all be over. Your belly will hurt, but you can have drugs for the pain, and the baby will be here, Phoebe. You'll finally get to meet your child." He squeezed my hand. "Any questions?"

I sniffed into the wadded-up Kleenex. "Lester, I am so not ready for this. How in God's name did I get myself into this fix?"

He pushed his glasses up the bridge of his nose and took a moment before answering. "Correct me if I'm wrong, but I believe the phrase was 'frequent, vigorous sex'?"

The memory of my saying that a lifetime ago almost made me smile. "Stay with me a few minutes," I said. "You can bill me for the time."

We sat together, quiet. There had been no breakfast tray this morning, and at lunch all the prodding physicians had put me off my feed. Instead of my dinner tray I had Lester's company, and now it all made a desperate kind of sense. We listened to the sound of visitors coming down the hall to visit the new gynecological patients. I worried they would move me to the maternity floor. I didn't relish the thought of that. Lester promised he'd make sure that didn't happen. I thought about when Sadie was dying, and how she didn't make sense a lot of the time, but I recalled with utter clarity how she went on about not having her own children, how she said James and I had made up for that, but I could tell that we were a Band-Aid for what she was missing. Her rich life—all that travel, the men, a variety of poinsettia named after her, her art collection—in the end all she wanted was kin. I'd thought that when the Bad Girls came to live with me, I'd made the best kind of family a person could, a chosen group to call my own. Some family. Ness had HIV, any minute now Beryl would be on her way back to Alaska, and Nance the anorexic was about to become my sister-in-law. Nothing ever stayed calm. A person could fall in love with a man, and against all odds that man could love her back. A person could become pregnant when it was so iffy an undertaking not even her own doctor believed in it, and still and always, there were more surprises headed your way.

"Lester?"

"Yes, Phoebe?"

"I wouldn't have your job for anything."

"So you've told me."

"Even if something goes wrong tomorrow, promise me, you won't let them put me all the way under. I want to be as awake as I can, even if it hurts. I know how crappy my odds are for a long life. Already I've gotten so much more than I expected. So I don't want to miss this. Especially if it compromises the—you know—baby."

In acknowledgment he squeezed my hand. After a while I feigned sleep, and Lester, good sport that he was, pretended I really was out for the night. He went home to his well-coiffed wife, his expensive view for which he paid so dearly, and the few hours between medical crises that allow him to enjoy what came along with his paycheck. Me, I lay there holding on to a version of myself that would end for good in just a few hours. I had nearly perfected the role of pregnant, bitchy whiner. I'd had to, in order to hold myself together. So why was it I suddenly didn't feel quite ready to let that "me" go? Think of Rome, I told myself. Wheeling myself along the cobbled roads where all that history took place. Everyone around me speaking another language so I didn't have to say anything. The sun. Surely on that side of the world the sun lit the sky in a much brighter arc.

SOMETIME TOWARD MORNING I felt the urge to talk to Sadie. Because pregnant women are forgiven any sort of strange cravings, I spoke out loud in a normal tone of voice to this aunt who'd left me a farm, lingered in death, and led me to love and loss and now this baby. "Okay, Sadie. I did it. I can't remember what you said to me, not all of it anyway, but I recall there were promises, and Juan and me, we had the shortest damn love affair on earth. Broken promises from you, who never once lied to me that I'm aware of, so this had better make up for it. Sadie? You hear me? I can stand the physical pain; hell, you're talking to the girl who got fitted for her first training bra in Shriners' Hospital, measured with a yellow tape by a freaking nun. I can take having to go back to the wheelchair full-time, that's no biggie; I could even picture dying if it means I get to be with Juan again. But that's it, Sadie. Anything more dramatic, like a stillborn baby, and heads are going to roll. I don't care if you're dead. I don't want to hear that this is God's will, or any of that. I will come and find you and God both, and you will be eternally sorry. So get on the horn, and tell him this baby has to be healthy. Tell him to take me if he has to, but too many people are counting on the baby. I think he'll agree we've had enough sorrow here."

Maybe the light in the endless hall flickered. Or one of my tired brain synapses momentarily sparked like a dud firecracker. Maybe it was my weakness for doors left ajar, and the promise of Juan about to enter through that space. More likely I was exhausted from being hungry and affecting such a witchy exterior all these months. The thing with the light happened so fast that no one, least of all me, could truly say whether it was a short in the electricity or God winking in agreement. Quickly, so as not to jinx anything, I shut my eyes and played possum. I was terrified, not of having the operation, but that my words might have been heard. I must have slept, because it felt like only two minutes later that the orderly guys were there with the gurney to take me to the OR. "Is it really morning?" I asked.

They pulled open the blinds to show me. Sure enough, the sky was starting to lighten. However, it wasn't Rome. It was the same old Bayborough coastline that I used to think was so beautiful I could hardly stand it when the sun set for the night.

IN THE OPERATING ROOM Lester promised they'd go light on the drugs, but even though he stood there in his scrubs right beside her, Dr. Jenkins apparently had other plans. When she ordered the anesthesiologist to push the medicine into my IV, suddenly I was standing naked on the surface of Mars. Chemical warmth spread throughout my limbs, slowing me to dream speed, taking me to Planet Peaceful in about three seconds. I turned my head to the right, which took about three days, so I could see just who it was administering these heavy potions. He was wearing a mask, but his dark, merry eyes peered above the pale blue of the paper. His skin was the color of coffee, his eyebrows expressive, and he looked so familiar, I was sure if I'd had my wits I could have remembered his name. "Juan," I said. "It's about time you showed up. Did you know that you almost missed everything?"

Before he could answer me, the room spun and we were in the greenhouse. All around us the flowers bloomed at light speed. To keep from passing out I had to shut my eyes and will the blossoms back into seeds, which rattled in their hulls as they rained down from Florencio's weathered hands into the rich, damp soil. "I love you," Juan said. "You are all I've ever wanted and then some." I tried to lift my hand to his, but my wrist had turned to lead. I watched my love spiral away from me until he was nothing more than a speck of dust in my eye.

"Give her some oxygen," I heard Lester say, and I breathed in what felt like the silver that stars are made of, something cleaner and sharper than plain old air could ever be.

"That's better," he said.

Meanwhile Dr. Jenkins and her company tugged away at my belly, a strange feeling, unpleasant and invasive. "Stop," I said, but they'd set a tent up in front of my face, which effectively kept me from seeing anything except blue rippled paper. I could hear the frighteningly liquid sounds of my own fluids, and the sucking of machines keeping the mess under control. "I think I might be sick," I told the doctor in the mask.

"Look at me," he said gently. I studied the crinkle of fine lines around his eyes. He began whistling, and I knew then that this was my bed, and I was waking from a dream that seemed so real I couldn't wait to tell Juan about it. Juan, who was in the shower, getting ready to start his day driving the brown van with the gold UPS letters on the side, earning his paycheck to buy me flowers I didn't need, chocolate my roommates swiped, and the new setting for his grandmother's diamond. Platinum. More precious than silver or gold.

"Do you know how much I've missed you?" I said. "Call in

sick today. Come back to bed and hold me. I'll make it worth your while."

"We're giving you two units of blood, Phoebe," Lester informed me. "Just as a precaution."

"That's nice," I said, as the loop I was traveling changed course once again. Red poinsettias lined the path, blooming as I walked by. Each flower's center held a hundred-dollar bill. I would wait until dinner to tell the Bad Girls that I was giving them bonuses, but, oh! wouldn't they be happy. "When's lunch?" I asked. "Can we have pad thai noodles?"

The melodic clatter of metal instruments against one another, but it wasn't Joey's band. Latin words, but not the names of flowers. At the center of my flower, someone was digging up a tree so old its roots held grudges that predated the dinosaurs.

I looked at the masked man. "You're not Juan, are you?"

He shook his head.

"I'm drugged up like a rock star, aren't I?"

He chuckled. The rest of them continued to pretend I wasn't there, but I knew I was. I could tell when it came time to lift the baby from me to the world, because the energy in the room increased, and everyone stepped closer to the table. Even the drug doc leaned away from me to see what was happening.

"We have a baby girl," Lester announced.

I concentrated hard on the questions I'd memorized. "How does her spine look?"

"Perfect. Straight. No abnormalities."

"Heart?"

"Beating at a normal rate."

Then I heard her cry. I shut my eyes rather than acknowledge this child in our midst. If I let her know my feelings—that just hearing her voice tore my heart in two—if she knew that I would trade her entire life for just one more day of Juan's—if we so much as made brief eye contact, I was sure she'd pull some dramatic life-threatening event just to get back at me.

"Want to see your baby?" Dr. Jenkins asked, her voice kind for the first time in our history together. No doubt she saved every shred of niceness for such moments as these.

"Later," I said. "I'm tired, and it hurts so much. Listen," I said to the gas doc. "How much do I have to pay you to send me to la-la land?"

"Free of charge," he said, and off I went.

"PHOEBE? SWEETIE, IT'S MOTHER. No need to open your eyes. I'm here. Bert is, too. You'll forgive James for calling me here, won't you? I've been aching to come, and I just couldn't miss this moment." Then I felt her whisper into my ear. "I'm so sorry about what happened. I'd give anything to change the order of things. I would. Darling, the baby is beautiful. She's so tiny and perfect. Bertram's out there snapping pictures through the nursery-room window. He bought this camera called a troll or an elf, I can't remember, all I know is it doesn't require a flash, and he keeps on crying and asking will you please allow him to be a step-grandfather to the little one."

My mother, Rita DeThomas Dunlap, could only bear to touch me through the sheet. Even then, she patted a safe place, not my cheek or my hand, but my foot. Oh, if I confronted her she'd claim to be afraid of dislodging the IV, and that she just wasn't a "toucher," but the truth was, acknowledging anything below my waist was a huge deal for Rita. Like bad Central Coast fog, her guilt filled the room. Since the day Juan died until the phone call here at the hospital, I had forced her to keep a distance. The Bad Girls told me when she called, and they kindly removed the flowers she sent. I chose to ignore everything in favor of holding on to the baby I didn't want. Now Mother was here, stepping naturally into the role of Grandma. And Bertram, the man I hardly knew, the continual reminder of what I'd lost by letting my mother and him marry first—what the hell, he could be grandfather to Nance and James's new baby. He might even do a good job of it.

Lester came into my room. "Hello, Rita. Nice to see you again. How've you been?"

My mother began one of her long-winded answers, and I couldn't bear to hear about her happy marriage, so I cut her off. "How long until I get out of here?" I asked.

"You're awake," my mother said.

Lester snorted. "Was she pretending to be asleep? For God's sake, Phoebe, stop this nonsense! We'll let you out in a few days. Your blood count's looking good, but we want to keep a close watch, avoid any post-op complications."

"Make it as soon as possible, Lester. I have plans."

"Sweetie?" my mother said. "What plans?"

"Michigan," I said. "I've never seen it. I'm going home with you."

Lester sighed. "You're not going anywhere for at least a week."

A nurse wheeled an isolette into the room, and I clenched my fists. "Here's your baby. You can feed her a little water from the bottle. Let me show you how—"

"Hold it right there," I said to the nurse. "Mother, is James here?"

"Yes. He's just out in the hall with that lovely girl."

"Take the baby to him," I said. "The baby. I'm not keeping it. Her. She's my wedding present to them. And Lester, can we see about getting me moved to a surgical floor? I really don't think I'm up to being around all these infants."

Beryl

16

Farm Journal

THE DAY EARL'S POSTCARD ARRIVED I was kneading the flaxseed I'd forgotten to add to my chocolate rye bread into the dough. Without the seeds I knew it wouldn't toast up with that nutty, irresistible perfume. Since it's the rare person who can't be tempted by the smell of fresh-baked bread, and Sadie's kitchen was the center of the house, I figured I was performing a service, so far as Nance was concerned. Yes, she was eating, but not all that much. Anyway, the postcard featured a robot breathing fire at no one in particular. It looked like a rough draft of a robot, such a great idea that it was hurried into production before it was structurally sound. Earl hadn't been introduced to Hallmark. In Alaska he had a drawer full of weird postcards—I mean hundreds of them. He also had a large collection of toys. At first I thought how weird that was, but pretty soon I was happy he had a thing for monsters and robots instead of something horrible like on-line porn. On more than one occasion he'd told me he loved cheesy Japanese horror films as much as he loved me. When he said things like that, I laughed, and he'd kiss me and outside our cabin the Canada geese flew overhead and made a wonderful racket. Alaska. I knew I was missing something wonderful by staying here at Bad Girl Creek.

Dearest B—my redheaded sprite, my well-read honey, my Arctic temptress,

Am off to Sweden for a few weeks with George and Tom to record a CD. Due to the time difference we'll probably play a lot of expensive phone tag, so I'm sending this card to let you know that every spare second I have I'll be thinking about you. Will try to send a card every day, and be back no later than Christmas. I promise to turn Stockholm on its head to find you something unforgettably Swedish, something as tacky as possible. Take care of Phoebe.

Love, E

Sweden? In November? Though we were currently enjoying a rainy day here in the valley, my heart felt like it had turned to ice. He was farther away than I had imagined. I pictured snow banked up against modern-looking buildings; tall blond women in fur-lined parkas entering and exiting said buildings with style, grace, and an overabundance of European sex appeal heading toward my Earl, and I was terrified he'd succumb to their wiles. But when Earl and his musician buddies made music, they'd stay up late creating arrangements and practicing different approaches, ignoring the world altogether. Until they chiseled out the one riff that made the music hum, made the compilation of sound not only their own but one step beyond that, nothing mattered. Not women, not food, not sleep. They'd record however many times it took to get each track right, then break for coffee and farmhand-size breakfasts at some diner run no doubt by big-breasted blond women who found aging musicians just about the sexiest thing to ever cross the fjords, or whatever the hell kind of landscape they had over there.

I hated feeling this jealous, but I did. So I took it out on the bread, and drove those flaxseeds into the dough like I meant it. When my arms grew tired of kneading, I shaped the loaves into rounds and covered them with a faded dish towel to let them rise. I sat by myself at the table, trying not to think of Swedish women, and wasn't terribly successful. What was it about the Nordic women? Okay, they had naturally blond hair and those relaxed sexual mores, but what else? What did they have that I didn't? Only everything.

An hour later, when the bread puffed up against the dish towel, the first thing I thought of was a breast. I punched it down a little harder than I needed to, gave it a mammogram with my hands. Then I reshaped it into baguette-shaped loaves and let it complete its second rise while I imagined completely crazy scenarios, like Earl having a Swedish girlfriend he forgot to tell me about, or flight attendants who put new meaning to the word *layover.*

I preheated the oven, folded the dish towel in thirds, and smoothed it flat with my hands. It took a lot of effort to keep a kitchen running properly. Lately my soul felt so worn that when I looked in the mirror I expect to see Auntie Em peering back.

As I had often done when I was in prison, I indulged in my parallel-universe fantasy. This was a realm that lagged far behind the annoying present. Back then it was Parallel Universe Beryl, who worked at the prison instead of being in it. She was the kind guard, the one who gave visitors extra minutes. She smuggled candy bars in and listened to the cons explain over and over why they didn't deserve to be there. Now I used the game to picture us Bad Girls like differently outfitted Barbies. For example, Parallel Universe Beryl Anne Barbie had never picked up a kitchen knife with evil in her heart, no. Cool, calm, and well dressed, she walked out of the room the minute an abusive man pushed her button, and continued her graduate studies. Likewise, Alternate-Time-Frame Phoebe Barbie said no to the mother who asked to marry first on what was supposed to be her wedding day, and had a ceremony so fabulous it made the eleven o'clock news. Think It Over Ness Barbie did not have unprotected sex with that handsome, cheating boyfriend. She held him at arm's length and said, *Buster, no wrapper, no nookie,* and he listened instead of sweet-talking her into the uncertain future; she went on to counsel AIDS patients, not be one. And instead of using not eating as a coping mechanism because grief was just too hard to give into, Nutritional Nance Barbie consulted the four food groups and partook of enough sustenance to remain her sassy, over-organized Southern self, and ran a food bank so precise that no child within five hundred miles went to bed with an empty stomach. But as my stepmother would say, *Wishes and dreams won't put sugar and cream in your coffee. You, young lady, will have to drink it bitter.*

The bottoms of the loaves got a little burned, and the crust came out a tad dry. I spread some sweet butter over it and that helped to soften it. I pictured Earl's shoulders in the summertime, brown and ropy with muscle. There were actually days in Alaska when it got hot enough to wear shorts. Earl in shorts, the waterfalls at the end of a long hike uphill, brightly colored mushrooms growing everywhere, and his admonition that the orange ones, the ones that looked the most like an illustration out of a fairy tale, were deadly.

The bread never got the chance to cool properly, because Ness and I stood there at the counter slicing slab after slab, slathering each with butter, and chowing down trying to fill the emptiness in our hearts now that Phoebe had gone home with her mother.

"Looks like I'll be spending Thanksgiving here," I said between bites.

"Hurray," Ness answered. "That means I don't have to watch Nance suffer over every bite of turkey by myself." This as she was consuming her fourth slice. "Lord, Beryl, I feel gross. Don't let me eat any more of this."

"Okay, I won't."

Ness rubbed her stomach and groaned. A minute later, she said, "Oh, hell. We might as well finish the loaf. We're pigs, Beryl Anne. We're absolute gluttons. Thank God no one can see us but each other."

"I know," I said. "That's why whenever I bake, I always make two loaves."

We sat there, two miserable, bloated souls. If we drank any water, the expanding bread would burst our bellies. On the bright side, flaxseeds were healthy, high in fiber. But in the sixteenth-century plant book I'd bought on my travels with Earl, flaxseed wasn't for eating. The book insisted it worked wonderfully as a poultice. Mashed to a pulp, cooked with mistletoe, gum arabic, and deer marrow, flaxseed was reported to draw pain from hidden wounds. Maybe all the seeds Ness and I had ingested would race around our bodies collecting various aches, like Cub Scouts finding arrowheads. Maybe a flaxseed poultice was just what Phoebe's heart needed. I still couldn't believe she'd done what she threatened: given the baby to James, gone home with her mother. Her *mother?* Why on earth, when she was the root cause of Juan's death? My mind ran up and down dead-end streets looking for answers. The only thing I remained sure of was that it wasn't good to separate a perimenopausal woman from her parrot.

"What's that awful noise?" Ness asked me. "It sounds like somebody smacking a big old wad of bubble gum."

"It's Duchess," I said. "I stocked up on toys at the pet supply when I thought I was going home. You know, Christmas presents for Verde."

Duchess, hearing her name, poked her head out from under the table. Her bone, some bizarre edible thing that cost me five bucks and looked like Soylent Green, was guaranteed to remove tartar from dog teeth. With Phoebe gone, Duchess had lost her task of guarding the pregnant one, and she seemed at loose ends. Her yellow muzzle had a tinge of white to it, and she slept a great deal. Like Nance, sometimes she wasn't interested in breakfast. I'd been taking her for walks, trying to perk her appetite while I made sense of things myself. For example, why wasn't I in Sweden, protecting my relationship from the tribe of big-breasted blond women?

"Well, I wish she'd chew more softly," Ness said. She checked her watch.

"Did you forget your pills?" I asked.

"No. Just wondering what you-know-who is up to over there with the baby."

Phoebe had shocked us all by going straight from the hospital to the airport with her mother and Bert. Old Bert sprang for first class all the way to Michigan. Rita said she'd send Phoebe home for Christmas, and in the meantime, to let James handle everything, including naming the baby. James said there was never any doubt in his mind that she'd be called Sarah after their aunt, and I suggested Juanita for her middle name and that was that, down in ink, on a permanent record. Phoebe behaved like her mother ordering us around was perfectly acceptable, and that a wee trip to the new homestead was nothing out of the ordinary. Rita cried as they waved good-bye—I'm sure already missing her granddaughter—but Phoebe's face was placid and calm. I wondered what would happen when the drugs wore off. According to Nance, Pheebs hadn't once seen that baby, let alone held her, not even at the hospital when the awkward task of checking little Sally out took place.

Nance said, "She asked the nurse, 'Where do I sign,' and then she scribbled her name like she was signing for a shipment of fertilizer. I thought James was going to have a heart attack when they handed Sally to him. He sat in the back of the car with her all the way home, made me drive, kept telling me to slow down, this wasn't Laguna Seca, like I was speeding or something. I mean, yes, we love her, but we have no formal training in child rearing. We're just two idiots who like the *idea* of babies."

"We should go over there and check," I told Ness. "Bring them the other loaf of bread."

She looked at me and smiled. "Only a criminal could come up with such a clever ruse."

I licked the butter from my fingers. "I got my degree at Chowchilla Women's Penitentiary," I reminded her.

Ness looked down at the glob of soy margarine she'd spilled on her shirt. "I have to go change," she said. "Don't you dare go there without me, promise?"

I nodded, and she left the room.

It fascinated me how James and Nance's wedding plans had suddenly become secondary to diapers and formula. While James's new house was finished except for some interior carpentry, and they kept the baby over there, Nance rarely spent the night. She'd wander home at all hours, the circles under her eyes so dark they looked like football makeup. I never saw her without a cup of coffee in one hand and a paperback Dr. Spock in the other, and usually a banana, which she claimed to eat for potassium as well as keeping up her energy. "How's the baby?" I'd ask, and she'd answer me in a monotone, "I swear, this is the first child in the history of the universe that does not require sleep." At night, when I got up to fetch a glass of water, I saw twin lights shining: one in James's upstairs window, and one under Nance's bedroom door, like Paul Revere warning the patriots. Did any of us get any rest?

When Ness came back in a clean sweatshirt, I stood up and slapped my leg for Duchess. "Come on," I said. "Let's go ask again if we can baby-sit Sally."

"Why bother? Nance will just say no."

"You have to think positive, Precious. It's been a whole week. She and James have got to be so sleep-deprived as to be about out of their minds by now. We'll take them the other loaf of bread, lay the guilt on about a dog who needs a walk, admire the baby, and when the moment arrives, and it will, we'll say, *Why don't you guys go grab dinner and a movie?*"

Ness laughed. "Bread might work on James, but what about Nance?"

I held up the mail, which included a new copy of *Bride* magazine. "The Martha Stewart issue," I said. "What engaged Southern girl can resist?"

SARAH JUANITA NAVA DETHOMAS—it seemed like a huge name to saddle a five-pound baby with—at least until she opened her mouth. Then she was a miniature Godzilla, her milky-sweet breath raining the loudest fire I'd ever heard. New babies make this funny, cute, yelping noise, *ooh-lah,* it sounds like, but coming out of Sally it was greatly amplified and not at all attractive. I couldn't see any of Juan's easygoing nature in her, though she did have his huge, dark eyes. If you turned Phoebe's patience on its head like a bad tarot card, Sally was definitely her daughter. Her little face, unspoiled by the C-section, seemed to be set in a permanent pout. When she opened her eyes and fixed on you, the look she delivered was pure accusation. This child was pissed.

James stood at the granite counter of his new kitchen eating the bread I'd brought. He had one of those Sub-Zero fridges big enough inside to store a whole cow, but besides opened cans of formula, it contained nothing. Nance sat on the floor by Ness's knee, running her hand through her stringy hair. Her designer jeans were spotted, and she smelled a little funky, but we pretended not to notice. Ness rocked Sally in James's Sam Maloof chair. Uninhabited, the rosewood rocker resembled the wooden spine of a dinosaur, but was actually quite comfortable. Ness crooned hymns to the baby, but eventually she grew tired of competing, and she let Sally roar on.

"Ah, motherhood," Ness said. "Let it be said that some things are overrated."

"Hear, hear," Nance remarked in agreement. "I believe I've worn out my Pappagallos walking the floor with her. Phoebe is no doubt sitting in a canopy bed being hand-fed banana pudding, milking her stitches for all they're worth, and here we sit, covered in spit-up and smelling of diapers, and this baby will not be silenced. Remind me to kill Phoebe if she ever comes back. That is, if I can find the energy. Beryl, will you kill Phoebe for me? Will you strangle her for leaving us? I'll pay you whatever you think is fair."

"Sorry," I said. "I only do knives."

James laughed, and at first it sounded like the real thing, no let's-be-nice-to-Phoebe, ha-ha-ha. Then he dropped his bread on the hardwood floor and stood there staring at it, his laugh meanwhile chugging along like a freight train that had just jumped its track and was about to buy a black leather jacket, a girly magazine, a pack of Camels, and head off to the bad side of town. Pretty soon he was sitting on the floor, laughing hysterically, pointing to the bread, which had landed butter-side down, and then he was crying, tears running down his cheeks.

Nance eyed him wearily. "James, you're doing it again," she said.

Ness and I looked at each other. Here it was, our opportunity to strike. Ness placed Sally against her shoulder and patted her back. The howling now had staccato blips in it, like some awful New Age music—Celtic annoying, was what Earl called that sort of thing. "You two," she said. "Out. Even if it's only to sleep in your cars. We'll watch Madame Foghorn. We'll put in earplugs and have us a merry old evening. Now go. That's an order."

Nance pulled James up from the kitchen floor. She swiped

her thumbs under his eyes, and he leaned against her. Her bones still showed in her face, and he was exhausted, making them look like a wised-up Hansel and Gretel as they left the bread on the floor and walked out the custom-made front doors with the Craftsman-era stained-glass inserts. Looking at the two of them, I had a gut feeling that once Nance got back on solid food, they might actually make it as a married couple. Already they'd learned one big lesson: Sex leads to babies, some of them quite challenging. And the free bonus: True intimacy includes things like baby vomit, intermittent hysteria, and an overwhelming desire for a nap.

"Quit hogging Sally, and give her to me," I said as soon as the door shut.

"Only if you let me dress her up in her cowgirl outfit first," Ness said.

"Not that awful thing," I said. "We want this baby to like us."

"Grab the camera from my bag," Ness said, already having stripped Sally down to her diaper.

Sally fought us, too. She may have been only a few weeks old, but already she had fashion opinions that did not include her gingham shirt, or her denim skirt with the adorable miniature suede fringe. She seemed especially disapproving of the camera shutter's click, but we shot a whole roll anyway. Ornery as she was, Sally was no match for two pent-up, well-rested aunts. Inside of an hour I had her sleeping on my lap, and Duchess finally stopped trembling; we were bored to death with James's Hemingway collection décor and sat paging through the Martha Stewart issue of *Bride* together, taking turns picking the tackiest thing from each page, declaring one another the winner.

"Oh," Ness said, "look at this." She pointed to a bridal ensemble that looked like an English riding habit. It was beige silk, with a pin-tucked vest and hand-tooled lace-up boots.

"You cheater," I said. "That's not tacky, it's beautiful."

"I know," she said. "Maybe I should ask David to marry me so I can wear this."

"Oh, yeah. Why not marry a gay guy? Certainly less trouble than the other variety. Plus, they have great taste. That's what I always say."

Ness looked at me like maybe Sally had absconded with my rational thinking. "Maybe it wouldn't be so bad," she said. "Maybe the best marriages are about friendship, really."

"Are you trying to tell me something?"

"Did Earl say when he was coming back?"

"That's right, change the subject," I said.

"Well, did he?"

"Christmas," I said in what I hoped was a blithe manner. "Which will be here before you know it." If he didn't fall in love with the Swedish tit factory I saw in my mind every time I closed my eyes.

"Ugh, the poinsettia sale is in less than a week," Ness said. "I suppose it's too late for me to score a Valium drip."

"Well," I said. "If we get tired of the customers, we can always bring out little Miss Foghorn. She'll drive anything away."

Sally, of course, was currently sleeping like an angel. We'd dressed her in the outfit David Snow had sent over, and who knew, maybe there were days Annie Oakley also had drool painting one cheek to a glistening sheen, and her six-shooter hands clenched in fists. Patiently I pulled each finger loose, but Sally must have been angry at the marrow level, because she tightened them right back up again. "Have you ever seen anything like that?" I asked Ness. "Is this normal?"

"The child misses her mother," Precious said.

"Jeez, Ness. It doesn't take a rocket scientist to see that."

"Let's kidnap her," she suggested. "Gather up all her paraphernalia, get her settled in Phoebe's room, and leave Nance and James a note to come fetch her in the morning."

I thought it over for a minute, but only that long. "I'll take the three A.M. feeding," I said. "I don't sleep all that much anyway."

DUCHESS WAS THRILLED to have someone to guard again. She stayed by the crib all night and day. When any of us came near to check on the baby, Duchess got to her feet and sniffed, checking that person's credentials. Sometimes I sat by the crib just to pet Duchess. Call it parrot deprivation, but I needed to stroke something with a simple outlook on life. When James and Nance saw how well Sally had adjusted, how much less she wailed, they caved right in, and we transformed Phoebe's bedroom into a nursery, signed up for shifts, and got that cranky little baby on a schedule just like the one I had in prison.

Everything was going fine. We got caught up on sleep. Sally relaxed enough to approach semicute, though she still had her moments when nothing seemed to make her happy.

The day of the poinsettia festival I stacked newspapers next to the card table where Nance had set up the cash box. Florencio let Segundo do the heavy lifting while Ness and James helped the customers make choices. Sally sat in her stroller and gathered admiring glances and compliments. One lady said, "Whose darling baby is this little sweetheart?" and we confused the hell out of her by answering in unison, "Ours." I'm sure she left thinking that Sadie's flower farm had turned into a polygamist commune. The day turned so warm we took off Sally's bonnet, and her dark hair wisped up into a curl.

It was when the lady in the red minivan that I remembered from last year pulled up that I got the shock. I had been folding newspaper around her preordered plants, when a headline on the entertainment page caught my eye. It read, TONIGHT, IN CONCERT, THE ONE, THE ONLY BUCKETHEAD. The date was this very evening.

Well, I thought. Unless Earl had found a way into my parallel universe notion, somebody was not telling me the truth.

Everyone

17

The Secret to a Successful Winter Garden

East Lansing, Michigan

Dear Bad Girls,

According to my mother, Michigan has wonderful malls, filled with every little item a heart could possibly desire. The wonderful new Buick Bertram bought her has fabulous leather seats. Bert also bought her an entire set of antique Spode china in the pattern she'd always craved—Buttercup. Yes, it's yellow—sunny, spirit-uplifting, yes-I-can yellow. And as I sit looking out the living room window at Mother's winter-charred garden, I find myself deeply relieved by the distinct lack of yellow.

Dino, Mother's full-time gardener, who is also a college student, is bundling up the canes he pruned from the forsythia. I feel certain he does not know thing one about how to shape forsythia, because this poor specimen is starting to look like an extra in a Tim Burton film. Had I the energy, I'd roll out onto the porch and give him a Florencio-inspired lecture. *For to cut, make proper angle, sí?*

Just like a crazy quilt, my belly is knitting itself back together. It will never look the same, but oh, well, who's gonna see it besides you guys? I'm doing PT at a private facility here in lovely, wonderful East Lansing, where everyone decorates for every holiday. Wonderful, wonderful. Do you suppose Lawrence Welk came from East Lansing? Bert drives me to my sessions (he has a Town Car with, you guessed it, leather seats), as Mother is busy with Christmas plans, which involve much baking of miniature banana breads, freezing mammoth amounts of cookie dough to be baked exactly two days preceding the holiday, and of course the elaborate penning of Christmas cards that explain her marriage and change of residence and hint at her daughter's tragic year without revealing too much, because tragedy is considered tacky in the Christmas card circle. I'm thinking this year mine should say, "Hey, it was a terrible year and I'm amazed the world's still spinning."

Whoops! The clock has just struck ten, so I must cheerfully wheel off to PT, where it's try, try, try, and no frowns allowed. If Santa were lucky enough to reside in East Lansing, Rita'd have him on a schedule, too. His suits would be pressed with a knife-edge crease, and his beard and fur collar would be bleached to a uniform winter white.

Pet the critters for me. Tell the poinsettias I hate them.

Love,
Phoebe

Bayborough Valley

Dear Phoebe,

Sweetie, a letter from you—actual words on a piece of paper! You licked the stamp and everything! But I noticed you didn't ask once about little Sally. I know it must hurt too much to allow thoughts of her into your brain. In prison it was next to impossible to keep thoughts like that out. But strangely enough, life became tolerable only when I let the troubling thoughts in. Anyway, Sally is fine. Growing, eating like a pig. We adore her.

Wish you were here.
Love, Beryl

From the Desk of Nancy Jane Mattox

Things to Do Before Thanksgiving:

Surprise drop-in at caterer's—make sure no oil

Double-check photographer

Videographer—number of blank tapes?

Give wedding planner notice

Order cake from Jacqui's—bribe?

Remind Ness of ribbon color change in bouquet

Find ribbon—San Francisco? Ask David

Final fitting for dress—see if it can be taken in another inch

Call Lester for some kind of stomach tranq Rx

Baby tranqs?

Telephone Gymboree

Catalog people—price herbal gift line

Clean greenhouse windows before wedding—Segundo?

Pediatrician appt. for Sally's next round of shots—James take her?

Farm Christmas card—address invitations—hire calligrapher?

Call Mother?

Pedicure

Manicure

Spa day—hot rock massage, herbal facial, deep-conditioning treatment for hair, milk bath, Brazilian bikini wax

Confession

Menu for bridal shower at David Snow's—nix the deep-fried thing in favor of crudités

Decide last name issue

Call diaper service—current batch gave Sally a rash; find alternative to horrid white cream that stains clothing

Read marriage literature from Father O'Reilly

Pray for Phoebe

Pray for Sally

Novenas for myself

Try not to think about Rick

Do not under any circumstances telephone Rick

No online *After-Hours*

Buy extra-small turkey for Thanksgiving dinner

Learn lullabies

Bayborough Valley

Dear Mary Madigan Caringella, whose name is nearly as lovely as her voice,

If only I knew where to send this letter, I'd use that Priority feature the post office boasts is as good as UPS. However, as far as we Bad Girls are concerned, UPS, which brought us Juan Nava, and Phoebe love for a short while, can never be replaced by speed or thrift, but that's an entire story I didn't have time to tell you. At least not in enough depth that you would see how just mentioning his name hurts my heart. If you were here now, I'd make us a pot of Mexican hot chocolate and grab a box of Kleenex and tell you the whole sad tale.

Why is it the holidays bring out this gloomy side of me? I have friends, a wonderful house to stay in, and a man who loves me. My tummy is full, there's plenty of sunshine, and in other parts of the world people are hungry and living in cardboard boxes.

Well, for one thing, it's Earl. He said he was going to Sweden. When I saw this ad in the paper for a gig under the name Buckethead, I assumed he hadn't left yet. So I show up at this concert (black satin panties under my jeans), and it turned out it wasn't Earl at all, but some other guy at least six inches shorter than him and didn't play any jazz whatsoever. Thinking back, he never really admitted he was Buckethead, but all his money and the mysterious musical career—well, I assumed—didn't you? What do they say? When you assume, you make an ass out of you and me? All I know is I had better get a postcard from him soon or "heads are gonna roll," which is what Ness says when something goes annoyingly wrong here at the farm. You'd love Ness. All sass and attitude.

Maddy, I wonder where you are this cold November morning. I imagine Galisteo probably has a fine covering of frost on all the trees, and your summer garden has been turned over to rest atop poor Harry's bones. I picture Rick hunched over the computer creating a spiral staircase of metaphors, the back of his neck needing shaving, the little-kid way the hem of his T-shirt used to catch on that hair. Or maybe you two have split by now. If that's the case, don't be sad, Maddy. You have a lot going for you—that voice in particular. Earl sure went on about it. Did you two ever talk about recording together? That night in Santa Fe when you sang while he played Steely Dan I will never forget. I think Rick was jealous. No, I know he was. Men and music—it's a touchy subject. Do you suppose that in their souls, men eternally stay ten years old? Is this well-kept secret only revealed to women standing on the brink of menopause, when it can do me no good whatsoever?

Since Earl left, I haven't had a single period. Of course I'm too old to be pregnant, but I bought a test anyway—deep down I might even have been hoping my body's last gasp included a baby of my own. No blue stick. Some days

I swear I can feel the hormones leaching out of my body the way the greenhouse plants suck the nutrients from the soil. When I don't even know where Earl is, and my life is on hold, what can I possibly feed myself to fill up the gap?

Love, Beryl

P.S. Sorry to whine. All I meant to say was wherever you are, I hope you're warm, safe, and on your way to happy, or even better, on your way here.

Love, B

Novel Possibilities—R. Heinrich

So say Tim is sleeping with this groupie that he meets in Oklahoma while he's playing various contests for money and what the hell, decides to take her along for the ride. After all, she's got a credit card, she's interested, and there's nothing like wild sex for unwinding after a midnight show. . . .

Or, he's down and out, fleeing heartbreak, and his car breaks down in the mountains of New Mexico, and way up there in the high altitude he finds a trailer he can stay in for free, where he holes up and writes great lyrics, and he meets this Indian girl at a general store where she cashiers and he wanders in one day needing to buy soup (it's all he can afford) . . . she invites him home to her adobe house and they have this giant fuckfest and everything is groovy until she starts drinking and he learns that she murdered her ex and he's buried out front in the garden. . . .

So what would happen if I outed Earl as Buckethead if it means I can get myself a halfway decent job? I know I promised Maddy, but how much freaking soup do we have to swallow to make it through this winter?

Dear Mom,

You know how you always send me that check for Christmas . . .

Idea: A mystery novel about a serial killer who chooses his victims at truck stops where they always serve Jell-O. . . .

Idea: Romance novel written under a pseudonym. How hard could it be? Koko the ape could do better than Nicholas Sparks.

Somewhere find a doctor to diagnose this stupid back pain. Psychosomatic? A slipped disc? Kidney cancer?

> *Dear Don,*
>
> *I know I left* After-Hours *on less than cordial terms, but time's passed and . . .*

Idea: A modern-day *Grapes of Wrath,* using the newsroom as a platform . . .

Idea: Maddy's story—whatever that is . . .

> *Dear Nance,*
>
> *Remember the time we lit all the candles in the house (including the birthday candles) and stayed in bed until they'd melted?*

"HEY, LADIES. DAVID HERE. Somebody call me back so we can get this shower menu confirmed, please?"

"This is Gina at Dr. Ullman's office calling to remind Ness of her appointment tomorrow. Don't forget to go to the lab first. Please call if you can't make it."

"Hello? Hello? Is anybody there? Pick up, this is Rebecca Roth calling. Phoebe? We'd still like to schedule that show of your work for this March. But I need to hear back from you, like, immediately? I don't mean to bother you this close to the holidays, but this is, like, my third message? I hate the holidays. I try to be on a plane somewhere else when anything major rolls around. So if you get my machine, you probably won't hear from me until after New Year's."

"Hey. This is Beryl. My bike got a flat and it's raining. Can somebody pick me up? I'm all the way in Sierra Grove under the awning for Java the Hut. The number is . . ."

"Hi, is this the farm with the black horse? I hope so. Anyway, I bought some poinsettias from you last year, and I'd like to order three dozen this year. Actually, if you have four, I'll take four dozen. Do you deliver to the Bay Area?"

"Hello, I hope I have the same farm that sold me the poinsettias recently? Regarding the plants, well, could you please tell me what would happen if say a child overwatered them?"

"This is Millie at Gymboree returning Mrs. Mattox's call. Ma'am, our policy requires that babies be able to sit up and crawl before we allow them to enroll in our courses."

"Rebecca Roth again. What, are you guys in Hawaii or something?"

"David here. I need to talk to Ness when she gets in, thanks."

"Valley Market calling to let you know we have one free-range, organic turkey available, a twenty-pounder. Call back by tomorrow morning if you want it, otherwise I'm selling it to the next person who asks."

"It's Phoebe. I guess you're not home. Hi anyway."

"This is Cora at the Family Counseling Center returning Nancy Mattox's call. Due to a cancellation, we have an opening for a consult, December ninth at eight A.M. Shall we tentatively schedule so you don't lose the slot?"

"David here. I think there's something wrong with your answer—"

East Lansing
The Café of Diminished Light
Dear Bad Girls,

Here is a modern-day fairy tale I ran across. Let me know what you think of it.

Once upon a time, a girl who couldn't walk fell down a rabbit hole and bumped into all manner of fairies. One was tall and had skin the color of hot cocoa, and braided hair that glistened like it was alive. Just by the sound of her voice, she could talk horses into lifting their heavy hooves and placing them in her hands. Another fairy was really a sprite (which is basically a fairy with a bad attitude), and more than anything in the entire world she liked dressing up in nice clothes and organizing all the other fairies in ways they didn't appreciate. But who could blame her? She was trying to rescue a magic garden that had been ignored and left to grow into weeds, and instead of a green thumb, her skill lay in public relations.

One of the more interesting fairies was the redhead. She didn't talk a lot, but concocted elaborate meals of honey mead, fiddlehead ferns, and fairy chocolate, which made all the other fairies happy and agreeable unless it was the week before their periods. Also, she could tame anything with wings, even the fabled gryphon that was always in a rank mood and letting everybody know about it.

The last fairy in this posse had a twisted back, so she couldn't fly unless it was in first class on American (with leather seats). She tried hard to work alongside the other fairies, but sometimes she got too sad to lift a trowel. One day she flew on a silver bird to a place where it was always winter. It was okay at first. I mean, what fairy doesn't need to catch up on her sleep, or lie on the couch and watch *Oprah*? Who in her right mind would turn down meals of bananas and graham crackers? Eventually, she found herself missing her tribe and scheming to get away from the mother of all fairies, who might have turned out not to be an evil stepmother in disguise, but still got on her nerves. Well, you know how they say one must always look beneath the surface in fairy tales? The crippled fairy came up with an ingenious plan, so simple that it earned her some glitter on her formerly drab wings. As fairies are wont to do, she wished and hoped very hard that the other fairies might forgive her for being such a freaking troll, and meet her at this secret place:

American Airlines, Flight 2683, 4:57 P.M., December 14th, San Francisco Airport.

Love, Phoebe

Rick and Maddy

18
The Silver Bullet

WE STOPPED THE TRUCK and stared in wonder at the Airstream trailer propped on cement blocks and surrounded by weeds. All those equal sections of aluminum, the rounded rivets seaming them together at precise increments, made it look like a patchwork quilt put together by aerospace engineers. "A diamond in the rough," said Maddy. "Just needs a little spiffing up."

As I stepped out of the truck, my foot encountered a beer can bleached pale by the sun, and I kicked it out of the way before one of the collies cut a paw on it. I'd expected us to part ways at the Greyhound station in Albuquerque, one sloppy kiss and "See ya," but instead Maddy'd driven south, past Truth or Consequences, probably the greatest name for a town since Faulkner came up with the unpronounceable, impossible to remember Yokna-whatever-it-was. "Spiffing?"

Her dark eyes shone back at me, always uncertain of my teasing. "Look it up, Hemingway."

"Plan to, as soon as somebody replaces my dog-eaten dictionary."

I watched Miss Mary take a breath and prepare to bitch me out, tell me that the last thing I needed was encouragement from

Mr. Webster to indulge in big words. But this time she was too busy staring at that trailer, imagining God knows what.

THERE'S SOMETHING INHERENTLY SEXY about watching a woman clean a house. All that energy and decisiveness, and the way their hair flies around as they scrub the sink, but I still doubted that mere spiffing would render the Landyacht livable. A layer of dust covered the beast, thick as what St. Helens had left on most of Oregon when she blew her top.

"My mom's side of the family has lived in these trailers since as far back as Airstream's been making them, Rick. They're well insulated, and they have the coolest bathrooms you've ever seen. Plus the bed folds up to make a kitchen table. People go wacky to own an old one in decent shape. They'll spend a fortune for anything original. This puppy's for sale, you know. Wish I had the ducats to buy it. Airstream freaks drive around in caravans all over the world, Europe even. They're like intellectual low-riders, strutting their coolness."

I frowned.

That set her off. "Listen, this is a perfectly reasonable place of residence unless you're some goddamn yuppie with a high profile and a client roster to impress. I really don't see the problem staying here."

"Did I say anything about having a problem?"

"You didn't have to. It's written all over your face."

Well, I did have a problem. The girl I lived with was sneakily emptying a fifth of vodka every week. I'd humored Maddy when she balked at leaving New Mexico. Agreed to stay on someplace cheap for the winter if she'd stop drinking. I'd write my novel and keep her company on cold days and worse, even though I was still puzzling out why besides my money she wanted a loser twenty years her senior hanging around. But living in a dented-up, twenty-four-foot '63 Tradewind out in the middle of nowhere? "Maddy," I said. "This thing looks like something that came off the set of *The Jetsons*."

She stared at me blankly. "Who?"

I sighed and uprooted a mouse nest from one of the cement

blocks by flicking the toe of my shoe. There were mouse nests in every cranny. "Not important. Never mind."

The rounded door looked like it belonged on the side of a turboprop. Inside, things smelled funky, and all those mouse nests outside had to have friends on the inside. It made me worry about hantavirus, about breathing in mouse scat while I slept, and croaking before I could figure out something worthwhile to make of my life. Maddy, meanwhile, found a broom and began sweeping. I watched as broom straw raked all traces of the past out of the trailer into the cold air beyond the door, Maddy urging history to hurry up and join what was already an ancient landscape. At some point I'd have to confront her about the drinking.

The great residential debate began the day we left Galisteo. "Look," I'd said—reasonably, I thought. "If we're going to blow this pop stand of a state, why not go someplace warm with halfway decent employment? How about California? I'm sure I could get a job at some paper, if nothing else, in copyediting."

Maddy bit her lip and pretended to think about it.

"Karaoke bars galore," I tempted, jostling the salt and pepper shakers on the table of the diner where we were eating our lunch of green chile burgers and cheese-smothered fries. "Not to mention that ocean you've always wanted to see." I didn't say twelve-step programs, but I was damn sure thinking it. For a part of every day in New Mexico since Beryl and Earl left, she'd holed up with a bottle and drank herself into a side of town so dark that even if I were armed, I wouldn't care to visit. She'd cry, and I'd ask her, "What is so godawful that you have to marinate it in alcohol?" She wouldn't answer. The most she'd stayed sober was two days. But those two days were golden: She'd sing to me, bead necklaces, and she was getting better at making dinner, and we'd made long, slow love that took us both to Valhalla. Whenever we got remotely close to discussing the drinking, she'd start running off at the mouth about any one of a hundred subjects.

"Rick, you won't believe this! I have this address of a place down south that Lee told me about," she'd said. "Guess what? It's free for the winter; all we have to do is pay for heat!" And followed up with straddling my lap, tightening her legs around me, and those hot little kisses that promised more. "I'll do better there," she'd whisper. "I know I will. And you can't give up on your novel. I won't allow it."

I'd try to ignore the twinges in my nether regions. "I'm tired of pretending I can write," I'd told her. "I can't write worth a damn."

"That's not true. Why are you always putting yourself down? I love your writing. It's gotten tons better since you stopped with the big words. Think of how much work you could get done in a small town. How quiet it would be. There aren't even any neighbors! A white Christmas," she said, and sang the entire song. Under the table she ran her bare foot up my ankle, and I wondered how she'd managed to remove her sock without me noticing.

She was making progress with the ratty old broom. I could see the speckled linoleum someone had laid on the floor. Between the speckles and the spots, it looked very retro. "Look," Maddy said. "Actual floor. I knew it was under here somewhere."

And she smiled that dazzling smile that nearly took my breath away.

I'd slept with my arms around Maddy for months now, and sometimes we had good sex, but we'd never made love in the way that lovers do. Yet I could tell if that kind of thing were ever to happen, it would change me. Maybe not her, but definitely me. I wondered what stood in our way. Was it Nance? The memory of her smart mouth? The way she'd lay down proof sheets on my living room floor and scrutinize each shot, mercilessly culling her photographic herd? That big dumb dog of hers at her side, that constant companion, the only being she was sure loved her without judging her on her many bad habits? I'd typed a list of them into the laptop. Secured the file with a password. What I didn't like:

The messes she left in the kitchen

Her jewelry all over the bathroom counter

Her spendiness—designer jeans when regular Levi's would do

The way she called me on my shit

Her habit of hanging up on me when I was behaving like a shit

The way she wouldn't let my shit just die, but insisted on talking it all out

The problem was, those were exactly the same things that I loved about her.

I never did delete that file.

"Sometimes where you sing, you sound like Emmylou Harris," I said on more than one occasion to Mary Madigan Caringella. It wasn't a line.

"Bullpucky," Maddy would answer. "I'm tons better than her."

But she was joking, and if I pushed the subject, the footsie playing or the hot kisses or her hand on my belt would end as abruptly as it had begun.

"HEY. DID WE FORGET ABOUT THANKSGIVING?" she asked me as we landed for the night in an Albuquerque motel that had seen better years. "What the hell day is it anyway?"

"Yeah, I'm pretty sure Thanksgiving's over."

"Damn," Maddy said as she fed her dogs sopapillas with honey. Mentos and Slim Jim leaped down from the second double bed in our rented room to partake of her offerings. I'd never liked them as dogs, but had to admit they got into a travel routine with less complaint than most humans. Mentos was a food swiper, but Jim was pure gentleman: He'd wait until he was invited to clean a plate or finish an unwanted taco. "Well," she said. "I wonder if we'll remember Christmas."

"Babe," I said, "I'll fill your stocking."

Maddy laughed. "Yeah, I've heard that promise before. Maybe Santa will bring you a dictionary."

"Very funny." I switched on the television, something I hadn't watched for months. The colors appeared garish, and the news anchors were trying too hard to look like movie stars. The news itself—substitute any year, change the names, and it was the same old war, murder, and cheating, with the obligatory feel-good sound bite to close out the hour. How could any of that matter compared to the war going on inside me? I turned it off and stared at Maddy, who'd fallen asleep on the other bed with the dogs. I got up and covered her with a blanket. Then I put on my jacket and took a walk outside in the bitter New Mexico night, Nance's cell phone in my pocket like a rabbit's foot. Above me there wasn't a single visible star.

I thought about all the hero shit my father had inadvertently laid on me. How a boy grows up thinking that that kind of effort is not only possible but his ultimate task—help win a world war, be there in time to save a life, turn himself from paperboy into a Pulitzer Prize–winner—complete one incredible deed and then he's off the hook, he can settle down, watch sports on TV, coach softball, learn how to barbecue hamburgers so that everyone can tell they came from his spatula. I knew that a reasonably educated man should be able to let go of this expectation and remain happy. Or recognize that heroic acts can be small, like helping out a woman whose purse got stolen at a goddamn memorial for the murdered. That the small heroisms could even potentially aggregate, form a larger chain, and therefore add to this man's sense of self-worth, his karmic résumé. But name one thing reasonable about unemployment at fifty-one, or losing the woman you love because you're too much of a chickenshit to grow up in the ways she needs you to. Even bullies learn the positive aspects of sharing their marbles.

A billboard advertising Acoma Pueblo winked at me as snow fell on my neck. Maddy once said she wanted to take me there, but we'd never gone. I fed her, I did her laundry, and I threw out her empty bottles. I walked her way-too-smart dogs, I held her at night, and I tried to write stories that fell through my grasp like trying to hold on to snowflakes. None of that would make me a hero, but maybe I could take her to the Pacific Ocean.

And, I could see Nance.

For a lark I dialed my old number into her cell phone. It had been disconnected for months, but like a cat escaping a car's wheels, here in the memory of her electronic wonder, those ten digits gained another life.

OUT OF THE BLUE I HAD A DREAM about Dalton Afterhart, and at first I thought, Hey, look who's here. Nice to see you again, but don't get any ideas about me going to bed with you. Instead, let's have a drink and smoke ourselves silly in this here bar. Later on we'll sing a duet, and people will throw us almost enough dollar bills to pay for the drinks. How fecking brilliant a plan is that? And we drank rum and Coke; and even in my dream state I could taste the sweetness of the drinks, feel the harsh smoke in my throat, and pit my voice against Dalton's wannabe Kenny Rogers. We ran though the list of country-and-western favorites: "The Gambler," "You Picked a Fine Time to Leave Me, Lucille," "Margaritaville," and then a voice shot out from the audience asking for "Amazing Grace." It was Maggot, sitting there with a smile on her face. When she was alive, I hadn't yet met Dalton. In fact, he was probably the only man in Oklahoma I hadn't slept with. But long before Dalton came on the scene, if I sang, Maggot listened. She got tears in her eyes when the song was sentimental. She clapped until her palms turned red. She said to me, "Mary Magdalene, if you ever put your mind to it, you could be somebody. You could sell records and everything. I'd give my left arm to sing like you do. Would you do 'Amazing Grace' for me one more time, please?"

Maggot, *I wanted to say.* For you I would sing it forever.

IN FRONT OF THE AIRSTREAM, the wind blew grittily across our faces, and I turned my jacket collar up. I kept forgetting that Maddy was twenty years younger than me. That references to world events I grew up with and the Beatles' impact on the music scene were ancient history to her. In a Hollywood film us being together wouldn't seem so out of the ordinary, but movies had plot. Things happened, things that led to other things, and eventually some important lesson grew out of it. If there was a happy ending, the moviegoer forgave the actors their age differences, because if there was one thing America ached for it was happy goddamn endings. To someone like my dad, however, it would appear that I'd taken up playing an extended game of house with a teenager in a never-ending attempt to avoid my responsibilities.

"Watch yourself," he used to say to me in that forbidding whisper. "A woman will get herself pregnant and trap you into marriage." I'd always wondered if my good Catholic mother had snared her "prize" that way. If I was the result of chicanery, they'd hidden the fact. Surely after fifty-plus years and three children, old Richard had softened on that score. So why did his dire predictions echo in my head?

When we were back outside, checking the trailer hookups, I said to Maddy, "Well, it looks livable to me. How about you?"

In answer, she leaped up and wrapped her legs around my waist. Around us, the dogs yipped and raced. It struck me that the weight of Maddy against my body was hardly anything.

FOR A WHILE WE COOKED EACH OTHER SOUP on the minuscule two-burner stove, deemed the Silver Bullet cozy, and talked grandly about living this way the rest of our lives. Who needs a bunch of material comforts? Want what you have, and all that. We rejoiced in taking walks all bundled up with only our noses showing, in watching winter transform the dull brown landscape into glittering frost over stark tree limbs. The dogs were at their happiest running around in the brisk air, and we lived far enough from neighbors that we could let them off leash. Then the truck blew a head gasket, and it cost a bundle to fix, and that put a sizable dent in my money, which got Maddy upset enough to finish a fifth of vodka in only two days. So she'd stop crying, I told her she didn't have to pay me back. I left the empty bottle sitting out on the counter, though, as a reminder of her slip. Neither of us said anything about it, but its presence was heavy. Anything in that trailer's minimal space took on deeper significance.

Then it snowed, snowed again, and there came the one day that I had to dig us out three separate times, from the drifts piled up against the door so high it gave me a bona fide panic attack. No matter how often I cracked the louvered windows to let in fresh air, the trailer made me sleepy. Outside, the wind whistled through its pointy little teeth, pelting the aluminum siding with snow so abrasive that just walking from here to the truck left my face feeling sanded. The tiny shower/bath lost its panache. I took to driving thirty miles to town (a relative term) to take a shower at a Laundromat, a place so scuzzy I invested in plastic sandals. There at least I could stretch my arms above my head, adjust the showerhead, and throw in a few more quarters if I needed more hot water. Our chemical toilet worked great, but when the door separating you from the person outside is so thin you can hear them breathing, it isn't terribly easy to relax. Peeing in the snow was fun the first couple times, but I missed having Harry to talk to.

"You happy here, Babe?" I'd inquire from time to time, and Maddy always gave me a smile. She'd moved on from stringing single-strand necklaces to working on a beading loom. In seed beads of various colors, she'd begun weaving intricate blanket patterns she was sure would fetch more money come next summer's market. Sometimes she'd appear by my side so silently it took me a few minutes to realize she was there. She'd take my hand and gently pull me to my feet, no words, just gestures that meant come with me. It wasn't really about sex, though we sometimes ended up there. She wanted holding, needed somebody kind inside her moving in that rhythm that assured her she was still alive. Sometimes it felt to me like she was making up for a lifetime of not letting anyone close, just like I'd done. What could I do? I started to like being needed. I rubbed her shoulders and brushed her hair with my fingers. I tried not to think, not to ask, "And when the snow melts? What happens then?"

Then there was the matter of her singing. I'd be laboring over the chapter I'd neatly outlined, certain that by following my ideas and by not straying outside the plan, I'd finally stumble across the narrative voice that eluded me. I'd hear her coming back from taking the dogs out, her voice wound up full throttle. I'd have to stop working and listen. When she opened her mouth, all I could think was that however small a thing like lightning may be, when it happens, there ain't no sky big enough to hold it.

TWO CHRISTMASES AGO I'd tried hard to find the perfect gift for Nance. I'd learned in our three years together that girls did not appreciate CDs, no matter how much they admired the artist you'd selected. Giving a woman a CD was the equivalent of saying, *You're my bud, not a person I know well enough to bring to orgasm.* No amount of shopping would help me pick out clothes she'd like that I could afford—so I scratched cashmere sweaters and Italian leather boots off my list. "Why not jewelry?" a clerk suggested, and after my cold sweat evaporated, I began my diligent hunt for the perfect item, something that would make her eyes light up and net me some really great sex as a thank-you. She had diamond earrings already, platinum studs she wore all the time, so earrings were out. I'd never seen her wear a ring, and rings were touchy things—prone to misinterpretation, so I bypassed that display case entirely. A bracelet, I decided. Practical, could be worn every day, something that fit her and wouldn't interfere in the darkroom. She had small wrists. I found a gold mesh bracelet—"tailored," the clerk said, which meant not too fancy—and had the clerk take out a couple of links. I knew the measurement of her wrist well because it fit between my thumb and index finger exactly. Department stores are great about gift wrapping. Gold paper, silver ribbon, they even include a complimentary note card. "Merry Christmas, with love from Rick," I wrote. Not in printing, either, but my best handwriting.

I still remember her face when she slid the ribbon from the box, so hopeful, so prepared to ooh and aah. How her mouth collapsed, just for a moment, then recovered so bravely that I knew she was faking.

CHRISTMAS MORNING WITH MAGGOT we woke up at first light, prodded each other from our twin beds, giggled and joked and generally anticipated our riches. When we were tiny, and Grandma Fawn was still alive, she'd given us moccasins decorated with beads, fringed with metal cones that clicked with every step. We knew it was important to thank her politely, and furthermore

that these items were never to be worn, but instead saved for some kind of murky posterity. When I got the jacket that Dalton ended up barfing on, I said feck it and wore the crap out of it. I was sick of beautiful things gathering dust in closets just so when I was too old and fat to fit into them I could show them to my relatives. Maggot used to chide me that I'd regret it someday, when the beads were lost and the elbows worn through. But even with the darker splotch on the front, putting on my jacket was like wrapping myself in a baby blanket, instant comfort. I wondered what Daddy'd done with Maggot's jacket. Probably made a shrine to it.

A FEW DAYS BEFORE CHRISTMAS, it seemed like Maddy and I had been breathing each other's air for so long the medium had actual edges. I shut my eyes and saw broken dreams, unrequited desires, and such a fierce restlessness now that even the dogs seemed to be pacing. Even I was ready to drink. I couldn't write a sentence to save my ass, and we'd been eating white rice all week because it was too icy to drive to town. I checked the calendar for the bazillionth time—still December 23. We didn't have room in the trailer for a tree. There was no way even the scrawniest turkey could fit in our stove. I was about to spend my second Christmas without Nance Mattox, who was no doubt spending hers with that James character. Felt like I wanted to put my fist through the roof of the *art moderne* behemoth, but I didn't want to deal with the cold air that would pour through as a result.

"I know," Maddy said. "I could put some soy sauce on the rice, scramble some eggs, make pancakes, aim for a kind of egg foo-yung thing, minus the foo and the yung, since I don't know what in hell they are. How's that sound?"

"Truthfully? Awful."

"Well, feck you, Heinrich. I'm just trying to be creative."

Creative: She knew the word would needle me. I refused to bite because I feared how deep my teeth might sink in.

"Well, we could go have Christmas dinner in a restaurant. Though I can't imagine what'll be open around here besides a HoJo with sullen waitresses. I know, how about I get a packet of turkey lunch meat, some tortillas, and make turkey fajitas?"

Was I getting old, suddenly turning sentimental, wanting a holiday with all the trimmings? In Portland there were always two Christmas parties at the paper: One was for management, and everyone showed up dressed nicely and behaved. The other party was strictly *After-Hours* staff, and those of us who were lonely drank ourselves into feeling less alone while listening to a punk band blast a racket in a local watering hole. "Sounds less awful," I said. "Am I supposed to buy you a Christmas present?"

She quickly glanced at the trailer floor. "The dogs might like something. Doesn't have to be expensive. Jim gets a kick out of tearing presents open no matter what's inside."

Shortly after, she took off for a walk, leaving me to wonder what in the hell it is one buys a Border collie. When I got sick of being alone, I wrote her a note and carefully maneuvered the truck over icy patches into town. We were in the southern part of New Mexico, a place so small it made Galisteo look like a veritable metropolis. Along the highway there were mom-and-pop groceries, feed stores, the occasional Western wear shop, but mostly assorted farms and wild-ass drunk drivers getting their ya-yas out by flooring the old Ford. I wasn't looking to buy a goat, so I passed up the farms and hit the feed store in Las Cruces. I opted for what looked like woolly-mammoth bones for the dogs—at twelve bucks apiece their weight almost made them seem worth it—and a sack of pig ears, which the clerk assured me could indeed be eaten without causing intestinal distress. For Maddy I chose one of those plastic Breyer horses I remembered my sister salivating over when she was ten years old. Figured girls never outgrew that kind of thing. Instead of the palomino in show-saddle regalia, which looked kind of like Barbie doll fodder to me, I went for the naked, rearing black stallion—more Maddy's type, I thought. I had the clerk wrap everything, and she didn't bat an eye, gave it the complete Christmas workup, so I guessed I wasn't the only one doing the last-minute thing.

But, sitting on the truck seat, the one package didn't seem like enough.

In the market I gathered up the latest issues of magazines I thought Maddy might get a kick out of, *Rolling Stone, People,* the *Star* and the *Enquirer.* I found a few *Archie* comics I was sure had already been read, and added them to the pile. I bought her a dozen candy bars, some cocoa mix, the most expensive hand lotion they had, and new ponytail scrunchies in a fetching leopard print that I knew would flatter her jet hair. The cashier laughed when I asked her about gift-wrapping options. She actually thought I was yanking her chain. We said Merry Christmas, talked about how cold it was, and I left. As I pulled onto the highway, a veering blue pickup with an exhaust leak forced me out of my lane and onto the shoulder of the road. I had to breathe deep to calm down enough to go back out there.

At home, I wrote out in longhand:

> Dear Maddy,
>
> On the way home from Las Cruces, I came pretty close to the big adios. All I could think was there had to be more to life than that old red dirt road and my face in some cowboy's pickup truck grille. So I took my time in coming back with my little Santa sack of presents and thought a lot about what we're doing here. I bought the presents because I know you won't expect them, no other reason, so don't feel obligated to do the same for me.
>
> Babe, all these months in the same bed and I hardly know you. How come? Asking you this, I feel like a man drinking his last glass of whiskey, making a new start after the last drunk. I'm thinking maybe you could try meeting me halfway on this. I'd sure like it if you quit the booze. I promise to talk more. Merry Christmas, Maddy. Soon it'll be a new year. What do you say let's drive your truck to California and see that ocean you're always talking about in time for New Year's?
>
> Rick

ON CHRISTMAS MORNING I woke to a web of Christmas lights tacked up inside the trailer. Immediately I thought of Nance's migraines, and how blinking lights sometimes set them off. That last Christmas together, she'd found pearl-shaped lights that could be dimmed but under no circumstances blinked. She decorated our tree entirely in white lights, and hung the various ornaments we'd bought over the years. I woke to the smell of turkey roasting in the oven, and her terrible singing voice proclaiming, "Merry Christmas, Baby," a blues song I'd wrongly assumed nobody could murder. No music today, but I could hear Maddy outside rattling around. I lay there awhile, my arm around Mentos, who lately considered me her new best friend. "Look at that," I told the collie, "Santa's elves must have had a busy night. Some watchdog you turned out to be. Not even one bark to let me know we weren't alone?" She licked my face and I allowed it, even though her breath was rank with pig ear smells. "Well, enough affection," I said. "I'd better hit the shower and get ready for the present unwrapping."

The charm of the Airstream's economy of space was impressive. One could, if one wished, sit down, take a dump, brush one's teeth, and take a shower at the same time. One did not generally care to do this, but it was good to know such possibilities existed. I rinsed off, soaped up, shaved, and was in the process of rinsing a second time when I heard a loud crash and the sound of glass shattering. I threw open the folding door and stood there naked and dripping while Maddy lay on the floor grasping the neck of what was once a whiskey bottle. The throw rug we'd bought had drunk most of the whiskey, but not all of it. Maddy's fingers were bleeding. "Good God!" I said, dropping my towel so I could wrap her hand. I pulled her to her feet only to have her stumble against me and send us both sprawling. "How much have you had this time?"

"Only a shot in my coffee," she insisted, picking glass shards from her hand. "It's a Caringella Christmas tradition, Rick. Honest. We always did it." She shooed the dogs away.

"Well, I'm not a Caringella," I said. "And I don't think much of your tradition." I spied my letter to her on the counter, the envelope torn open, the single piece of paper lying there flat. Was this unattractive slip my fault for being so candid? Of her mother's drinking, Nance used to say, "You cannot tell a drunk to quit. It has to be her idea, her time, and her decision because in the end, it's her struggle."

No matter how reasonable that sounded, I unloaded both barrels. "Jesus Christ, Maddy, drinking before breakfast? Hurting yourself? What if I wasn't here, and you slashed a fucking artery? You think those dogs are going to drive you to the hospital?"

"I don't need the hospital," she said quietly. "Just a couple of Band-Aids. And I was having a drink because it's my thirtieth birthday."

"Some birthday. You need rehab, Maddy, not a cake. Trouble is, you can't afford either."

That set her to sobbing like I've never heard. She rubbed at her eyes, leaving blood streaks like war paint on both cheeks. When I tried to get her to wrap her fingers in the towel, she shoved me away hard. "Get out of here," she said. "Go. I know you want to. I'm not that perfect girl you lived with in Oregon, the one who knew how to dress right and keep a job and not drink too much. All's I am is a rode-hard Oklahoma slut who should have died by now but for some reason God's torturing by keeping alive. Leave, Rick, you have my blessing. I can't even believe you stayed this long."

I dried myself off and listened to her. Surely the twenty years I had on her afforded me the maturity of separating drunken emotions from what fears lay behind them. I wondered if this was what it felt like to be a dad, and that thought made my stomach squirm. Women—no matter what age they are—they say they want you to be open, to mean what you say, but they don't really mean half of what they say themselves. I watched her pace the Airstream and cry, rambling on about Christmases past, every so often wiping her bleeding fingers on her jeans, and wondered how much more of this I could—or should—stand.

"Take me to bed," she begged me at one point. "Just help me get to that other place and I'll be fine."

"Maddy, you're drunk. I don't want you when you're like this. I can't imagine who would."

Down she went on her knees, pulling at my jeans. "Rick, please. It's my birthday. It's me and Maggot's birthday. We're thirty. We made it to thirty."

I lifted her to a standing position and leaned her up against the wall of cupboards. "Maddy, I'm sorry, but I have to get out of here. I've tried to ignore the drinking, but I can't anymore. What we're doing here, it's wrong."

When I let go she slid back down to the floor, and the magazines fell on top of her. She carefully stacked them up, smoothed the wrinkles from the covers, but held on to the *People.* On the cover was a photomontage of the decade's biggest disasters. Was journalism really at so low a point that they couldn't throw Julia Roberts's smile on there to ring out the old year instead of the stone-faced Timothy McVeigh?

I dressed, threw on my jacket, petted a shaking Mentos, and opened the door.

"Don't leave like this," Maddy said, suddenly sounding sober. "If you'll give me another chance, I'll tell you about my sister."

"MAMA DIDN'T LEARN she was carrying twins until she was in the delivery room and up on the table, groaning to push out what she was sure was the single fattest baby in the entire history of women giving birth. She loved to tell the story, loved to dramatize the moments of our births, because for one thing, it was her chance to hog the spotlight. She and Daddy hadn't thought babies were in the cards for them. They'd never used birth control, but she kept on getting her period regular as the full moon. So her pregnancy was that much more special. Not that Mama would ever use it, but Grandma Fawn traded a friend one of her best beaded shifts for the cradleboard anyway. She had him use the finest wood to make it, lace it in rawhide cut in a single strip from a good cowhide, decorate it with beads in yellow and orange, and leave a space to paint the baby's name in so he'd know it was his alone. She made a quilt, too—MayAnn helped to stitch it—this tiny pieced thing ten stitches to the inch, and Mama intended to wrap her baby in that quilt right off, so that the first thing the infant would know was the kind of softness that comes from women's hands. I can see them all in the waiting room: Daddy, who was squeamish of people blood, but could wring a chicken's neck no problem; MayAnn hearing Mama's screams and deciding right then and there that even if her sister Nita could stand it, there was no way she was putting her own self through that; and Grandma Fawn busy thinking up names because Mama and Daddy liked that tradition of the grandmother naming the baby.

"Margaret was born, Mama said, in a river of clear fluid, a slippery fish that sailed out of her body into the doctor's hands. Once they suctioned out her mouth and put the drops in her eyes, Mama swears she smiled, cooed, and lifted her hand to Mama's face. She lay there beaming in the glow of the miracle of birth, Maggot nestled close, when suddenly she felt a cramp, cried out, and then, as she put it, *'Along came Mary.'* I arrived rafting my own river, not of salty amniotic fluids, but of bright red blood.

"Mama said the nurses snatched Maggot away so quickly that she started crying, and she was certain that kind of treatment scarred a baby, that Grandma Fawn was smart to have hers at home, where things moved slowly and naturally and babies sort of yawned their way into the world.

"The trouble didn't end with the blood, which came from her tearing while having me. Halfway out, I got stuck. The doctor used forceps, which left dents in either side of my head, and the way Mama told it, those instruments were what led to 'fetal distress'—a fancy term for a baby that's born blue and refuses to pink up. They worked on me right there. The nurse handed Maggot back to Mama because the doctor needed the nurse's hands for me. That nurse was the one who pressed her index finger against my heart, gently pumped for forty-five minutes until she got me jump-started enough to take my first breath. Mama said she held on to her firstborn and thought, I never expected more than one baby. If that one doesn't make it, maybe it wasn't meant to be. I mean, look at Elvis. He lost his twin brother, but he ended up giving a gift of music to the world so large that maybe it was God's plan all along. Did you know that it was Rudyard Kipling who said, *Great music speaks a noble language*? And that folk music is the heart of that language?"

"No, Maddy, I didn't."

"For weeks the doctor speculated over whether or not I'd

have brain damage, and who knows, maybe all that's why I am the way I am, the unplanned soul who wasn't supposed to be here. I was the spare, not the heir. Ha-ha."

ALL THAT DAY AND INTO THE NEXT, I made Maddy cups of coffee. I wiped her tears, I tended the dogs, and I read out loud to her articles on fashion dos and don'ts just to make her remember that she knew how to laugh. She told me enough so that I could picture her twin sister at any age. This Margaret—she'd be Maddy's replica in the face, but possess none of her attitude. They'd both come home from school with pictures Crayola'd on that rough brown paper, and what they'd drawn would be interchangeable—stick figures, houses, puppies. But without fail Margaret's picture would go one inch higher on the refrigerator door. Margaret would rate the pink hair ribbons; Maddy the blue ones past their prime. Margaret would end up married to someone dependable like my insurance salesman brother, and pay off her mortgage early, while her sister Maddy would flit from watering hole to watering hole, singing her heart out until her voice dwindled to that rasp that meant it was time to move to the business side of the bar, to tend to making drinks instead of inspiring the people who drank them.

Except it didn't happen that way. Margaret showed up on time for work, hung up her coat, remembered all the children's names, who liked apple juice and who preferred orange, and died anyway, achieving a kind of sainthood that demoted her sister to something that made her parents wrinkle their noses.

"My father," Maddy said, her throat raw from talking, "has to concentrate to remember who I am. Oh, hell, I don't blame him. He and Maggot were like this." She crossed her fingers. "Me, I was always nosing my way out of the bridle."

"And your mom?"

She shut her eyes and Mentos moaned. I patted the dog, attempting to comfort her. "You promised to tell me the whole story," I prodded. "Don't start hiding now."

She opened her eyes. The tears were gone. This bone-dry truth no longer stuck in her throat. "You know those people who can't take a breath without reading their horoscopes? The ones who look suspiciously at every fallen leaf, at what the newscaster says, and sees conspiracies all over the place?"

"I suppose."

"Well, that's her. She will not speak to me. She talks to others about me, but not me directly unless she's accusing me of something."

"Jesus Christ, Maddy. Why the hell not?"

She shrugged her shoulders and pressed her face against the dog. "I'm a reminder of what she lost when McVeigh blew up the building."

"How about being a reminder of what she didn't lose?"

She snorted. "As if," she said, feigning a teenager's callow slang.

"Somebody ought to kick your mother's ass."

She snorted again, this time ending in a laugh. "Oh, that would be a sight. Mama'd knock you unconscious, big guy."

I pulled her down on the mattress. Kissed her forehead, cheeks, chin, and lips. She tasted like salt and faintly of coffee. I took her clothes off and touched her everywhere. I cupped her breasts and kissed them, reveling in the responsiveness of her flesh. I lifted her into my arms and let every pore of our combined flesh make contact. I parted her legs and ran my thumb over the straight black hair that curled over her sex, and kissed her there so long and so skillfully that I made her come twice. In the back of my mind, the image of that unwanted blue baby would not go away. Of the nurse's steady finger, pressing just hard enough, of knowing a fact like that. When no one else cared, total strangers who subscribed to the Hippocratic oath had persuaded Maddy to live and now she was thirty years old, each of them so hard won her knuckles were bloody. Making love to her now wasn't all that different than giving her CPR. All I had to do was show her that each inch of her skin was equally important, not just the nerves that burst into song, but all of it. That the reason I was there at all was to make her believe it.

THAT LAST CHRISTMAS WITH NANCE, I did the dishes, including scouring the turkey pan until it gleamed. I wrapped the leftovers in foil,

stashed them in the fridge, and not once that night did I turn on the television. I sat by my girlfriend on the couch, the Christmas tree lights our only source of illumination. I thanked her for my fisherman's knit sweater and the first edition of Pete Dexter's *Paris Trout* that she'd been hiding from me for months. I told her I loved her, and could tell she felt secure in my love, that I meant what I said. That night, I even felt worthy of her love, like maybe we were good for each other. I made love to her on the couch. For once I didn't care about anything except hearing her come.

ALL TWINS DO IT—*switch places, just to see if they can get away with it. We grow up being taken for each other, hating that, aching for autonomy, and then, boom! one day we saw the advantage of confusion and went for it. With Maggot, it was taking the mandatory civics and economics exam that you had to pass to get your high school diploma for me. I expected her to turn me down flat when I brought it up, that technically being cheating and a sin and all, but she said yes. We stood in a stall in the girls' room changing clothes. I put on her plaid jumper with the loose yellow T-shirt, her socks and penny loafers, and the single-pearl necklace no one ever saw her without. She pulled on my black fishnet stockings, my black miniskirt, and the tight black shirt that, when I lifted my arms, flashed a gleam of midriff. I ratted her hair up, helped her apply makeup, and when she looked in the mirror, she nearly caved in a moment of doubt.*

"Is the eyeliner absolutely essential?" she said.

"Yeah," I said. "Otherwise it'll look fake."

She got a B, deliberately missing some answers so the teachers wouldn't suspect.

That night, as we lay in our twin beds, she whispered, "I kind of liked wearing your skirt, Mary Magdalene. Boys looked at me like I was pretty, like they might ask me out."

"They would if you'd give them a chance. And you are pretty," I said, reaching across the space between our beds until I found her hand and squeezed. "Maggot, any time you want to, you borrow that skirt."

I still had the skirt. When I wore it, Rick whistled at me.

MADDY WOKE ME AROUND TEN. The trailer was clean, one might almost say spiffy. She'd loaded the dogs and our things in the truck. She'd propped the stallion between the windshield and the dashboard, his rearing legs pointing forward. "Get in," she said. "We'll celebrate New Year's in California."

Phoebe

19

Visitors

DECEMBER 26, BRIGHT AND EARLY, I sat in the bulkhead of first class, in a window seat on the right side of the airplane. If I shut my eyes I could almost imagine I was my aunt Sadie, traveling flush, off to a torrid affair with some man who spoke only broken, sexy English, or headed home because she needed a break from his ardor. Surely sometimes she tired of the effort it took to maintain passion. There had to be seasons when she wanted nothing more than to dig in the dirt at her farm, to talk to Florencio about weather trends and what kind of fertilizer to try this year. Even a legend took downtime. More often than not, though, Sadie was running around downtown Bayborough-by-the-Sea campaigning for sea otters, or telling the appliqué-sweater-and-khakis crowd that no, Bayborough did not need another golf course and under no circumstances were they to count on her support, financial or votes. Her opinions fueled the gossip column in the *Blue Jay*. The moneyed conformists pretended not to take notice, but it only took one brave soul in the midst of all that sameness to reveal the Emperor in all his nudity. When Sadie'd send the car for me at college, suddenly I was no longer invisible to my fellow students. Did I care? No, I looked forward to one of our movie marathon weekends spent on her couch, to the easy company. To me my aunt seemed totally normal, and simultaneously, the most exotic creature in the world, like a passionflower pushing through boring old ivy. However she behaved, it seemed to me that Sadie did things first and foremost to please herself, but now I wondered if that truly had been the case. How easy it was to love a memory. In the midst of this crazy year, those thoughts remained my constant comfort. Every time I tried to evoke Juan's memory, to find solace in remembering the slope of his shoulder, or the half moons in his fingernails, it seemed I fell off a cliff.

At Sadie's funeral people had remarked to me, "How sad that your aunt died alone, with nobody to hold her. I can't think of anything more tragic." So I wasn't a man, and I didn't hold her in some movie-star way. I loved her with all my heart, and she loved me back. I held her hand until the life ebbed out of her. Just like the girls at Bad Girl Creek, Sadie and I had made a community of two. We had our own government, and screw death if it thought it could change that.

The flight attendant tapped my shoulder, and I opened my eyes. "Do you need to use the restroom?"

"No," I said, a little confused, and wondering if that was a stock question for first-class passengers. "But I think it's empty right now, so you go ahead."

After she left I realized she was asking me as a cripple, not as a girlfriend. How far I'd come. I laughed out loud, not caring who heard me, a Bad Girl at last.

ON CHRISTMAS EVE I had wheeled myself into the spare bedroom my mother had turned into Gift Wrap Central. She sat in a brocade wing chair, bending over a package covered with jumping reindeer. Beside her at least a dozen unwrapped boxes waited their turn. "Mother?"

She pressed a hand to her chest. "Oh, Phoebe, you startled me. Is everything all right? They didn't work you too hard at therapy, did they? Did you remember to tell them about your stitches?"

I didn't bother to reply to her questions. She asked them

every time I returned from my sessions, and by now my stitches were dissolved. On the occasion of my last workout, all we'd done was eat date bars and listen to Christmas carols while the therapists sneaked nips from a bottle of brandy, flirted with one another, and complained about the meager amount of time they got off for holidays. I took a roll of gold ribbon from my mother and looped it around my fingers, making a bow, then let it fall back to a straight line. "Remember how you always made me wrap the presents?" I said. "You called me your special elf. Took me years to figure out it was just a job you hated doing."

She bristled. "That's not true. I asked you because you were so much better at it than anyone else. Your father used to say your packages looked like works of art. That it was a shame to open them."

Even then, apparently I was trying to find my way into something arty. "I was only teasing, Mother."

"Oh. I know that."

I leaned forward in my chair. "You know, everything's not all right."

"Oh, my God. I knew it. Do you need me to call those physical therapy people?"

I set the ribbon down. "Of course not. I feel stronger than I did before the surgery. It's the other stuff I'm not managing very well."

"Grief is hard," she said, her mouth firmly set. "I'll never get over losing your father."

"At least you have Bert."

She nodded her head. "Yes, and he's a dear, but did you really think he could replace your father? Daddy was my life partner, the love of my life."

I'd never called him Daddy. It was always Father. It made me uncomfortable to hear her speak of him in such familiar terms.

She smoothed the wrapping on a package, coaxing a wrinkle from the paper. "Every morning I open the closet and expect to see his plaid golf pants hanging there—you remember, the ones I told him were in terrible taste. And his argyle socks on the closet floor. Somehow he just couldn't remember to put them in the hamper. Those rolled-up knots of socks I used to yell at him about. I miss that."

I completed a loop on my second bow. This one I finished, but it came out a tad lopsided. I'd known my mother loved my father, that when he was alive she deferred to him in most decisions, but that she missed him this much? That she'd kept hidden. "Look at this bow, Mother. Present-wise, it appears I'm losing my touch."

She taped a seam. "It's fine."

I swallowed hard and went for it. "I want to talk about you and me. About how we can never talk about anything unless it's about me being in a wheelchair. Do you think we can discuss that?"

My mother looked out the window to where her butchered forsythia waited for spring. "I'm your mother, Phoebe. We can talk about anything. Although I'm not sure how to begin."

"That makes two of us. Well," I said, "let's keep it simple. I'll condense what's been on my mind for thirty-nine years, and you give me the *Reader's Digest* version of what's been on yours for—how old are you, Mother?"

"I'm in my seventies."

"Mother! What's the difference if you're seventy-one or seventy-nine?"

"Women of my generation just don't discuss that sort of thing."

I laughed. "You've earned your years. Why not be proud of them? Sadie always was."

She was silent.

I knew that by saying that I was comparing her to my aunt, which she'd always suspected. But I was also throwing out on the table my own pathetic odds for longevity. Okay, there were still some pieces of furniture covered with sheets, and maybe they'd stay that way. But I'd come this far, so I pressed on. "First off, I want you to know I don't blame you for—" I swallowed hard. "Juan's death. I miss him. I wish we'd had more time together, but what happened was an accident. It hurts a lot more than I thought it would, but I'm getting used to it. I think we need to talk about it, though, to try to move it out of the way, so maybe we can become friends. How's that sound to you?"

My mother began to weep quietly. Maybe that too was her generation's edict on grief—to show as little of it as possible, to keep those tears in the multipurpose guest room of life. Sadie once told me that ever since Allen Ginsberg had written that poem, *Howl,* it seemed to her that people all over the world did just that, that Allen had given them permission to mourn proudly, and even if the hurt was there forever, at least they shouted and got it out of their systems. I reached for my mother's hand, but remembering how she'd rubbed my foot in the hospital, settled for grazing her knee.

"It's hard work taking care of a baby," she said. "But worth the effort. Even when the child has problems."

I frowned. "See, now there you go. Problems, like me in a wheelchair—"

"I was speaking about your brother!" she exclaimed, and I sat back in my chair, chastened. "James was such a little scaredy-cat, never wanting to play with the other boys, always in his room arranging his army men or polishing his damn coin collection. Did you know he used to sneak food between meals and hide it in his bookshelf? When he was in third grade, I had to put him on a diet. He hardly fit into the Husky Boy sizes! And he was forever listening to your father's old Rosemary Clooney records. For a while we speculated that he might be homosexual."

James, in eternal pursuit of bedding Nance, would die hearing this. "A gay son wouldn't have been so awful. Or maybe to your generation, it would?"

She sniffled. "Oh, for goodness sake, Phoebe, I don't care if my children dress up in clown regalia or have torrid e-mail romances or take vows of silence like monks. I just want them to lead safe and happy lives. I want them to settle down so I can stop worrying. I'm old, Phoebe. I'm tired."

Somewhere-in-her-seventies old. But I knew well how tiredness had very little to do with age. I set the bow on the coffee table and started another. I finished three before either of us said anything more. Multitasking like mutes, we wrapped the remaining packages, taped on bows, tied the gift tags securely to the knot in the ribbon where it wouldn't slip off and get confused with someone else's pile. Tomorrow, we'd tear them open. Just like when I was a child, I'd wrapped all my gifts. "I'll tag these later," my mother would say, as if I were so dense I thought the flannel nightie, the vegetarian cookbook, the socks with moose on them, and the book on women painters were for someone else. I knew what I was getting for Christmas. I'd always known. For that golden span of time I had with Juan, things had been surprising. Surprise after lovely surprise. In my body, in my heart, and in the way his presence broke the boundaries of what had been my practical, manageable world. But now I was back to flannel and bath powder. More than some get, I told myself as I decorated the packages. "I'm tired, too. Shall I put the bows on these packages?"

She nodded. "If you don't mind."

I thought about how my mother and I communicated. I said things that shocked her; in return she gave me her silence, which I was then left to dissect and interpret. So maybe it wasn't girl talk, like with Sadie. It was still a connection. I tied the ribbon on to the package in my lap. "You more than anyone know how much love hurts, Mother. That a person can't open her heart without leaving that gap for grief to crawl through. How in some cases it isn't worth it."

She looked at me, indignant. "Are you saying it's better not to try? This from my brave girl who insisted on going away to college, who took on that godforsaken farm and turned it into a business?"

I hadn't expected her to turn my words against me. "Excuse me?"

Then she let go the sixty-four-thousand-dollar question. "Phoebe, explain to me how can you be so certain you don't want to keep your baby when you haven't even held her?"

In the area of my solar plexus, something caught on fire. I tried to listen to my heart, to detect if there was a problem, but this wasn't an electrical misfiring, it was a burst of shame. "Because I know that I'm the wrongest person in the world to be taking care of her right now. Because I don't know how to love someone who made it impossible for me to cry over loving the man I loved. Isn't that enough reason, Mother? Isn't it?"

My mother slipped a Polaroid from her sweater pocket. She studied it and smiled, but did not show it to me. Did she carry it around all the time? "Such a perfect little face. Cesarean babies are lucky that way, even if it is hell on their mothers. James said they named her Sally. Short for Sarah Juanita. Her first Christmas, and you missing it. Too young to know what's going on, but next year that'll be a different story."

She looked me directly in the eye, daring me to argue, and it was my turn to shy away. Sally. As a verb the word meant to go forth, to venture out. Don't dilly-dally, Sally. God, I hoped she would. Sniff every flower, dip her toes in the ocean, stuff her pockets so full of seashells that they made her pants hang low. For Juan's daughter, I needed to believe in a world full of possibility, one long trail with good surprises at every bend in the road. It occurred to me that possibly my mother had wanted all that for me, but in the wanting of such happiness also came the price of knowing there would be hefty bruises along the way.

"It's a nice name," I finally said.

BERT HAD BOOKED MY FLIGHT through to San Francisco instead of Bayborough. When I asked him why, he said, "Larger airports have jetways. Much easier for wheelchairs to traverse."

The flight made one stop. I used the bathroom then, while the cleaning crew was vacuuming and filling the seat pockets with new issues of in-flight magazines, and I knew my crutches wouldn't get in anyone's way. We dropped off passengers and new ones boarded. A woman with a one-year-old settled across the aisle from me, securing the baby into a carrier seat on the aisle. The tension in first class raised a notch. Everyone had paid good money for the comfortable seats, and now this rotten little baby was going to scream all the way to San Francisco. Earphones in place, I waited to see what movie they'd show next. Give me a Jackie Chan movie, I pleaded silently. Nothing romantic, and no tearjerkers, please. Meanwhile, the snacks were good, my vegetarian meal was entirely edible, and my aisle seat sat blessedly empty. The baby was quiet until takeoff, and then fussed a little. Out of the corner of my eye I watched the mother try all sorts of tricks to quiet him. She sang, she jiggled the car seat in a kind of rocking motion, and finally stuck her pinky in the child's mouth so he could suck on it.

Seeing that gave me a funny feeling in my stomach, the same way the cesarean section had felt real and not real all at the same time. Just like then, I had to turn away, to pretend it was happening to someone else. I looked out the airplane window and studied the clouds.

I loved takeoffs, the huge body of the plane hefting itself into the sky. The unlikeliness of a hunk of steel moving through the air like a feather seemed no less bizarre than me sitting inside, and no less hopeful. Below, the landscape blurred in the jet stream. The wings of the plane shredded clouds on its way to that eight-mile high. How anyone could be afraid of flying baffled me. Even traveling in winter, waiting for the deicers to thaw the wings, even with so little to see out the window, it was fun to me to be hurtling through the sky. The inflight movie turned out to be some awful crap with Richard Gere once again dating a teenager. I closed my eyes and tried to sleep, telling myself to dream about Juan, but dreams are headstrong things, and rarely listen.

"PARDON ME," the woman across the aisle said, pulling me out of my half-slumber. "Would you keep an eye on my baby while I use the restroom? I'll just die if I can't go right now. Thanks."

She sprang out of her seat and disappeared behind the lavatory door before I could protest. The baby turned his face and looked at me, all wide blue eyes and drool-covered chin. Then it burst into tears, and I heard the man seated behind it swear and throw down his paper.

"Why do they allow children on planes?" he said, loud enough for the entire compartment to hear. "Isn't it bad enough we're stuffed in here like sardines?"

The baby began to howl. Allen Ginsberg would have

cheered at this baby's pitch and stamina. "Shh," I said, and reached down to unhook my seat belt. I scooted into the aisle seat, reached across and jiggled the baby carrier the way I'd seen his mother do, but he—blue jacket, so I assumed boy—cried on. I looked around for the flight attendant, but she was probably in the cockpit feeding the pilots. The baby wound up, and the crying continued. What was his mother doing in the bathroom? Washing her hair? "Listen," I told him. "Don't you know that you have your whole entire life ahead of you? Well, you do. I'm sorry to have to tell you this, but lots of sad things are going to happen, and you're going to need those tears you're wasting now. Trust me, you'd better save them."

The cranky businessman sighed loudly. "Why don't you read him a little Kierkegaard while you're at it? Good thing you're not his mother."

His words stuck in me like darts, and I wished for Ness with the sharp tongue, or the quick-to-respond Nance. I patted the baby's arm, and tried not to flinch when he clutched onto me with his damp hand. When his sobs had finally turned to hiccups, his mother came out of the restroom. "What's the matter, Jake?" she asked. "Did you think I went away forever? Oh, Sweetie, I'm sorry." She took out a wet wipe and began to clean him up.

"Excuse me," I said to the businessman. He wouldn't look at me. I raised my voice as loud as it would go. "Yes, you. What you said a little while ago? Well, I'll bet all the flowers on my farm you're no blue-ribbon father yourself." I scooted back to my window seat, latched my belt, and listened to the blues channel until we landed in San Francisco. You don't fuck with a mother, I wanted to say to him. No matter how removed she is from her child, she still is one.

"I HAVE NEWS," Ness said, grinning at me as she fetched me at the airport gate. The terminal was packed with Christmas travelers returning home, but a six-foot-tall black woman pushing a wheelchair can pretty much part any sea.

"Oh," I said. "Are you moving in with David?"

She gave me a shocked look. "Why on earth would you think a thing like that?"

"You're there all the time. Sometimes you spend the night."

She laughed. "I love my room at the farm. I've even been doing a little redecorating, which is David's fault. Gay men—they can't let anything alone, you know. Rest assured, I'm not going anywhere."

Not that I had expected fanfare, but I was surprised to see Ness alone. "Where's everybody?"

"Nance had a photo job, Beryl woke up cranky and said she didn't want to drive all this way, and so she's home making dinner."

"So tell me your news."

She pressed the button for the elevator. "In time, Sweet Cheeks. Just know that it's good news, and it's going to make everyone happy, okay?"

"Come on. If it's good news, why wait?"

"Phoebe, be patient. Anyway, we must prioritize. First I have to brief you on Operation Honeymoon."

"What?"

"The surprise bridal shower for Zelda and F. Scott. We're having it on the twenty-ninth. There's lots to do yet. We need your help."

"So the wedding's still on?"

"It's on, all right. I don't think Miss Nancy Pants has slept in months for all the planning."

"Did she eat anything on Christmas?"

"That she did. A small piece of turkey, no stuffing. She ate the green beans but not the potatoes. Also she grazed the celery stalks and the kalamata olives. Did you know it burns more calories to chew celery than you get from eating it? Beryl told me that. Poor old celery. Maybe we should just let it grow."

"Well, at least she's eating more than she was. Did she agree to see a therapist?"

"Yes, after the honeymoon. And believe me, I for one cannot wait until this wedding hoopla is over. How was Michigan?"

"Oh, you know. Midwestern. Snow. Funny accents. My

mother has a terrible gardener. Bert is a sweetie pie. I felt like I had a manservant the whole time I was there. He took me out to lunch every day I had physical therapy."

"How was therapy?"

I sighed. "Sucks no matter what part of the country you do it in. I kept up, though. It was a good way to get out of the house. How'd the poinsettia sale go?"

"We kicked poinsettia butt. Raked in the dollars. James thinks we should build another greenhouse so we can grow more of the little boogers."

"Really?" That had never occurred to me. I thought of the places on the property where another greenhouse might fit. There were several. If we built one in a clever way, it could become the focal point of the farm, and maybe with a little rearranging, the poinsettias could move to an older greenhouse. The new space could be a place for customers to shop, or store their winter plants to make sure they lived through the season.

Ness and I drove the three hours south to Bayborough and talked the entire way. Leroy was fine. Duchess was on that new arthritis drug for dogs, and racing around like a puppy. Beryl was still hanging around, waiting to hear from Earl who, despite his promises, remained in Europe over the holidays. She was pining for Verde. She called Furry Paws in Eagle River every day, Ness said. Could a parrot really understand the telephone? And how could Earl miss their first Christmas together? David Snow had responded amazingly well to a new medication, though there were some side effects, like weight gain, and he was terribly upset about not being able to fit into his clothes. . . .

I won't ask after the baby, I told myself, looking out the window at what passed for a California winter. Michigan had snow—piled up and dirty on the berm. Here the hills were a vivid grassy green; anything on the ground was litter. If there was a problem, someone would have informed me. Sally. I tried to fit that name to the bump I'd carried around for nine months. I laid my hand over my belly, which still had the funny sewed-together feeling. It was so empty without the kicks. All she'd left behind was stretch marks.

At the farm Ness warned me not to spill the beans about the

shower. "Go lie down a little before dinner," she said. "I'll tell you the rest of the plan tomorrow. We'll spring it on her at the last minute, so she doesn't have a chance to back out."

"Or worse, reorganize it."

"Right," Ness said. Then she paused. "I hope we've seen the last of this not-eating thing. A person can only take in a wedding dress so many times before it ceases to be a dress, you know?"

I knew from dresses. As I wheeled myself to my room, I wondered what had become of my own wedding dress. I'd worn it for a solid week after the day I was supposed to marry Juan, so that over time it became a dress, a nightgown, mourning clothes, and finally, the worst kind of heirloom. I was sure someone had it cleaned and packed away, and someday, like a psychoanalyzed Miss Havisham looking for the odd thing in the closet, I'd come across the dress and have a good cry.

The scent hit me the second I crossed the threshold—a kind of sweetness I failed to identify with any flower I knew. My indoor plants were flourishing—the Easter cactus green and healthy, the variegated pothos trailing nearly to the floor. A planter of those golden mums the girls knew I liked sat on the dresser, but even a novice knew they didn't smell like something between spring lilacs and French soap and possibly some vanilla extract. Nance probably tucked sachets in the bureau, I told myself as I hefted my overnight case on my bed to unpack. She'd do something like that. I undid the case's latches and dumped the contents into the center of my bed. A shoe bounced off the bed onto the floor. When I bent to retrieve it, I spied the tiny washcloth halfway under my bed. I picked it up as if it was nothing more than a tissue that had missed the wastebasket, but the moment my fingers closed over the yellow terrycloth I knew. Its nap was disturbed, stiffened, like a cat's fur halfway through cleaning. This cloth had been used to bathe the baby. They'd kept her here, in my room. The mystifying scent was her essence, that pure, undiluted new-baby smell that can't be bottled, and lasts just long enough to make you forgive her dirty diapers. From the kitchen I heard someone calling my name, so I didn't have time to decide if I was angry or sad. Unsure of how to dispose of it, I tucked the washcloth under my pillow.

THE NIGHT OF THE BRIDAL SHOWER Nance was in a particularly impressive dither. Her final day's work before the wedding was a family photo session on the beach in Bayborough-by-the-Sea. The wind had played havoc with everyone's hair, the client was unhappy, and Nance was grousing about ending up taking alumni pictures at high school reunions when her career took the inevitable nosedive. "You watch," she said. "I'll be the dumpy blond telling the even dumpier blonds that they don't look any different from their senior portraits, and God will hear me and send me to the special liars' corner of hell."

"At least you'll have interesting company," Beryl said. "I mean, think of all the people who'll be there—Nixon and Clinton, Jon Lovitz, the Baron von Münchausen, and Pinocchio. All of them running around hell in their fiery little knickers."

Ness laughed so hard I had to pat her on the back.

"There is nothing funny about hell," Nance sniffed.

"Yes, there is," I said. "You *know* a man thought hell up to keep a woman in line. What's got into you, Beryl Anne? I've never heard you talk this way."

She shrugged. "I'm tired of being the peacemaker around here. I miss my damn parrot. It's Nance's fault for talking about hell and damnation all the time," she said. "I need some major comic relief."

"You're a heathen," Nance started.

"Oh, is that so? You're obsessed with archaic ritual."

"Hey, you two," Ness said. "No fair using Scrabble words."

"Everybody calm down," I said, and delivered my agreed-upon lines that would set the bridal shower in motion. "I know. Let's light a fire in the fireplace, make popcorn, and have a girls' night."

"I really need to go spell James," Nance said sourly. "He's been alone with Sally all day."

The baby's name rang out like the sound of wind chimes,

echoing through the room. Up until now we'd so carefully avoided saying it.

"I thought you guys hired a nanny," Ness said, stalling her so David and the other guests could arrive.

"We did. She called in sick. We need her well so we can go on our honeymoon."

Funny how just one second ago I was part of the pack, but now no one would look at me.

"Call him and tell him to bring the baby up here," Beryl said. She looked directly at me, and I tried not to blink.

My heart raced around the track a couple of times, and finally leaned against the fence of my ribs and gave in. I could see her looking at me. I was not going to fall apart.

"Sooner or later," Beryl went on, "you have to get used to it, Phoebe."

I felt like I couldn't get enough air. "Jesus, Beryl. Don't you think I know that?"

"Then what's the problem?"

"Nothing. It's just that this was supposed to be girls' night."

Ness said calmly, "Check out her diapers. Sally's a girl."

I took deep breaths. Fine. This would not defeat me. I'd stay long enough to give Nance my present, then excuse myself and lock the door to my room.

Nance made the call.

I busied myself by clearing the dishes. I wrapped our dinner leftovers and tidied the kitchen counters. The lights on the Christmas tree bathed the living room in a red glow that felt more like simmering anger than postholiday happiness. My heart was tense in my chest, as if it were about to burst loose from my rib cage and go looking for a fight. I recalled the smell of the washcloth I'd found days earlier, and sometimes clutched in my hand as I slept. Since I'd been home I spent a lot of time in my room, at my workspace. With clay and tools, I'd begun a new obsession—legs. I made fairies with dimpled thighs, knees as round as a summer moon. I shaped ankles to fit into slippers, beach thongs, and cowboy boots. I held them up in the light and turned them, not certain what they were, but they weren't the clay ladies of old. These dears had a menopausal wisdom, a knowing look, and they took no nonsense from me. Several times during the workday I'd open my bedside table drawer and study the photos of Juan and me—so few—only a dozen or so. Cheek to cheek, mugging for the camera. With Leroy, and in the background, Florencio on the tractor. Juan's face looking into the camera soulfully, as if there was no power on earth strong enough to separate us. Our affair felt as brief as the season when the tulips bloomed. I thought about how Sadie had fed me folktales involving various flowers, and that heartbreaking legend about the tulip, but I knew that every good story generally had a small root in fact.

The back door creaked, and James came into the kitchen holding the baby. "Sorry, Phoebe," he said as he walked past me. "Only for a couple of hours. I have to make some phone calls or I'll lose out on this deal I've been brokering." He handed the baby to Nance. The look on her face as she tucked the blanket around Sally burned through me. She loved that baby like it was her own. That was what I'd wanted all along, right? I wheeled my chair into the living room as fast as I could spin the wheels. The doorbell rang, and in walked David Snow, bearing gaudily wrapped presents. "Happy naughty bridal shower," he said, and kissed Nance on the cheek.

"Happy *what?*" she said.

"Surprise," Beryl and Ness said in a muted unison. "This is it, Baby Cakes. Your very own personal lingerie shower. Sit down and expect racy presents, because we traveled to the ends of the earth to find the sleaziest stuff they make."

"At least to the bad side of town," I added.

Nance looked to James, who tried hard to pretend he didn't know a thing about it and failed utterly. "I didn't make up the part about the nanny crapping out on me," he said. "Will you forgive me for the other lie?"

She pressed her lips together, and I could tell she was moved; in fact she was inches from crying.

David removed one of the intricate bows taped to a package and gently affixed it to Sally's head. She slept on, adorned but unaware. "Let me have that baby," he said, and settled into the Eames chair with her in his arms as he began singing some Billie Holiday. I couldn't take my eyes off her.

Nance said, "I can't believe I didn't figure this out. Usually I know everything that's going on around here."

Ness said, "Not everything," and smiled so widely I knew she was about to spill the good news she'd mentioned at the airport.

"What's that supposed to mean?" Nance said.

"Just a sec. I have to get something from the kitchen." Ness brought in a pitcher of margaritas. "Damn, I forgot the glasses. Well, we can each take a sip from the pitcher, I guess. Brace yourselves for my miracle news. My blood tests from a few weeks ago? The ones I had to have repeated? They can't detect the virus anywhere in my system. Lester says maybe it's the investigational meds, maybe next month it'll be back again, but right now, I have normal blood counts every which way there is. How's that for a belated Christmas present?"

Beryl leaped across the couch and sat in her lap, hugging her. "Finally some good news," she said.

James cleared his throat. "That's the best news ever, Ness."

Nance wiped her eyes and smiled. "God bless," she said, then to all of us, "I suppose you ordered one of those ridiculously fattening cakes?"

"From Jacqui's," David said. "Jacqui and me, we're buds. The box is in the car. Somebody else will have to get it because no way I am letting go of this sugar." He jiggled sleepy Sally, and her bow bobbled.

Sally. Baby face—chubby, dimpled, like the clay I worked. That shock of dark hair the color of Juan's. Her hands seemed useless, they were so small. The sadness that cloaked me was massive. It seemed absurd—my hormones were back to normal, I'd made and stuck by a truly logical decision, and my one and only brother was about to marry the girl of his dreams. In two days they'd walk outside and stand in the same place Juan and I were supposed to, make their vows, finally sleep with each other—halle-freaking-lujah—and Sally would have legally wedded parents with normal life spans and this great future with everything a girl could possibly hope for. I checked my pulse, and found it near enough to normal that I thought I was going to survive. The doorbell rang again, and Nance, leaping up to answer it, said, "If there's a Chippendale's dancer standing on the other side of the threshold, I'm sending him back where he came from."

"Damn, wish I'd thought to order a dancer," Ness said as Nance disappeared into the foyer.

We heard the door open, Duchess squealing the way she does when one of us returns from an extended time away from her view, and the crash of Nance hitting the floor. James got there first. He began arguing with the man who knelt next to Nance, and I heard this woman's voice saying, "Back up and let me look at her; I have first-aid training."

By the time we were all in the foyer, James had his hands on Nance's cheeks, patting them, the black-haired girl had her ear pressed to Nance's chest, and the handsome guy I'd never seen before was standing up, a little to the side of the action, his arms folded across his chest and his mouth held in a tight line. "I think she should go to the hospital," he said. "She hit her head. You don't mess with head injuries." Then, "Hey, Beryl. How's it going?"

"Hello, Rick," she answered, just as Nance came around, looked at him, and, groaning, closed her eyes.

"Rick?" Ness said. "Rotten Rick?"

I looked at her and nodded. "Apparently."

"I'll drive," James said gruffly, and this Rick—it was truly Rotten Rick, there in our foyer—shook his head no.

"How can you drive and watch her at the same time? You sit in the back with her. I'll drive. Maddy, can I have the truck keys?"

The black-haired girl had a name—Maddy—where had I heard that?

"How in the hell will you all fit in there with my dogs?" she asked.

Ness pushed her way through all of us and knelt beside Nance. She flicked margarita mix on her face. "You wake up, Nance. You come back to us right now, you hear me?"

Beryl's postcard. She'd mentioned the girl might come see us, but she'd left out the Rotten Rick aspect.

"I think I can drive my own fiancée to the hospital," James said stiffly. He was heating up, his face reddening. I'd never seen my brother raise his hand for anything except a champagne toast, but I had the feeling all that was about to change.

"Nobody's saying you can't," Rick said. "Just that it's a stupid idea when you have all these capable drivers standing around. Ones in control of their emotions, I mean."

"Oh, there's no one more in control of their emotions, is there, Rick?" Nance said.

But that was a lie. I could hear it in his voice, and see it in his body language: The journalist still loved her. The only question was why he had waited until now to tell her.

"Listen, asshole," James began, while poor Nance sat up on the throw rug and rubbed her head, and her hand came away with some blood.

"I think I'm going to need stitches," she said. "Does CHOP have plastic surgeons?"

"The two of you!" David said, standing up from the Eames chair at last. "I will drive. Carry her to my car, and we will go to the hospital together."

Ness stood there with her full pitcher of margaritas. "Call us the minute you hear anything," she said.

The front door shut, and we heard a tiny wail from the other room.

"What's that?" Beryl said.

Back in the living room, David had deposited Sally in the Eames chair, and she was awake now. She did not look or sound happy. Ness started to go to her, but with one outstretched hand, Beryl stopped her. "Phoebe, Ness, meet Mary Madigan Caringella. Call her Maddy. Maddy, these are the Bad Girls." That done, she took hold of Ness's arm and steered her toward the kitchen. "Ness, we have to get the glasses, remember?"

This Maddy girl looked at me. I wondered what she was doing here, and more important, why she was with Rotten Rick.

"Isn't anybody going to see to that baby?" she asked, in a slight twang.

The shower presents, the leftover Christmas trappings, the fire in the fireplace, the pitcher of margaritas, all of it looked festive, but the guest of honor was missing, the men had departed, and the political struggle to deal with Sally's escalating crying had rendered me mute.

Maddy looked at me and smiled.

"Beryl!" I yelled. "Hurry up with the margaritas. I need a drink."

"Somebody really needs to pick that baby up," Maddy said. "I know that some people think it's okay to let a child cry, but that's bullshit. If the baby is sad, give her a snuggle. Life is damn short, you know?"

Then she picked Sally up and set her in my arms, which immediately stiffened as if they operated independently of my brain. "Why are you doing this to me?"

"Geez, it's nothing personal. Don't have a heart attack, okay? I just thought the baby might want her mother. Do you know where the bathroom is in this place? I have to pee like a racehorse."

"You get back here," I called after her, as she disappeared down the hall. "I have no clue what to do with this child. I'm not her mother. Get back here. Ness? Beryl Anne? Somebody, please?"

I jiggled Sally. I tried to find comforting words. The Bad Girls left me alone, and still that baby cried on. Her fretful crying graduated to full-fledged sobbing. Finally, reluctantly, I let her have my little finger. Her mouth latched on, and it might as well have been my breast she sucked.

Once she made the connection, I knew there was no giving her back.

Rick

20

Beach Grass

In the great room at the flower farm, there was a book on the coffee table called *The History of Flowers.* While I waited for Nance to change clothes so we could go someplace and talk things out, I read enough to learn that the cyclamen—from the Greek, meaning "circle"—was a bulb with poisonous roots. Handy fact to know if faced with cyclamen at the salad bar. Yet the next sentence went on to explain that if toasted, the bulbs were not only safe to eat, but legendary for helping even the most stubborn person to fall in love. In journalism a reporter learns which sources are trustworthy; he also develops instincts. Where to probe, when to avoid. I wondered if that was how some old farmer figured out the cyclamen. When it came to loving somebody, it was always thus: The difference between love and death depended on enduring fire.

"Ready?" she asked, her face unreadable. There was a Band-Aid on her hand from last night's IV. They hadn't been able to get a vein in her skinny arm.

She was dressed in pale denim jeans and an oatmeal-colored sweater she'd stolen from my clothes years ago. "I'm ready," I answered.

She walked ahead of me, and it was like old times, me admiring her butt. I wondered if she could sense me checking her out, or if she minded. Without turning, she said, "You might as well bring the collies."

"I'd planned to."

We drove around looking for a coffee place, and then ended up at the beach. She'd handed me the keys, and stayed silent in the car. I wasn't familiar with the area, just kept turning down streets that all apparently ended at the ocean. "This okay?"

"It's fine," she said, and got out of the car and shooed the dogs out too.

A ways down the sand, some kids were using the last few days of Christmas vacation to create an old-fashioned bonfire out of the piles of available driftwood. A spectacular privilege, I thought, getting to play with matches, maybe the only time in their lives that kind of thing would be tolerated. I caught up with Nance, who was standing facing the water.

"What's the deal?" she asked me as Jim, Mentos, and Duchess ran loose on the stretch of sand known as Dog Beach.

"The deal about what?"

"You and dogs. I thought you couldn't stand big dogs. Particularly smart ones. In case nobody's told you, border collies are practically the Ph.D.'s of the canine world."

In order to hold back the smart answer I wanted to give her, I sighed and shut the door to the Rodeo. "They're Maddy's."

She looked at me with that old what-am-I-going-to do-with-you look. "Maddy. That was my next question, after the dogs."

"What am I supposed to do, tell her to get rid of them?" The minute the words exited my mouth, I knew they were a mistake.

Nance launched, and let me have it. "You used to have no problem telling me how much simpler life would be without Duchess, Rick. You used to tell me to *give her away.*"

"I never—"

"Yes, you did. You said it at least once a week!"

"Nancy, I think I'd remember if I said something that awful—"

She let out a yell. "Goddamn it, Rick! This is what you always do! Deny you say the things you know hurt me! You drive me freaking crazy, and then I start trying to prove to you what I already know is true, and you deny it! You said it, Rick. You said it all the time. You told me to get rid of Duchess for no reason at all."

"Well, say I did, which I'm not admitting. So maybe I had my head wedged for a while there. Is that a mortal sin?"

"For a *while?*"

She was on fire, and I worried if she got all worked up again, she'd pass out. "All right, maybe it was wedged for a long time. Maybe it still is. I'm sorry."

"You're *sorry?*" She folded her bony arms across her chest and smiled a smile I knew was not born of happiness. "Oh, Lord, let me stand here and savor that. That's maybe the third time in my life I've heard you say those words. You must be in love with that girl. How old is she, Rick?"

"Come on, Nance. I've been sorry for a lot of things. Just because I don't say so out loud doesn't mean I don't feel remorse."

"I'm supposed to be a mind reader?"

"Maybe if you tried running on logic instead of credit cards, you might notice what other people are feeling."

"Don't you dare throw credit cards in my face, Rick Heinrich. I'm not the one saddled with long-term debt preventing me from enjoying what other people call a regular life. I'm not some hardass hipster hanging onto his youth by avoiding responsibility. I'm not—"

I cut her off before she could add any more to the insult list. "A regular life? What in the fuck is regular about your setup? You're living on a farm with a bunch of strange women and their animals. In Portland you couldn't keep a houseplant alive. I can tell all this really agrees with you, since you look worse than I've ever seen you. What do you weigh? Eighty pounds? Ninety? You're about to marry some investment counselor you don't love and move in next door to Dysfunction Farm for good? What then? Fuck him until his heart explodes? Inherit money? This is about money, isn't it? I bet you can buy a lot of really comfortable Band-Aids with his kind of dough. Do they make them with Louis Vuitton logos these days?"

Her face crumpled, and I wished I could take every angry syllable back. This was how we always fought, the same verbal abuse. Only the words changed.

"You are the meanest person ever to walk this earth, Rick Heinrich."

It was a terrible habit of mine when cornered to smirk and laugh, and like some kind of autonomic faux pas, I did both. It was no good telling her what I meant was exactly the opposite. Once upon a time Nance had known how to read me, had known how to coax me from the cave where I hid in order to avoid my feelings, but it appeared she'd forgotten or no longer cared.

She stood there looking at me, waiting for me to take it all back.

I didn't.

That sweater of mine, a nubby old thing, nothing special. Why did she keep it? She probably had a hand-knit sweater from Ireland bearing a three-digit price tag. At one time the wool had embraced her body, flattered her breasts, and made her look downright boneable, but right now it hung on her like a thrift-shop find. I looked away. The school kids settled down by their bonfire. One of them threw a stick for Jim to retrieve, and the dog ran full out to find it. Duchess and Mentos wandered nearby, investigating piles of kelp.

"Tell me," she said, keeping her voice steady, "why you're here. Did Beryl tell you I was getting married? Did you plan this grand entrance two days before the event to make me doubt myself?"

"Jesus Christ, Nance. You think I'm that cruel?"

She continued to look at me, saying nothing.

"Well, should you be getting married if you're not a hundred percent sure?" I could tell she still loved me, and it scared me that she would after all I'd put her through.

"You rat bastard. How about the girl you slept with last night? Is it my business? No. Do I ache to take her aside and warn her that the Heinrich maneuver will not save her life but just might kill her? Hell, yes. But I see the way she looks at you. That I understand. You have this way of making women love you. I don't know what it is, but you have it in spades. You think I don't know that you fooled around while you were living with me? The girl in accounting? The features writer with the long hippie-girl skirts? Newsflash, Rick, I'm not a complete idiot. Not anymore, anyway. For once tell me the truth. Put aside your seduction, your clever games that always trip me up and make me think things are my entire fault. Are you here just to mess up my life? If so, congratulate yourself. You're the first guy to send me to the hospital. Put that on your résumé. I'm sure it'll net you another job."

She started off toward the dogs. All this time she knew about the women at work? Inside my socks the beach sand sifted.

This was like getting my James Taylor story tampered with, rewritten as if I had no morals, guilt by association. No way was Nance going to believe that I'd accompanied Maddy this far just to watch her face as she saw the Pacific for the first time. She didn't want to hear that, and besides, it wasn't entirely true. I did want to see her. I'd always want to see her, to know her. I dreamed about what might have been. Ours was the perfect romance—fights, make-ups, and great sex, none of the warts that were part and parcel of life. I deserved this. Let her gloat over my idiocy in letting it all go if it made her strong. Last thing I wanted was to make her faint again.

Last night the ER doctor had insisted she needed to be admitted for observation, and that she should only leave the hospital to go directly into a treatment program for eating disorders. Nance stood firm. She'd go there after the wedding. When the doctor said he didn't believe her, she asked him if he wanted her to write it in blood.

He shooed us men out so he could speak to Nance alone. James, David, and I sat in the waiting room trying to be cool. "Relax," I said before James could wind up his fist. "I'm not here to steal your girl."

"You'd better not be," he said.

"Don't you think if that was what I wanted, I'd have done it by now?"

"I think you're a little shit who gets his jollies making my fiancée cry."

"Can you boys hold on a second?" David Snow said. "If you two are going all John Wayne on me, I have to run to the hospital gift shop and pick up one of those throwaway cameras. Nance would kill me if I missed a photo op like that."

We stopped talking and sat in the molded chairs watching CNN with the sound muted.

Nance stayed in the ER long enough to undergo an EKG, have blood drawn, listen to all the stern lectures, and then she checked herself out AMA. "Take me home," she said to James, and he guided her into the passenger seat of the car. James and I sat in the backseat, looking out our windows, saying nothing—what was there to say? Somewhere out in the dark the Pacific Ocean rolled on. It had no problems with anorexia, or whom to love, or what in hell to do about losing someone you loved for all the wrong reasons. When we arrived back at the farm, Beryl was the only one up. She showed me where the spare room was and said that Maddy had already gone to bed. The house was silent. It smelled like the sea, and babies, the essence of women. I tried to take the couch for the night, but all that expensive furniture intimidated me, and eventually I slid into the sheets beside Maddy in the guest room. Immediately she draped herself over my chest. It was how we'd been sleeping for months, but tonight it felt illicit. Down the hall, I knew Nance was in her own bed, but I was pretty sure she wasn't sleeping. I thought about getting up, sneaking down there just to talk, but the next thing I knew it was morning, and she stood there in my doorway, ordering me around. "Get dressed, Heinrich. We're going to talk and settle this once and for all." Always practical, Nancy. Why had she been starving herself? Because of marrying a guy she didn't love, or was it because she wanted to be marrying me? Was her not eating, like I used to tell her all the time in Portland when something was bothering her, her own damn problem to solve by herself? She was skin and bones. Her jeans hung on her like she was wearing a pair of mine. Did it matter whose problem it was when it was a serious problem? I jogged down the beach to the shoreline to catch up with her, put my hand on her shoulder to turn her around, and before I knew it, I had pulled her into my arms.

There are some women you go to hold for the first time, and

your bodies sort of clash. One of you reaches upward for an embrace, and the other reaches at the same time, and it's like you're already fighting. Not so with Nancy Jane Mattox. From day one, my chin rested comfortably on the top of her head. Her arms slipped easily under mine, so I had this wonderfully reassuring sense of male dominance. Her hair in my nose gave off the perfume of expensive shampoo and the barest hint of her body beneath. I knew that smell. I would recognize it in a crowd. I knew how she heated up when we made love; how when she was cooling down afterwards, a shred of leftover pleasure would tremble through her body, and how she'd smile and shudder all at the same time, and how we called that her encore. I wondered if she had it with James. Did he notice how amazing that was? If she didn't have it, would she miss it, and think of me? Sometimes the scent of her in the morning would make me stand still as I was shaving, just amazed at how there were certain places in my condo where her perfume lingered. I'd stand there and breathe her in, touch things I knew she'd touched, retrace her steps. After so much traveling, I felt like I'd come home, and if that isn't love, I don't know what the fuck is.

We used to spend Sunday mornings at Powell's, the city-block-long bookstore, drinking coffee and reading all the major newspapers along with the other bibliophiles. I'd skip shaving, and Nance would leave off the makeup. Every once in a while I'd glance up at her just to see her face, pale and childlike, engrossed in the *New York Times*. Sometimes we'd walk through the stacks together, holding hands, checking the shelves for hidden treasures. Other times we'd split up and agree to meet in an hour. The best part of those separations was that we'd usually end up bumping into each other before the time was up.

"Hello," she'd say shyly. "Do you come to this bookstore often?"

I'd answer, "I'm glad I came today," and that was the cue to start the game. We'd pretend not to know each other, flirt a little, end up pressed against the books kissing shamelessly, touching each other just enough to get riled up, and then go back to searching the stacks again.

"It's not too late for us," I said into her hair as the wind kicked up, and sand blew against my legs. "I've changed. Really. I'm not the same person."

She was quiet. Listening, I thought. Wanting proof.

"I quit my job. Left it all behind. I'm writing now. Really writing, like I always said I wanted to. Of course, financially I'm a ruin, but I'm thinking a part-time gig will be enough to get me by."

She hadn't moved. Not a good sign. I felt a coldness move through me that had nothing to do with the ocean breeze. "You're going through with this wedding, aren't you?"

"If you let me."

I tried to break loose then, but she wouldn't allow it. There was so much strength in her small body as she held on to mine that I pictured us tied into a Gordian knot. I could see every loop of historical thread that bound us together and probably always would. No matter whom I slept with, argued with, maybe even married, Nance would be on the edge of the picture, looking back at me, loving me from a distance. Did it really have to be that way? Why couldn't I change some more? I'd already changed a lot. Left my job, sold the car, stuck by Maddy when she wasn't terribly pleasant. . . . I took a breath and almost said what I knew she wanted me to say: *I've never stopped loving you. There's nobody else like you in the world. Don't marry James. Marry me. I'll knock you up, we'll settle down, buy a house, and every night I'll be home by six*. But the trouble was, none of that would ever be true, and I didn't really know if it was Nance I loved anymore, or maybe the idea of Nance. If the reason I wanted her so much just now was because she was marrying someone else, then I truly was a scoundrel. "I won't get in the way," I said. "If you'll start taking care of yourself. Eating. Go into the treatment program."

The ocean smelled of salt and fish—cleansing smells, like a good scrub with a rough washcloth. Nance let go. She walked down to the water, stood there awhile, and then called Duchess to her side. The old dog's hind legs moved a little stiffly; arthritis, probably, and I knew it would devastate Nance when the dog died. I could have been nicer about the damn dog. I wished I had been. I liked Mentos and Slim Jim. I even liked Duchess, but for some stupid reason I just couldn't let her see that. *You made this bed,* I told myself. *Now you get to lie in it, lumps and all.*

I watched her walk back to me, and for the first time I saw how thin she really was. A person doesn't just contract anorexia, like the flu or chicken pox. It's one of those diseases that lurk. I knew that score. When we lived together, Nance would nibble at her food for a week, then prepare these elaborate repasts for me but eat nothing herself. She had dozens of excuses. *I'm full. I snacked while I was making this. I made the sausage and potatoes for you; I'm just having salad.* Dozens, and I fell for every one. All the literature said it was a control issue, a way for the overwhelmed to harness the chaos. I knew I overwhelmed her. Hell, maybe that was part of what I liked about being around her, watching her struggle to keep her balance. Watching my forge-ahead blond princess lose her footing, drop the Leica, collapse into tears, doubt her very soul—to be honest, when I could boost her back up, that was what had made me feel like a hero.

"Let me drive, Nance."

She nodded, and we loaded the dogs into the Rodeo.

Nance directed me to Katy's Diner in the valley, where the dogs had bacon and eggs on the porch. I drank coffee and fed the woman I loved oatmeal off a spoon while she tried not to gag and I tried not to cry.

MADDY WAS RIDING THE BLACK HORSE bareback around the arena, and the horse was bucking every couple of strides. I expected her to fall off or scream, but instead she was laughing hard, maybe even encouraging him. She took time out from one particularly spine-jolting bump to wave at me. "He's running out of gas," she hollered. "In a few minutes he'll start listening to me."

Women and horses. I could live to be a hundred, and I would never understand the attraction. I leaned against the fence and watched her while all around me, the farm went about its business. The old Mexican guy was loading plants onto a handcart; his helper had some elaborate spraying mechanism taken apart and he was cleaning it, talking Spanish to himself. Beryl came out of the greenhouse and stopped by me for a second.

"How'd it go?" she asked, as Maddy endured yet another buck.

"It went," I said.

"Is the wedding still on?"

"That it is. In two days hence Nance will marry the rich guy."

"So, are you and Maddy leaving tonight or tomorrow?"

"Wow, Beryl, get right to the point, why don't you?"

She cocked her head and studied me. "It's simple math. I want Nance to be happy. You do not make her happy. Therefore you need to haul ass and stay permanently away."

"Talk like that only makes me dig in my heels."

She thought that over. "Do you love Maddy?" she asked.

I shrugged.

She took hold of my sleeve and twisted it hard. "Do not shrug at me, Rick. Do not make the mistake of thinking your pathetic games would ever work on someone like me. I went to prison for killing a man you're practically an understudy to. If you don't have Maddy's best interests at heart I will lock her up here and hire a deprogrammer. Don't think I'm kidding."

Here came my smirk again. I bit down on my lower lip to keep it from escaping. "While it's none of your business, I can see you mean what you say, and I appreciate your being so upfront. Beryl, I do not know if I love that wild thing out there teaching a half-ton animal his manners. However, I do know that I love Nance, and that the best thing I can do for her is to let her go. So that's what I'm doing. I hope that's good enough for you, but if it isn't you're going to have to find a way to live with it, because Nance said I could go to the wedding. Ask her if you don't believe me."

She shook her head wearily. "Don't screw this up," she said. "Don't screw Maddy up, either. That girl has had enough heartache in her for two lifetimes."

"You mean losing her sister?"

Beryl's tired expression softened. "Well, well. If she's told you about that, I guess there's more to you two than I thought. But be warned, I'm keeping my eye on you."

She walked away, and Maddy brought the horse from a wild gallop to something close to a slow, easy trot. "You look good up there," I called to her over the lump in my throat.

The smile that broke over her face reminded me of a sunflower, wide open, heart completely exposed.

THAT NIGHT AFTER DINNER, Maddy and I walked down the cobbled streets of Bayborough-by-the-Sea. It was dark, and there were hardly any streetlights in the wealthy section of town. I wanted to give Nance the space, and fully intended to use this walk to either talk Maddy into leaving or asking her to drop me at the Greyhound station in Salinas.

"I have something I want to say," I told her. "I need to explain—"

She cut me off with a hand pressed softly against my mouth. "They asked me to stay," she said, stopping in front of a boulder that straddled the end of the tarmac and the beginning of the sand. "Beryl told me they voted, and they think I'd make a halfway decent Bad Girl. Unanimous."

"Are you going to take them up on it?"

"I'm thinking about it. Okay, that's my news. Go ahead and tell me yours."

It had changed now. There was no longer any urgency if she was staying. But I owed her the truth. "I don't know where to start, Maddy. She was my girlfriend for a couple of years. She left me because I treated her like—well, how I treated you. I made her stop eating, I made you drink. Guess I'm a dangerous guy to hang around."

She laughed. "Oh, yeah, you're badness condensed, Rick. Hey, I think I can hear the ocean. I wish it wasn't so dark out. I wonder if this is how a blind person feels. Do you think that's what it's like to be blind, all heightened senses and wonderful smells?"

She stood in front of me with her arms outstretched, breathing in great gulps of sea air. I wanted her so badly I reached for her arms, and held them just above the elbows, where I had once held on to Nance to keep her from leaving me. "I have no idea what blindness is like, Maddy. Come here. I feel like kissing you."

She turned, and I planted one on her.

"Mmm," she said. "What was that for?"

"Maybe to see if I could still do it."

She slid her hand inside my jacket and toyed with the back of my jeans. "Trust me, partner, you can still do it. I bet you can even do it on the sand. Wanna try?"

"Jesus, Maddy. There are cops patrolling the beach. You want to get hauled in for indecent exposure?"

She gave my behind a pinch. "Sometimes I plain forget you are fifty. Come on, Gramps. Let's get out of here and go on home, leave the fun to the young ones."

"That's reverse psychology," I said. "Play fair."

She unbuckled my belt and slid her hand in. "How about we just play instead?"

"Dammit all," I said, giving in.

"WHAT DO YOU WEAR to a wedding where your old girlfriend is marrying a guy you think is a dipshit?" I asked David Snow, who was here to give Nance away. We were in the guest bedroom, and David was tying his tie.

"A tremendous amount of restraint," he answered.

"Yeah, right. What if all you have is black jeans?"

"Then you wear black jeans, but you iron them first. A nice crease helps just about everything. All eyes will be on the bride, Rick. What do you care? Oh, sorry. Not that in any way I intend to encourage you, but how did you let someone that wonderful get away?"

I imagined us in ether. Standing on the deck of a cruise ship throwing those paper streamers to the people on shore. How in the end, they break, because what they were made of was paper, and paper, whether streamers or printing the news, didn't last. "If you want to hear the whole sad story, Dave, it might take a while. How long do we have?"

He smiled. "You, entire decades. Me, it all depends on my monthly T-cell count. I don't know you very well, Rick, but I can tell you that James is a stand-up individual. He'll worship that girl. Give her babies and diamonds and a place in the social register. Isn't that for the best?"

I sat down on the bed and studied my socks. "If she wants to settle for a perfectly ordinary life."

He laughed, and behind the thin face, prematurely aged by illness, I could see the strong man he used to be. "Oh, Buddy. We all start out thinking we're so damn unique, bucking the trends, making our imprint, our ideals so fresh and new that any moment we're sure we'll make the cover of *People* magazine. Then you lose a job because you're not twenty-one anymore, or you wake up with a virus nobody knows how to cure. Your hairline recedes. You realize that perhaps spending your retirement savings on high-tech stereo equipment and trips to Cabo might not have been the greatest idea after all. It's *living* your boring old life that gives a person wisdom. Believe it or not, that so-called ordinary life is all we get. Now let Nancy have hers without making her feel guilty. Chances are things will turn golden. You're not the loser here, you know. Isn't it enough that she loves you more than she loves him?"

"No."

He finished knotting his tie. It was one of those Jerry Garcia nightmares; why anybody would wear one was beyond me. "Why, you're pouting. That's almost cute, except it isn't." He patted my arm. "Behave yourself at the ceremony. James may look like a teddy bear, but I happen to know he can bench-press two-twenty."

I tied my shoes and went to find Maddy. She'd spent most of the day hanging out in the barn, grooming the horse, so I wasn't surprised to find her there, braiding his mane. She looked fabulous in a borrowed blue dress. "Hey, Babe," I said. "Need an escort for the wedding of the century?"

Her dark eyes bore down on me. "Feck you, Heinrich."

"What did I do now?"

"Duh."

She was wearing the purple lipstick, though it didn't go with the dress. It gave her a youthful, punky air that cheered me up a little. "Ever thought about trying a different shade of lipstick?"

"Ever thought about trying life without testicles?"

"Since I met you? Frequently."

She smiled. "And?"

"I've decided to keep them. You look beautiful. Come on."

"Where are we going, Rick?"

"To watch what should have been my wedding, I guess."

She pulled on my sleeve and looked up at me seriously. "And then what happens? Do you walk offstage with a broken heart? Come on, Buddy. You know what I mean. Where are we headed?"

"To get in line for cake, and the most expensive brand of champagne, undoubtedly."

"Ricky, sometimes I think you tick me off royal on purpose. Is that some stupid trick you tried on the blond girl? It doesn't play with brunettes." She threw the mane comb down in the dirt. "Goddammit, Rick. What happens next? Where are we going? You, me, us?"

The horse moved away from us to investigate his hay pile. "To see the ocean?"

Maddy looked at me, and what I saw in her face scared me.

"Where's all this coming from? I thought you liked keeping things simple. Day-to-day and all that. Occasional sex on the beach."

"I do. Well, I did. Fecking A, I love you," she said, and blushed. "Oh, Sweet Jesus. Forget I said that. I don't know what's the matter with me."

"You don't want to love me, Maddy. Look what I did to Nancy."

"Oh, I get it," she said. "You're the rogue horse, the one man who can't be tamed, can't be ridden? Give me a royal fecking break! Do you know what a crock of shit that is? Do you? Save the drama for your novel."

I ran my hand down the horse's neck, envying all that muscle designed to do nothing more than hold up such a magnificent face. What was I supposed to tell Maddy? That I loved Nance more than I could ever possibly love her? That I had fucked up the one thing in my life that could have meant something because it was my nature to throw roadblocks in front of myself? "I didn't put those awful things in my story," I said.

She took my hand in hers. "Don't you think I know that?"

"I don't know anything."

"Jesus Christ, Heinrich."

She kissed me. I let her. The purple lipstick—I knew how hard it was to wipe off. Didn't matter. I held on to Maddy and listened to the horse working on his hay. This farm—not a place I'd figure for Nance, who was more the leather couch, manicured landscaping, and Nordstrom's-within-a-short-drive type of girl. It did something to a person. I could see why she'd stayed. Maddy was going to stay, too. Suddenly, for no good reason, I missed that Airstream trailer for all I was worth—which was that couple of thousand dollars I had left from selling my car.

I'd heard it said that some people aren't meant to be with anyone; I'd never thought it was a saying that applied to me. Music drifted through the air. "I think they're starting," Maddy said, and dragged me toward the main house.

THE TREES WERE STRUNG with twinkle lights, even though it was high noon. Two hired musicians, a violinist and a cellist, both dressed in tuxedos, began setting up their instruments and music stands. This gathering of her friends—and outsiders, Maddy and me—was under way. There would be music, the words from the minister, the kiss, and then this agony would be over.

"Nice music," Maddy whispered as the strings started up something classical I didn't recognize. "All this moisture in the air, I'm amazed they can stay in tune."

When the cellist played the first few notes of "Ave Maria," from out of nowhere came Maddy's voice, joining in strong and clear, causing everyone's head to turn. Damn, the girl could sing! Nance gave her an uncertain smile. The wheelchair-girl's baby fussed a little, but with a change of position, shushed right down. I listened while Maddy steadily explored octaves. There was nothing operatic in the song beyond her range. At any moment it felt like she would choose a lower register and growl out some blues, but she stayed where she was. She finished singing, and Nance and James held each other's hands and made their vows. When it came time for the kiss, I turned away, my jaw so tight it hurt. I told myself David was right, that I could be happy for her eventual life, the dream she was always reaching for but never had with me. Maddy gave me a little pinch on the butt. "Almost through," she whispered. "Then we've got a date with an ocean, my friend."

We stayed long enough to watch the newlyweds eat cake because I had to see it for myself—the pointless calories go into her mouth, and her swallow. I knew then she would make it. She didn't need me. She had exactly what she needed. While Maddy slipped away to change into her jeans, James danced with Nance. She let him lead, which was more than I could ever get her to do. I drank a glass of champagne and watched the beautifully dressed guests move from table to table, like characters out of *Gatsby*. It truly was another world, one I neither cared to join nor would ever be invited inside.

And then something came over me. I found myself walking boldly out there on the dance floor, tapping James on the shoulder. "Mind if I dance with her one last time?"

He stopped. "Actually, I would. I don't think it's such a good idea, given the circumstances."

"It's okay, James," Nance said, moving into my arms. "Really."

"You come right back to me, Mrs. DeThomas."

She looked him in the eyes. "Don't you ever worry about that."

"Thanks," I said.

I held her carefully. In this dress she looked like something spun out of glass, fragile, beyond sweet, something to keep on a shelf rather than use up. "You look incredible," I said.

"I hope so. This dress cost a fortune."

"I wouldn't expect anything otherwise. I hope this guy gives you everything you need, Nancy."

Her hair, her makeup, the diamond earrings glinting in her lobes—it was a perfect exterior, but who could say if it matched her insides. "Don't worry about me. I'll be fine. I worry about you, though."

I looked out beyond her shoulder at this farm, the fields of flowers, and the greenhouses with the cloudy glass, the eucalyptus trees tall and swaying, the air clean and chill—California and its balmy winters. Nance was as far from fine as I was. Why do people come into each other's lives, I wondered. What fucking lesson is there in this much upheaval when things end so badly? I squeezed her hand and she squeezed back; there was history in the flex of every finger. When the music stopped, I held her close and whispered in her ear, "Go have babies."

For a moment she trembled. "You be nice to that girl."

"I'll try." I pushed her toward her husband and walked away without looking back.

MADDY HELD HER HANDS OVER HER EYES the last block before we reached sand. I was taking her to the same beach I'd been to with Nance. I didn't really know the other beaches, and last night, well, we could have been standing on the surface of Mars. "Oh, God, oh, God," she kept saying. "I know I've seen it from the car, but I cannot fecking believe I am going to set foot in the Pacific Ocean. Wait. I have to take off my boots."

"It's the middle of winter, Maddy. You'll catch pneumonia."

"No way," she said, keeping her eyes shut while she worked her laces loose. "It's like summer out here."

I'd found a parking spot right at the end of the street. Nobody else was thinking of the beach, not with New Year's Eve approaching. The sound of the ocean was roaring. "Maddy? You can uncover your eyes now."

But standing outside the truck, she kept her hands pressed over her eyes a while longer. The dogs were barking madly, wanting her to give them the cue that they could take off. Her chin trembled, and I could tell she was thinking of her sister. "On second thought," I said, and grabbed her up in my arms and raced with her down the sand to the water, her shrieking in my ear the entire way. Tomorrow my back would kill me, and we'd both have colds, but right now, this moment, as I ran into the small waves and felt the salty chill penetrate my clothes, I saw the look on her face, half-childlike, half-ravaged with grief, and I knew any subsequent discomfort was entirely worth this now.

We ran out into the surf, up to our thighs. In my arms, she turned and looked at me, splashing water my way, her hair swinging. She was laughing. I could do that—make Mary Madigan Caringella laugh. Suddenly that seemed far more important a feat than bringing her to orgasm. I let the dogs out of the truck, and like a pair of bodyguards scared of the water, they raced to her side.

The farm was nice, but it couldn't hold a spirit like hers. Somehow I'd find a way to convince her to go with me.

Beryl

21
Farm Journal

DEAR EARL,

Here are some things I've been thinking about since you left me at the farm and boarded your plane for Sweden.

Every time I think I have love figured out, something happens to change my mind, like Phoebe taking little Sally back. Nance marrying James after all. And Rotten Rick—Maddy choosing him over a life here with us. Who would have predicted that? Nance would say it's God working his mysterious ways. Me, I call it the power of love, and Ness laughs and says, "You nut, they are one and the same. God is Love and Love is God. Let it go already." I try.

I try to say, *So what that you didn't keep your promise about Christmas and I spent it playing gin rummy with Ness?* It's not so bad. I know a whole prison full of women who managed to get along without counting on love. They did their time. They stayed hopeful, like dogs at the pound, peering out the chain link hoping to hook up with somebody kind enough to feed and water them. They lived, until they didn't anymore, like Juan, or my mother, or the birds I tried and failed to save when I worked at Bayborough Bird Rehabilitation Center. *If it'll fly, we'll surely try,* we used to say.

I tried with those birds, and I tried with you, my love.

Earl, when you came into my life, I had closed off the part of my heart that dared to hope for anything kind from a man again. I helped everyone except myself. Then you started calling me and playing that music, and eventually we talked, sometimes for so long my ear would go numb. Inch by inch, you made me love you. You sat behind the counter at the bookstore dressed in your nothing-special clothes, saving me books, taking my hard-earned money, and all I saw was a man who had shouldered great hurt, like me. I saw a man who smiled at little kids, and sometimes even flipped them a quarter for the gum machine for no reason at all, and a man who liked to eat hamburgers and listen to the seals out in the harbor, even though he might have ketchup on his face and couldn't see the seals. I was like that. You were, too. Maybe I still am. But you, Earl? You were the mystery then, and you're still this mystery.

You have more money than I can comprehend. You go to Europe like some people go to the mountains for the weekend. You hang out with these legends—I haven't told the Bad Girls who, don't worry—but how does a man get to know people that famous? Are you Buckethead? I don't think so, unless you can shape-shift, because that guy in Santa Cruz wearing the KFC bucket and the mask wasn't you at all. I know your arms, your hands, the way you cradle that guitar, the way you two become one, like lovers in some Greek myth that hasn't got to the tragic ending.

Who are you, Earl?

Why do you love me?

What is there worth loving in plain old me that you couldn't find in these places you go to—Amsterdam, Munich, Stockholm—places I know exist, because there are maps saying so, and sometimes you send me postcards, but certainly places I've never visited or expect to.

I'm sending this letter to our P.O. box in Palmer. I hope you get it, and I hope you'll let me know—by letter, phone call, carrier pigeon—whether you are ready to be honest with me. If you are, then maybe we can have a life together.

But if you're not ready to be honest, I'm going to arrange to have Verde shipped back to me at the flower farm and stay here. Give my things to the women's shelter.

Let me know, Earl. Think about it and let me know.

I'll always love you,
Beryl

Rosemary

The herb of fidelity. Scattered in living quarters, *Rosmarinus officinalis* is said to bring good luck, or even to change bad luck. Greek scholars wove rosemary into their hair to increase the power of recollection. Appropriate at weddings, funerals, baptisms, and to ward off illness, rosemary makes a memorable appearance in Shakespeare's *Hamlet,* when Ophelia says, "There's rosemary, that's for remembrance." Legend insists that it wasn't the prince's kiss that woke Sleeping Beauty, but instead a sprig of rosemary he held beneath her nose, and bruised until it released its scent.

Phoebe

22

Overwintering

"ARE YOU SURE YOU'RE GOING TO BE ALL RIGHT HERE BY YOURSELF?" Ness asked me for the fiftieth time that morning as we stood in the foyer, me leaning on my crutches, her in newly purchased travel clothes that came with a wrinkle-free guarantee.

"To repeat, I am not alone; Sally's with me. James and Nance will be home in two days. Alice will be here tomorrow for my physical therapy. And I haven't forgotten how to work a telephone."

"I wish Beryl hadn't gone."

"She had to go, Ness. Earl called, she's in love, and she doesn't live here anymore."

My friend and roommate frowned at me. "You could both come with us. David says Arizona's wonderful this time of year. Warm, but not too warm. We could stuff ourselves on *calbacitas* burritos. Buy turquoise jewelry. Order custom-made cowboy boots, for both you and Sally."

Arizona sounded tempting. Outside the winter landscape was wearing a tad dull. It wasn't an El Niño year, but we'd had enough rain that some days Florencio and Segundo spent more time in the barn playing dominoes than they could working the fields. "Someone needs to stay here and mind the farm, Ness. We have deliveries coming, bills that need paying, and show me one week when no equipment breaks down. I'll see Arizona eventually. Right now I just want to spend time with Sally."

Ness still had that look. It went way past my wheelchair, that look. "If you're sure."

"What? Do I have to evict you to get you to take a vacation?"

We heard the honk of a taxi outside, and Ness picked up her suitcase. "There's David. I'll call home every night to make sure you're okay."

"If I'm busy with the baby I might not answer the phone."

"You'd better, or I'll fly directly back and get in your business big time, Girlfriend."

Didn't I know it? In the year and a half since Ness Butler had come to live with me at Sadie's farm, I'd learned that when she set her mind to something, whether it was growing flowers or shoeing horses or befriending me or returning to her Baptist roots, she did so with style and determination. "Send me a postcard of a jackalope," I told her. "Bring Sally back some beaded moccasins."

The screen door banged shut, and I was alone with my daughter.

Motherhood was still a concept that held me in awe: that tiny human being with the damp little fingers complete with miniature fingernails, those twelve pounds of piercing cries and adorable coos, that perfect being capable of the wettest, smelliest diapers imaginable, had issued forth from my crippled body. Nobody, least of all me, expected a miracle like that could happen. Every time I got dressed, I ran my fingers over the cesarean scar and remembered refusing to see her when she was born. At the time, letting her go to Nance and James seemed as logical as elementary school addition. Two people who could think straight plus one baby to love without resentment equaled a good life for Sally. It wasn't Sally's fault Juan died in that car crash, but for me the two events were forever connected. I had been too angry with her to see beyond the narrow confines of my heart. Whenever I thought about blaming her, my cheeks flushed and my heart beat hard, and I thanked my stars for second chances.

The night of James and Nance's wedding, they'd stayed out on the dance floor until guests began leaving. I went indoors to check on Sally, and ended up sleeping in the rocker next to her crib. James had arranged for a cab to pick them up early, since they had a seven A.M. flight. So it was still dark out when Nance slipped into Sally's room, dressed in her traveling clothes. She bent over Sally's crib and touched her lightly. "You were my little girl for a while," she whispered. "But I knew your mother would never sign you away. As soon as we tear up those papers I'll be your aunt. I'll spoil you rotten, and teach you the proper way to shop, and give you cousins you can boss around. Sleep tight, little angel."

It was a golden shining moment I wanted to keep intact, so I kept still until she left.

My brother and his new bride were on their honeymoon in Hawaii, exploring various islands with no particular set itinerary. The month they planned to stay was nearly over. They'd moved at a snail's pace, James told me, making sure Nance was resting, and eating right. As Stinky had said in his last phone call home, "I probably won't make her fat, but I've definitely made her happy." I pictured Nance in a flowered shift, focusing her camera, happily recording on film exotic flora and my brother's dopiest grin. There were two things I hoped for: that Nance would come out of the treatment program that lay ahead of her with some of the issues that triggered her anorexia put to rest. Now that the wedding was in the past, I began to think that Rotten Rick showing up wasn't so awful, that maybe it had been the turning point, that night she had to go to the hospital. I knew that she loved my brother. And that brought me to the second thing: I prayed it was a deep enough love to make the marriage thrive.

When I thought of them necking on beaches, I couldn't help but selfishly ache for my own honeymoon. Juan had said he wanted to show me "the real Mexico, not the tourist stuff, *Cara,* but out-of-the-way places where people live simply and having family is considered the only real wealth." Even though it hadn't lasted, Juan was my family. We'd planned to drive south in the very same car he ended up dying in. How strange to think we might have had the fatal accident ourselves, and all three of us could have perished. Instead, here Sally and I were, months later, coming to terms with having lived in spite of losing him. Some days I woke lost in the fog, his name on my lips, and it took Sally's smile to break through my sorrow. Other days the farm business distracted me enough that I forgot to dwell in that deepest of wounds. Sally made a funny noise, and her expanding view of the world pulled me in tighter than any lover's embrace. I'd catch a glimpse of one of the owls sailing out of the barn at dusk, like a new dad sent out for pizza because Mom's too tired to cook, and stand there lost in the awe of all this amazing commitment going on all around me. Every now and then a flower Segundo had given up hope on would bloom in a far corner of the greenhouse, and those small wonders were reminders that life, no matter how lonely, was still the perfect, singing gift, and capable of surprising me. I told myself that Juan and I had enjoyed our honeymoon beforehand, kind of like indulging in dessert before the main course is served. Nothing wrong with that. Sometimes I believed it. Memories of our bodies together were starting to come back to me in small doses. When I least expected it this shiver would travel over my skin, and I'd stop whatever I was doing, humbled by the memory of the way flesh could sing, how lovemaking had left echoes in my flesh for days. I'd hug myself and for the briefest moment, moving my hand in a certain way recalled Juan's fingers on my skin. A stranger might say hello to me on the street, passing by, and in that instant, it was as if a trace of Juan had traveled through him, this puff of familiar, warm wind, gone as quickly as it had arrived. It felt sweet and painful at the same time, and completely out of my control. At night my dreams tossed and pitched me into such sexual want that occasionally I'd wake certain Juan was in bed beside me, touching me where he—oh, suffice to say I had no regrets that we'd rushed into making love before marriage. That I'd been allowed a taste.

At the door of Sally's room I listened. My daughter was teaching me, among other things, that like puppies, babies make noises when they sleep. I held on to the rocking chair by her crib and watched her in her slumber. As usual, her thick, brown hair was sticking up in sweaty cowlicks. One hand curled into a fist clutching the satin hem of her blanket. Her mouth pursed itself as if she were nursing on whatever dream she was having at the moment, and finding its taste irresistible. Part of me ached to sit there forever, but I was determined not to become the kind of hovering mother my own had been to me. Of course, I was failing miserably, but I hadn't entirely rejected the notion that it was possible to let Sally make and eat mud pies, swallow the occasional bug, crash a bicycle, and fall in love.

The thing was, there weren't any books on how to get motherhood right. It was a day-by-day proposition, and error filled. The best I could do was lead with my heart, forgive myself when I screwed up, and think what lucky ducks animals were to have kept their instincts and fur coats and left the hard work of civilization to us idiot humans. What a mess we'd made of things. I envied Duchess her predictable routine.

Nance's yellow Lab lay in a patch of sunlight shining through the bedroom window, warming her old bones. Sensing me looking at her, Duchess lifted her beautifully shaped head and looked up at me with dark, questioning eyes. "You babysitter extraordinaire," I told her. "Minding Sally, keeping me company, you deserve the Nobel Prize. Nance will be home soon, I promise. I bet she brings you lots of presents. Doggie Hawaiian skirt, puppy poi, and a lei made entirely of biscuits."

Duchess thumped her tail, sighed contentedly, and settled down again to guard the baby.

Every now and again I thought about why Sadie had left me the flower farm, and I had come to believe there were lots of reasons besides getting me out of my wheelchair and into the larger world. I supposed that deep in her marrow she knew I would revive it, begin the never-ending task of coaxing flowers to grow, and maybe that was what she had wanted. Had she known that it wouldn't really become a farm until my roommates moved in with their various critters? How had this place existed without pets? If Ness and Nance were the heart of the farm, their animals were the life that caused that heart to keep beating. I'd heard foolish people dismiss dogs as nonsentient beings. Those months I lay in bed trying not to cry, when I was about to dissolve into self-pity, Duchess had wisely bumped her head against my hand, channeling my sorrow into practical affection. Leroy had his cantankerous days, kicking holes in his barn stall, and sometimes early in the morning when he'd beg for his hay I entertained fantasies of the glue factory, but when Florencio rode him at a stately pace, I swore it was as if we owned a living, breathing da Vinci. Had Sadie loved the birds like pets, her faithful barn owls and the occasional hawk, the visiting Canada geese? Did her heart leap up when a migratory bird passed through? Mine did. I knew she planted entire rows of sunflowers for the crows. She stocked the feeders with the highest-quality birdseed. She installed pumps in the birdbaths so that the water bubbled up, and the birds didn't have to fly all the way to Bad Girl Creek just to take a sip. Lately one dog and a horse hardly felt like enough. Sally was a huge presence, and wonderfully distracting, but sometimes I fiercely missed that cussing parrot of Beryl's. I'd tried calling her, but gotten no answer. I supposed that there were all manner of fun things to do in Alaska. Snowy glaciers, sled-dog races, Arctic chili cook-offs, places where you couldn't take a baby. Sooner or later she'd be home. Then we'd catch up.

WHENEVER SALLY SLEPT, I did a few chores. I grabbed the baby monitor, transferred myself from crutches to my wheelchair, and washed dishes, ran a load of laundry, made up her bottles. If she napped after lunch, I took the monitor with me and rolled down the newly paved driveway to fetch the mail. In the winter it arrived early, while UPS and Airborne deliveries usually showed up in the late afternoons. Before everyone left on their various trips, I'd signed releases so that the drivers would just leave the packages on the back step. If a box was too heavy for me, Segundo would deal with it the following Monday. It was a workable system, and I felt sure we'd left nothing to chance that a phone call couldn't solve.

I looked forward to the mail. There was always something interesting in the mix of circulars, say, a card from Stinky, or Nance's Martha Stewart magazine that I found to be amusement of the highest order. Any day now I expected Ed McMahon's face to smile up from a great big check so that I could buy a new John Deere tractor that didn't break down once a month. With money like that, I could go completely wild, buy a commercial-size juicer, get myself some high-end sculpting tools, order Sally some glittery red shoes, and have enough left over to buy Picasso's *Monkey on Horseback,* a print at Rebecca Roth's gallery that struck me as a good investment, at least so far as the eye was concerned. Weekdays Florencio brought the mail up to the house, but he had weekends off, and I welcomed the exercise as I rolled along, thinking how many times Sadie must have made this walk, surveying her plants, listening to the neighing of the neighbor's horses, watching rich people in fancy cars cruise by admiring this valley. Her inventory had become my inventory: flowers and crop cycles. She had money; I had chores and money worries. Of the two of us, I knew mine was the richer life.

Postcard from Anchorage

Hello, Bad Girls!

Earl bought me a *house!*

It's huge and beautiful and there's a view from every room and it's mine, the deed is in my name, I am a homeowner, I really, truly am. See enclosed picture for details—I'm the giant smile in earmuffs with the parrot on her shoulder.

The reason Earl didn't come back by Christmas was that he was recording a CD in France. He's going to Amsterdam this spring, and then his musician friends may come up here for the summer. But I'll be busy—he wants me to decorate the house and pick out furniture and have the kitchen remodeled until it's just like I want it. It's staggering to think about. I don't know where to start except wish you guys were here to help me. Every day I look at the hardwood floors and the old windows and think, Do I try to make something elegant, or keep the place woodsy? I keep thinking that if only Sadie was alive, she'd know what to do. She'd be able to see into the bones of this place, to know what it is the house wants.

Well, in the meantime, I sit on the floor and listen to Verde's new cuss word, which is in Tlingit. I have the kennel attendants to thank for that. He's happy I'm home. I set his parrot gym near the front window and he sits there all day checking out the scene. I swear the ravens come along just to tease Verde. Yesterday he came unglued when a red fox walked across the property. I wish you'd been there to see the paw prints left behind in the snow—so perfectly intact I could have made plaster casts of them.

Last week we got some new snow, so I skied into the backcountry and startled some ptarmigan. It was like an explosion of snow and feathers and wild bird spirit. I thought to myself, I could stand here forever, but I ended up skiing ten miles without seeing another person. The view of the mountains was incredible.

How strange to think that the hundreds of bulbs we planted before I left should start coming up soon, but I won't be there to see them. I love my house—my house! But it's hard to leave one landscape I was beginning to understand for an all-new vista. It seems like everything up here has to try so hard! The flowers, the animals, and me—I'm taking driving lessons, and I suck at left turns. I know, I said I never would, but a person can't live in Alaska without knowing how to drive. While skidding on ice is not the entertainment you might imagine it to be, I'm learning not to scream every single time it happens.

Many kisses to Miss Sally, and hugs for the rest of you, at least until you learn to do better tricks.

Love,
Beryl Anne (homeowner!)

I felt as if I were reading a computer-generated Frommer's guide. It was her same old cramped handwriting, but something about the words didn't ring quite true. She'd left us a few days after the wedding, flown on up to Alaska after Earl called.

I studied the picture of her house. It was enormous, and surrounded by spruce trees. She looked happy enough, dressed warmly, Verde on her shoulder. I tried to picture her driving, but it didn't fit. I could easily see her on her bicycle; she was always so deep in thought and bikes allowed for that kind of distraction. I guessed if I could learn to be a mother, maybe she could learn to drive. What the hell, maybe even I could drive again one day. Pick Sally up from school, take her to the mall . . . what I had trouble picturing, however, was Earl traveling to Europe what seemed like every other month. What was that all about? When he lived in Sierra Grove and ran the used bookstore, it seemed like he never went anywhere, and was always pressed for cash. Then we found out he was rich, and everything changed. The only typical information in Beryl's letter was Verde increasing his scatological vocabulary. I promised myself I'd call her tomorrow morning, after Sally's bath. Clean and dressed in a new nightie, my baby girl was full of gurgles and in a good mood for at least twenty minutes. I could hold the phone over her crib, give Beryl a baby fix, and suss out the truth.

"WE'RE HAVING SO MUCH FUN," Stinky hollered to me on the crappy cell phone connection, "that unless you need us to come home, we're staying another week."

"I'm fine," I said. "How's it going, anyway? Is marriage all it's cracked up to be?"

"Oh, Wingnut," my brother told me. "There aren't any words big enough to describe it. I honestly did not know people were allowed to be this happy."

I knew what he meant. Did I ever. But what I said was, "Good for you, Stinky. Kiss Nance for me, and feed her lots of pineapple."

"I will. Kiss the baby."

We said good-bye and hung up, and I felt a pang of guilt at what I'd put my brother through, insisting he take Sally, then so abruptly yanking her back. As if she'd heard my thoughts, Sally began to wail. Quickly I wheeled in to see her in her crib, red-faced and flailing her arms. "What's the problem?" I said, checking her diaper, which was dry, and smoothing her covers, freshly changed this morning. She cried on, until tears pooled at the corners of her eyes and my heart was racing. "What?" I said, trying to project an air of absolute calm, taking her into my arms and sliding her into the front pack I wore so she could nestle close to my worried heartbeat. Momentarily she quieted, but all that afternoon she was fussy.

I took her temp with the stick-on strip, I rubbed her back. I did her what I considered the biggest favor of all by sparing her my singing voice, and then I took her into the living room, turned on the television to all the talk shows, the courtroom dramas, and the infomercials. In between I offered her formula, then water. None of that was what she wanted. "Please stop," I said softly, stroking her cheek. Her cries sounded angry, but I didn't know from babies. Maybe she was ill. I telephoned the pediatrician, another Dr. Jenkins, a cousin of the annoyingly cheerful Dr. Jenkins who had been my obstetrician.

She was clipped, as if I were interrupting something important. "Does she have a fever?"

"No."

"Have you offered her water?"

"Yes. I've fed her, rocked her, and promised her a Porsche when she turns sixteen. I think she's holding out for a Ferrari."

Dr. Jenkins didn't laugh. "Sometimes they just need to exercise their lungs. Call me back if she doesn't settle down within the next couple of hours."

A couple of *hours* of this?

At hour two Alice called to cancel our physical therapy appointment. "I have a nasty cold, Phoebe. I don't want to expose either you or the baby," she said. "Hey, is that Sally I hear crying?"

"She's not crying," I said. "She's exercising her lungs. There's a difference. I'm not sure what, but supposedly there is. Alice, do you know anything about babies?"

Alice sneezed. "Well, I know that one sounds loud. Want me to send my husband over? Babies and dogs really like him."

"You need him there to take care of you," I said, hoping she'd argue and insist.

"Did you call her doctor?"

"Yeah. She says not to worry."

Alice sneezed again. "I could come if you really need me to."

"That's okay. Feel better, Alice. See you next week."

Sally cried and cried. If she could have punched me, I swear she would have. I thought about calling the crisis hot line. But what did I say? Help, I'm a handicapped new mother who can't figure out what the hell is making her baby cry, and I'm losing my mind? At the start of hour three, I felt guilty stuffing the cotton in my ears, but not guilty enough to stop. I tried Billie Holiday, which had worked for David Snow, but he had a good singing voice. So I tried some very strange world music CD Beryl had left behind that was filled with birdcalls and might have been titled *This Is Your Parrot on Drugs* if only I knew how to translate the dialect.

Sally and I probably sounded like somebody on the first day of alcohol rehab. I laid her down in her portable crib and shuffled through Ness's CDs until I found Puff Daddy, or whatever he was calling himself these days. When he started rapping, Sally's eyes grew big and her sobs dwindled to whimpers. "Look at you," I said. "Not even six months old and already rebelling. You're going to be a handful."

But after only a few "songs," Puffy apparently bored her, and she resumed crying. We were heading into hour four, and if I wanted the doctor I'd have to go through her exchange. Calling her for every little thing made me sound like a terrible mother, but I was so tired I feared I was in danger of some hysteria of my own. If only Ness were here, or Nance, or sensible, calm David Snow. I leaned over Sally's crib and pleaded, "How about a nap?" Her little mouth trembled with rage like I'd set her first curfew.

I rolled around the great room in confusion, and then remembered the stash of cash I kept in the desk drawer, and called a taxi service. "Do you have any female drivers?" I asked the dispatcher.

"Is this call from OSHA?" he wanted to know.

"No, it's from a mother who has a crying baby, and who

doesn't want to have to listen to any complaints from a male driver," I said.

"The call goes out to whichever driver's closest," he said.

"Fine." I recited my address, held on to Sally, and waited. She wailed, I jiggled her, and when the cab lights crossed the driveway I wheeled us onto the porch.

When I saw that the driver was female, I wanted to cheer. I felt certain the gods were with me, and this plan would work.

"You need a hand?" the cabbie said, eyeing my wheelchair and straining her voice to be heard over Sally's piercing cry.

"If you could just help me lift the chair into the cab," I said.

Our driver was tall, Latino, and had a wonderful smile. On the back of her visor, her license picture was smiling. She was strong, too, because she lifted my raging daughter with one arm and pushed the folded chair in with the other arm. "Got a baby seat?" she asked.

"I was planning on holding her."

She frowned. "That's against the law, ma'am. I have one in the trunk. It'll only take me a second to get it strapped in."

When we were finally settled, she got into the driver's seat, and flipped the meter. "I'm Mimi."

"Phoebe," I said. "And the one with the lungs is Sally."

"Where to, Phoebe?"

I felt the folded bills in my pocket, a couple of hundred dollars. Sally wailed. "Just drive around, I guess. I'm trying to get this one to stop crying, but I imagine you don't need me to tell you that."

"So. Anywhere in particular?"

"Right. You decide."

Mimi made a left onto Valley Road, and we crossed the highway. Soon we were in Bayborough-by-the-Sea, maneuvering down the tiny streets, the cab tires bumping rhythmically along the cobbled stones. Sally's cries faded to intermittent, and as I petted her damp hands, I dared to hope this ride had done the trick.

"Want to take the fifteen-mile drive?" the cab driver asked.

The thought made me smile. "You know, I haven't been on that since I was in college. A long, long time ago. Sure."

Like every cab driver on earth, Mimi knew shortcuts, and how to get through the gate without paying the fee. She took the road at a steady pace, and I was spellbound by how the world can change so drastically, but some things, like this drive, managed to remain untouched. There were fabulous homes I'd dreamed of owning since I first visited my aunt. One particularly Italian structure sat at the edge of the cliff and when I rolled down the window, I could hear the surf. Years ago the parks system had stopped visitors from hiking out to the lone cypress, but it was still there, the gnarled root system clinging to the cliff, growing against all odds.

"Have you lived in the area a long time?" I asked the driver.

"No. Just moved here."

"Where did you come from?"

"All over."

"Oh," I said, uncertain if I should keep the conversation going. "Does it bother you when your fares ask you questions? I mean, would you rather just drive and listen to the radio?"

She laughed. "Usually they keep pretty quiet. But sometimes they like to hear the local history. I don't mind."

We were quiet the rest of the drive, and when we exited the scenic stuff, she drove along the oceanfront in Sierra Grove, stopping at a turnout where a boardwalk led down the hill to the beach. When she cut the motor, Sally woke up yowling. "You mind if I try something?" Mimi asked me. "It's an old trick my *abuela* taught me."

"Who am I to disagree?" I said. "Try away."

Mimi wrapped Sally in her blanket as tight as a burrito. She walked down the boardwalk with my baby until they were indistinct shapes, and my heart pounded in fear. If she walked away with my baby, what would I do? I couldn't run after her, and I had never been able to walk on sand. When Sally's yips faded and all I could hear was ocean, and the bark of an occasional seal, jealousy replaced my fear. They stood there long enough for me to remember I didn't have legs or an *abuela*. The most I knew to do was call an ambulance. I would never make it as a mother unless I got help.

"Don't suppose you're looking for a job as a nanny?" I said

when she came back to the car and strapped Sally into her seat.

"Thanks, but I already have a job driving a delivery truck. This is my son's cab. I drive it when he has something else going. Tonight he's studying for a big test. He's a fireman, working toward his paramedic's license."

"That's nice," I said. "So, you're a mom. What the hell is this crying thing about? One minute she was perfectly happy, the next, Armageddon. They didn't cover that in the baby book."

Mimi looked at me in the mirror. "They're babies," she said. "What do they know from books?"

SALLY SLEPT THROUGH THE NIGHT, and so did I. Sea air or plain exhaustion, I didn't care so long as I got some sleep under my belt. We had a nice, quiet day, even though it rained, and I actually got a little work done on my clay ladies, The brown clay I shaped into a mermaid could have been anyone until I thought of adding a blocky Checker Cab for her to sit on. Odds were that I'd never see that woman again, but for quieting Sally, she deserved a sculpture.

At three P.M., just after Florencio and Segundo went home, Sally started in. Right away I considered paging Lester. After all, Dr. Jenkins was frightfully young. How did she know it was *really* okay to let a tiny baby cry herself to sleep? I knew firsthand the long-term psychological effects of inconsolable grief, and didn't want my daughter to experience one minute of that howling vacuum. Duchess, fed up, began to pace the floor and howl. That was all I needed, a hysterical dog in addition to a crying child. I picked up the phone and, without thinking, punched in my mother's number in Michigan. Factoring in the time change, I figured she and Bert were probably just finishing supper, which put her at the kitchen sink, prewashing dishes before she put them into the high-end dishwasher she didn't trust to get things clean. She answered on the second ring.

"Mother," I said, when I heard her voice. "Do you know how to make a baby stop crying?"

She laughed. "Well, I think I remember a few tricks. Tell me when it started and what you've tried."

I laid out the last few days, starting with Ness leaving by cab and Mimi fixing things by cab, and even asked my mother what she thought would happen if I bought a defunct cab and took Sally out to sit in it. Rita ignored that, and walked me through all the possibilities: colic, croup, diaper rash, dehydration, bad dreams, tantrums, and hyperactive bowels, which sounded so horrible I didn't want to ask what it meant. "You really have tried everything, haven't you?" she said. "Oh, honey, this is when I wish I didn't live so doggone far away. I could drop in, let you take a nap, make you supper."

"Stop," I begged. "You're going to make me cry, too."

"Maybe you need to," she said. "You've spent a long enough time not crying that maybe it's time to let it out. Put that baby in her crib. No child ever died from crying. Then you get back on the phone with me and talk."

I did as she said. Sally hiccuped and flapped her arms. It killed me to leave her there alone, but my mother had managed to raise me, so I believed her. "I'm back," I managed to say before the dam gave way, and the most awful noises began to come out of me.

"Oh, honey," she said. "Let it all out. I promise I won't go anywhere. And if you need me to get on a plane tonight I will do that. You just say the word."

If I'd been capable of speech at that point, I would have said yes, plane, now, hurry. But with tears and snot and the effort of holding on to the phone, I couldn't produce normal speech.

"When your father died," my mother said, "I thought I might as well lie down and die myself. You're too young to remember, Phoebe, but your father took care of everything. The bills, the taxes, whatever needed doing. The night he died was the first night I'd slept alone in decades. I cried until I was empty, and then I stared up at the ceiling and told myself, 'Now, Rita DeThomas, you have two children in this house who still need bringing up. Jim would absolutely be horrified if he saw you carrying on this way. He was a sensible man, and he's left you more than enough money to finish the job. So what's it going to be? Poor, pitiful widow woman, or are you going to make your husband proud?' That's what I told myself, Phoebe."

"Did you believe it?" I managed.

"Not one single bit."

We were silent a moment, and I could hear Sally crying again.

"The important thing is to tell yourself you will get through it," she told me. "Wait, I know one thing that you could try. Do you have a hot water bottle?"

"I think so."

"Go fetch it," she told me. "Fill it with warm water, place it across your knees, pad it with several layers of blanket, and lay Sally belly down on top. Take care to make certain her face isn't covered in blankets. Do it now, and I'll hold on."

I laid the phone down and did as she advised. When Sally quieted, I picked up the receiver. "Mother?" I said.

"What is it, honey?"

"I love you," I said, and then I started to cry all over again. "But the truth is I don't think I'm up to this. I should have left Sally with James and Nance."

"Why, Phoebe," my mother gently chided. "You stop that business right now. Crying for no reason is only the tip of the iceberg with daughters. Trust me, there will be broken arms and missed curfews and questionable friends and that first failing grade to use your tears on. And just when you think you've survived the worst, something new will come along to challenge you. Crumple up now and you won't make it five years, let alone until she turns twenty-one."

"Oh, Mama," I said. "What if I don't live that long?"

My mother didn't hesitate one second. "By hook or by crook, you will. Having children only increases your grip on the world. It's like reading a thriller. You can't put it down because you have to know how the story turns out."

Then, as if baring our hearts to each other was an ordinary thing, she began telling me how Bert was taking her on a trip to Italy in the spring, and this wonderful shade of blue of the water along the coast. I tried to listen, but everything she said floated by me, like a dream that I found pretty but was too tired to enjoy. When we finally hung up, I dragged myself onto the couch and slept right there, one hand on Sally's portable crib, the other within reach of the phone, and I hugged the hot water bottle to myself.

"CARA? *COVER YOURSELF WITH THE AFGHAN. Can't have you catching a chill. Let me stoke the fire, get it going good again. There, that's better. Hey, I like what you've done with the place. The new paint in the guestroom—very sunny. The driveway—you know, that was the first thing I planned to do after we got married. Plus install more ramps for you. And I see you're back to making clay people. That's good. The world needs your clay ladies. Remember how I said my mother would be shocked to see them? Not anymore, my love. Would you believe this? Heaven* erases *prejudices. A person comes here; he begins to see the beauty in all things."*

The Juan who finally came to me in my dreams did not look like the man I'd last seen in his wedding clothes. He was graying at the temples, and his face seemed careworn with age lines. His eyes, though, they were the same dark coffee brown, so deep and soulful as to pull me into a place I'd forgotten existed. *"Juan? You look so different. What happened to you?"*

"Up here you get to pick your age," he told me. *"This is me at fifty. I tried age ten, that's when I hit my first home run, and twenty-one, when I was cocky, but fifty is nice, it suits me. As time goes by, you'll understand why."*

"I miss you so much," I said. *"I can't stand taking a breath without you."*

"Shh. Enough of that, Pheebs. I'm here. I'm right next to you all the time."

Oh, in dreams anything is possible. A bear puts his arm around you. You make love to Johnny Depp, and he thinks you're the most exquisite creature he's ever seen. You fly across the sky and understand the secrets of the universe as they spin by in a kaleidoscopic whir too swift to learn from, that rough spin of subconscious and fulfilled wishes. *"Juan, I have to ask. Did dying hurt?"*

"Nowhere near as much as leaving you."

"God, I hate it that it hurt you at all. Not a day goes by that I don't wish it had been me instead. It seems crazy that I'm here and you're not. And your mother, Juan. It's my fault she died."

"Phoebe, my love, that's just plain silly talk. Mami's happy here. Where I am now is incredible, you can't imagine the people I meet. Every moment I had on Earth is precious, even the hurt and suffering. It's hard to explain, but you have to trust me. Escuchame, Bebe. *I don't have much time. You're going to wake up soon and not remember any of this. So let's move on to the important things."*

"You mean Sally."

"Sally, yes, but you, too. Look at our girl, Phoebe."

"I do. Look at her temper."

He laughed. *"In Mexican culture, we celebrate the woman's lineage. Their strength exists separate from the men, you know, like a river is part of the earth, but two different elements? Our women are so precious to us that men envy and respect them equally. Women have a knowing. Lucky for Sally that you possess such a strong spirit. You will give her so much."*

"The hell I do, Juan! You should have heard her crying. I had no clue what to do. If it wasn't for my mother, I swear one of us would have gone mad. Sally needs a father."

"She'll have one."

"Oh, I know. She has Uncle James, and Uncle David, and three grandfathers in Segundo and Florencio and Bert, but they're not you. There will never be anyone else for me like you, Juan. You were it. Don't get me wrong, I'm not complaining. You were more than enough. I will love you until the day I die, and after that I will love you even more."

"I'm flattered, my sweet, but I'm not so special as you claim."

"Yes, you are. Every word I said is true."

"Now you listen to me, Phoebe DeThomas. You will go on and love somebody else. That is what it means to live."

"No way, José."

"You don't think such a thing is possible, but you will see."

"Not even your ghost talking can make me love somebody else."

He sighed, a sound like the wind whistling down the chimney, blowing ashes across the carpet. "Cara, *love comes to you when you're least expecting it. One day you will be sitting in the kitchen pinching clay in your hands, or maybe on the porch nursing a slight headache. Maybe it will be one of those bad days when your sorrow runs as deep as Bad Girl Creek. There will come a knock at the door, Duchess will bark, and you will go to open it, and what you see there will cause your heart to leap up. I have to go now. I'm taking Florencio's daughter to the park. Then we'll have an early supper with Sadie.*"

"Don't leave me, Juan. Stay with me."

"Be open to the possibility, Phoebe. Promise me you won't grow bitter and sour and root bound. Be the girl I fell in love with, daring me to race her in her wheelchair. And please? Never, ever cut your beautiful hair."

EARLY THE NEXT MORNING Segundo's phone call woke me. I half listened as he told me how his car had broken down, and that he would be delayed at least a couple of hours. "Don't come in," I said. "It's all muddy and looks like it might rain again. Take that girlfriend you're always telling me about to the movies."

Until I could hang up I studied Sally in her crib, looking at me with wide eyes, her expression deceptively docile. I heated her bottle and fed her, then took her into her room for a sponge bath. "Well, well," I said. "See what a little sleep does for you?" I was still groggy from my own fretful night. I'd had one of those slumbers thick with dreams I couldn't remember to save my life.

I was pondering the logistics of taking my own shower—where I could stash Sally safely, how feasible it was to wash with the shower door open, all those considerations that would eventually make me settle for a swipe with a washcloth—when someone started hammering hard at the front door. With each knock, my head pounded twice as hard, and Sally began to fuss again. "Dammit," I said, putting her in the front pack and wheeling to the door. From the window I could see a brown UPS truck, and in the split second it took me to remember how I used to feel when Juan drove up, I felt my heart tear in half. I yanked the door open and started in before I gave the woman driver a chance to explain herself. Then I saw that it was Mimi, the cab driver.

"I signed the release form for deliveries to be left out back," I said.

In the daylight I could see she was Beryl's age, her glossy brown hair chopped short in one of those really cute styles I could never pull off. Like Juan, she was Hispanic, and like Juan, her smile was welcoming. Seeing her in the UPS uniform caused me to remember him so strongly I put a hand to my throat. Mimi was wearing a lot of makeup, but she was one of those women who knew how shadow and blush could make the most of her eyes and cheekbones.

"I apologize, Phoebe. I did drive around to the back, but nobody was there, and as you see, this package is marked perishable. It's going to rain, and I didn't want to leave it to get soggy."

Sally resumed her wailing from the night before, and the sky opened up so hard I expected hail. I wanted to throw myself out into the mud and wallow like the saddest pig ever. "Excuse me," I mumbled, fighting tears. "I'm kind of a wreck here. Can you just leave the package on the front porch? I can't really manage it on my own, and my farm foreman won't be back in until Monday."

Mimi hefted the box, which was about three feet long, and looked heavy. "If you don't tell anyone, I can take it inside for you. We're not supposed to do that, liability and so forth, but I don't mind." She looked back at her truck, then opened the door and pulled the box inside. "Where should I put it?"

"I don't know. Anywhere. Wherever I won't trip over it."

"The box says orchids. From Hawaii?"

James and Nance. "The kitchen table," I hollered over Sally's crying.

Mimi placed the box at the table's edge where I could open it. As she turned to go, she hesitated, a thoughtful expression causing her to frown. "I'm a grandmother," she said. "Would you like me to hold Sally just until you catch your breath?"

It wasn't like I didn't know her. We'd spent half the night driving around Bayborough together. But I was still a bad mother.

I didn't bother to find out if she was a kidnapper, or contagious, or anything else. I handed Sally right over and marveled at how light I felt when she was in the UPS driver's arms.

"Is driving for UPS your other job?"

She nodded. *"Que pasa?"* she said to my daughter. "What is so upsetting that you have to complain so loudly? Look outside at the rain. You're so loud you're getting the sky all upset." She jiggled Sally and looked at me.

"I wish I could say she takes after her father," I said.

"Sientirse la mama de los pollitos. Sientirse la mama de Tarzan," Mimi said in a singsong Spanish. I closed my eyes. Maybe Juan's mother would have said exactly this same thing to Sally. Maybe Juan himself had lullabies committed to memory. I didn't know except that I would never hear him sing them.

"What did you tell her?" I asked, because Sally was once again reduced to hiccups.

"That she makes me feel like a mother hen, that she's a wild thing, and I feel like Tarzan's mother trying to quiet her. It doesn't mean anything. Just the sound of my voice she likes. Maybe the Spanish."

Juan's Spanish—he hauled it out when we made love. He could have been telling me the vacuum cleaner needed a new bag, but the sound of his words made me melt inside until my heart was a puddle of chocolate and he was lapping it up. "I wish I knew more Spanish," I said. "I mean, more than just to say please and thank you."

"Spanish is easy," she said, "except for the verbs."

I put the kettle on for tea and took a box of gingersnaps down from the cupboard because it seemed the polite thing to do. "Will you stay awhile?" I asked.

"I'd love to."

By the time tea had steeped and we'd both had a couple of cups, the box of cookies was empty. We sat in a time period that seemed to exist all of its own. Never once did Mimi leap up, moving at Mach 1 the way Juan used to. Where he had been energetic, she moved slowly. There was a peace about her as she held my cranky daughter in her strong arms, as if she knew exactly what she was doing. I wondered if there was any way I could match UPS's salary and get her to come to work for me. And there was this: When I squinted, when I narrowed my vision so that Mimi's uniform up against Sally's skin was blurry, I convinced myself that this is what it would have looked like when Juan held his daughter.

"How many grandkids do you have?" I asked.

"Two. But I'm not allowed to see them."

"Why not?"

"Oh, a bitter divorce. My son tried for custody, but he lost. His ex is into punishing him. I'm just an extension of that."

"That must be really hard."

She cooed at my whimpering daughter. "Yeah. Everybody has a sad story, and that one's mine. Too long to tell."

I wanted to say I had time to listen to that story, but I didn't know her well enough. "What about another time?" I asked.

The rain pounded the earth, and I knew that come Monday morning Segundo would be knee-deep in mud. "What's your last name?" I asked. "Mine's DeThomas."

"You promise you won't laugh?"

I crossed my heart.

"Bravo."

I laughed. "You're just saying that to cheer me up."

"Nope, it's my name, and my mother's name, and hers before that. I sound like one of those miracle cleaners they sell on infomercials, 'Folks, try some Mimi Bravo for those really tough stains!'"

She handed Sally back to me but didn't take her eyes off my daughter.

I recognized the sorrow in her eyes. I could tell she was so tough that no one else would see it but me. Was it the grandchildren? Her own broken heart? In a way she reminded me of Ness. I poured her another cup of spice tea.

"I really don't have time to finish that," she said.

"Just a sip for the road," I said. "Sally's dad was Mexican. I pictured her growing up bilingual."

"Really?" Mimi Bravo said. "Did you two divorce?"

"No. He died before she was born."

"I'm sorry."

"Yeah, that's *my* sad story."

"Spanish isn't so hard to learn," she said, sipping the tea. "I could give you lessons. Your girl is beautiful."

"I'm sorry I was such a witch to you. Please forgive me."

"Done and done."

As she rose to leave, I asked, "Is this your regular route?"

She nodded. "I think it was a fluke I got assigned to it—one of those promote-the-minority things. It gets me out of San Jose, so I'm not complaining. It was nice to meet you—again."

"Will you come see us another time?" I asked, ashamed at how desperate I sounded.

She looked at me frankly. "I'll try."

MIMI CAME BACK SEVERAL TIMES. Once she left a bag on the porch. Inside was a CD of Tish Hinojosa's lullabies. Another day she ran in at lunchtime and left me oranges. "They're good for juice," she said, and I hardly had time to thank her before she was out the door and I heard the van start up. We exchanged phone numbers after that, and she called me the next day to offer to sit with Sally while I took a nap. "Unless I'm imposing," she said.

"How is letting me nap an imposition?" I asked her.

"Well, I heard about your Juan from the other drivers. Me showing up here like that must have reopened the wound in a terrible way."

I grinned bravely over the phone line. "I know what it looks like, me in this chair. I've spent my whole life dealing with people feeling sorry for the poor cripple. But Mimi, take a look at my life—I have this farm, my baby, friends, I'm rich. Miserable maybe, but embarrassingly rich. I miss him, but seeing your van pull up, for a second there it felt like old times."

"I can come over tomorrow," Mimi said. "How about I bring lunch? Nothing fancy, a salad and some bread. Sound okay?"

I wanted to say yes, but now that I'd had some rest, I was starting to think like a mother, protective, suspicious in endless ways. "No offense, Mimi—"

"Oh, Phoebe," she interrupted. "UPS drivers are like firemen or cops. If one of us needs help, two will show up."

I don't know if I ever welcomed sleep as gratefully as I did the first day she baby-sat. I was so tired that I felt certain Juan would come to me in my dreams, but if he did, I didn't remember. All I know is that when I woke, Mimi was sitting on the couch reading *The History of Flowers,* Sally was clean and fed and lying on the floor on a blanket happily amusing herself by drooling all over toys that she was too young for. There was a fire going in the fireplace, Duchess lay in front of it, and I thought I could smell macaroni and cheese baking, and I had been living on crackers and cookies until that moment.

"*It Happened One Night* is on TNN in a half hour," Mimi said. "Do you like old movies?"

"Love them," I told her. "But I'd rather talk."

"So we'll talk during commercials. Tell me about this place. It's like something out of a fairy tale, all these flowers. You'd never know it was there from the highway."

I regaled her with a brief history of Bad Girl Creek. "So I advertised for roommates and ended up with best friends," I said.

"That's a great story," she said. "A happy one, for a change."

A FEW NIGHTS LATER I dreamed Mimi was there again, sitting on the couch, teaching me Spanish.

"Casa," *she said. "House."* "Cocina," *she said. "Kitchen."* "Amigo," *she said. "Friend."*

"Flower?" I asked.

"Flor. *And flower shop,* florería. *Farm,* granga, finca."

"Please move in with us," I said. "Not as a baby-sitter, as one of us. A Bad Girl."

"Chula?" *she said.*

"Chula. Para siempre, eternamente, todo los días de la vida," *I rattled off, suddenly fluent.*

She smiled. "Thanks, but you wouldn't want me, I have these mangy cats."

"You have pets?"

"Two cats. Sumo and Homer. Sumo's nineteen and has three legs. Homer's only three, but he's blind. Some gang boys thought it would be amusing to deprive him of his sight. What am I sup-

posed to do? Take them to a shelter? They are so grateful to have a home."

"Mimi, I swear, you and the cats, you'll fit right in."

"Phoebe?"

"Now what?"

"I think I should tell you. I'm gay."

My dream self thought a minute and watched the fire crackle in the grate. This fire, it smelled like the woods, ancient and deep.

"Mimi," I said. "I'm crippled, Ness has HIV, Nance is Catholic, which some people consider a mammoth character fault, and Beryl, our last roommate, went to prison for killing her husband. Now she's living in Alaska, which might be more of the same, depending on how you feel about cold weather. I'm telling you, gay is way down the list of undesirable qualities."

"Well, I do love babies," she said.

"And babies love you. Bring on the cats and let's see what Duchess thinks."

BY THE TIME NANCE AND STINKY ARRIVED HOME, tanned and relaxed, I'd talked Mimi into giving us a try. She had the guestroom fixed up and had set up a loom in the corner of the great room, and was already at work weaving a blanket in the Zapotec design. I could see from Nance's face that she'd left Rick behind, maybe on one of those lava beds, like a remote passion that would burn forever, but in exile. She had put on weight, not much, but definitely some. We'd have her for a few nights, and then she was going north to a treatment center in Saratoga. Ness came back from Arizona saying that David wanted to rent a place there, and my alarm bells went off. I'd already lost Beryl and didn't want to lose anyone else. One clear night we gathered around the kitchen table with our various foodstuffs and laughed and told stories until our cheeks hurt. Outside, flowers were working their way up toward the sun, determined, imperfect, and the result of our hands in the soil. The barn owls' babies learned to fly. Duchess and Leroy welcomed the cats, and seeing little Homer with the ruined eyes trailing after Duchess was about as good as it gets. We took turns propping Sally up on our knees, jiggling her until she let out her first giggle, and fought while each of us tried to claim responsibility. When she went back to acting like a regular baby, I thought it was the perfect time to bring up what had been weighing on my mind. "Ladies, how would you feel about a trip to Alaska?"

"Alaska?" Ness said. "I will not visit that frostbitten wilderness unless it's summer."

"Summer would be okay," I said. "But we'd need to hire some salespeople to keep up with orders."

"Summer?" Nance said. "We'll miss the valley's best weather. And what about James? Don't you think that whenever we go, James should come along? I mean, it's Alaska, a wild place, and having a man along makes good sense."

"Makes good sense you want to get laid," Ness said.

"You shut up," Nance fired back. "I'm a married woman, and sex is a sacrament."

"Give me a break," Ness said, turning to Mimi and me. "Ladies, did you hear that? A sacrament?"

Mimi watched the fracas and shook her head. "I think you are all off your rockers."

At that time Mimi had been with us a few months. Every day I scrutinized her manner, worried that she would decide we were too strange a lot. On her night to cook she made such mouthwatering enchiladas that Nance had actually asked for and eaten seconds. She smiled at the shocked looks Nance and Ness sent her way, and just like I imagined my aunt Sadie might have responded when faced with an adventure, she said, "Oh, what the heck. I'm up for anything."

At that moment we pinned on her wings, and she flew up from new roommate to official Bad Girl, and I had no doubt she would stay.

Mary Madigan

23

Meanwhile, Heaven

"I THOUGHT WE WERE TAKING THE NORTHERN ROUTE," I said, waking up crabby and stiff from a nap on day three of our meandering drive to no place in particular. Rick was at the wheel, the collies asleep and wedged between us, and out the window I could see southern New Mexico in full winter plumage. Long expanses of pale brown prairie were broken up by patches of dirty snow. "You said you were all hot to see the Tetons," I told him. "Of course, being a writer, you probably know that Teton means breast. No wonder you're so fascinated with them. Men and tits, I just don't get it. How are breasts so different than regular flesh?"

"Trust me," Rick said.

"So, breast man, why the hell are we going south?"

He smirked at me, which was Rick-ese for *I'm not going to answer until I'm damned good and ready.* Even at age fifty-one he liked guessing games, which I found strange, but if I wanted to know anything I had to play along. I held the map up to my forehead like a fortune-teller and shut my eyes. "I know. We're going to Margaritaville, where it's mandatory to dress in ugly Hawaiian shirts and waste away looking for the saltshaker. No, wait, we're going to El Paso, so you can walk the streets and sing a lovelorn lament since your old girlfriend got married even though you're nowhere near a cowboy. Am I getting close?"

"Very funny, Caringella. We're going back to Las Cruces."

I sputtered with laughter and petted Mentos, whose head was in my lap. "Oh, sure we are. You hated Las Cruces."

"That's entirely true," he said. "I find it a town without pity. Or beauty, for that matter. Not enough breastlike mountains for my taste."

"So why, pray tell, are we going there?"

He downshifted to make the grade and looked at me with those brown eyes that burned straight through me. I hated how bad I wanted him. He hated how bad he wanted me. We were locked on the horns of the horniest dilemma and not trying very hard to get past it. "There's this Airstream trailer for sale there. Well, actually, it's sold. Since I called the owner from the last gas station."

I screamed and leaped over the dogs to hug him. "You fecking hate that trailer!"

"Give me some credit," he said. "I just told you I hated it to piss you off."

"I love that trailer!"

"What is it you're always saying to me, *'duh'*?"

"Dammit, Rick."

"Damn what? Why do you swear so much?"

"Because it gets your attention."

"Maddy, you already have my attention."

I guess I did. "Well, there's lots of things I love, but you don't buy them for me."

"Well, I guess this just goes to show you that you never know what I'm going to do, do you?" He adjusted the rearview mirror. "Besides, I need that trailer. It helps me write. A clean, well-lighted trailer, that's important to a writer. Plus, where else can you pee, wash your hands, and take a shower at the same time?"

I stared at him. "Heinrich, if you're lying to me, if you are kidding, I will kill you dead."

"Caringella, if you had killed me dead as many times as you've threatened to, I'd be dust in the wind by now."

"So, what exactly are you planning to do with that trailer?"

"I told you, I'm going to write in it. And pee, and take showers, though probably not at the same time."

"You booger. All by yourself?"

More smirking. Sometimes I hated it that he was so good-looking. It opened doors for him that the rest of us had to spend years knocking on. Everywhere we went, into a diner for a burger, or a convenience store for a bag of chips, a national park to take in the view and use the restrooms, some woman smiled the *Hey, if she doesn't work out, I'm available* smile at him, and I sent her major hate rays that had no discernible effect. "So, how are you planning to move your new trailer from Las Cruces, the town lacking in tits and beauty?"

"With your truck."

"Oh, *my* truck. What if I say no?"

He pulled over to the side of the road, and the dogs perked up, certain this meant a pit stop. "Maddy, if you don't want the trailer, tell me now. I can spend the money on a big-screen TV, a new stereo, or the bass guitar I've always wanted to learn to play."

"I want the trailer! I want the trailer! But it'll take extra gas to pull it, and gas costs money, it's winter, and if I don't get a job pretty soon how can . . ." I didn't even want to hear myself answer that question so I let my words fall away.

"Tell you what," Rick said, pushing my chin up from where it was resting on my chest. "Let's just buy the fecking trailer and put it in Slim Jim's name."

I opened my door and the dogs piled out. "You said fecking."

"I did not."

"Yes, you did."

"Maybe I did. I'm not saying I did. Maybe you rub off on me. I'll have to work on that."

"You'd better not. I love you," I said again, and this time there was no question in my voice. I waited to see what effect my words would have on the cranky unemployed trailer owner who was finally being nice to my dogs.

All he did was smile. We let the dogs have a few minutes, then he whistled them back to the truck, and said, "Load up," and they minded him the same way they minded me. Love. No way was he going to say it back until he was ready, if ever. I guessed for now a trailer would suffice.

We drove another hour, and bored by the silence, I fiddled with the radio buttons until I caught a country station. "Not country-and-western," Rick moaned. "Anything else, please."

"Shut up," I said. The station was playing the original recording of Dalton's "When You Stopped By," and I turned it up. "You know this song, Heinrich?"

"I've heard it a few times."

"Well, once I sang it at a rodeo just like this." I launched into the words I'd loved ten years earlier, and then grown so weary of I'd made merciless fun of them. It was easy to harmonize with Dalton's youthful and strong voice, not yet marinated in alcohol.

Rick said, "I may have mentioned that tune in a column once. Guy was way ahead of his time. Wonder why he stopped with that one hit?"

"Lots of one-hit wonders out there," I said. "Everyone knows it's the second song that makes a career."

Rick nodded. "Dammit, Maddy, you can just sing the shit out of that song. Earl told me you should be recording."

"Oh, yeah, me a musician, that's fecking brilliant," I said, as more prairie passed us by. "I'm all right. But nothing special."

"You're special," he said. "Earl gave me the name of a couple of people in Tennessee he wanted you to meet."

"Stop lying."

"I'm not lying. I never lie."

I gave him double fisheyes. "Everyone lies. Just don't lie to me about singing or trailers." Or love, I thought, but did not say.

"I swear to you I'm not."

I thought that over. Since we'd left California, I'd begun to feel the itch. It was getting on rodeo time, and while I should have been breaking camp in Arizona, the only part about it I genuinely missed was the singing. What if Earl really had given Rick the phone numbers? What would happen if I went to Tennessee and just met some of those record people? "I want to meet your parents," I said.

"Good God, why?"

"I just do. I want to sit on your dad's lap and tell him jokes, and catch a glimpse of what you're going to look like in thirty years. I want to help your mother with the dishes. Think they'll like me?"

"Sure. It's me they have a problem with."

"Well, that's ridiculous. You're fecking wonderful. You were my hero in Oklahoma, finding my purse, giving me that money. And now you're buying me a damn trailer. And Tennessee! Damn. Let me have a talk with your dad. I'll tell him how great you are. How you always put the toilet seat down after you pee, and how you buy me dinner without complaining, and of course, how you make me squeal in bed."

He nodded. "That last bit should convince him."

Mentos nosed my hand. I petted her and kept humming Dalton's song. Slim Jim sat up looking out the window, as regal an outlaw as the man next to him.

"I can't write a hero, much less be one," Rick said. "And I'm not fishing for compliments here, I'm truly confused. Chump, yes, hero, no."

"Bullshit. You let that Nance girl do the right thing, kept your nose out of it, which I find incredibly heroic. And you stayed with me when I fell off the wagon, for another thing. But most of all you quit your stupid job rather than let those people bully you into apologizing for something you didn't do."

He looked at me. "That job paid my bills, Maddy. I liked it."

"There's lots of ways to earn money, Heinrich. And way more other stuff to like. It's time for you to see the world. That's what heroes do, you know—they set out on crazy journeys, and they end up in strange places, and they meet all sorts of people and animals, and when things are tough they—"

"Buy Airstream trailers," he said.

"Silver Bullets," I said. "Did you notice how I'm trying to sound like a writer?"

THAT NIGHT AS WE SNUGGLED CLOSE in the fold-down bed of the trailer, he asked me to sing Dalton's song for him again. "I can't sing without instruments," I said.

"Try."

"I don't want to."

"Please."

It was the first time he'd ever said that word to me. Well, well, well, well, well. I thought about that time in Santa Fe when we had walked down the street and come upon the wedding party, and how he'd asked me if that was in my future. Then I thought about how he stood up so straight and tall while Nance said I do to that James character. I had told Rick I loved him not ten minutes earlier, and I knew it was a big risk, but he hadn't tried very hard to talk me out of going with him. Saying the words, I was scared, but I was also fecking tired of biting them back after we made love, or he reached over and rubbed my shoulders when it was my turn to drive. I wanted to know what was going on inside his heart if, as I suspected, he liked me in the way that might turn into love, or if this was truly a short-lived flingy-thing we were doing, and if so, how in the hell was I going to get used to living life without him. But I thought of the Chinese cook I'd once dated, who told me that when the moon is full, you just try to catch a glimpse of it in the river, you don't go asking it where it goes every other night of the month.

So I shoved past my embarrassment and sang. While I reached for the high notes, he ran his fingers up and down my throat, feeling the muscles expand and contract. It felt like he was a blind person and I was the Braille. I didn't think it was possible to feel this nervous singing something I knew so well, and when my voice shook, the touch of Rick's fingers calmed me down. When the song ended, and my throat went still, I swallowed once, and Rick kissed me lightly on the forehead.

"Musicians," he said. "Do you realize that I've spent half my life writing about them? And why? Once I wanted to be one, but I had no talent. Even if I'd had talent, I couldn't have stuck with it. You either have it or you don't, Madigan. And you do. What I have is so many CDs I could open a store. I've shilled for new artists I liked, criticized the arrogant, and now I'm listening to you and I think everything I wrote was a voluminous prologue."

"There you go with those big words again," I said. And for a brief second, I imagined him bed with that Nance, giving herself to him, intent on wearing him out, her skin slick with passion, but I didn't think about that very long, because what he said made me almost cry, and pretty soon our touching each other was all about accidental meetings and staying put when your head told you the smartest thing to do was move on, and this endless skein of forgiveness so necessary to loving somebody that it unwound and gathered you up all at the same time. Rick knew me well enough to know certain things. That during sex I liked my breasts kissed ever so gently, but that when he wrapped his hands around my wrists, I liked him to hold me tight. He knew that when he parted my thighs with his knee I was pretty much done for, and he knew that I liked kissing best of all, so there were always lots of time-outs from the main event to kiss and kiss and kiss some more. And he hadn't forgotten that my favorite thing of all was how he kept his eyes open, focused on mine at the moment when he finally entered me, looking deeper inside me than flesh could ever penetrate. He did that now. For one heart-stopping moment I thought maybe I knew what Dalton meant in that line about not wanting a certain chunk of time to end.

February

The official opening of the Murrah memorial was too crowded, plus the president was flying in for the dedication. I was exhausted from the recording sessions in Tennessee, which had gone okay, I thought, but to listen to those people helping out with all the technical stuff I was in line for sainthood, right. I sure as hell didn't want to be anywhere near where one fecking nut job had already blown things up, not when the presence of the leader of the free world was there giving all the other FNJs another reason to act crazy. Rick and I went to Nightwalker, where we parked the Airstream in Aunt MayAnn's side yard.

On the day of the opening we sat close on her couch and watched the news coverage. We listened while all kinds of people made heartfelt remarks, and I wondered whether McVeigh was watching this from his prison cell, or staring at the walls while he waited out the days of his sentence: Life. Ha, what a joke! *Tell that to my sister,* I wanted to say to his attorneys. *Tell that to the babies.*

"Terrorism is the worst kind of cowardice," one of the news anchors said. "Hopefully, we as a nation will never see such a heinous act again."

Aunt MayAnn shook her head. "Listen to that pure fool. Right now there's another idiot out there cooking up a worse plot. People don't change just because some white man in a five-hundred-dollar suit says they should."

"It's journalism," Rick said. "His speech is all about sound bites and resonant endings, not the truth."

"I thought I told you to quit that writer talk," she said. "You don't fool me, Ricky boy. You want to write a book people will buy and read? Watch *All My Children*. Now that's a show and a half."

Rick flashed her a smile and reached over to pat her hand. MayAnn adored him. They rode horses together. She had a pretty good selection of cowboy music, and sometimes they listened to that and traded stories. When we brought the boom box into the house and played her my demo CD, she put her hand to her throat and swallowed hard. That was all the assurance I needed to take my ass out on the road and go for it. Only one thing stood in my way: Mama.

She'd had herself a little breakdown a while back, and ended up in the hospital for "a rest," MayAnn had told us. She might have been released to go home, but so far as I could tell she was held together with Band-Aids that were about to lose their stickum.

After a while, when I couldn't stand looking at the news coverage anymore, I went outside on the porch to where she sat wrapped in a blanket, her horoscope book in her lap. The book was five years out of date now. Some of the pages were so thumbed they were disintegrating at the corners.

"Mama," I said. "Sometime soon, maybe tomorrow, Rick and I are going to the memorial. You can come if you want to."

She didn't answer, but this time her stare didn't seem quite so vacant. I sat down next to her and put my head on her shoulder. "I lost my twin, Mama. For a long time I thought that was the hard part, but it's not. You and me trying to figure out how to live the rest of our lives, how to still love each other when all we can think of when we look at each other is Maggot, that's the challenge. Don't need a star chart to know that."

My mother took a cigarette from her pack, placed it between her lips, but did not light it. Big River, MayAnn's bloodhound, looked up mournfully, but sad was his regular look, so maybe he was happy, who could tell? Far off in the distance I could see two black specks that I was pretty sure were my collies running around like chickens with their heads cut off, no doubt trying to herd grasshoppers or whatever dared to move. They loved it here, where they could run free and chase whatever and not get yelled at. The ratty Appaloosas whinnied from the corral, hoping that we'd forgotten how to read clocks, and would feel them dinner a couple of hours early. Like them, I figured I'd just keep chipping away, only I was chipping at my mother, hoping to find her center, the place where she could use a spare daughter.

"I love you, Mama," I said, and I sang her the one song I knew she would like, "Amazing Grace."

No applause, but she did set the book down, and for me, that was a start.

A WEEK LATER Rick and I shuffled through the crowds in the parking lot. I held it together past the countless memorial wreaths laid by the chain link fence. We'd seen all that before, on the day we'd met, but each flower still stabbed like a fresh wound. All that color in the winter landscape was as startling as blood. We'd come for the newly opened exhibits, things that had been under construction the first time I'd been here. I knew they'd be hard to look at. One hundred sixty-eight smiling faces yanked from their lives because a single troubled boy decided a bomb made a statement. "Collateral damage," he called the dead babies. My sister had lost her life trying to save them. My pockets were stuffed full of Kleenex.

"You hanging in there okay?" Rick asked me as we went inside.

I nodded.

We read each carefully worded statement introducing the exhibits, and tried not to cry like all the people around us were doing. I pointed out to Rick the photos of search and rescue dogs. "There's River," I said, pointing to a blurry image. "Auntie told me that if she made him stop before he found something, he'd get all depressed, so they just kept going, even when his paws were bloody."

Rick said, "You want to know how stories are chosen to go nationwide, Maddy? The hierarchy of editors?"

I looked at him. "Uh, not particularly."

"Good, because I don't feel like remembering that anymore."

Then we linked hands and almost laughed, until we came to the photo display. Blown up to wall size were images of the rubble, layers of stuff that had been left behind after the bombing and since cleaned up. First thing I noticed was how a bomb can reduce all kinds of colors to that universal gray-brown ugliness. "If you stand back, it looks like any old landfill," Rick said, and put his arm around me.

And he was right. It did—chunks of concrete and rebar and the occasional recognizable bits of office equipment—a computer keyboard, telephone cords, and bits of paper. It could have been the trash piled up when the sanitation people went on strike. But the longer I stared at the photos, the more they transformed, until I flashed on standing at the bottom of Canyon de Chelly years ago, when I was still bouncing back and forth across the West hoping to find my belonging place by working the rodeos and sleeping with any old fool who asked. I remembered looking up at the layers of strata packed into rock formed by various ages in history, battles, massacres, the inevitable process of human beings living and dying and hopefully evolving, and wondered if when I was part of it if anyone would remember me. Someday Rick's body and mine would be part of that vein, our lives mere specks of dust in the larger landform, maybe even side by side, if we didn't blow ourselves up first, like that fecking McVeigh had my sister. Then, of its own accord, this enormous trembling began in me, and nothing I did to stop it—not deep breathing, not thinking of summer—none of it worked.

"Hey," Rick said. "What's going on?"

"Talk to me," I said, hyperventilating from the panic I felt at what I saw. "About anything. Just talk. Say words. Fill up the space so I won't pass out."

He pressed his forehead to mine, and I could feel his breath on my face. "Steinbeck had a trailer. Did you know that? And a dog. There wasn't one musician I interviewed over the years who wasn't superstitious. I'm a sap for love stories. And I think I've finally figured out what *not* to write about."

"Tell me," I whispered, while inside me my blood jittered like a coffee percolator.

"Some stories seem to be meant for living, not for writing."

"You can write about my sister if you want to."

He shook his head no. "Do you remember the last time we were here? You said I was your hero. Well, the tables have turned, Maddy. You've saved me."

I wanted to say, "Oh, knock it off," because sentimental things made me feel so damn lost, but the picture in front of me would not allow me to do that. I clutched his arm and stared at the picture, not wanting to believe it.

"Oh," he said. "I recognize that. It's one of the wire photos. I'm pretty sure it ran across the nation."

Already the tears were coming. I pointed a shaking finger toward the rubble where the pointed toe of a hot pink shoe stuck out, looking so nearly whole that it was hard to believe there wasn't a foot in there, a leg attached, the whole person just having a brief lie-down. I'd been with her when she bought those shoes at a discount place in Tulsa. They were on sale because they were such a ridiculous color. She knew the day-care kids would like them.

"Why'd her shoe survive the bombing, but not her?"

"Come here, Maddy." Rick pulled me to his chest, and held on while I cried.

We studied that photograph for how long I don't know, maybe an hour, maybe it was only a few minutes, but we stared until we knew each scuff and scrape and the painful angle at which the pink shoe lay. We stood there visiting with Maggot until I felt my sister in every fiber of my being, the same way I felt when I sang. Her presence was there, and it felt like whatever I was missing was now filling up with her.

Rick said, "It's like the color of a sunset, Maddy."

I smiled gamely. "Like sticking out your tongue at Catholic school uniforms."

He nodded.

Then, at exactly the same time, we said, "Like somebody planted a seed," and we laughed.

That was how I wanted to remember my sister, her pink shoe an emblem of something larger and better to come, deep in all that trash, a small flower poking through to announce the end of one very long winter.

Acknowledgments

WHEN I ENVISIONED THIS BOOK, the September 11, 2001, attacks had not yet occurred. Afterwards I was concerned that the subplot of the Oklahoma City bombing might appear gratuitous. In the end I left it in because unfortunately, after September 11, it seemed more relevant than ever to explore what it means to survive such unspeakable pain. It's my sincere hope the story does not come off as treating terrorism lightly, offend anyone directly affected by the Oklahoma incident, or reopen wounds that have begun to heal.

My writing mistakes are my own, and I take full responsibility for them, but not to thank those who helped me along the way would be like not finishing the book. To that end, thanks first to Deborah Schneider, my agent and friend, for her constant care, long-range vision, and never-ending supply of kindness. To Marysue Rucci, my wonderful editor, your support, your keen eye, your challenges, and your gentle humor are gifts I can no longer do without. To her assistant, Tara Parsons, my publicity assistant, Tracey Guest, and to my copy editor, Sue Llewellyn, much appreciation.

To my doctors, Michael Armstrong, Laurie Dahms, Ron Feigin, Michele O'Fallon, and Gerry Sagahun, much gratitude for keeping me upright in many ways. To my writing students, for teaching me far more than I teach them: Cathy Fallon, Ernestine Hayes, Jason Hoefel, Mike Howarth, Chris Kennedy, Pat O'Hara, Michael Queen, and Paul Tinsley, hurry up and finish your books—the world needs your stories. To my colleagues, Linda McCarriston, Sherry Simpson, and Ron Spatz, thank you for your company and your support, and above all, your friendship. My writer friends never let me down: Earlene Fowler, Judi Hendricks, Caroline Leavitt, Joyce Weatherford. Jodi Picoult, critic extraordinaire, cybertherapist, and general commiserator, bless you for your careful criticism and Bad Girl humor. I swear you care as much about my writing as you do your own. My Alaska girlfriends have given new meaning to the words "kick butt." Susie Blandin, Gail Boerwinkle, Jacqui Carr, Ellen Cole, and Susan Morgan, thanks for everything from crème brûlée to crying on one another's shoulders.

My family offers steadfast love; my doggies, the unconditional variety. My husband, Stewart, defines love. He makes dinner, listens to my midnight rambles, rubs my back, draws me maps so I don't end up in Barrow, and best of all, always remembers to kiss me goodnight. I know what a lucky girl I am, Buddy. Thanks for everything.

Beryl Anne

1

Peter Jennings and the Bear

THAT SEPTEMBER, Anchorage had more moods than a menopausal woman. The sun shone one day and disappeared the next. The leaves began to turn russet and gold, but instead of falling hung on to branches, unwilling to let go. When the first frost came, and the last of the columbines shriveled, people sighed with relief at the return of what seemed like normal autumn weather. Then, a week later, it was warm again, and pansies close to the earth shamelessly opened their petals to take in the shine. Perhaps most troubling of this out-of-season business was the bears. By the end of the month they were usually bedded down for the winter, and stayed that way until spring. This year, however, bears ventured out long past their usual hibernation dates. Programmed to fill their bellies in preparation for sleep, they got into trash, foraging like ravens, and were seen taking dog food from dishes left out for retired huskies. The newspaper's gardening column warned bird lovers like Beryl Reilly to hold off filling feeders with thistle and sunflower seeds for the chickadees for fear of attracting ursine visitors. A bear encounter was the last thing Beryl wanted. Life was hard enough already.

She sat on the leather living room couch with her journal in her lap. It was a small book, its cover a map of the world. For the last five years she had marked in red pen every place she and Earl had traveled. The western United States, their slow drive through the South and up to New York and Canada, and then beyond the Atlantic, where the line stopped, and they'd flown to Europe. Earl wasn't the "see the British Isles tour" kind of traveler. Despite his casual clothes and fondness for diners, he flew first class wherever he went. He knew cutting-edge places to eat, where to shop for French jeans, and most of all, where to listen to the best live music to be found. He had friends in far-flung places, places he often traveled to on a moment's notice. But since the middle of summer, when he'd announced that he wanted to stay home for a while, Earl had spent most of his time in the basement, which he'd converted to a music studio.

Beryl uncapped her pen and wrote down exactly what she was thinking:

> Earl's going to leave me. He thinks I don't know, but a woman can tell. When I walk into the kitchen and he's reading the paper, he tucks the sports section under his arm and heads downstairs to the studio. A shrink would call that "cave time," and advise me to "take care of my needs myself," but a shrink doesn't live with Earl, I do. He spends more time down there with the guitars and recording equipment than he does with me. Clear through the kitchen floor I hear him teasing notes from his guitars and keyboards. I imagine him adjusting the knobs and plunking the strings with the tenderness and attention he used to shower on me. With the flick of a switch he can loop a chord progression into a never-ending spiral, infuse an electronic drumbeat without a drummer within a hundred miles. Just the other day I heard the chugging sound of a locomotive passing underneath me sounding so real I ran to the window to look for a runaway train.
>
> An extra inch separates us in bed. My lover, who has always turned to me in his sleep, now sleeps on his left side, turned away. When I ask, "Do you want spaghetti for dinner," he looks at me as if I've asked

him to account for every single day of his life. No matter what I say, it puts him on edge.

Okay, so I've skipped a few periods. Maybe I *am* in menopause, the practical joke nature sics on woman so fiercely we wish our cramps and embarrassing accidents and water weight back again. Does he think I'm happy about hot flashes, mood swings, and my faltering libido? And lately I admit I cry at television commercials showing a tender family moment, and the one-legged chickadee hopping around our deck hoping for some crumbs tears my heart as if it's made of tissue paper, but is that necessarily a bad thing? I've been around the block. I know that in a man's world problems exist to be solved. What if I don't know what the problem is? "Just let me be sad," I say, and off he goes, alone, to the studio, to the bookstore, or to hike away from me, and I'm afraid he's never coming back. Yet sometimes we have sweet reunions. He whispers in my ear as he undresses me, and I feel the very pores of my skin open to take him in. And I want to say it doesn't matter, but it does, because I know Earl's going to leave me.

Five years back, when Earl had bought her the house, Beryl had imagined growing old there, the two of them, their life worn to softness by the years they'd weathered. Bohemian Waxwing, the oddly constructed house, was an Anchorage landmark high on the Hillside with its curving roads and occasional seventy-five-miles-per-hour winds. The builder had been a sculptor, married to a woman who was a serious bird-watcher. He'd set down his chisels to design a house that embodied his beloved's favorite bird. The roofline made up the arch of the bird's spine and connected two window-filled wings. To be sure, it was an unconventional dwelling, but the bank of windows struck Beryl as particularly illogical, since a week didn't go by without her hearing a fatal thump and finding a cooling feathered body lying on the deck. The house's story had its dark side as well. When the artist's wife developed a particularly aggressive form of breast cancer and died, the husband left town, and for years the house sat empty. Apparently nobody wanted to take a chance on hand-hewn beams if they came with the specter of love cut short.

But after walking through the empty rooms, Beryl told Earl she didn't believe in curses. She'd never thought she'd own a home, but she began to warm to the idea of decorating with earth tones and soft linens, making this place a reflection of the two of them. "Every house has a history," she said, "and every history holds its measure of sorrow." It was a house, for Pete's sake; Earl had put it in her name. Real estate, like lingerie, wasn't returnable.

Many nights she stood on the balcony wrapped in a blanket watching the northern lights shimmy across the evening sky. The aurora rippled and waned, varying from green to purple to—on rare occasions—nearly red. Supposedly, way out in the bush, if the conditions were right, you could hear it hum and whistle, but Beryl had never been that lucky. The lights almost made her believe in God again, but come daytime her confirmed distrust of the Creator of the universe came rushing back. There was too much sorrow on earth to believe that a Supreme Being would allow that kind of pain. Beryl told herself she believed in concrete details, in evolution, in matter she could touch, like the rich, dark earth, and her foul-mouthed parrot. Now that she lived where she could experience seasons, she believed in the earth all the more strongly.

Beryl studied the Alaskan landscape, the names of the mountains and glaciers—Sleeping Lady, Denali, the Knik, and Matanuska. She memorized the names of flowers like the periwinkle blue forget-me-not, assorted columbines, and the frankly yellow butter-and-eggs. She cooked reindeer sausage and tried salmon jerky, but Earl preferred plain old meat loaf, mashed potatoes with a puddle of butter in the center, and lima beans straight from the can. When he said thank you––like a man who after years of unwrapping ties and leather wallets finally receives the big red tool chest from Sears—that was enough for her. They sat together at the kitchen table eating while Hester Prynne, Earl's tabby cat, peered down from atop the fridge, and Beryl's parrot Verde muttered obscenities to himself from his elaborate, toy-filled cage. She loved her life, even if her boyfriend didn't love her.

The morning she'd decided to confront Earl, he was up before she was. She washed her face, ran her fingers through her curly hair, and poked at the bags beneath her eyes, which, like unclaimed luggage, appeared to be there to stay. She heard the downstairs television switch on, and sat on the end of her bed, tying the belt of her pale pink chenille robe while gathering her nerve.

I will get through this, she told herself. *It's time I took control of my life anyway. I'll learn to drive a car. Make an effort to find new friends. I'll let my emotions out instead of filing them away for that rainy day that never comes. I'll*—what was it her friend Maddy had said the last time they talked on the phone? "Fake it until you make it." A mantra for recovering alcoholics, it would work for newly single women as well.

Downstairs she stood in the kitchen and called his name. Her knees shook and she felt her stomach turn over. "Earl? Honey? We both know things can't go on like this. Can't we talk about it?"

For a long time he didn't answer. Rather than ask again she stared at the screen and watched Peter Jennings narrate in his strong, clear anchorman's voice over footage of whatever the latest world crisis was—teenage mothers stuck in the welfare system, drug cartels financed by unwitting Americans, a war that was always brewing someplace—oh, the specifics didn't really matter. Beryl stood at the kitchen table holding on to her elbows while Earl, on the living room couch, leaned forward concentrating on any news but hers. When he didn't answer her question, she sighed, swallowed against her nausea, and went upstairs to take her shower.

Later she could hear Earl bumping around in his studio, but she didn't go after him. She tried to work on some embroidery, but she had a headache, so she took a nap. She dreamed of her friends in California on the flower farm where she'd once lived.

It was a typical, sunny autumn day, and the smell of chrysanthemums was thick in the air. Phoebe, who had inherited the farm from her aunt Sadie, was telling them all something Sadie had said about growing roses, and Beryl couldn't help but smell the soft, dusty petals even deep in her subconscious. When she woke, the September sun was waning outside her bedroom window, bathing the birches in failing light.

Downstairs the kitchen lay half in shadow. While she could have turned on any number of lights, she didn't want the scene to have sharp edges. Earl was bent over the kitchen table writing checks from one of those enormous checkbooks, four of them to a page. He paid all their bills, and every month he gave Beryl more money than she knew what to do with for "household expenses." She hardly ever spent it unless she was buying him a gift. After all this time she had a bank account well into the mid–six figures, which didn't seem quite real when she opened her statement and examined the balance. "My buddy," she said as she rubbed his shoulders, "buddy" being her term of endearment for this skinny, gray-haired virtuoso who collected signed first editions and traveled to Europe as easily as people around here drove to the Kenai Peninsula for the weekend. "Tell me what's wrong."

Earl reached up and patted her hand. "Nothing's wrong."

Beryl took a breath, let it out, and spoke before she lost her courage. "Earl, don't do this."

"Do what?"

"Retreat from me," she said. "Go all icy and distant and pull away when I go to touch you. If there's something wrong, let's talk about it. Fix it. You know I love you, right?"

He stamped the envelopes and stacked the bills in a neat pile before he answered. "Beryl, I'm as fine as anybody is these days," he said. "The economy's in the toilet, and Bush is in the White House. Ask me again in four years." He closed the checkbook and stretched his arms above his head, neatly moving away from her in the same movement. "I need to get out. Winter's coming. It makes everyone feel a little claustrophobic."

Just then Verde squawked from the front room. Beryl's severe macaw didn't appreciate being left out of any conversation, and this one was no exception. Beryl opened a cupboard to get him some peanuts. "There's still some light. We could hike Powerline Pass trail if we hurry," she said. The hike wasn't exactly challenging for someone like Earl, but it wore Beryl out. The views were stunning, but unless you were looking inside a Wal-Mart, gorgeous scenery pretty much set the standard for south central Alaska.

The set of Earl's shoulders was stiff. Maybe this *was* all about impending winter. Maybe she was, as her stepmother used to say, "borrowing trouble." But deep down she felt sure he was trying to figure out how to leave—how a man could do that after promising a woman "forever." It gutted her legs, but she took a breath and forged ahead. "Look. I can tell you want to leave, and not just for a little while. So let's get it out in the open. Be grateful we had five years."

He stared at her, measuring her words.

"This isn't a trick," she said. "I'm sad, but I won't fall apart. Why don't you go take your hike? I'll stay here and make some bread. That rye you like. And soup. When you get home, we'll work this out like adults."

Earl smiled in such plain relief that Beryl fell for him all over again—the shy, reluctant grin, the slightly overlapping front teeth, and the crinkly lines near his eyes that smoothed out when they made love. "Are you sure?" he asked.

Sure? About dismantling her life? Well, it wouldn't be the first time she'd done it. "Why would I lie to you?"

"No reason. Okay, then. I think *I will* go. On the hike."

As if she'd signed his permission slip, Earl was out the door in twenty minutes. No perfunctory goodbye kiss, just him grabbing his daypack and jacket and a terse "See you later." Beryl glimpsed a wave of the hand with the callused fingertips she loved to feel travel across her skin—though she hadn't in quite some time, and now she was going to have to say goodbye to all that. He'd return less burdened. They'd eat dinner and push their plates aside and open their mouths and behave like civilized people. *You love that couch, so you keep it. I know how important your books are to you, so I'll help you pack them up so they won't get damaged,* when all she wanted was to sidle up close, unbutton the top of his Henley and run her hands over his chest until he got the idea that using bodies instead of words was a much better form of communication—and medicine to heal most rifts.

Instead she put on her winter jacket and gloves and set out for her own walk. A spattering of rain, typical of the autumn season, darkened the tarmac. Soon, enough moisture would collect in the graveled places and turn to frost. They lived too far up the Hillside to have streetlights, but it was still a fairly spendy neighborhood, complete with a homeowner's association she continually worried would discover her past felony conviction and boot her out as undesirable. Beryl tried to imagine who lived in the houses on the acre-plus lots. Some were styled in a postmodern box shape, with paned windows like staring eyes. Others were massive log-home forts, and when Beryl looked at them she pictured entire forests giving their lives to become pretty lumber. Rarely on her walks did she encounter a neighbor. Oh, sometimes a dog walker would give her a brief nod, but nobody spoke beyond "Hi," or "Cold, isn't it?" If you lived this far up the hill, people figured you didn't want to be bothered. She had her hands in her pockets, her head down, the posture of brooding, and was trying to reconcile what had happened in her kitchen half an hour ago with what would happen when Earl came home. Menopause had delivered her a unique method of reasoning, such as, "If Hollywood can make such authentic love stories, films that make a person cry time after time, then why can't human beings stay in love for longer than five years?" Furthermore, was the whole idea of finding one's soul mate doomed to failure? A beautiful pipe dream with a hairline crack? Could anybody sustain a relationship and maintain a sense of herself? Phoebe had nearly lost herself when Juan died. The love of Ness's life had left her with HIV. And why couldn't Nance, who would make the best mother, have her baby instead of three miscarriages?

After she'd thoroughly depressed herself, she pictured Peter Jennings, his handsome face, the dark hair graying at the temples, his professional calm, and wondered if he was like that in real life, if he was married, and who the lucky woman might be.

In fact, she was so caught up in her thoughts she didn't see the bear. To her it looked as if her neighbor's front-yard spruce tree had suddenly sprouted a goiter. What the hell, this was Alaska. Anything could and did happen, people falling into glaciers, the legalization of marijuana, the mayor shutting down a harmless library exhibit because he wanted to pretend there was no such thing as gay pride. But in the next instant, the tree goiter was on the ground on all fours, breath steaming from his nostrils, looking as surprised by Beryl as she was by him.

She tried to remember bear etiquette—were you supposed to run, like you did with moose, hauling ass as quick as possible from those deadly hooves? Bear claws were huge and thick, scar makers of the highest order. Maybe she was supposed to stand absolutely still, or was she supposed to make noise? Bear bells and pepper spray—just about every Alaskan store had them for sale—and a joke to tell along with them—but it didn't take a rocket scientist to know they wouldn't do diddly against a pissed-off bear. Should she back away? She didn't see a cub. Sows with cubs were the most dangerous. Was it a black bear or a brown one? It was hard to tell in the shadows. She remembered a Tlingit tale she'd read in a book she'd bought at Title Wave Books.

> "A woman is out gathering berries with her family. Surprised by a bear, she drops her basket. The bear takes her away. He becomes her husband. She makes his dinner. From their passion, children are born. Her husband treats her well. It's a good life, except for her occasional wondering about her life before this one."

Then, depending on the version, her brothers return for her and kill the bear, which by now she loves with all her heart or, seeing how bearlike she's become, they kill her, too.

Beryl closed her eyes and thought of the people who might possibly miss her should this bear take her life—her girlfriends back in California, definitely. Earl? Of course he would, for a while anyway. She smelled the bear's harsh odor, or maybe it was her own fear rising. All she knew for certain was that when she opened her eyes, she was home, having run all the way and seeing nothing. But even standing on her own front porch the feeling of safety eluded her. Peter Jennings, she thought. Peter would have known what to do.

To calm herself she would make bread. First she sifted the rye flour with wheat, shook anise seeds from the spice tin into the mix, and in another bowl she stirred blackstrap molasses with melted butter and warm milk. Then she spaced out for a moment, staring at the bowls, trying to figure out what was missing. Her mind returned to the bear. She remembered that her neighbors had hung a bird feeder in the tree. The poor bear was hungry, that's all. He was looking for something to fill his stomach before hibernation. Maybe he didn't like the taste of fifty-three-year-old women. Maybe he had a good laugh at her running down the street like her hair was on fire. Oh my God! Yeast! How could a baker forget the leavening? Outside it had begun to rain.

The six-burner restaurant stove was so powerful and efficient at baking that the bread was done and cooling on the wire rack in three hours. Its perfume filled the kitchen, and made Beryl so hungry she went to work on a white bean soup, taking time to chop shallots and then to lightly caramelize them before adding them to the soup. Such careful attention made the difference between an okay soup and a meal so wonderful that she knew Earl would ask for seconds. There was sour cream to dollop on top of the soup, and chopped green onions to sprinkle across. Why not put as much care into this dinner as all the others? She had just finished washing her hands when the phone rang.

"Are you channeling Martha Stewart?" her friend Phoebe asked when Beryl explained the dinner menu.

"I hope not," Beryl said. "Didn't she run over her neighbor or get really fat?"

"According to the rumors," Phoebe said. "At least you aren't being investigated for stock shenanigans."

Beryl could hear Phoebe's five-year-old daughter, Sally, screaming in the background. "What's wrong with the little princess?"

Phoebe sighed. "Her highness is making sure everyone

knows that she is not pleased with her dinner menu. How can any child of mine hate vegetables, I ask you? Suddenly all she wants is bacon or cheeseburgers, even for breakfast."

Beryl thought about how a change in appetite could be an omen, and how the words *omen* and *ominous* and were so obviously related, but how did the English language go from there to the word *augury,* or the queen of them all, *portentous?* She got so distracted that Phoebe had to startle her back into joining the conversation. "Beryl Anne? Are you still there?"

Hormones. The answer had to be hormones. She'd find a doctor and get a prescription and start taking them immediately. "I'm sure picky eating's just a phase, Pheebs. Sally won't perish if she eats a hamburger now and again."

"Over my dead body. They put all those nasty growth hormones in meat nowadays," Phoebe argued. "I don't want this child needing a bra by second grade. Oh, my God, Beryl. Think about it. My daughter is going to have bigger tits than me by the time she's thirteen years old! Probably even before that."

Now the rain had turned to snow—the first flakes of the season. They'd melt before they hit the ground, Beryl thought. She and Phoebe laughed, and for the moment things were so nearly like the year Beryl had lived at Bad Girl Creek that she felt as if Phoebe were down the street, or in the next room, even, instead of a six-hour plane ride away. She flew down to see them twice a year, but this winter she'd asked Earl if they could stay home. Winter in Alaska was slow and quiet, cozy. Beryl wanted to read, play with Verde, and cross-country ski along the Coastal Trail. If they traveled at all, she wanted to head back to New Mexico, where Earl performed music in out-of-the-way bars, tried out his new material, and where Beryl had first met Maddy, who was now living in Nashville, sans Rick, whom Beryl never thought was good enough for her anyway. When Earl left she would be alone for winter. Well, alone wasn't necessarily a bad thing. She took a breath and decided not tell Phoebe about the breakup. The last thing she wanted was to add to her friend's burdens.

"The reason I called," Phoebe said, "is my love life."

"You have a love life? That's wonderful, Phoebe. Who's the lucky guy?"

"Hang on. It's not what you think. I went on a movie date with my Rolfer, Grant. He's very nice, and he's handsome, and the movie was pretty good, too, but Beryl, am I nuts? The whole time we're sitting there in the theater all I can think is I'm sitting next to the man who knows my misbehaving muscles intimately. Not to mention he's seen my"—she paused and lowered her voice—"my bird's nest peeking out from my underwear a time or two. Honestly, I was so nervous I couldn't eat my popcorn."

"Your bird's *what*?" Beryl asked.

"Think metaphor," Phoebe said. "Precocious little pitchers have big ears, remember. Well, anyway, it was a tense evening. And he asked me to go again next week. Do you think that means something? Or is he just lonesome? I wonder if maybe he parked in a handicapped space and got assigned community service and I'm the service? Oh, enough about boring old me. How's the love of your life, you luckout?"

"Earl's fine," Beryl said.

"Pass the phone so I can say hi."

"He's out for a little hike, otherwise I would."

"He goes for hikes a lot, doesn't he?" Phoebe said.

"Well," Beryl said, looking out the kitchen window at the fat flakes illuminated in the porch lights and wondering where he was, if this would be the last time she had a right to feel this way. "Hiking's a religion up here. If it's a nice day, you go fifteen miles. If it's a crappy day, you only do seven."

"Wait. Isn't it dark all the time now?"

Beryl craned her neck to see if she could catch a glimpse of the driveway. Earl was probably in his truck, driving up the hill this very minute. She'd explained Alaska's light-and-dark peculiarities a thousand times, but her friends in the Lower Forty-eight persisted in believing that Alaska had two seasons, light and dark, so she'd finally quit trying. "How's Nance doing?" she asked. "Ness? Mimi and Dayle? David? Anyone heard from Maddy?"

"Maddy sent us a CD," Phoebe said. "Mostly cover songs, but man, she can really belt it out when she wants to. Did you hear that Rotten Rick had to go back to work? He got a job writing for that retirement newsletter! Ha. Everyone else is fine. Mimi and Dayle are currently broken up, however."

"That's too bad."

"It's a stalemate with those two. Dayle misses Alaska and wants Mimi to move there with her. Mimi refuses to leave Bayborough because her grandkids are here. Of course, her daughter-in-law still won't let her be a part of their lives, but Mimi persists in thinking that will change."

"Tell Dayle she can come stay here if she wants. There are whole rooms I haven't explored. Sometimes I feel like I live in Manderley."

"I loved *Rebecca,*" Phoebe said. "I was maybe ten when I read it for the first time. It was so creepy and romantic all at the same time. Kind of like love, actually."

Beryl said, "I think I read it in prison."

Both were silent a moment, and Beryl felt the shift in tension even before Phoebe spoke. Prison had ended ten years ago, and her friends loved her through and through, but every time Beryl made a reference to it, there was this momentary awkward hush. "There is one thing I wanted to tell you," Phoebe said. "Before you hear it from someone else."

The receiver suddenly felt leaden in Beryl's hand. "Oh, God, Pheebs. Save the worst news for last. Tell me what happened."

"Nance lost the baby."

"No. Oh, not again."

"Yeah, she did. Yesterday."

In her nearly five years of marriage to Phoebe's brother, James, Nance had been pregnant three times and miscarried three times. This made attempt number four. Beryl had watched Phoebe make the transformation from "Eh, who needs a baby" to a darned good mother, but Nance's maternal impulse ran clear to the core. Beryl'd never known anyone who wanted a child so badly.

"And she made it so far this time," Phoebe said.

"What's the doctor say?" Beryl asked.

"Time to give her body a rest."

"How long a break does she have to take?"

"Actually he said to stop trying altogether."

"Does that mean they're going to adopt?"

"Sally, you put that video down this minute!" Phoebe

sighed. "Sorry to sound like such a crab, but I cannot bear one more viewing of *The Little Mermaid* today. I should probably hang up. Poor Nance. They really thought this time was going to be the charm. The ultrasound looked good. It was a boy."

Beryl didn't want to think about it, but now the picture was in her mind, a tiny boy waving from across the creek that ran behind the flower farm. His face was in shadow, and he pressed his palms together and dived into the water. "Is she eating okay?" Beryl asked. Nance was anorectic, and too much stress could potentially send her back to the days of apple skins and half-cup cottage cheese entrées.

"James says she is. He made her go back to the shrink. Says she just needs time to grieve the loss. That's the one thing I suck at, you know? I'm just not a patient person. Never have been, never will be."

Beryl understood that, probably better than any of the other women who lived at the farm, but they had no idea why, and she hadn't gone out of her way to tell them. All Beryl'd revealed of her past was hints that a series of long-ago obstacles had kept her from having a career as a teacher. She'd closed off that portal, kept it from the world, and living in Alaska had only reinforced the wall. "I'll write her a card," Beryl said, hearing the sound of a car pulling up. "I have to hang up now, Phoebe. Earl's back. I have dinner ready."

"Keep in touch, Martha," Phoebe said. In the background there was a crash, and she sighed again. "I'd better go sweep up before one of the animals cuts a paw. Love you, Beryl."

"Love you back," she said, and hung up. In the time they'd talked, the weather had turned bad, one of those freezing rainstorms that made Alaskans stay indoors and light the woodstove.

Beryl waited for Earl's whistle as he took the stairs, the familiar clink of his key in the front lock, which generally triggered Verde's explosive greetings—a cussing parrot never ran out of things to say—and for Hester Prynne to jump from her perch atop the refrigerator, but instead, the someone rang the doorbell. Who would it be at this time of night? Maybe Airborne Express. Earl was always getting packages. She answered the door and instead of her true love, she met a state trooper. Snow and rain had dampened the shoulders of his extra-large jacket. He looked so young for someone that tall, his face unlined, his cheeks as smooth as a boy's. "Yes?" she said. "May I help you?"

The trooper removed his hat. "Ma'am, does an Earl Houghton live here?"

"He does," Beryl said. "But he's not in at the moment. Is there something I can do for you?"

The trooper had one of those military-short haircuts. Beryl invited him in to the foyer, where true Alaskans took off their shoes without a moment's thought as to the state of their socks. Only a *cheechako*—a newcomer, like she had once been—would stand there shod and dripping. But even though this man clearly wasn't a *cheechako,* water puddled around his boots on the slate tile. "I'm sorry to tell you, but we found his truck by Eklutna Lake."

Beryl looked at him. "Eklutna Lake?" No one went there after summer's end. The roads were impassable in snow. "No, he went for a hike up the Powerline trail."

"Ma'am, we found his truck off the road in the trees. Keys in the ignition, motor running, no sign of him. What with this ice storm—"

Beryl shook her head no. "You're mistaken. He'll be back any second."

The trooper looked at her sadly, as if his mouth were brimming with a speech he'd memorized from training, only to realize it was not going to make things any easier for either side of the equation. Beryl's knees began to buckle. "Ma'am," he said, catching her by the arm to steady her. "Is there someone I can call for you?"

However long it took to fall, Beryl had time to remember when she had been the one delivering bad news, six years back, on Phoebe's wedding day. Her fiancé, Juan, had been killed in a multiple car wreck on his way to their wedding. The pain of seeing the mangled cars and the devastation of Phoebe's life lay right below the surface, and if Beryl thought about it for longer than five minutes, she broke down. But now other memories began crowding in, demanding time and attention and recognition. Right then she would have given both her arms if that state trooper would just put his Smokey the Bear hat back on and go deliver his bad news to the house next door. He held her upright, struggling to maintain eye contact, to let her know just how serious this was.

He could have gone to Eklutna, Beryl reasoned. It was a beautiful lake. In the summer they'd kayaked there. Portaged their gear to a quiet spot, made love on grass so green it seemed to glow beneath their flesh. The trooper helped her to the kitchen table and got her a glass of water.

After she drank, Beryl pulled herself together. She could hear the soup bubbling on the stove. "Tell me," she said. "Even if it's really bad. Don't leave anything out."

Jo-Ann Mapson is the author of eight novels, including national bestsellers *The Wilder Sisters* and *Bad Girl Creek.* She teaches fiction in the MFA Program at the University of Alaska, and lives with her husband and four dogs in Anchorage, Alaska, where she is at work on a new novel.

From **"one of the most gifted writers of the contemporary urban west"** (*Los Angeles Times*) comes Jo-Ann Mapson's Bad Girl Creek trilogy.

Four female strangers responding to a "Roommate Wanted" ad created a minor miracle when they moved onto Phoebe DeThomas's flower farm and wound up saving it from financial ruin. But perhaps their greatest creation was that of a bond of friendship among vastly different women—women who all felt that life had turned its back on them. Their motto? Live life to the fullest. Love as often as you can. Regret nothing. Eat hearty. Laugh often. Plant flowers. And don't forget to dance.

0-7432-1771-3
(paperback)

0-7432-2462-0
(available in paperback, January 2004)

0-7432-2463-9
(available in hardcover, January 2004)

"A valentine to oceans of good women who survive bad beginnings and worse men."

—*USA Today*

"There's not a woman alive who wouldn't want to spend time with the ladies down at Bad Girl Creek. Mapson's women are complex and caring, funny and fierce, strong and fragile."

—*Booklist*

For more information please visit www.simonsays.com.